Seven Days of Us

. . .

Francesca Hornak

piatkus

PIATKUS

First published in Great Britain in 2017 by Piatkus
This paperback edition published in 2018 by Piatkus

1 3 5 7 9 10 8 6 4 2

A CIP catalogue record for this book
is available from the British Library.

ISBN 978-0-349-41561-1

Typeset in Garamond by M Rules
Printed and bound in Great Britain by
Clays Ltd, Elcograf S.p.A.

Papers used by Piatkus are from well-managed forests
and other responsible sources.

Piatkus
An imprint of
Little, Brown Book Group
Carmelite House
50 Victoria Embankment
London EC4Y 0DZ

An Hachette UK Company
www.hachette.co.uk

www.littlebrown.co.uk

Stylist. Her column History Of The World In 100 Modern Objects first appeared in the *Sunday Times* Style Magazine in 2013 and ran for two years, later becoming a book. Francesca is also the author of a second non-fiction book, *Worry with Mother.*

@FrancescaHornak

For Felicity and Charity

Seven Days of Us

Prologue

17 November 2016

Olivia

. . .

Olivia knows what they are doing is stupid. If seen, they will be sent home – possibly to a tribunal. Never mind that to touch him could be life threatening. But who will see them? The beach is deserted and so dark she can just see a few feet into the inky sea. The only sound is the swooshing drag of the waves. She is acutely aware of the tiny gap between their elbows, as they walk down to the surf. She wants to say, 'We shouldn't do this,' except they haven't done anything. They still haven't broken the No-Touch rule.

The evening had begun in the beach bar, with bottled beers and then heady rum and Cokes. They had sat under its corrugated iron roof for hours, a sputtering hurricane lamp between them, as the sky flared bronze. They had talked about going home for Christmas in five weeks, and how they both wanted to come back to Liberia. She told him about Abu, the little boy she had treated and then sobbed for on this beach the day he died. And then they'd talked about where they'd grown up, and gone to medical school, and their families. His home in Ireland sounded so unlike hers. He was the first to go to university, and to travel. She tried to explain how medicine represented a rebellion of sorts to her parents, and his eyes widened – as they had when she confessed to volunteering at Christmas, to avoid her family. She had noticed his eyes when they first met at the treatment centre – they were all you could see, after all, behind the visor. They were grey-green, like the sea in Norfolk, with such dark lashes he might have been wearing make-up. She kept looking at his hands, as he picked the label on his beer. Like hers, they were rough from being dunked in chlorine. She wanted to take one and turn it over in her palm.

By the time the bar closed the stars were out, spilt sugar across the sky. The night air was weightless against her bare arms. 'Will we walk?' said Sean, standing up. Usually she stood eye to eye with men, but he was a head taller than her. And then there was a second, lit by the hurricane lamp, when they looked straight at each other, and something swooped in her insides.

Now, ankle deep in the surf, their sides are nearly touching. Phosphorescence glimmers in the foam. She loses her footing as a wave breaks over their calves, and he turns so that she half-falls into him. His hands reach to steady her and then circle around her waist. She turns in his arms to face him, feeling his palms on the small of her back. The inches between his mouth and hers ache to be crossed. And as he lowers his head, and she feels his lips graze hers, she knows this is the stupidest thing she has ever done.

THE BUFFALO HOTEL, MONROVIA, LIBERIA, 2.50 P.M.

Sipping bottled water to quell her stomach (why did she have that last drink?), Olivia waits to Skype her family. It is strange to be in a hotel lobby, a little bastion of plumbing and wi-fi – though there is no air-con, just a fan to dispel the clingy heat. And even here there is a sense of danger, and caution. In the bathrooms are posters headed SIGNS AND SYMPTOMS OF HAAG VIRUS, with little cartoons of people vomiting. The barman dropped her change into her palm without contact – guessing, rightly, that most white faces in Monrovia are here for the epidemic, to help with 'Dis Haag Bisniss'. Another aid worker paces the lobby, talking loudly on an iPhone about 'the crisis' and 'supplies' and then hammering his MacBook Air with undue industry. He's wearing a Haag Response T-shirt and expensive-looking sunglasses, and has a deep tan. He's probably with one of the big NGOs, thinks Olivia. He doesn't look like he'd ever brave the Haag Treatment Centre or a PPE suit – not like Sean. Last night keeps replaying in her mind. She can't wait to see Sean on shift later, to savour the tension of No-Touch, of their nascent secret. Anticipation drowns out the voice telling her to stop, now, before it goes further. It's too late to go back anyway.

Olivia realises she is daydreaming – it's five past three and her family will be waiting. She puts the call through and suddenly, magically, there they are crammed onto her screen. She can see that they're in the kitchen at Gloucester Terrace, and that they have propped a laptop up on the island. Perhaps it's her hangover, but this little window onto Camden seems so unlikely as to be laughable. She looks past their faces to the duck-egg cupboards and gleaming coffee machine. It all looks absurdly clean and cosy.

Her mother, Emma, cranes towards the screen like a besotted fan, touching the glass as if Olivia herself might be just behind it. Perhaps she, too, can't fathom how a little rectangle of Africa has appeared in her kitchen. Olivia's father, Andrew, offers an awkward wave-salute, a brief smile replaced by narrowed eyes as he listens without speaking. He keeps pushing his silver mane back from his face (Olivia's own face, in male form), frowning and nodding – but he is looking past her, at the Buffalo Hotel. Her mother's large hazel eyes look slightly wild, as she fires off chirpy enquiries. She wants to know about the food, the weather, the showers, anything – it seems – to avoid hearing about Haag. There is a lag between her voice and lips, so that Olivia's answers keep tripping over Emma's next question.

Her sister Phoebe hovers behind their parents, holding Cocoa the cat like a shield. She is wearing layered vests that Olivia guesses are her gym look, showing off neat little biceps. At one point, she glances at her watch. Olivia tries to tell them about the cockerel that got into the most infectious ward and had to be stoned to death, but her mother is gabbling: 'Have a word with Phoebs!' and pushing Phoebe centre stage. 'Hi,' says Phoebe sweetly, smiling her wide, photogenic smile, and making Cocoa wave his paw.

Olivia can't think of anything to say – she is too aware that she and her sister rarely speak on the phone. Then she remembers that Phoebe has just had her birthday (is she now twenty-eight or -nine? She must be twenty-nine because Olivia is thirty-two), but before she can apologise for not getting in touch, Phoebe's face stretches into a grotesque swirl, like Munch's Scream. 'Olivia? Wivvy? Wiv?' she hears her mother say, before the call cuts off completely. She tries to redial, but the connection is lost.

· 1 ·

17 December 2016

Andrew

THE STUDY, 34 GLOUCESTER TERRACE, CAMDEN, 4.05 P.M.

· · ·

SUBJECT: copy 27th dec
FROM: Andrew Birch <andrew.birch@the-worldmag.co.uk>
DATE: 17/12/2016 16:05
TO: Croft, Ian <ian.croft@the-worldmag.co.uk>

Ian,
Copy below. If this one goes without me seeing a proof, I
will be spitting blood.
Best,
Andrew

PS. Do NOT give my 'like' the 'such as' treatment. It's
fucking infuriating.
PPS. It is houmous. Not hummus.

The Perch, Wingham, Berkshire
Food 3/5
Atmosphere 1/5

By the time you read this, my family and I will be under house arrest. Or, more accurately, Haag arrest. On the 23rd my daughter Olivia, a doctor and serial foreign-aid worker, will return from treating the Haag epidemic in Liberia – plunging us, her family, into a seven-day quarantine. For exactly one week we are to avoid all contact with the outside world, and may only leave the house in an emergency. Should anyone make the mistake of breaking and entering, he or she will be obliged to stay with us, until our quarantine is up. Preparations are already underway for what has become known, in the Birch household, as Groundhaag Week. Waitrose and Amazon will deliver what may well be Britain's most comprehensive Christmas shop. How many loo rolls does a family of four need over a week? Will 2 kg of porridge oats be sufficient? Should we finally get round to Spiral, or attempt The Missing? The Matriarch has been compiling reading lists, playlists, de-cluttering lists and wish lists, ahead of lockdown. Not being a clan that does things by halves, we are decamping from Camden to our house in deepest, darkest Norfolk, the better to appreciate our near-solitary confinement. Spare a thought for millennial Phoebe, who now faces a week of patchy wi-fi.

Of course, every Christmas is a quarantine of sorts. The out-of-office is set, shops lie dormant, and friends migrate to the miserable towns from whence they came. Bored spouses cringe at the other's every cough (January is the divorce lawyer's busy month – go figure). In this, the most wonderful time of the year, food is the saviour. It is food that oils the wheels between deaf aunt and mute teenager. It is food that fills the cracks between siblings with cinnamon-scented nostalgia. And it is food that gives the guilt-ridden mother purpose, reviving Christmases past with that holy trinity of turkey, gravy and cranberry. This is why restaurants shouldn't attempt Christmas food. The very reason we go out, at this time of year, is to escape the suffocating vapour of roasting meat and maternal fretting. Abominations like bread sauce have no place on a menu.

The Perch, Wingham, has not cottoned onto this. Thus, it has chosen to herald its opening with an 'alternative festive menu' (again, nobody wants alternative Christmas food). Like all provincial gastropubs, its decor draws extensively on the houmous section of the Farrow & Ball colour chart. Service was smilingly haphazard. Bread with 'Christmas spiced butter' was good, and warm, though we could have done without the butter, which came in a sinister petri dish and was a worrying brown. We started with a plate of perfectly acceptable, richly peaty smoked salmon, the alternative element being provided by a forlorn sprig of rosemary. The Matriarch made the mistake of ordering lemon sole – a flap of briny irrelevance. My turkey curry was a curious puddle of yellow, cumin-heavy slop, whose purpose seemed to be to smuggle four stringy nuggets past the eater, incognito. We finished with an unremarkable cheese-board and mincemeat crème brûlée which The Matriarch declared tooth-achingly sweet, yet wolfed down nonetheless.

Do not be disheartened, residents of Wingham. My hunch is that you, and your gilet-clad neighbours, will relish the chance to alternate your festive menu. We Birches must embrace a week of turkey sandwiches. Wish us luck.

Andrew sat back and paused before sending the column to Ian Croft – his least favourite sub-editor at *The World*. The Perch hadn't been bad, considering its location. It had actually been quite cosy, in a parochial sort of way. He might even have enjoyed the night in the chintzy room upstairs, with its trouser press and travel kettle, if he and Emma still enjoyed hotels in that way. He remembered the owners, an eager, perspiring couple, coming out to shake his hand and talk about 'seasonality' and their 'ethos', and considered modifying the lemon sole comment. Then he left it. People in Berkshire didn't read *The World*. Anyway, all publicity, et cetera.

The main thing was the bit about his own life. He felt he had made his family sound suitably jolly. The truth was, he wasn't much looking forward to a week at Weyfield, the chilly Norfolk manor house Emma had inherited. He never quite knew what to say to his older daughter, Olivia. She had a disconcerting way of looking at him, deadly serious and faintly revolted, as if she saw right into his soul and found it wanting. And Emma would be in a tailspin of elated panic all week, at having Olivia home for once. At least Phoebe would be there, a frivolous counterpoint to the other two.

Sometimes he felt like he and his younger daughter had more in common than he and Emma – especially now Phoebe worked in the media. Hearing about the hopeless TV production company where she freelanced, and where all the men were in love with her, always made him laugh. He was about to shout upstairs to Phoebe, to ask if she'd like to help him review a new sushi place, when an unread email caught his eye. It was from a name he didn't recognise, indicating some unsolicited rubbish from a PR. But the subject, 'Hello', made him pause. It read:

Subject: Hello
From: Jesse Robinson
<jesse.iskandar.robinson@gmail.com>
Date: 17/12/2016 16:08
To: Andrew Birch <andrew.birch@the-worldmag.co.uk>

Dear Andrew,
I understand that this message may come as something of a shock, but I wanted to connect because I believe you are my birth father. My late birth mother was a Lebanese woman named Leila Deeba, who I imagine you met as a reporter in Beirut, 1980. She had me adopted soon after I was born, and I was raised by my adoptive parents in Iowa. I now live in Los Angeles, where I produce documentaries, primarily on health and wellbeing. I will be in Britain over the holiday season, researching a project, and I would very much like to meet you, if you'd feel comfortable with that.

Yours,
Jesse

PS I'm a big fan of your columns!

'Are you all right?' said Emma, coming into his study. 'You look like you've seen a ghost.'

'Really?' said Andrew. 'I'm fine. Just fine.' His laptop was facing away from her, but he shut it anyway. 'I've just filed my column. And how are you?' Andrew had always been surprised by his own ability to sound composed, even genial, when his mind was reeling.

'Fab!' said Emma. 'I look forward to reading it. I'm just nipping out to John Lewis. I need to get some last things. Well, not last, but some more things for, um, Olivia's stocking. And I, I should get some more wrapping paper,' she tailed off, looking over his head at the clock. Andrew registered that his wife was speaking too quickly. But shock was still pounding through his body. She said something about what time she'd be back, and left.

Andrew sat, rereading the email again and again. Here it was, the voice he had been half-dreading, half-expecting. He thought back to that sultry night in Beirut, 1980, the one he had tried to convince himself had never happened. And then he thought of the strange little letter that Leila Deeba had written him, eighteen months ago, which had been forwarded from *The World*'s offices. He still had it, hidden from Emma. 'My late birth mother was . . . ' So the glorious, firm-bodied woman he had fucked between hotel sheets was dead. He stood up and stared out of the rain-flecked window. 'Frosty the Snowman' came floating up from the basement kitchen. How had he reached an age when a woman he had slept with could be dead – and it wasn't even remarkable? It was a bleak train of thought, and he forced himself back to the present. What, if anything, ought he to reply to this man? And, more to the point, what on earth was he going to tell Emma?

Emma

. . .

Mr Singer's waiting room, high above Harley Street, seemed to have been designed to cushion the blow of bad news. Everything was soft, carpeted, beige. There was always a plate of untouched biscuits by the tea and coffee, and piles of soothingly trashy magazines. Looking at a spread of a soap star's wedding, Emma wondered whether *OK!* was kept afloat by private doctors and their creepy diagnoses. Don't hope, Emma, she kept telling herself. Ever since childhood she had made the same bargain with Fate. If she wanted one outcome, she had to make herself expect the opposite – to really, truly expect it. Then, the other outcome would come true (the one you'd wanted all along). It was like paying insurance – prepare for the worst, and all will be well. Of course, when her daughters were afraid she told them to 'hope for the best', and 'cross that bridge when you come to it'. That was what mothers were supposed to say. Although only Phoebe confided in her, these days. If Olivia had any worries, she hadn't shared them for years. Perhaps, thought Emma, she could draw her older daughter out over the quarantine.

'Mrs Birch?' said the receptionist with the cartoonish lips (did she drop by the cosmetic surgeon on the ground floor in her lunch breaks?). 'Mr Singer's ready for you.'

Emma walked into his room. It was a grim combination of heavy mahogany furniture and medical equipment. Behind the curtain she knew there lay a narrow couch covered by a roll of blue paper, where she'd first shown Mr Singer the hazelnut-sized lump in her right armpit.

'I'm afraid it isn't good news,' he said, almost before she had sat down. 'The biopsy showed that the lymph node we were concerned about is Non-Hodgkin Lymphoma.'

Emma wondered if he had found this the most effective way to tell people that they were dying. No beating about the bush, straight out with it before they'd taken off their coat. He kept talking, explaining that further tests were needed to determine whether the tumour was 'indolent', or 'aggressive'. Funny to define tumours like teenagers, she thought, as he moved on to 'treatment options', fixing her with his pebbly eyes. Emma sat nodding as he spoke, feeling disembodied. Why hadn't she tried harder not to hope? She must have assumed, deep down, that everything would be fine, and now it wasn't fine at all.

'As I said, we need to do further tests and wait for those results before making any decisions, which is likely to be after Christmas, now,' said Mr Singer, 'but either way you'll need to start treatment in January. OK?'

'Does cancer wait for Christmas, then?' said Emma. It was meant to sound lighthearted, but it came out slightly hysterical.

Mr Singer (no doubt used to patients saying odd things) just smiled. 'Anything you wanted to ask?' he said.

Emma hesitated. 'Just one thing,' she said. 'My daughter's been treating Haag in Liberia, and she'll be quarantined with us over Christmas. Is that a risk, I mean, in my situation?'

'Haag?' said Mr Singer. For the first time she saw him look ruffled. 'Well, yes, my advice would be that, in view of the biopsy, you should avoid any risk to your immunity – particularly something as serious as Haag.' He shut her file, as if to signal that the consultation was at an end. 'Have a good Christmas. Try not to worry.'

Emma pushed open the door to 68 Harley Street, with all its little doorbells for different consultants. It was a relief to leave the hot, expensive hush of the lobby, and be out in the December air. Across Cavendish Square she could see the reassuring dark green of John Lewis. She had arranged to meet her oldest friend Nicola there, after her appointment, because, as Nicola said: 'Everything is OK in John Lewis.' Emma had secretly thought that La Fromagerie in Marylebone would be nicer, but now that the bad news had come, dear old John Lewis seemed just right.

Nicola was the only person who knew anything about Mr Singer and the lump – the lump that had just become cancer. Emma hadn't told Andrew, or the girls, because there hadn't been anything concrete to tell them, or to worry about. Usually Emma delighted in department stores at Christmas. But today, the lights and window displays and people criss-crossing her path were exhausting. She just wanted to be sitting down. She had already sent Nicola a text – *'Bad news'* – because she couldn't bear to see her friend's face waiting, poised between elation and sympathy. It took for ever to reach the fifth-floor cafe – every time she got to the top of one escalator she had to walk miles to the next one. Then they couldn't speak properly for ages, because they had to push their trays around a metal track, like a school canteen, asking nice young men for Earl Grey and fruitcake. Nicola kept a hand on Emma's arm the whole time, as if she was very old, and kept shooting her sad little smiles. Nicola does love a crisis, thought Emma, and then felt guilty.

At last, they were seated. 'Right,' said Nicola, 'tell me.' And as Emma explained how she was to have more tests tomorrow which would come back after Christmas, and would quite likely need chemotherapy in the new year, she heard the diagnosis taking shape as the story of her sixtieth year (Lord, how could she be so old?). By the time she had been through it several times, her mind had stopped galloping, and she felt more able to cope. Nicola was full of fighting talk, promising Emma, as she grasped her hand, that she could 'beat this thing' with her friends and family's support.

Emma swallowed a last mouthful of jammy cake and managed a smile. 'I'm not going to tell Andrew and the girls until after the quarantine,' she said.

'What? Why not? But you must! You can't be shouldering this all alone!' Nicola's voice shot up the scale with dismay.

'I can't. Olivia won't come home if I do. I know it. He said it was a risk, to be spending Christmas with her. But I have to, Nic, she has nowhere else to go.'

'Emma! This is silly. She'll understand – she's a doctor, for God's sake. The last thing she'd want is to be putting you in danger.'

'But – look, you know how it is with Olivia. This is the first Christmas she's been home in years, even just home for more than a few hours. It was the Calais camp last year, Sudan before that, the Philippines before that. I want her there. I don't care what Singer thinks. It's only a risk – a tiny risk at that. If she goes down with Haag, my creaky immune system will be the least of our worries.'

'But Andrew? Surely he ought to know.'

She knew Nicola was right. But she was loath to go into how little she and Andrew shared these days, or how self-sufficient she had gradually become. Ever since the psychotherapy course Nicola had taken after her divorce, she was apt to counsel one at any opportunity. And it wasn't as if Emma and Andrew were in trouble. Whose marriage was still wildly intimate after thirty years? Easier to blame Haag again.

'He'll say the same – that Olivia can't do her quarantine at home. And what if it *is* my last Christmas? I'd never forgive myself if I turned her away, and missed a chance to have one more Christmas with just the four of us. I've been so looking forward to it. The girls being at Weyfield again, like when they were little.'

Nicola's eyes were moist. 'OK, sweetheart,' she said. 'You know best.'

Phoebe

. . .

Here it was, Room 131, an executive suite. Phoebe knocked, the sound deadened by the thick wood and plush carpet, and stood wondering if George was looking at her through the spyhole.

He opened the door. He was wearing a white waffle robe and smiling with his lips closed and eyebrows raised, the way he did when Phoebe had proved herself endearingly incompetent. Behind him, dozens of tea lights flickered. George took her hand, leading her into the dark, candlelit suite. Crimson petals were scattered over the fortress-like bed. She decided to edit out this detail when she described the scene, as she already knew she would. Concentrate, Phoebe, she thought. It's actually happening. The thing you've been waiting for. There was George, down on one knee. From the robe pocket he took a little blue velvet box, and opened it with a flourish that she suspected might be rehearsed. The ring was a huge sapphire surrounded by diamonds, like Kate Middleton's. It looked nothing like any of her jewellery. She pushed down a surge of disappointment, and its accompanying shame for being so awful.

'Phoebe,' he said, his head level with her crotch. 'Will you – would you, be my wife?'

'Yes!' she squealed, hugging his head awkwardly as he staggered slightly to stand up. His knee clicked, and they kissed. 'I'm so happy,' she said into his mouth. 'I love you.'

'Me too,' he said, taking the ring, pushing it onto her finger and kissing her hand. He began manoeuvring her towards the bed.

'George,' she said, 'sorry – just I really needed to pee when I arrived.' He rolled his eyes fondly, and she walked to the bathroom. It was palatial. She wondered how much the suite had cost.

Sitting on the loo, she studied the ring. It had probably cost loads, too. She turned her fingers in the light, thinking how grown up her hand looked. A cork popped outside. She stood in front of the huge three-way mirror, excitement pooling in her stomach, hoping she looked somehow different. You're engaged! she told her reflection silently, as she pondered who to tell first, and whether she'd say it had been a shock, or admit that she'd suspected this when George's text had summoned her to a hotel. Visions of an engagement party, and wedding-dress shopping, and a hen weekend in Paris, or maybe Ibiza, blossomed in her mind. She stripped to her underwear and pulled on the second white robe. Its thick folds made her look pleasingly delicate. After examining the freebies by the marble sinks, she tousled her hair and padded out. George was sitting on a pert brocade sofa, photographing two champagne flutes with his phone.

'I had this on ice,' he said. 'It's Moët Rosé. Chose it specially. To my beautiful bride to be,' he said, offering her one of the glasses. He sipped, making the rasping noise he always did when he drank special wine. 'Wow. Good stuff.'

Phoebe grinned. 'You know I can't tell the difference between this and Prosecco,' she said, even though, after six years with George, and going to so many nice places with her dad, she could.

'We can work on that, Titch.' He reached over and ruffled the top of her head.

'It's beautiful, by the way,' she said, waggling her hand so the ring flashed.

'Knew you'd like it,' he said. 'It's very you.'

Later, lying in the crook of George's armpit, she felt herself beginning to believe she was engaged. Dinner in the Michelin-starred restaurant downstairs, and the free champagne the staff sent over, had helped. It must have been the shock, before, that had made it seem a bit unreal. Shock could numb responses, she was sure she had read that somewhere. And now that flurries of Likes and Congratulations!!!!! were appearing on Instagram and Facebook, she'd started to warm to the ring, too. Maybe it was time she graduated to 'lady jewellery' (her friend Saskia's shorthand for dainty, diamondy stuff). She checked her phone – the selfie she'd posted earlier captioned *Engaged! And modelling his 'n' hers bathrobes #BlindDateThrowback* had got 224 Likes, a personal best. She showed George, the little image of them clinking champagne flutes lighting up the dark suite.

'Awesome,' he said. 'But I don't get it – blind date?'

'Duh! Cos the couples on *Blind Date* always used to wear white bathrobes, and be, like, drinking champagne and being really cheesy. Remember?'

'Oh, right. Huh! Yeah!' he said. She wasn't sure he got it. Sometimes references like that went over George's head. He'd captioned the same photo #Moët #LTD #lifegoals. Loads of people had commented on what a pretty couple they made.

'That steak was genuinely amazing,' said George, into the dimness. 'Gym tomorrow!'

She didn't reply. She was thinking how silky the sheets felt against her legs, and how much she loved hotels, and how the rest of her life, with George, would be a series of places like this.

'I wish,' she said, 'someone would come and turn down my bed every night.'

'I'm sure that can be arranged, Princess,' he said, propping himself up on one elbow and smiling down at her.

'You do realise Mummy is going to be an absolute nightmare over the wedding,' she said. Her mother had sounded so emotional on the phone earlier. She'd actually started sobbing with happiness. A bit extreme, but sweet. 'She's probably desperate for grandchildren,' Phoebe carried on. Usually the whole topic of babies felt off limits with George, but this evening had given her courage. She snuggled in closer.

'No wonder, with your sister,' said George.

'Hey! Olivia's saving the world. She can't help it if she's too busy for men,' said Phoebe, slapping his chest. Funny, she thought, how she often moaned about Olivia herself, but didn't like to hear her criticised by anyone else. George wouldn't understand, being the third of four siblings whose main aim seemed to be to insult one another. Their younger sister, Mouse (real name Claire), was mostly talked over.

'When's she back anyway?' he said. 'When does lockdown start?'

'The 23rd. It'll be nice to have her back at Christmas, for a change.'

George did his snorty laugh.

'What?'

'Nothing. Has she even replied to you yet?'

'She will. Not sure she has signal there.'

They lay in silence for a while. A strip of fake Christmas light from Knightsbridge, far below, glowed above the suede curtains. After a while, George's breathing slowed, and his arm relaxed around her shoulder.

She looked at him, asleep. It occurred to her that her overwhelming feeling was one of relief. No more waiting. No more hoping, every time they watched a sunset, that *now* might be the moment. No more fighting back ungenerous tears, with each engagement paraded on Facebook. At last, it had happened. She lay, fingering the jewels on her hand, trying to absorb the idea of 'married'. The cumulous duvet was suddenly too hot, and she stood up for water from the minibar. An opened envelope on top of the fridge caught her eye. She guessed it was the bill, and teased out the sheet of paper inside to see how much George had spent. It was sweet of him to have gone to so much effort. The thought of him lighting all the candles, even strewing the tacky rose petals, was so unlike him it was touching. The paper read:

'THE PROPOSAL' PACKAGE:

Advance ring consultation and delivery £500

Room preparation including candles, rose petals,
Moët & Chandon Rosé champagne, fruit basket,
disposable camera and personalised chocolates £350

Executive Suite, including breakfast £1,000

She turned, not sure if she should make a joke of it, or not. But George was snoring.

Jesse

. . .

Jesse re-checked his email while he waited for Dana, his younger sister. She'd suggested they meet for cocktails when he'd called earlier – rattled but jubilant – to say he'd sent the message to Andrew Birch. That had been twelve hours ago, but there was still no reply. Could he have missed it? His birth father didn't seem like the type to miss emails. Plus Jesse knew he'd been online, because at 6 p.m. British time @ABirchReviews had tweeted: *Why must health writers invariably describe nuts as 'nutritional power houses'? Lazy and meaningless.* At 7 p.m. he'd been back on Twitter to say: *Please make Christmas 2016 quick.*

Wow. Sometimes the guy seemed so negative. Surely reviewing restaurants for a living couldn't be that bad.

When Jesse had first Googled 'Andrew Birch', exactly one year ago, and found hundreds of Andrew's articles online, many with an email byline, he'd been psyched. Here was a way to get to know his birth father, secretly, safely, before making contact. Researching Andrew had become his late-night hobby. His mind now contained a bulging file of Birch Trivia, each new fact bringing Jesse a detective's thrill. His therapist, Calgary, had warned that while this research was a 'safe space', he must not confuse knowing *about* his birth father with truly knowing him. Jesse knew she had a point. But the voice in Andrew's fortnightly restaurant reviews for *The World* magazine sounded so critical – so unlike Jesse's adoptive dad, Mitch – that the prospect of meeting his birth father in the flesh had become unduly daunting. Plus the column was a goldmine of information, since Andrew never gave the food more than a paragraph, filling the rest with glimpses of his personal life and past.

Jesse knew, for example, that Andrew was an only child, born in 1950 and raised by a single mother. She was named Margaret and had worked as an English teacher to support them both. When she died Andrew had written a moving tribute to her, as the preamble to a review of a new curry house in Willesden Green, her hometown. In it, Andrew revealed that his father had walked out on them when he was born. The piece had moved Jesse to tears, and given him hope that this absent father might make Andrew more receptive to a son of his own. Several times, Andrew had mentioned that he'd gotten a scholarship to private school and studied history at Oxford University. He'd been one of *The Times*'s Middle East correspondents from 1977 until 1987, mostly based in Lebanon, at the height of the civil war. Jesse guessed this was how his birth parents had met. This phase in Andrew's career seemed to have loomed large. Whenever he reviewed Middle Eastern food, most recently a falafel truck in 'hipster Dalston', he referred to it.

Not everything Jesse knew came from Andrew's column. A quaint British website called ThePeerage.com revealed that Mr Andrew Birch had married Hon. Emma Hartley in 1983. They had had two daughters (Jesse's half-sisters!), Olivia Frances Birch, born 1984 and Phoebe Gwendoline Birch, born 1987. In his reviews, Andrew referred to Emma as The Matriarch. That was cool, Jesse thought. He liked the idea of an aristocratic stepmother.

Better still was a clipping he'd found online, from an obscure eighties gossip column called 'Sloane's Snooper'. It revealed that Emma and Andrew had first met at the Royal Wedding, July 1981, where Emma was a guest and Andrew a reporter. This fact, besides being pure British rom com, was a coup. Since Jesse's 1980 birth date comfortably pre-dated Andrew and Emma's meeting, he felt confident he wouldn't cause tension by making contact. Hopefully, Emma would be cool about her husband's past. Still, he couldn't get complacent. For starters, Jesse had no clue if Andrew was even aware of his existence. There was every chance his birth mother had never told Andrew she'd gotten pregnant. All his adopted mom and dad could tell him was that, when he was two weeks old, they'd taken him from a Lebanese orphanage. Calgary kept reminding him to limit his expectations. She said the entire Birch family would likely be profoundly shocked when they discovered that Andrew had fathered another child – even if it happened long before meeting Emma. They would need time and space to process their emotions.

There were photos to study, too, mostly of Andrew at various media functions – often with Phoebe on his arm. But beyond his height, Jesse just couldn't see himself in his birth father. There was the shadow of his own hairline in Andrew's byline picture, but his birth mother's Lebanese genes were the dominant force in his DNA. Andrew had sandy, freckled colouring and wincing eyes, whereas Jesse's high-school nickname had been Aladdin, after the Disney movie. Andrew's hair grew straight back in a slick, silver plume – Jesse's curls had to be tamed daily. Even his birth father's hawk-like nose – perfect for damning an inferior Merlot – looked discerning. Jesse's straight, Roman profile hailed from his birth mother, like the rest of his features.

He'd scoured photos of his half-sisters for some physical likeness, too, but this was even less evident. Phoebe's Instagram and Twitter were tantalisingly private, but Jesse could see from the pictures with

Andrew that she was cute. She had a kind of imperious, English Rose face with sulky pre-Raphaelite lips, unusual green eyes and a fine aquiline nose. Nothing like Jesse. The only photo he could find of Olivia was her Facebook profile, which showed a female Andrew. They had the same long face, deep set eyes and fair skin – but on a woman, and without Andrew's sceptical gaze, it added up to something different. Homely, Jesse's mom would have said. Beyond this, Olivia seemed to exist in a social media vacuum. He didn't even know what she did for a job.

Emma must be too old to show up much online – unlike her media husband. The only photo Jesse could find of her was the one on 'Sloane's Snooper', from 1981. It showed a pretty, grinning brunette with big hair and shoulder-pads – a lot like a young Rachel Weisz. He could see the likeness between her and Phoebe, although Emma looked curvaceous, where Phoebe was actress skinny. But the photo was so old that he had no mental image of Emma, today.

Other trivia: Phoebe worked in TV (Jesse clung to this fact as some semi-common ground) and always ordered fish when she accompanied Andrew on his reviews. She sounded fun, and witty, in a dry, British way. Emma adored dessert, and Elvis, and wanted a dog but had to make do with a cat because Andrew didn't like dogs. This fact bothered Jesse. Who didn't like dogs?

Today, the Birches lived in Camden (home of Amy Winehouse!), but holidayed at the gloriously British sounding Weyfield Hall. It was Weyfield that had started the whole plan to head to Norfolk in December – specifically a Christmas photo-shoot of the house on Countryliving.co.uk. When Jesse had seen the roaring fires, family portraits and dark panelling, he'd realised how badly he wanted to be part of it. He'd started to feel quite romantic about the fact that his roots were part Arabian Nights, part Downton Abbey (never mind that Weyfield was on Emma's side). He became convinced it was his rare, cocktail blood, and not just the fact that he was gay, that had made high school such a bitch. And so he'd told everyone that he was heading to Norfolk, England, over Christmas to research 'a confidential project'. Only Dana knew the full story. Still, it wasn't technically a lie. The journey to meet his British birth father, in a country manor house, could make an incredible documentary. It would be his first film of his own, but he had a good feeling about it. He'd already shot some preliminary footage, just of himself in his apartment, talking about his life in LA, his childhood in Iowa and his expectations of meeting Andrew in Norfolk, England.

'I was thinking, don't you find it kind of strange how Andrew's a food critic, but he's super skinny?' said Dana, as the waiter brought their drinks. 'It's like he doesn't actually enjoy food. He literally never says "that was yummy". It'll just be, like,' she put on a snooty British accent: '"The jus was *well wrought.*" He described a sorbet as *deft* last week. What does that even mean?'

Jesse sipped his Beet Bloody Mary. He didn't usually drink, but hitting send on the email had frayed his nerves.

'I like his prose,' he said. It was crazy, he thought, how defensive he felt of Andrew already. Dana was right, though. His friends, cell phones poised over every green juice, were more into food than Andrew was.

'I'm sorry, I don't mean to be bitchy,' said Dana. 'I'm just pissed that he didn't reply yet. Anyway, now we know where your metabolism comes from.'

'Guess so,' said Jesse.

'He looks like he could be even skinnier than you.'

'Uh uh. We're identical – six foot four, 170 pounds.'

'Stalker.'

'Hey – it's all we have in common. Physically.'

'You say that like it's a bad thing. You should be thankful you wound up like your model birth mom.' Dana was always teasing Jesse about his freakishly pretty face.

'Phoebe looks nothing like him, either,' said Jesse.

'I noticed he mentions her a whole lot more than Olivia,' said Dana, after a pause. 'Do you think she's his favourite?'

'I think she's just more, like, the type of person you can write about,' he said. 'She always says funny stuff about the food they order.'

'Right,' said Dana, draining her drink and avoiding his eye. He wished he didn't get the feeling Dana was wary of Jesse's birth father, and family. Calgary had suggested that since Dana wasn't adopted herself, she might be reluctant to share her big brother. It made sense – he and Dana were so close that she followed him to LA after college. But her attitude still bugged him. Especially because he'd thought the exact same thing about Phoebe and Olivia himself. Only Phoebe seemed to accompany Andrew to his reviews and star in his anecdotes.

'I can't believe you won't be home for Christmas,' said Dana. She always got sentimental with vermouth.

'We only just had Thanksgiving.'

'When are you going to tell Mom and Dad this "confidential project" is a big lie?'

'Once I've heard from him. He's probably just working out what to say. He's not going to write straight back.'

'Sure,' said Dana. 'He has to soon, though. Or he'll have me to answer to.'

Jesse knew Dana was only keeping his secret out of loyalty, and would have preferred everything out in the open. But it felt safer this way, in case the search ended badly like last time. Jesse hadn't expected his mom to be so upset when he had tried to contact his birth mother – after years of deliberation – only to find that she had recently died. Nor had he expected to be so upset himself. This time he would wait until after he'd met Andrew to tell Mom and Dad. That was better than getting everyone involved before he knew the outcome. At least his birth father was definitely alive.

But by midnight West Coast time, there was still nothing from Andrew. Surely he would reply tomorrow, thought Jesse, sitting at the kitchen counter in his briefs with the air conditioner on full. He flicked from his email back to the Virgin Atlantic website. He should wait, he knew. To book now, before he had a reply, would be premature. But flights for the holiday season were only getting more expensive. He hovered over the Purchase Tickets tab, for a second, then clicked.

· 2 ·

23 December 2016

Quarantine: Day 1

Emma

. . .

Emma had arrived at Heathrow madly early, having left Norfolk before dawn. Every time she went to the loo (which was often, thanks to a large, muddy cappuccino from Costa) she felt terribly anxious that Olivia would emerge to find nobody to greet her. She used to have the same horror of being late to collect the girls from school. It was also very awkward to manoeuvre the sign she had made, in and out of the tiny Heathrow loos. She had painted it on a rug-sized sheet of green card from the art shop on Holloway Road. It read *Welcome home darling Wiv, you heroine*. Holding it now, she feared it looked silly. Olivia didn't like a fuss. And was it still OK to call her 'Wiv', her childhood nickname, coined by an infant Phoebe? But Emma needed to mark Olivia's safe return somehow. And busying herself with the sign had taken her mind off the lump for an hour.

A tall young man wearing a baseball cap sat down near Emma, and she moved the sign on to the floor, so the corner wasn't poking his thigh. He looked down at it, and then at her. 'Cute sign,' he said, in an American accent. If he hadn't spoken she'd have assumed he was Mediterranean, with his olive skin and dark eyes. He had the kind of chiselled, regular features that might make an actor or male model. 'Dishy,' she would have said, when she was young.

'Are you Wiv's mom?' he asked.

'Yes, she's been in Liberia, helping with the Haag epidemic. She's a doctor.'

'Woah. That's incredible. You must be so proud.'

'Of course! It's wonderful what they're doing out there.' Emma did like the way Americans were so enthusiastic. She'd always felt she'd have fitted in rather well in the States.

'For how long?'

'Just since October. But it's felt like centuries!' She giggled, and his face opened into a film-star grin.

'Incredible,' he repeated. 'I'm like in *awe* of those guys. What they do is so cool. Will she be OK, afterwards?' he said, after a pause. 'Do they offer them, like, therapy?'

'Gosh, I don't think so. No, I think they just get on with it,' said Emma, suddenly wondering if she should have organised some sort of counselling for Olivia. She'd seemed all right after her other volunteer trips, hadn't she? Though she'd never been anywhere so dreadful-sounding before.

'And what about you?' she asked, looking at the bag at his feet. 'D'you have English relations?'

'Kind of.' He paused for a moment, and she hoped she hadn't made some faux pas. Perhaps he was escaping a nightmare family Christmas in America.

'I'm visiting friends in London today, but I'm actually trying to meet with my birth father. He's British, but I'm adopted, so . . . My birth mother had me adopted. She and my birth father weren't, like, officially together or anything.'

'Golly, how brave,' said Emma, trying not to look taken aback. 'And presumably your father knows you're coming? Your birth father,' she corrected herself.

'Uh, I emailed him, but he didn't reply, and I already booked my flight. I'm not sure he even knows I exist. So. I'm kind of in a dilemma.'

'Goodness. Yes, I see. That's tricky.' She couldn't help thinking it was rash to fly all the way here, at Christmas, before getting a reply. 'Are you sure you had the right email address?' Emma had a deep mistrust of technology. How could anyone rebuff this sweet man? His eyes were just gorgeous – Marmite coloured, and fringed with a child's luscious lashes. Andrew had had terrific eyelashes when he was young, too. But Andrew's were fair, she thought, as the American man talked, so you had to be right next to him to notice.

They ended up chatting for quite a while, because the rather hopeless-sounding friend who was picking him up was late. Emma hadn't pressed him on the birth father stuff, since it all seemed a little dicey, and he'd obviously geared himself up to meet this man and was terribly nervous. So they talked instead about LA, where he lived, and his job, which was something to do with making health documentaries, and that had led to talking about health in general, which he was very interesting about. He was so easy to talk to, in fact, asking her all sorts of questions about herself – not her daughters or Andrew, as most people did – that she found herself telling him about her diagnosis. It was funny, the way one opened up with strangers. Perhaps she felt able to confide because he'd told her his own dilemma, she thought, as he talked about a documentary he'd helped to make on cancer. Or perhaps it was the safety of knowing she would never see him again. It was only when his friend arrived and he gave her a quick, squeezy hug goodbye (Americans were bonkers, but so sweet), that she realised they hadn't even introduced themselves. 'Good luck!' she shouted, as he walked away. He turned and smiled, and she'd wanted to rush after him and tell him if it didn't pan out with his birth father he must come and spend Christmas with them – but then she remembered that they would be in quarantine.

Olivia

. . .

Olivia willed her rucksack not to appear on the luggage carousel too soon, but it was the second bag out. Sean lunged for it and she wanted to tell him not to, to eke out their last moments. Arrivals was blinding. Everything looked so new and efficient. World Duty Free shimmered with oversize Toblerones, pyramids of perfume, and towers of amber bottles. 'Who *buys* that stuff?' she said to Sean. And how can all this be normal again, she wondered.

The airport, after the chaos of Monrovia's streets, sounded strangely muffled. And her feet, calloused in sandals, looked utterly out of place. Almost worse than the onslaught of consumerism was the dingy room where all aid workers were herded to have their temperatures checked. This must be where unlucky drug mules were interrogated, she thought, noting the contrast between the stained walls and the glitter outside. It was like seeing backstage. Sean looked at her and smiled. Not touching him for the entire flight had felt like an unscratched itch. Last night, knowing that they couldn't even shake hands today, they had lain together on the low bed in her apartment, limbs entwined so that she forgot where her skin ended and his began. She'd pressed her forehead into his chest and said: 'We will, y'know, carry on, once we're home, won't we?' It was easier to say it to his nipple than his face.

'For sure, you idiot!' he'd said, his mouth finding the top of her head. Lying there, fan whirring until the generator stopped, she'd felt like they were in a bubble, sealed off from the world. But looking at Sean now, she feared the bubble might have been an illusion. It was only five weeks since they'd first kissed. And for all they'd witnessed together they'd yet to share real life – yet to tell anyone they were a couple.

It was her turn. The security guard held up the non-contact thermometer, eyes wary. This, she supposed, was what she was in for: suspicious looks, people surreptitiously sanitising their hands after coming close. The thermometer beeped, and she was waved through. Sean was cleared next. They stood outside the room, facing one another, the requisite two feet apart. 'Bye, for now, then,' he said. Her throat seemed to have closed over. She wasn't like this, usually. Sean reached out to touch her arm, and she backed away instinctively – a reflex in public, after weeks of the No-Touch rule.

'It's fine, nobody's watching,' he said, smiling. 'Going to miss you so much, Olivia.' She liked the way her name sounded in his mouth.

'I'll miss you too,' she said. It had been ages since she'd let someone in this close. In fact, she wasn't sure she'd ever told Ben, her lukewarm boyfriend at UCL, that she'd miss him.

She heard a familiar shriek. 'Wiv! Wiv! Olivia!' It was her mother. She came stumbling up, impeded by a huge welcome home sign, hugging and kissing her without hesitation. 'Oh sweetheart,' she said into her shoulder. 'You're so thin!'

'Hi Mum!' she said, trying to sound pleased. 'You're not really meant to kiss me,' she added, extricating herself.

'Oh come on darling, don't be silly.'

She remembered her mother's mortifying habit of embracing her outside school, long after Olivia had grown to tower over her.

Emma stood gazing up at her as if she was an apparition, oblivious to Sean.

'This is Sean. We were working at the centre together,' said Olivia.

'How lovely!' said Emma, as if Olivia had said they'd met playing croquet.

'Lovely to meet you, too,' said Sean. 'Bet you're glad to have her home?'

'Oh yes, heaven!' said Emma, her voice ringing out over the hubbub. Already the claustrophobia of home was taking hold. Nobody said anything for a second.

'Well,' said Sean, scooping up his rucksack, 'Guess I should go, I've a follow-on to catch.'

'Bye, then,' said Olivia. Their goodbye wasn't meant to be like this. Why had her mother chosen now to appear?

'See you, O-livia. You have a very merry Christmas,' he said to them both.

'You too, Shane,' said her mother.

Olivia watched him walk away, head bobbing above the crowd with his endearing bouncy stride.

'Well, he seemed very nice,' said her mother. 'Can I carry anything?' She wondered for a second if her mother had guessed, but Emma was squinting to read the exit signs. 'Now, you have to get home quick as a flash, is that right? I've got snacks in the car – what about the loo, will you be OK?'

'Yes, I'm fine, Mum.' Her patter was as grating as it was touching.

'Don't you need some proper shoes? It's freezing outside.'

'We're just walking to the car, aren't we?'

'Good-oh.' She always said 'Good-oh' when she was on edge.

Her mother's VW Golf smelt of apple cores and Chanel No. 5, a queasy echo of childhood carsickness. Stuffy, artificial heat soon fogged up the windows until all she could see of the world outside was a waterlogged grey. The passenger seat was set for Phoebe (who still couldn't drive), so that there was no leg room. Olivia sat, trying to balance the Thermos of tea and Tupperware box of flapjacks that her mother had brought for her. 'I just *knew* you'd be missing proper tea,' Emma said triumphantly, as they stopped at a red light. Olivia hadn't the heart to tell her she'd been able to buy PG Tips at a little shop in Monrovia called The Hole In The Wall, that sold British imports like Marmite and HP sauce and KitKats that bent in the African sun. Or that, after weeks of stew and soft drinks, she was craving salad and tap water.

She looked sideways at her mother, who was wittering about how she intended to re-read Nancy Mitford while they were in quarantine. She seemed unduly excited about the entire prospect. By the time they were on the motorway her commentary dwindled, and Olivia leaned her temple against the cold window and closed her eyes to put Emma off talking. She knew she would never be able to convey what she had seen over the past weeks. Her mother seemed to take the hint, and they drove the rest of the way in silence.

As the roads got bumpier and twistier, some instinct told her that they were almost at Weyfield, and she half-opened her eyes to see the yews and cobbled wall that circled the house. The car swung round through the gateposts and up the drive, and the sound of tyres on gravel told her she was really back. One gate had come off its hinges and lay lamely against the gatepost – the whole thing overgrown with nettles and ivy.

'Must sort out that gate,' said her mother. 'It's like *Sleeping Beauty* here! Did you have a nice snooze, sweetheart? You must be shattered. Now let me get Daddy to carry those bags, you run on in.'

Olivia pushed open the front door, with its grinning lion knocker.

It had been left ajar, as usual, because the latch always jammed. Still, the disregard for the environment grated. She wrenched the door firmly shut behind her and walked into the hall, where old Barbours hung on one wall and an army of wellies flanked the skirting board. The Weyfield smell hit her – woodsmoke, dusty carpets and Lapsang Souchong tea. She stood for a second, looking at the sepia photos of the 1953 flood, which hung below the cornice. They were the only pictures in the house she really liked, the rest being fussy Hartley portraits.

After a moment Phoebe darted in. 'You're back! Yay!' she said. Her sister put out her arms in a careful, triangular hug so that she kept her feet and body as far from Olivia's as possible. Whether it was fear of infection, or the awkwardness that had dogged them since adolescence, Olivia wasn't sure. 'You're so thin!' said Phoebe admiringly, though her eyes were dismayed – Olivia was meant to be the bigger sister.

'PPE in thirty-degree heat will do that,' she said.

'PPE?'

'Personal Protective Equipment. The hazard suits.'

'Oh right! Like Bikram?'

'Bikram?' said Andrew, appearing behind Phoebe.

'Hot yoga, Daddy,' said Phoebe. 'The room's boiling, so you sweat loads and lose loads of weight. That's why Olivia's so skinny.'

'Sounds ghastly,' he said, striding towards Olivia, gripping her shoulders and making 'mwah' noises into the air, inches from either cheek.

'Probably not as ghastly as a Haag treatment centre,' said Olivia.

'Quite,' said Andrew. 'Now, where's your luggage?' He looked at her legs, and for a moment she waited for him to make a wry comment about her trousers. She had bought them with Sean for Africana Friday, a weekly Liberian ritual where everyone dressed in joyous, printed textiles – even when the Haag crisis was at its height. But he just took a coat from the wall, swearing as he wrestled with the door and strode out.

It was disorientating to be back in the big, cluttered kitchen, the dresser groaning with pink lustre and eighties Emma Bridgewater, alongside newer additions like the Dualit (a tiny victory for her father, after lengthy debates about the merits of toast on the Aga vs a toaster). Cocoa lay asleep under the table. Olivia had an odd feeling that only he could ever understand the weeks she had spent in Liberia.

'Cokey!' she said, crouching to tickle his chin and hear his Darth Vader purr.

'Careful!' said Phoebe.

'It's OK. Haag isn't spread by tickling.'

'But he's twenty. He's, like, a feline OAP. He might have a doddery immune system.'

Olivia bit back the snap rising in her throat: 'Who's got an MSc in infectious diseases?' and forced herself to say: 'He's tough, aren't you Cocoa?' Why was it easier to talk to a cat than her sister?

'Now, cup of tea?' said her mother, bustling in.

'I'm fine thanks, I had that one in the car.'

'Coffee? Might help with the jetlag? I always find it's better to just stay up, and try to get back on track.'

'Liberia is almost on the same meridian as Britain, I think you'll find,' said Andrew.

'Golly, yes, silly me,' said her mother. 'Now I'm doing roast beef for lunch, is that still all right? Two thirty-ish?'

'Great!' said Olivia. 'I'm going to go and have a shower.'

'OK darling, you're in the Shell Bathroom. I've put out shampoo and towels and everything.' She said 'Shell Bathroom' in the special loud, deliberate voice she used for foreigners.

Olivia was already in the doorway, so she kept moving to avoid saying: 'It's safe to share a bathroom with me.' How, after overseeing a Haag treatment centre, could staying at Weyfield make her feel fourteen again? Why couldn't she be the adult she was at work, with her family?

Her limbs felt leaden as she walked up the oak stairs and over the threadbare, olive-green carpet in the corridor – probably unchanged since those pictures of the flood. She turned left into her bedroom, which her mother called 'the Willow Room', as if they were in a period drama. Across the landing she could see Phoebe's much bigger room, which they used to share. It had been redone at Phoebe's insistence a few years ago, and now had to be referred to as the Grey Room. The huge bed was piled with slate-coloured throws and wreathed in fairy lights, the floorboards painted white. Olivia realised she had forgotten to say anything about her sister being engaged.

Her own room seemed to have been prepared for a guest. A sherry glass of hellebores sat on the dressing table, and by the bed was a carafe of water and stack of paperbacks. On top was a book called *Love Nina*. Phoebe and Emma had been obsessed with it a few years ago, and she had disappointed them by not reading it. They had kept pointing out that it was set in eighties Camden, as if this was a mark in its favour. Why would she want to revisit her own, blinkered childhood? Olivia liked books she could escape into, fantasy and thrillers. She looked at her reflection – never easy at Weyfield, where every mirror was spotted with age, like an over-ripe banana. Phoebe was right, she had got skinny. Too thin, in fact. Watching her undress last night, Sean had said she was wasting away. The medic in her knew he was right – her periods had stopped last month, just as they had when she'd lost a stone during finals. But she had secretly enjoyed the novelty of feeling fragile. Which was stupid, she knew. Why had she succumbed to some ideal of daintiness – of Phoebe-ness – when she had long ago made peace with being tall and strong? Anyway, she'd be back to normal within weeks, if Emma kept feeding her like a foie gras goose.

Andrew

. . .

The three of them stood near the Aga for a moment, after Olivia had gone upstairs. Emma looked slightly deflated. 'Very tired,' she said, half to herself.

Phoebe slipped onto the bench by the long farmhouse table. Her ethereal face, uplit by her laptop, looked rather eerie. 'George thinks Audettes for the engagement party,' she said.

'Oh yes, gorgeous!' said Emma. 'I'll just see if she wants a hot-water bottle,' she added, moving towards the door.

'She's fine, Emma,' said Andrew, more curtly than he'd meant to. His wife used to flap this way when he came back from Lebanon, bombarding him with snacks and hot drinks, and discreet enquiries after his digestion. It was her way of coping, he knew. One of the only good things to come from quitting foreign correspondence had been an end to Emma's stifling concern. Even so, carrying Olivia's rucksack into the house he'd felt a tug of nostalgia, and something like envy.

'Who's the PR there?' said Phoebe.

He knew this was Phoebe's way of asking him to get Audettes, an overhyped Mayfair restaurant, for free. 'At Audettes? I believe it's one of the unfortunately named Natasha Beard's. But I gave them two stars, so I don't imagine she'll be wild about hosting your shindig.'

'Uuuurgh.' Phoebe slumped forward, so that her little chin sat on the table, and looked up at him. Her eyes were like flowers.

'I'll see what I can do,' he said, walking across the dim passage to the smoking room, his unofficial study.

Bloody George. It still rankled that he had proposed to Phoebe without Andrew's permission. Emma joked that it wasn't like Andrew to be so bourgeois (which, he felt, was true) but it implied a lack of deference. Still, Phoebe mustn't know their misgivings. It might drive her away. Andrew should know – Emma's parents had never approved of him, and their hostility had only added a certain frisson to proceedings. But that had been rather different. Sir Robert and Lady Hartley weren't objecting to Andrew per se – though they'd have preferred Emma to marry a toff. It was Andrew's scoop on Bunty Hartley in 1978 that had been the problem. Emma's uncle Bunty was a Tory MP, outed by Andrew for his connection to a dodgy arms deal in Iraq. The story had been published long before Andrew met Emma – there was nothing he could do to un-write it, and no way the Hartleys would forget the name of 'that dreadful hack' who had shamed Bunty. Always, at Weyfield, he felt their froideur afresh. Not least because one of Emma's ancestors seemed to be glaring at him from a gold frame at every turn. Thank God Emma's parents had died before Andrew became a food critic. That would have been the last word in nouveau, in their eyes.

Andrew sat at the bureau in the smoking room, its innards bunged up with yellowing postcards and bent photos and inexplicable magazine cuttings. The garden outside looked bleakly soggy, walls punctuated by naked pear trees. He tapped out an email to Natasha Beard, and immediately got her out-of-office. That would satisfy Phoebe. He attempted the cryptic crossword, but Emma's voice kept fluting through from the kitchen, over her CD of dirge-like carols, making it impossible to think. He laid the draught excluder along the door to dull the noise. It looked about two centuries old. Why did Emma keep these things? He read *The Economist*, and found himself hugely irritated by a glowing review of a book by a man in his year at Magdalen. Finally, he pulled an envelope out of his wallet – the letter he had received eighteen months ago. He read it again, despite knowing it by heart.

Andrew Birch   *P.O. Box 07-2416*
The World Magazine   *Riad El Solh*
Bedford Sq   *Beirut*
London   *1107 2002*
WC1B 3HG

20 June 2015

Dear Andrew,

It has been many years, but I hope you remember meeting me, Leila Deeba, in Beirut. I am writing to tell you that, after we met, I discovered I was pregnant with your baby. He was born 26 December 1980. I chose to have him adopted, as I felt unable to raise a child alone. I would like to sincerely apologise for not having informed you. I was young and afraid, and my career, at that time, was my obsession. Beirut was a dangerous place for a child. I thought it would be easier for you if you didn't know.

But I am writing to you now, Andrew, because I am sick. I have a terminal disease. I have accepted that I will probably die without meeting my son. For many years I hoped he would try to find me, but he has not. I never had any other children.

If, some day, he contacts you, please tell him that not a day passed when I didn't think of him. My dying wish is that he has been happy. Please believe this letter, for his sake. You will know him if you see him. He was beautiful. I named him Iskandar.

> *Yours,*
> *Leila*

I wish you well, and I hope that life has been good to you.

Andrew thought back to when he had received the letter, in June last year. It had been lurking in a Jiffy bag of post, forwarded to Gloucester Terrace by an intern at *The World*. Initially, Andrew had doubted its authenticity. The sceptic in him wondered if it was a hoax, or the start of a dismal plea for money. Even if this was the Leila Deeba he remembered, the stunning Télé Liban presenter with whom he had had a one-night fling, how could she be sure the baby was his? The voice sounded distinctly melodramatic, possibly unstable. And the handwriting was all over the place. The woman might well be delusional.

And so he had decided, with very little deliberation, to say nothing about the letter to Emma. It would only open a whole vat of worms. The thing was, he and Emma had already been together when Andrew had shagged Leila. Admittedly, he had only been taking Emma out for three months. And, at the time, their romance had been a secret, because of the Uncle Bunty awkwardness. Even so, allowing himself to be seduced by Leila Deeba was wrong. So when Leila's uncorroborated letter arrived, years later, it had seemed pointless to show his wife. It would just upset her. She would wonder, if he couldn't keep his hands off other women then, what else he'd been up to. The truth was, nothing. Meeting Emma at the airport after his night with Leila was torture. Emma had been holding a banner that read: *A Hero Returns*. Even worse were the ensuing weeks when she had nursed his injured leg (he always thought of his shrapnel wound as a punishment from Allah). Afterwards, he knew that he never wanted to feel that heinous again. Within a year he'd proposed.

But now that Jesse's email had proved Leila's letter true, Andrew wished he had shown it to Emma when it had arrived. By saying nothing for eighteen months, he'd dug himself into quicksand. He opened his draft reply to Jesse. It was a week since the man had written. Andrew had to say something. So far, he had:

> **Dear Jesse,**
>   Thank you for your email. While it would be a pleasure to meet you, I am afraid December is not a good time, as my family and I are presently in quarantine. My daughter Olivia has been treating Haag victims in Liberia and we have been instructed to avoid contact with anyone but immediate family.

He sighed. He couldn't really say 'immediate family' to Jesse. That was crass. Besides, the draft implied that in normal circumstances Jesse would be welcomed with open arms. He stood up and stared at one of the porcelain spaniels on the mantelpiece, and his own face in the mirror. He suddenly looked about eighty. Then, to clear his mind, he played a long game of online Scrabble.

'Lu-unch!' trilled Emma. He would try again after a drink, he decided.

Emma

. . .

Emma was determined that Olivia's first meal at home should be perfect. Ordering a special cut of topside, baking the crumble (Olivia's childhood favourite) and prepping everything so that it could be on the table within ninety minutes of her arrival had been a good distraction from the lump. The horrid thing was, it wasn't just 'the lump' any more. But after this meal, she could start planning Christmas Eve supper and Christmas dinner. Then, in the days between Christmas and New Year, Emma had decided they would all tackle the attics. And then quarantine would be over, and she could tell everyone. If she pressed her left arm against her body she could just feel the little nodule, tucked away, in secret. Nicola had made her promise to call if she felt low, which was sweet. But having both daughters home had given Emma a boost. Besides, she knew that if she stopped to think, panic would catch her in its undertow and sweep her away.

They were eating in the rarely used dining room. It was such gloomy weather that Emma had switched on all the lamps, which somehow made the room look even darker. And she'd had Andrew light a fire, but some poor bird must have made its nest in the chimney, because an eye-watering mist hung over the table. Looking at the linen napkins and special wineglasses (given a hasty rinse and check for dead flies), she wondered if it wouldn't have been better to sit in the kitchen. The dining room was meant to feel festive, but now it looked unduly formal. She had spaced four chairs equally around the long, conker-coloured table, but with the places so far apart and the joint of meat yards from either end, it reminded her of *Beauty and the Beast*. She shunted all four plates and chairs up to one end, so that they were just using half the table. That was better. They usually had more people here, since Emma liked a full house. Guests made everyone behave better. She knew Andrew resented this, especially when Nicola dominated dinner with her psychotherapy theories, but it diluted the silences that were apt to descend when it was just the four of them. She quickly dismissed this thought and shouted again to the others.

The food, at least, was a success. Olivia had helped herself to more garlicky green beans, and the roast potatoes were a triumph (good old Delia). Emma was just anxious that the beef had come out a bit dry. That was the trouble with doing roasts in the Aga, as Andrew never failed to point out. But the Aga was as much a part of the house as the panelling, or the smoky fireplaces, or the big oak staircase. They couldn't just rip it out and put in a shiny Smeg, like in Camden. She watched Andrew take a mouthful. He frowned slightly as he swallowed, but didn't look up from his plate. Sometimes she wished he'd never got *The World* column – it made cooking for him nerve racking, when it hadn't been before. She used to enjoy the whole process, the chopping and weighing, taking down her faithful orange Le Creuset, stirring comforting stews at the stove. When Andrew was young, returning from war zones, he used to say he dreamt of her Chicken Chasseur. Now that he had eaten at Michelin-starred places for years, it was different.

Phoebe was meticulously cutting bits of fat off her beef, before putting a tiny piece in her mouth. She had refused even one Yorkshire pudding, saying that they reminded her of flannels, which made Andrew snort with laughter. Phoebe's bon mots made up the bulk of his column these days.

Olivia smiled at Emma, and said, 'This is delicious, Mum.'

Emma realised she was sweating, with heat, or nerves, or relief to have Olivia back safely she wasn't sure.

There was a silence that lasted slightly too long.

'So, Olivia,' said Andrew. 'High points?'

Olivia looked at him, hands paused mid-cutting. 'It wasn't really that kind of trip,' she said.

Andrew's neck coloured. 'Well. There are always highs, to any travel,' he said, taking a sip of wine. It was a special Bordeaux, retrieved from the cellar after much deliberation between wine and champagne.

'We so enjoyed your blog,' said Emma, before Olivia could answer him.

'Thanks,' said Olivia. 'It was helpful to write.'

'It's not easy, to write about such horrid things and be entertaining,' said Emma. 'Why did you make it anonymous, though? Wouldn't it be nice for everyone to see what you're doing?' Olivia looked terribly thin. She had Andrew's rangy build, unlike Phoebe who was small like Emma – and might have had Emma's bosoms and hips, if she weren't so disciplined about food. Emma had never managed to diet. Perhaps cancer would help, she thought grimly.

'Blog . . . ' said Andrew. 'Such an ugly word.'

'It's blogs that people read now,' said Olivia.

'I still like to hold a page,' said Phoebe.

'Quite,' said Andrew. 'That's exactly it, Phoebe. Besides the fact that the majority of blogging is tripe. Most of these people can't write for toffee. Not yours, of course,' he added. 'I thought the one about Haag stigma in rural areas was particularly good.' This was the blog that Emma had forced under his nose yesterday, since he'd holed himself up in the smoking room. He had told her he didn't want to hear what Olivia was doing, because it was 'too hellish to contemplate'. She sympathised, of course. But considering his years in foreign correspondence she'd expected him to take more interest. She'd even hoped the two of them might bond a bit over Olivia's African adventure – this being the first time Olivia had come home immediately after a trip. Now, she didn't feel this would happen.

'I liked the one about the locals calling your friend "Pekin doctor",' said Phoebe. Emma could tell she was nervous.

'Thanks,' said Olivia, helping herself to more gravy.

'George used to get called "Mzungu" when he was in Kenya,' said Phoebe.

'And what was George doing there?' asked Andrew. 'Defending the Empire?' He still said George's name as if he was trying it out for the first time.

'Building a primary school or something, I think. Some Gap Yah cliché.'

'Well that sounds wonderful,' said Emma.

'It's what everyone does,' said Phoebe. 'When they don't know what else to do before Edinburgh.'

'Kenya's quite different to Liberia,' said Olivia.

'I know, I just meant, it's also in Africa,' said Phoebe.

'It's quite a big continent . . .' said Olivia.

Emma wished they were still young enough for her to say 'Olivia, don't be condescending', but how could she, now they were grown ups?

'Remind me, why did it stop being Keen-ya?' she said, instead. For some reason, Olivia visibly clenched her jaw. Emma hoped she hadn't inadvertently served her gristle.

*

The crumble had salvaged lunch – the hot, spiced fruit seeming to thaw Olivia, and tempt Phoebe to chance a few calories. Even Andrew, who disliked pudding on principle, complimented the star anise in the custard. Emma had thought they might all walk round the grounds before it got dark, the way she used to with her parents, but once she'd cleared the sticky plates everyone had gone separate ways. Phoebe flopped on the sofa in the back sitting room, 'too full to move'. Olivia had already vanished, iPad in hand, saying she needed to read the news.

'Wouldn't you like a break from it all?' Emma had asked, but Olivia had stared at her, as if she'd said: 'Forget those dying people. You're here now, with us.' Which was what she had meant, in a sense. It was like when Andrew used to come home from Lebanon and sit glued to the TV. At least in those days the news used to stop.

Andrew was determined to go and uproot the Christmas tree, while it was still light. They used the same tree every year, dug up on the twenty-third and replanted on Epiphany, as Emma's parents had done. It was rather sweet, how seriously he took this one masculine job. Besides, it was the only Hartley tradition he seemed to embrace, so she left him to it.

Olivia

· · ·

Reaching for her phone to text Sean, Olivia remembered there was no signal at Weyfield. In some ways, Norfolk was more backward than Liberia. It already felt like they'd been apart for ages, that she'd stored up a hundred things to tell him. She'd got used to having him close, or just a WhatsApp message away. For the past fortnight he'd spent every night in her room, the two of them sleeping naked under her lightest sarong. She knew her bed was going to feel too cold, and too big, tonight. She started an email to him instead.

SUBJECT: Home Sweet Home . . .
FROM: Olivia Birch <olivia.birch1984@gmail.com>
DATE: 23/12/2016 16:30
TO: Sean Coughlan <SeanKCoughlan@gmail.com>

Hi Pekin,
Missing you already! How was the rest of your journey? Hope you got back OK, and it's good to be home. Wasn't quite planning for you to meet my mother like that . . . Pretty certain she didn't twig about us, luckily. It's really strange to be here (though I did have the best shower of

my life – hot AND cold running water! That you can drink!).
I think I'm in some kind of reverse culture shock. I'd got
used to the chaos I guess, and now Norfolk seems too
quiet. Having said that, the house here is pretty chaotic,
but in a very British way. It's all a bit Miss Havisham ... my
mother can't bring herself to change anything because
this is where she grew up. No point texting or calling, by
the way, my phone doesn't get signal. So it's emails only,
for now. Normal for Norfolk ...

Nothing to report so far, got home and then it was
straight into family lunch. Do your folks get it in any way?
Mine don't ... Or not so far. My mother is fussing over me
constantly, but can't bear to really hear about anything.
And my sister is just completely wrapped up in her little
universe. She doesn't mean any harm, but I still want to
shake her. My dad and I don't really talk, like I said. As far
as he's concerned, a new sushi bar is headline news.

Anyway. It feels wrong to be so far away from you! I'm
not telling anyone about us, by the way – promise you'll
wait till the week is up too? Write soon, I have a feeling
this is going to be a long, long seven days ...

Kisses and more,

O x

Andrew

. . .

Lunch had been interminable, thought Andrew, back at the smoking-room desk. He'd pretended he was going to fetch the tree, to get Emma off his back. He would do it later. He felt a twinge of guilt over the way he'd dismissed bloggers. Especially since Olivia's blog had in fact been rather well written. What was it that stopped him just saying so, straightforwardly, the way Emma could? And why did reading it bother him so much? It wasn't that he couldn't stomach blood and guts. He'd seen as bad and worse in Beirut for years.

He opened his draft to Jesse, and his mind set off on a habitual loop. He was curious to meet his son, of course. And if he cut him off now he would doubtless lose the chance. Besides, it was the decent thing to do. It must have taken courage, on Jesse's part, to write at all. And Leila's pathetic letter, with its 'dying wish', was tugging at his conscience. But how would Emma react to Jesse? He could hardly expect the man's birth date to remain secret. Emma would count back nine months and realise, instantly, that Andrew had been unfaithful. The trouble was, she had so little tolerance for withheld information – for lying, as she saw it. And how would his daughters view this bastard son, fathered while Andrew was technically with their mother? Olivia already seemed to be looking for excuses to avoid him. And Phoebe, who worshipped him, would be so disappointed she'd probably cut him out, too. He couldn't bear that. You did hear of it happening. Men in their sixties, living alone because of some idiotic misdemeanour. The thing to do was to be firm and absolutely transparent. The wine at lunch had given him conviction. He started a new message and tapped out:

Dear Jesse,
  Thank you for your email. While it would be a pleasure to meet you, I must ask you to accept that this is sadly impossible for me. I do not take this decision light—

The door clicked behind him. He shoved Leila's letter under a pile of books and minimised the email. But the photo he'd been looking at was still open on his screen. It was a young man with dark curls, in black tie, captioned *Jesse Robinson, Help For Syria Fundraiser*. Something told Andrew that this, out of the many Jesse Robinsons that Google Images offered up, was his son. He closed it, quickly.

'Who's that?' said Phoebe, coming in. 'He looked hot.'

Andrew's stomach recoiled. 'Uh, an actor I've got to interview.'

'Who? Let's see?'

'Now, now, you're a married woman – almost,' said Andrew.

She looked at him and laughed. 'Daddy!'

'I emailed La Beard about your party, by the way, but I doubt we'll hear back until into the new year.'

She sat on the arm of his chair. He'd have preferred her not to – it was an expensive, ergonomic throne bought on Wigmore Street, at odds with the Hartley bureau and ancient sofa. Emma always looked pained by it, even though she rarely came into the smoking room. Still, she had the last say on any new object in her childhood domain.

'OK,' sighed Phoebe. 'It'll have to be next year now anyway. When everyone will be doing Dry January.' She sat, picking at a ladder in her tights, the rock on her ring finger all wrong with her chipped, turquoise nails. 'We could've had it tonight if we weren't stuck here,' she added. She sounded faintly accusing, although what she wanted Andrew to do about their quarantine he couldn't think. But that was the way with Phoebe. He always seemed to be conceding to her, or promising to meet some outlandish request. Ever since she'd been tiny, he'd wanted to make her happy – the way she made him happy. She had that effect on everybody, except, perhaps, for Olivia.

'Bloody nuisance this quarantine, eh?' he said, giving her narrow back a perfunctory rub. 'What about Claridge's? I know the Maybourne Group pretty well.'

'Maybe ... I was thinking somewhere a bit newer ... Could you try Sexy Fish? Claridge's is a bit, like, Park Avenue pensioner.' She pulled her skin taut and pouted, miming a surprised, Botoxed woman.

'Ha! You're wasted behind the camera, Phoebe. I might have to borrow that line.'

'Any time, Papa,' she said, sliding off the arm and walking out. 'Or maybe try Dean Street Townhouse?' she shouted from the passage. 'They have a private room.'

Andrew unclenched his entire body. That had been close. He would have to be more careful. He cleared his screen, and erased his browser history. He would send the reply later. Phoebe had interrupted his concentration – he didn't trust himself to say the right thing to Jesse now. Besides, the urgent thing was to get rid of Leila's letter. It was madness to have it lying around. But the rubbish or recycling was too risky – the binmen seemed to come once a year in the country – and the fire in the dining room had expired faster than the conversation. The chimney was probably filthy – they all were at Weyfield.

After a moment's thought, Andrew climbed the stairs to the attics. It was freezing up there, the single light bulb over the main room reminding him of a TV interrogation scene. He soon located a 1980s briefcase in a pile of his obsolete belongings (flak jacket, bulky camera, hard hat, notepads) that Emma had retired to Weyfield. His fingers flicked through the combination lock, his birthdate and their Camden alarm code. One Nine Five Zero. He stuffed Leila's letter into the secret pocket in the lining and relocked the case. That was safe for the time being. He knew Emma would demand a post-Christmas bonfire – a Hartley tradition – and that he could burn the letter then. Slipped between other, innocuous papers and thrown on the pyre it would furl into secret ashes. Nobody need ever know of its existence. There was an old-fashioned finality to the act that appealed.

The sound of footsteps coming up the stairs made him freeze. Bugger. He nipped into one of the garret bedrooms and held his breath.

Emma

. . .

Emma knelt in the main attic, holding the box of Christmas decorations. Originally it had held a gingerbread-house kit, bought one Christmas when the girls were small. On the lid was a photograph of two children in wonderfully retro jumpers, marvelling at their perfect gingerbread house. She remembered trying to copy it with her daughters, and their attempt looking nothing like the box. The roof had kept slowly sliding off, making the girls shriek with gleeful dismay, until Andrew ingeniously secured it with bamboo skewers.

Both girls had been thrilled by Christmas then. Phoebe still enjoyed it (she welcomed any excuse to shop), but at some point Olivia had outgrown the excitement. Emma missed seeing them revel in something together. It didn't seem that long since they were counting down the doors on the Advent calendar, glossy heads pressed close – Olivia's blonde, Phoebe's dark. She remembered assuming they were going to be the kind of sisters who were close as adults. A noise in the little bedroom next door made her jump. She did hope they didn't have rats again. Or that Father Buxton, the priest said to haunt the house, wasn't back. Feeling rather spooked, she clattered downstairs vowing to give the attics a spring clean after Christmas.

Still, it was comforting to be back at Weyfield. Walking into the drawing room she greeted her mother's portrait, as she always did. It showed Alice Hartley as a young mother, not much older than Olivia, and although it was a rather bad likeness, it always made Emma feel Mama was still here. Two days ago she'd stood looking at it for ages, silently telling her mother about the lump. Yesterday, seeing all the things that needed fixing in the house, she'd found herself apologising to it instead. Just last night she'd spotted an ominous dripping in the servants' passage – now the utility room – as she tried to dry out extra blankets for Olivia's bed.

She knew her mother would forgive her the lack of funds to redecorate. But she feared Mama would be sad that neither of her granddaughters seemed to feel much attachment to the house. Phoebe liked showing Weyfield off to friends, but that was slightly different. She made no secret of the fact that she'd have preferred it kitted out with en-suites and reliable heating. Emma guessed that the house's faded grandeur made Olivia uncomfortable, just as it did Andrew. He never said so, but it was obvious by the way he hid in the smoking room. When they were a young couple, she had hoped that one day Andrew would stop looking out of place at Weyfield. But he never had, even after her parents died, so she'd trained herself to ignore it. That way she could indulge in private nostalgia when she was here. Perhaps that was why she didn't really want to do the house up, she thought, looking fondly at the worn cushions and rug. She liked things as they were. She just wished the others did, too.

Sitting on the piano stool, Emma opened the box of decorations. There was something delicious about the clumps of tissue paper, softened by years of hands unwrapping and rewrapping. She knew the Hartley heirlooms by touch – baubles, round and smooth, spiky stars and the padded angels studded with tiny beads. Then there were newer Birch decorations, like the sparkly New York taxi, the Science Museum robots and the ogee-shaped bells Andrew had brought back from Lebanon. Her favourites were the nineties glass balls from the Conran Shop, like huge soapy bubbles. There had been two dozen originally, and there was a time when one got smashed each year, but things were more sedate now. She remembered the girls having a special order in which they hung the decorations, Phoebe passing them to Olivia, who had stopped needing a stepladder when she was twelve. They'd demanded a particular Mariah Carey song on repeat, which Emma secretly rather enjoyed, and which had always driven Andrew from the room. That reminded her, he'd been gone ages. It was already dark outside. How long could it take to dig up the tree?

Andrew

. . .

After Andrew heard Emma go downstairs (he knew it was her, by the panting), he had stayed hidden for a while. It would be a bore to encounter her on a landing and have to invent a story about why he wasn't outside getting the tree. While he waited, he looked idly through a kind of portfolio on the floor. It was full of Phoebe's old drawings and collages. She'd shown promise as a child, but lacked the focus to go to art school. Now her aesthetic eye was evident only in her extensive wardrobe, and the way she told him which shirt to wear. He recognised a school Father's Day card that had charmed him at the time. It was titled *My Father The Hero*, and around the edge a seven-year-old Phoebe had drawn different dishes – spaghetti, and salad and steak frites, like an illuminated manuscript. The written part read:

> My father is a hero because he tests out restaurents, and tells people
> if they're good or bad. He also makes people laugh a lot, because
> he writes very funny things. I often go with him to the restaurents,
> and he writes down what I say about the things we eat. Last time I
> ordered a hamberger that was disgusting, and I said it tasted like a
> plimsoll with ketchup, so he wrote that in the magazine. We also

laugh a lot at the other people in the restaurents, and sometimes we speak in a secret code that Mummy and my sister dont understand. I love him, because he is so funny.

It was amusing to see that they'd had shared in-jokes, even then. Phoebe might look like Emma, but she'd certainly inherited his humour – and his turn of phrase. He remembered being touched that she'd seen heroism in a food column, while he was still feeling like a sell-out for quitting foreign correspondence. But that was always Phoebe's gift. She could make you feel special – or, at least, she made Andrew feel heroic. Speaking of which, he must go and uproot the bloody tree, before Emma sent out a search party.

Phoebe

. . .

Phoebe lay on the sofa, looking at simpering models in *Condé Nast Brides* and *Wedding*. Her mother had bought them as quarantine reading matter, which was sweet, though Phoebe knew she wouldn't want anything in a bridal magazine. Her plan was a winter wedding this time next year – either all candlelit and Scandinavian and hygge, or brilliantly glittery and kitsch. Whichever, it wouldn't be at all meringuey.

Her mother had been obsessed with a summer date and kept saying, 'But you don't want to wait ages!' which was totally unrealistic. No way was six months long enough to get everything sorted. Besides, Phoebe loved the run up to Christmas, and, as she'd agreed with everyone, it would make the wedding very 'her'. Both magazines had an exhausting 'Pre-Nuptial To-Do list' on their back pages, each slightly different. Wedding planning looked like a full-time job – which was just as well because her contract on *Dolemates* would end soon. Phoebe had been a casual researcher at Bright, a 'boutique TV production company', for a year. First, she had worked on a series about diet and exercise in the Middle Ages, causing her parents much hilarity. Now she was stuck on *Dolemates*, a dating show for the unemployed. It was a dire blend of *Jeremy Kyle* and *First*

Dates, and her colleagues found it very funny that 'posh Phoebe' was involved. Her mother always made a valiant effort to sound enthused, but usually got the name wrong. Her father delighted in calling it Benefit Cheats, Phoebe's own joke, and one she went along with to save face. She doubted Olivia even knew about *Dolemates*. She wasn't sure if this was annoying or a relief. Olivia probably still thought she worked 'in fashion', because of that beauty internship at *Vogue* years ago.

Her mother appeared in the doorway, looking anxious. 'Have you seen Daddy?' she said. 'He's vanished. The tree's still in the garden. I can't find him.'

'Maybe he's escaped. He was in the smoking room after lunch.'

'Phoebe – I'm serious, he's not there, he's not outside and he's not anywhere in the house.' Her voice was getting the panicky note it got in train stations.

The sound of someone yanking the front door, and the scrape of branches against wall, answered her.

'Andrew, thank God, where were you?' she said as he came in, nose red with cold.

'Getting the tree.'

'But when I went out a moment ago you weren't anywhere!'

'Had to send a text. Bloody Vodafone only works at the bottom of the drive. Now, are you two going to help me?'

For some reason, Phoebe immediately wondered if her father was having an affair – simultaneously feeling disgusted by her own mind. He'd never do that. Though he had seemed a bit weird in the smoking room earlier. Why do you have to think such psycho things? What's wrong with you? she asked herself. Intrusive thoughts, she remembered Nicola calling them. She hoped she wasn't going to end up as stressy as her mother.

*

Once the three of them had got the tree up, slightly lopsided in a copper coal scuttle, she felt better. The drawing room was freezing, as usual, but Phoebe had always loved its terracotta walls, rococo cornice and film-set chandeliers. She and Olivia used to sock-skate across the expanse of polished floor, and set up house in the huge fireplace. It was a shame her parents let the decor at Weyfield get so tired. The house could have been amazing if they spent money on it. She stood by the tree and took a deep sniff, the rush of piney resin transporting her back to seven years old – shaking presents with Olivia and praying for a Sylvanian Families windmill.

'Wiv! We're decorating!' called her mother. The opening chords of 'Once in Royal David's City' rang out from the ancient hi-fi, as Emma put on *Carols From King's*.

Olivia walked in, holding her iPad. She didn't stop looking at it as she sat down. 'Seventy new cases, diagnosed today,' she said.

'Oh, how dreadful,' said her mother. 'Those poor people. I must donate.'

Phoebe wanted to say: 'Can't you stop talking about Haag, for a second?' but she knew she couldn't. Olivia had only just got back. She was wearing her Cambridge college hoody, the one Phoebe found inexplicably irritating. It was like she still had to rub her high achiever-ness in everyone's face. At least she'd taken off the backpacker harem pants.

'It's not that simple. Corruption is so endemic there, the charities can only do so much.'

'Well, it's still terribly sad,' said her mother weakly.

Phoebe knew better than to offer an opinion. Not that she really had one. It was awful, of course, when you read the news, or thought about how some people had to live. But what could you do, unless, like Olivia, you were prepared to give up on your own life to go and help them? And hadn't George said the only way to genuinely help Africa was to stop sending money, so that the countries had to sort out their own problems? It all made her head spin.

'Now,' said her mother, after a pause, 'bigger decorations low down, delicates at the top.'

Phoebe began laying the familiar trinkets out on the rug. 'Ooh, *this* one!' she shrieked, finding the Elvis Santa she'd bought on a road trip from Vegas to San Francisco. Christmas Tree Decorations were listed, truthfully, on her Instagram profile as one of her Likes. She loved the excuse for glitz, the way the tree was the same, yet different, year after year. 'George's family have a colour-themed tree every Christmas,' she said, to nobody in particular. She always felt slightly depressed by this when she visited George's family on Boxing Day. His parents also had a second home in Norfolk, a barn conversion in nearby Blakenham. In fact it was this common ground, discovered at a sticky student club, that had led to their first kiss. But despite its proximity, the Marsham-Smiths' house couldn't have been less like Weyfield. It was brand new, with whole walls of glass like cinema screens, and dinghy-size sofas.

'Gosh, how smart,' said Emma, in her polite voice. 'But I rather like our mish-mash.' Phoebe knew that she probably thought a co-ordinated tree was a bit naff, just as she did herself. She wondered why she had mentioned it at all.

'I love our mish-mash,' said Phoebe. 'It's the only thing hotels do wrong. Artificial Christmas trees and tinsel.'

Olivia looked up and raised unplucked eyebrows.

Phoebe knew what she was thinking. She wanted to snap, 'I was *joking*. And could you either go away or help?' but turned back to the tree.

Olivia picked up one of the large glass baubles, and hung it near the top.

Phoebe automatically moved it to a lower branch. 'The big ones go lower down.'

'Right.'

'I just meant, we've always done small ones at the top.'

'Always . . .'

Phoebe couldn't tell if she was teasing or picking a fight. She stopped herself saying, 'You'd know, if you weren't always working at Christmas.' There was no point. Olivia was an expert at holding the high ground. She'd just say something about junior doctors' hours, or how Phoebe would be glad to find A&E open if she broke her arm tonight.

'Now, who shall we have at the top – the angel or Elvis?' said Emma.

'I need to check my email,' said Olivia, walking out.

An hour later, Phoebe lay in the bath in the Green Bathroom (so called because of its mint-coloured lino). She had put the heater on full, but forced open the little window so it didn't get stuffy. There was something delicious about the wafts of snowy air mingling with the scented steam, like a kind of après-ski spa. But she couldn't quite relax. Having Olivia at home always put her on edge. And this year, with her mother hailing her sister as a saint (which, of course, she *was*), would probably be worse than ever. Why did Olivia have to ruin anything fun with her po-faced glares? Just because she was so politically aware, so obsessed with Africa. Tension balled in her throat – a groping, too late, for a just-cutting-enough retort. Just enough to make Olivia reflect on how patronising she could be – and how she, Phoebe, was the pretty one who was getting married, who had the buzzy job and hectic social life and loads of Instagram followers. Although Olivia probably wouldn't care about any of that.

She stood up, feeling the blood rush to her head with the heat, and reached for the landline phone, which she'd brought in. Lying back down, she stuck boiled-lobster feet out of the water, and tried to cool them against the old, curly taps. It was impossible to get the water temperature right at Weyfield: it either came out scalding or tepid. She'd long had a campaign to get all the bathrooms redone, or at least the one that she used, but her mother seemed to have a bizarre attachment to the house's awful plumbing. It was a running joke she had with her father – Emma's insistence on Weyfield remaining as uncomfortable as possible. Phoebe's room was so cold she'd slept in a jumper last night.

'Hey you,' said George, just as she was thinking he wasn't going to pick up, and that maybe she couldn't be bothered to talk.

'Hiii.'

'How's quarantine?'

''noying. Already. We were just decorating the tree, and—'

'Hang on a sec, Titch.'

Phoebe waited while George said 'Cheers mate, have a good one,' in the voice he used for cab drivers and people in shops. He must be paying for something. She hoped it was the Dinny Hall earrings she'd told his sister she wanted – and then remembered he'd already given her a wrapped present for Christmas Day. It was small and square, but she had a feeling it wasn't the hoops. Trust Mouse to mess it up. She didn't get that kind of thing.

'So quarantine's a mare, you were saying,' he said.

She'd lost the urge to rant about Olivia now. It would be hard to explain anyway. 'Yeah, just, you know. Families. When are you driving down?'

'Tomorrow morning. Back for New Year's. Short and sweet.'

'Cool.' She couldn't think of anything else to tell or ask him, so she said, 'OK, well, talk later.'

'Talk later, Titch. Chin up.'

'Love you.'

'You too.'

She hung up, pushing away the thought that, in six years, George had never actually said 'I love you'. He'd proposed, for God's sake. The 'I love you' issue was becoming another intrusive thought. She reached for a towel –it was rough and smelt of festering laundry, like all the towels at Weyfield. She made a mental note to keep it in her bedroom, just in case Olivia used this bathroom. Whatever her sister said about there being no risk, she was still a teeny bit nervous about catching Haag. At least she'd lose loads of weight for the wedding, if she did.

Jesse

. . .

Sheringham (did you pronounce the h? Jesse had no clue) was the end of the line. Jesse trundled in from Norwich on a ludicrously small train, practically a toy train. There wasn't even a station, just an unlit platform, with a rickety gate separating it from the sidewalk. He inhaled cold, salt-spiked air, thinking how crazy it was that he had started this day by the Pacific, and now here he was beside another ocean in Norfolk, England. No, wait, in Britain there was no ocean. Just the quaint-sounding 'seaside'.

Sheringham High Street had the trippiest Christmas lights – twinkling red shrimps and yellow crabs revealing a time warp of shop fronts below. He took a couple of pictures on his phone to WhatsApp to Dana, before seeing he had no signal. There was a tiny cab office, signed 'Cliffords Taxi's' by the platform, and he was soon in the back of a beaten-up Ford, headed for the Harbour Hotel, Blakenham.

'You from A*meeer*ica?' asked the driver, as the car looped round the coast road. His accent was like nothing Jesse had ever heard. It had this insane lilt, rising at the end of every sentence – not Kardashian-style, just kind of wistful. He would have to interview some locals for his film.

'Yeah, but I have English blood. I'm visiting family here,' he replied. He was about to explain that he was looking for his birth father, but the man just grunted and turned on the radio. That was cool. He had to learn to hold back some more, anyway. He'd already gone and told the lady in the airport the whole thing, in a red-eye stupor. He and Calgary were always working on this need to blurt. Or, as Dana put it, his 'Obsessive Compulsive Sharing Syndrome'. But somehow, it still happened. He'd see something like the cute sign, and hear himself remark on it, before he'd even realised he was thinking out loud. It was like the emotional outbursts he'd worked hard to tame, but which still – on occasion – erupted. His adoptive parents, both so measured, jokingly blamed these traits on Jesse's 'hot-blooded' Lebanese heritage. Now, Jesse wondered if he'd inherited them from Andrew. His birth father had no problem sharing his personal life, and he definitely had some anger issues.

The car slowed as they entered Blakenham 'town'. This turned out to be two tiny, winding streets – literally cobbled – leading to the quay and his hotel. Getting out, he saw an ornate facade like a Victorian seaside postcard, overlooking a moonlit harbour. Inside, the lobby smelt of bleach and stale beer, the floor carpeted in maroon swirls. The Band Aid Christmas song chanted quietly in the background. A girl with painful-looking acne, wearing a Santa hat, gave him his key.

'What number is room service?' he asked. He was starving, having shunned all the junk in Norwich station. She looked blank, and he had to repeat the question three times, asking first for 'concierge', then 'the menu' and finally 'dinner'.

'Ohh,' she said. 'Kitchen's closed, sorry. Closes at eight.'

'Can I get, like, some chips?' he asked, feeling slightly desperate. Clearly, his standards would have to drop.

'Chips? No, kitchen's closed.' She was starting to look at him as if he was very stupid.

'I mean, crisps, potato crisps,' he said, remembering that chips meant fries in Britain.

'Ooooh, crisps. Yeah, we got Pringles in the minibar, if y'like? Or, I s'pose we could do you a soooup?' she said, seeming to take pity on him.

'Soup would be perfect! Thank you, you're a doll!' he said, putting a note on the bar. She looked bewildered. 'We'll put it on your bill,' she said.

'No, that's for you. I appreciate it.'

'Ooooh. Right, thanks!'

He set off down miles of musty corridor, hoping he'd be able to communicate more smoothly with his father.

The room was done in the same maroon as downstairs, the bed covered in a glossy quilt and the curtains swagged, like a puppet theatre. There were little signs everywhere. 'Please do not throw anything other than toilet paper down the toilet.' 'Please re-use your towels, wherever possible.' 'Kindly note that a late checkout will incur an extra charge.'

He considered documenting his arrival on camera, but right now a shower was priority. It was over a bathtub, the water pressure pitiful. He heard a knock and got out quickly, grabbing a towel. The girl from the lobby was standing outside with a tray. She blushed, looking for a second like she might drop everything, before handing it over and scurrying away. Clearly, what they said about the Brits being uptight was true. Although perhaps it was a little cruel to greet a teenage girl fresh out the shower, he thought, catching sight of his torso in the mirror. Dana and his mom were always reminding him that being gay wouldn't stop him breaking female hearts. Cross-legged on the bed, he tore the spongey bread roll and took a cautious sip of tangerine-coloured soup. It was tepid, custard textured and so sweet it might have been dessert. Too bad. He couldn't expect Whole Foods here. He dug out his iPad and emailed Dana.

SUBJECT: So far so good
FROM: Jesse Robinson <jesse.iskandar.robinson@gmail.com>
DATE: 23/12/2016 20:40
TO: Dana Robinson <danar_1985@hotmail.com>

Hey,
So I'm sitting in my room in the Harbour Hotel, Blakenham, overlooking a beautiful harbour. Spent an awesome day with David Rubin, who relocated to London in June. We had brunch near his apartment in Shoreditch, it's a really nice neighbourhood.
   Still no reply from The Birth Father ... What do I do?? Not sure how many days' sightseeing Blakenham Town has to offer!
   Wish me luck with the jet lag.
   J xoxo

The truth was, this wasn't at all how Jesse had envisaged his first day in Britain. Pressing send triggered an intense wave of *What the fuck?* What was he doing in a provincial hotel, eating terrible soup when he should be doing shots at La Descarga, or walking Dana's dog Flynn on Santa Monica Pier – or back home in Iowa already, helping his mom cook. No, forget that, right now he should be welcomed, with open arms, at Weyfield Hall. Or, at the very least, brushed off with an email. But he wasn't going to say any of this to Dana, who'd been mad when he'd booked his flight before hearing back from Andrew. He considered resending his original email, but would that look desperate? He was pretty sure his birth father had received his message. Before leaving LA, Jesse had sent Andrew a message from a fake Gmail account, posing as a food PR in Brooklyn to see if this would elicit a response. Andrew's one-line reply had been almost instant: 'I don't cover New York, as you'd know if you took the trouble to read my column.' Seeing an email from Andrew, but not addressed to him, was unexpectedly painful.

Maybe now's not a good time, he told himself – again. It was Christmas, after all. Maybe Andrew had replied, but for some reason his reply hadn't delivered. Perhaps he was so overwhelmed, he didn't know what to say. This whole thing was like the misery of dating, multiplied. He'd steeled himself for a guarded response. Calgary had helped him to accept that he and Andrew might have totally different energies, despite their genetic link. But he'd never expected to be cut dead. He was starting to wonder if it wouldn't have made more sense to suggest meeting in London. He had no clue what he was going to do in Blakenham for a week, if this silence continued. He lay back on the static quilt, trying not to think about how many greasy heads had lain on it, and reached for the 'Positivity Meditation' podcast in his iTunes.

· 3 ·

Christmas Eve 2016

Quarantine: Day 2

Olivia

. . .

A vivid dream about Abu, the little boy who had died in her care, made sleeping in impossible. Olivia came down to find everyone already in the kitchen, talking over the white noise of Radio Four, the ticking toaster and the coffee machine. Her mother jumped up, asking how she'd slept, and whether she'd like eggs, and would she prefer tea or coffee, and how about a croissant?

Olivia had never liked chatting in the morning. She still felt foggy with sleep and shaken by the scenes she had revisited. Sean hadn't replied to her email. It was bothering her more than she'd expected. Don't get too attached, she told herself. It might be different back home.

'Your temperature, you did remember?' asked Emma.

'Of course. It was normal. I'm fine, Mum,' she said, stepping over a bank of carrier bags, spilling with an obscene amount of food. For a second she feared Emma had broken quarantine to go shopping, before realising it was Waitrose online. Her eyes must have adjusted to an alternative, Liberian reality, because everyday things kept striking her as near-futuristic. She found herself gazing at some bagged spinach on the worktop, the little leaves all cleaned and trimmed as if they'd never seen soil, until a quizzical look from Phoebe stopped her. Everything seemed so safe, so sanitised. She poured a bowl of muesli and tried to remember where the spoons were kept. The first drawer she opened was inexplicably full of gold pinecones and ribbons. She tried a cupboard, and a melamine picnic set nearly fell in her face. This house was ridiculous. Why was there so much stuff everywhere, piles and piles of it? She wished she'd spent quarantine alone in her tiny flat, which she'd never fully unpacked and now preferred that way.

'What kind of tea would you like?' asked her mother.

'Just normal, please,' she said. She wished her mother would let her make her own, sparing her the inevitable questions about how long to leave the bag in and how much milk she wanted. 'English Breakfast, then? Or Earl Grey?' asked Emma. 'Or Lapsang?'

'Lapsang smells like Frankfurters,' said Phoebe, without looking up from a magazine.

'Christ – you're absolutely right!' said Andrew. 'Couldn't think why I've never liked it.'

'Ze *Wurst* Tea In Ze Wurld,' said Phoebe in a German accent. 'There's your headline.'

'Ha!' said Andrew. 'Maybe I'll pitch an April Fool on a new sausage-derived tea.' When Olivia sat down he stood up, saying: 'Well, I'll leave you ladies to it,' and walked out with *The Times* crossword. Olivia pulled the main paper towards her, so that she wouldn't have to talk. Phoebe was looking at her again, her doll-like head tilted.

'What?' said Olivia.

'Nothing. Just, that bowl's, like, for pasta.'

'Does it make a difference?'

'Nope. Just looks a bit weird.'

Olivia went back to the paper. Being 'weird' had always been Phoebe's big fear. Even breaking bowl conventions was cause for concern. She turned the page and froze. For a second, she thought she might be sick. A photo of Sean in the bottom left-hand corner sat under the headline: 'Irish Doctor Diagnosed With Haag Virus'. She skimmed the text, heart bounding. Then she read it all again, slowly, as if knowing everything might undo it.

Irish Doctor Diagnosed with Haag Virus

An Irish doctor who is the first person to be diagnosed with the Haag virus on British soil has been named as Sean Coughlan. Mr Coughlan, a paediatrician, was among a team of 50 aid workers who volunteered with the charity HELP to treat Haag victims in Liberia, one of the hotspots of the current outbreak.

The doctor reported symptoms, and later collapsed, while waiting for a follow-on flight from Heathrow to Dublin yesterday. Mr Coughlan was checked on arrival at Heathrow at 9 a.m., but was subsequently delayed for ten hours due to fog. Following his collapse, he was transferred to the high-level isolation unit at Royal Free Hospital in north London, accompanied by a team of health workers in full protection suits. He tested positive for Haag last night.

Mr Coughlan, 33, will be kept in a high-level isolation ward at the hospital while he is treated by Dr Paul Sturgeon, one of the leading experts in the field. His condition is said to be critical.

The total number of cases of Haag worldwide is more than 15,420 and 9,120 deaths have been reported in four countries — Liberia, Guinea, Nigeria and the US.

There is no vaccine against Haag, and healthcare workers are particularly at risk as they come into direct contact with patients. Public Health England has confirmed that it will notify members of the public who may have had contact with the doctor while he was infected with the virus, though experts said the risk of transmission was low.

The health secretary chaired a meeting of the Whitehall Cobra contingencies committee and said that there would be a review of the procedures adopted by aid workers and other officials working in Liberia. The Prime Minister, who will be chairing another Cobra meeting on the situation later today, said that everything would be done to support the patient and protect public health, adding that 'Our thoughts and prayers are with this courageous young man's family.'

'He can't!' said Olivia out loud. Her mother and sister both looked up from *How To Spend It*.

'What?' said Phoebe.

'Sean. Sean has it. He has Haag. No. No, he can't! Fuck!' she said. Her mind bloomed with catastrophe: Sean dying, his funeral, getting Haag herself, the two of them lynched by the *Daily Mail* as the feckless 'Haag Couple'.

'Haag?' said her mother, springing up.

Olivia pushed the paper towards them, grabbing her iPad. She needed more facts. 'He was working with me at the centre. You met him yesterday, remember?'

'Oh darling, how awful.'

'How come?' said Phoebe, eyes alarmed. 'Weren't you all wearing the special suits?'

'Nothing's a hundred per cent,' said Olivia, willing Weyfield's painfully slow wi-fi to hurry.

Her search brought up hundreds of results, but it was just the same report over and over, same stats and phrasing, same photo of Sean doing a thumbs-up in terracotta-coloured scrubs. Behind him she could make out the centre's familiar concrete floor, tarpaulin roof and the door into the Red Zone, plastered in hazard signs. She knew that early Haag symptoms presented gradually, sometimes over several days, before worsening abruptly in a matter of hours. It was one of the cruelties of the disease, often resulting in late diagnosis. But still, Sean had seemed his normal self right up until they'd said goodbye. Hadn't he? She remembered how he'd refused the plane meal at 3 a.m, and her chest seized. The idea that he might have been shielding her, putting on a brave face, was unbearable. She needed details, but all she had was Sean's own email and mobile number – no use while he was in isolation. She had no contact for his family, and besides, they had sworn not to tell anyone their secret until quarantine was over. She wanted to scream out loud. She'd known they were being stupid all along. Should she say something – let her family or Public Health England know? Almost simultaneously she decided not to. Not yet. She would just be extra vigilant. After all, they'd barely touched since their last morning in her room. Haag wasn't highly contagious until the later symptoms began. She should be fine. Sean had been asymptomatic when they parted. As far as she knew.

'Oh, his poor parents,' said Emma.

'Did you know him well?' asked Phoebe.

'Reasonably. Not really.'

She looked relieved. 'I'm sure he'll be OK. Sounds like he's in safe hands.'

'Yup,' said Olivia, taking her bowl to the sink and quickly leaving the kitchen, before sobs choked her.

Jesse

. . .

After an unsatisfying yoga practice wedged between bed and mini-bar, and breakfast downstairs ('freshly squeezed' meant something different here), Jesse went for a walk. It was a dazzling day, the sky an upturned bowl of blue, the ground sugar-coated with frost. He took a few mindful in-breaths, noting the ozone marshiness of the air, different from the beach back home. The total lack of hills in Norfolk was freaky. The place was like an infinity pool. A raised path across the marshes lay straight ahead, a spinal cord through the flatness, to the sea. On his left, an ocean of feathery reeds nodded and whispered in the wind. The entire panorama would make an incredible opening shot to his film.

A middle-aged couple passed him, both wearing Gore-Tex jackets and stabbing the ground with totally unnecessary Nordic walking sticks. His 'Hey there!' in reply to the woman's 'Mornin' sounded brash in the stillness. He hadn't felt this out of place in a long time. If he did get to meet his birth father – and the possibility seemed more remote with every moment – he needed to get his shit together. The steady thump thump of approaching feet made Jesse turn. A guy around his age, maybe a couple of years younger, was jogging towards him. He was actually kind of hot. As he got closer, Jesse took in his icy Siamese-cat eyes, and the kind of tawny hair and skin Dana spent hundreds of dollars trying to fake. His arms and chest were built, but his flushed cheeks gave him a boyish air, too. He reminded Jesse of a football player from college named Brad Ackland. Or a British Leo DiCaprio. Jesse didn't risk another 'Hey there,' and just grinned, making a big dorky gesture of letting him pass. 'Cheers, mate,' said the guy, on an out breath. His warm, soapy smell hung in the crisp air, as Jesse watched his back view pound down the path. So not all the cute guys were in Shoreditch, then.

Olivia

. . .

Subject: No subject
From: Olivia Birch <olivia.birch1984@gmail.com>
Date: 24/12/2016 10:00
To: Sean Coughlan <SeanKCoughlan@gmail.com>

Baby,
I know you won't get this, or not today anyway, but I can't not write.

She couldn't think what to say next. It wasn't fair to dump her own terror on Sean, much as she wanted to. If she wrote at all she should be reassuring, upbeat. But what was the point, either way, since there was no chance of Sean reading emails at the moment. Even if his condition stabilised, he wouldn't be allowed any hand-held devices until he was out of isolation. Which could be days. Because he would get better, wouldn't he? He was in the Royal Free, not Monrovia, she reminded herself. He'd have twenty-four-hour care, from the same fat-cat consultants who should have come to help in Liberia. Immediately, any comfort in this was extinguished by shame. She thought of all the patients she'd admitted to the treatment centre, where there were no beeping monitors or new drugs or assisted ventilators. There was no divine hand to medevac them to safety. Nobody to report their particular case in the papers.

What had she been thinking? How could she have lost control like this? She'd seen other aid workers do the same – living for the moment, like they were in a war zone. And she'd judged them. She even remembered discussing it with a fellow volunteer at the Calais camp, last year. They'd agreed that the way to meet emotional challenge was through focus on the work, practical care, applied learning. What a pompous twat. Now she'd gone and done exactly what she disapproved of. She'd put everyone at risk. Everyone and everything. Her own career, Sean's career, HELP's reputation in Liberia. Why hadn't they held back, followed the protocol, instead of acting like teenagers? She dug her palms into her eye sockets.

There was a knock on her door. 'I'm doing Mummy and Daddy's stockings,' said Phoebe.

Olivia paused. She wanted to tell Phoebe to go ahead, to do them without her. But she needed to carry on as normal. Her family suspecting her secret would only make things worse. 'I'll be down in a bit,' she said, brushing away tears even though Phoebe couldn't see.

'OK, I'll be in the Porch Room,' said Phoebe, footsteps fading along the passage.

The Porch Room was directly above the front door, a child's narrow bedroom. Olivia wasn't sure whose. Phoebe would know. For as long as Olivia could remember, it had been the present-wrapping room. The chest of drawers by the little cast-iron bed groaned with recycled Christmassy paper, carefully saved gift boxes, and special pens that didn't work or suddenly glooped out gold blobs.

As children, she and Phoebe used to hover outside on Christmas Eve, asking to come in, and delighting in a stern order to 'Go Away Immediately'. How unfair, she thought, walking down the passage, that some children are born to such privilege, others to shantytowns. Weyfield was a different planet to Liberia. At least there was the whiff of reality in Camden, when you chatted to the *Big Issue* sellers.

She found Phoebe on the floor of the Porch Room, surrounded by carrier bags, chocolates, paperbacks and beribboned soap.

'OK, here's what I've got,' she said. 'This is Mummy's pile.' She pointed to the frothier and pinker of two heaps. 'And this is Daddy's. We're short on non-edibles for him. It's, like, practically all condiments. He's so hard to buy for.' She sighed dramatically. 'Annoying we can't just go to Holt and buy extra stuff.'

Did Olivia detect a hint of reproach? She sat down beside Phoebe, inwardly calculating that each pile probably cost over a hundred pounds.

'Wow! Good job, Phoebs,' she said. It felt outrageous to be fussing about an adult man's stocking, when forty-eight hours ago she had been comforting an orphaned toddler. She thought of Sean, and felt like someone was slowly, slowly squeezing her insides.

Phoebe looked up, her eyes suspicious. 'What did you get?'

'Just these,' said Olivia, unwrapping two wooden bottle stoppers, carved into a giraffe and zebra, that she'd bought on a rare weekend off with Sean in Fish Town. They looked incongruous among the luxury littering the floor. Their paper bag still smelt of the spices that had hung in the air that Sunday.

'That's all?'

'Yes.'

'OK. What are they for – wine?'

'Yeah, just, for bottles, I guess. Any bottle.' She hadn't really thought about what they were for. Sean had been buying them for his parents, so she'd followed his lead. How could he be interred in a Trexler tent now?

'Are they, like, safe?'

'What? Yes! They'd need to have been in a Haag patient's bed to be a risk.'

'OK.' Phoebe took them in a pincer grip, added one to each pile, then swapped them, then swapped them back again.

'Yeah, I think that's right. Zebra for Mummy,' she said to herself, frowning.

'Sorry I didn't have a chance to shop,' said Olivia. 'It was pretty full-on out there.' She needed Phoebe to register that she hadn't just been on holiday. 'You're so good at this stuff, though. You've done really well,' she added, in the voice she'd perfected as a trainee at Great Ormond Street.

Phoebe said nothing and kept tinkering with the heaps.

'I did get these,' said Olivia after a long silence, bringing out the six DVDs she had ordered, almost at random, last week. It was all Sean's idea. He'd insisted she use his Amazon Prime account to deliver to Weyfield, when she admitted she hadn't bought any proper gifts. 'I was going to put them under the tree,' she said, 'but have them for the stockings if you need them.'

'You can't have more than one DVD in a stocking.'

'Why not?'

'Because. It's not balanced, it's too many. And they watch stuff on Netflix now. Anyway, what will you give them for their main presents?'

'I'm sure they'll manage without. And they'll still be getting them, just not under the tree.' This conversation needs to end, she thought. She suddenly felt very tired.

Phoebe studied each DVD case, took two and began silently stuff-ing the pair of long woolly socks on the bed without looking at her. At first, Olivia tried handing her gifts, but with each offering Phoebe said something like: 'No, I've just put a soap in. We need something edible,' so she gave up and sat watching, until the stockings bulged like just-fed pythons. This, thought Olivia, was why she avoided Christmas at Weyfield.

Andrew

. . .

Emma was evidently more anxious about Haag than Andrew had realised. She had barged into the smoking room earlier, jabbering about the unfortunate Irish doctor who had the virus. Trying to explain that this didn't mean Olivia was next was a lost cause. Emma kept saying, 'But Andrew, she *knew* him. *I* met him, at Heathrow, when I fetched her.'

'And did she know him in the Biblical sense? Did you lick his eyeballs? Did Olivia bid him a passionate farewell, with tongues?'

'Don't be facetious. This is serious.'

'I'm deadly serious. Haag isn't an airborne pathogen. You need to exchange bodily fluids to contract it. And the other person needs to be symptomatic – I presume he wasn't foaming at the mouth? Weren't they all checked on arrival?'

'Well, yes, but the whole airport stage seems terribly badly organised. I can't think why he was hanging about waiting for a follow-on flight. Surely he should have flown directly to Ireland in the first place?'

'Well, I doubt he had a choice. I don't imagine Aer Lingus lays on daily flights to Liberia.'

She didn't look convinced. It still mystified Andrew how he – a rational, broadsheet journalist – had married a woman who leapt on any scare story the tabloids dreamt up. Besides, he had his own real crisis to deal with. Jesse Robinson had emailed again this morning. Worse, he was actually here – in Norfolk. In this second message, Jesse politely mooted the possibility that his first email hadn't arrived, reintroduced himself, and then explained that he was staying in Blakenham. At first Andrew read this as some kind of frightful, Shakespearean coincidence. But the next line revealed that Jesse knew Andrew 'holidayed' near Blakenham and had taken the liberty of 'booking a trip' there, adding an implausible excuse about a documentary he was researching. Why were all young men obsessed with documentary? wondered Andrew.

Jesse even went on to suggest meeting at Weyfield or 'taking a walk on the beach'. What had possessed the man to fly all the way here after receiving no reply? How did Jesse know about Weyfield? How much else did he know? Bugger the internet. Had anything wrecked families, relationships, bloody normality more efficiently than the internet? Andrew didn't think so. He made a mental note to write a column on this one day. Then he remembered that, over the years, he had probably divulged all the information any estranged child could hope for in *The World* – freely available online. Had he mentioned Weyfield by name? Google revealed that, yes, he had, on numerous, rather boastful, occasions. Also online was that god-awful *Country Living* shoot which supplied the exact location of the house.

He was sunk. He really ought to reply. The trouble was, the Haag excuse sounded terribly unlikely. Besides, what if Jesse decided to risk Haag and join them in quarantine? It was a distinct possibility. He seemed pathetically keen. If Andrew was to protect Emma and the girls from the whole business, the only sensible option was not to reply at all. He deleted both Jesse's emails with a swift tap and stood up. He needed to get out, to escape the house that had caused this mess – and he was damned if he was going to pace the grounds like a prisoner. Surely a stroll along the coast road would be safe. They were miles from anywhere. He walked quickly to the hall, grabbed a coat and left, just pulling the door to so that the others wouldn't hear. Then he slipped back in and pulled on an orange balaclava, knitted by Emma in the eighties. He squinted into the mirror by the door – he looked mad, but unrecognisable. Should he be unlucky enough to encounter Jesse Robinson (he didn't put it past Fate these days), at least the man wouldn't clock him.

Andrew strode along the road to the beach. He had always found the Norfolk landscape oppressive. The unbroken horizon and dome of sky imprisoned one in a bell jar of rural stillness – bar the occasional 'Coo-*coo*-coo, coo-coooo' from a wood pigeon. Christ, even the pigeons sounded depressed here. Andrew had never been, would never be, a country person. But Emma was still in thrall to Norfolk. She wanted the girls to experience the same childhood summers and Christmases she had. For a while, Andrew had campaigned for their daughters to see more of the world. Emma had interpreted this, not inaccurately, as Andrew's own yearning for travel on leaving *The Times*. When her father died, leaving her an orphaned only child, Emma had only grown more attached to Weyfield. There was no question of selling. As the years passed, the place had become ever more shrine-like. There was now a spooky sense of time warp in the frozen carriage clocks and taxidermy birds. Even the air tasted decades old. Andrew had stopped suggesting improvements long ago – it was easier to hibernate in the smoking room. Emma probably imagined he was still intimidated by the house, as he had been at first. He wasn't any more. If anything, the place was rather embarrassingly dilapidated – not that they could afford to restore it.

A rust-coloured bull in the field to his right threw him a bulgy-eyed stare, then let forth an accusing moo. Damn you, thought Andrew, noting the animal's penis. I'm sure your calves don't email you out of the blue. You're free to sow your studly oats with impunity. He took out his phone to note down this phrasing and, when he looked up, wished he hadn't. George was jogging along the raised dyke that ran parallel to the road and had recognised him, despite his headgear. Bugger being six foot four. The boy was bound to tell Phoebe that he'd seen Andrew out walking, leading to all kinds of awkwardness. George leapt down from the dyke to the road and came to a stop, hands on his powerful thighs, panting and squinting up at Andrew. He was wearing a Lycra get-up that left nothing to the imagination.

'George!' said Andrew, yanking off the sweaty balaclava. 'Keep your distance!' he added, with a crossed-fingers plague gesture. Too bad he couldn't do so every time George offered his aggressively macho handshake. 'You well?' said Andrew, after a pause, since George was still panting in his odd squat.

'Yah, good thanks,' said George, eventually. 'Nice disguise! You AWOL? I thought Phoebs said you guys couldn't leave the house.'

Andrew hated modern youth's substitution of 'good' for 'very well'.

'Technically,' he said. 'But, uh, a man needs to escape all that oestrogen now and then. I'd appreciate it if you kept this between the two of us, old boy.' What was this man-to-man tone he had adopted?

'Got it. Hard work, then, quarantine?' said George, straightening up. It gratified Andrew that he still towered over George, even if he couldn't compete with his scrum-half physique.

'Well, not unlike every other Christmas here,' he replied. 'And you? Preparing for the coming excesses?' He indicated George's trainers, wondering how long they were expected to make chit chat.

'Huurh, yah, no, training for Paris. The marathon.' Andrew had forgotten George's tedious marathons. He made a point of ignoring the boy's money-grabbing emails, detailing the latest 'challenge' he was attempting – though he knew Emma donated fulsomely. The thought crossed Andrew's mind, as so often since Phoebe's engagement, that his grandchildren would be part Marsham-Smith. It wasn't a comfortable idea.

For a moment, they both stood looking out to sea. A cascade of church bells rang into the silence. Bloody churches on every corner in this county.

'Well, better make a move – Mum's doing a roast,' said George, jigging up and down like a boxer preparing to punch.

'Send my regards to the Marsham-Smiths,' said Andrew, stepping back to let him pass. Couldn't you say 'my mother', not 'Mum'? he thought.

'Will do, cheers,' said George, thudding off.

Andrew stood, pretending to admire the landscape, until George was a safe distance away. The air here, near the beach, was tangy – the way fish should taste, commented the part of his brain that was always writing his column. He knew George never read his reviews, and that this – rightly – annoyed Phoebe. Jesse probably read them religiously, Andrew thought. What if, in deleting those emails, he was throwing away his one chance of a father-son relationship – the kind he hadn't had with his own father or Emma's, and never would with George?

He remembered his secret disappointment at Olivia's birth, on hearing the baby was a girl. Andrew had wanted a boy. A son, he believed, might smooth the scar left by his own absent father. But Olivia was not a boy, and nor was Phoebe – although it hadn't mattered with her. Thinking of Phoebe, of that Father's Day card in the attic, his thoughts swung full circle. Deleting those emails *was* the right decision. To imagine that he and Jesse might strike up a paternal bond now was pure fantasy. And if Andrew said nothing, did nothing, Jesse would have to go back to the States, and that would be an end to it. The alternative was too messy.

Approaching the gateposts, Andrew caught Emma's voice. She sounded slightly hysterical. Stopping, he heard her say, 'But it would ruin Christmas,' and then, 'I don't *owe* it to them. Anyway, I will, soon.' He realised with surprise she must be talking on her mobile – he'd thought she only used it in crises. What would ruin Christmas? Probably some undelivered-present she'd got her knickers in a twist about.

He hid behind the gatepost, wondering what to do, as a DHL lorry stopped at the bottom of the drive. The noise startled Emma. She rushed towards the driver making wild 'no' gestures and pointing to the note she had put up which read: *Please leave all deliveries here, as we are unable to sign. Thank you.* Andrew watched the driver stare at her in confusion. 'We can't sign, we might have Haag!' shouted Emma. The man looked horrified, dropped a parcel on the drive and jumped back into his lorry.

Emma

. . .

Symptoms of Haag, Emma typed. Even the word sounded like someone dying, she thought. She knew the symptoms, vaguely, but now that Olivia's colleague was ill she needed details. Google returned thousands of results. At the top was a row of grisly pictures of people, or perhaps corpses, on stretchers. She clicked quickly on the NHS website, a beacon of first-world safety, to escape the images. It read:

Symptoms of Haag Virus

A person infected with the Haag virus will typically develop nausea, vomiting, fatigue, breathlessness, excessive saliva production, a headache, and sometimes, but not always, a raised temperature.

These early symptoms start gradually, between two and seven days after becoming infected. They may vary from mild to severe.

Dizziness or fainting, profuse sweating, a raised, bluish rash and impaired organ function follow. These later symptoms develop rapidly, often within a few hours.

Haag is fatal in 70–80 per cent of cases. The sooner a person is given care, the better the chances that they will survive.

Haag is infectious and is passed by contact with bodily fluids. A patient is most contagious once they develop later symptoms, so special care should be taken to isolate anybody who may have the virus, to avoid risk of infection.

It went on to state the importance of calling 999, should one have been to West Africa, and believe one might be symptomatic. Emma closed the tab, anxiety flapping like a bird behind her breastbone. Then, knowing it would be upsetting, but unable to stop herself, she went back to her original search, and clicked on one of the stamp-sized images. It was a child – the head huge in proportion to its body, tiny limbs covered in blueish blisters. The look of surrender in its eyes was heartbreaking. She felt a new awe for Olivia, facing these things in the flesh. She would watch her daughter closely for early Haag symptoms, she decided, Googling 'donate to Haag crisis'. She felt rather peculiar herself and tipped the Stollen she'd been nibbling into the bin.

The trouble was, the news about Olivia's poor colleague was inescapable. Radio Four seemed intent on working it into everything, and the sprawl of papers on the table was seething with Haag stories. Even P. G. Wodehouse didn't help. She had tried to distract herself by arranging holly and ivy over all the paintings – attempting a little boogie to Elton John's 'Step Into Christmas' while she did so. But Olivia had walked in and looked appalled, and Emma had worried that perhaps dancing was terribly insensitive. Finally, she had rung Nicola, which meant a shivery mobile call at the bottom of the drive to avoid being overheard on the landline. This hadn't helped, either. Nicola had been very alarmed about Olivia knowing the doctor with Haag, and begged her to tell Andrew everything in view of 'the increased risk'. Emma had banked on Nicola promising her that Olivia would be fine, and not to panic.

Having donated £50, and then, feeling that was mean, another £200, to Save the Children's Haag appeal, Emma started the borscht she always made on Christmas Eve. As she chopped beetroots, fingers turning fuchsia, she kept thinking about the American she had chatted to at Heathrow. She remembered Nicola telling her this was called 'projection'. Apparently fixating on some tangential worry, in times of high anxiety, was the brain's way of protecting itself. This didn't lessen Emma's concern for the sweet man. What if his biological father never replied or didn't want to meet him? Or what if the father had a new family who were unkind to him in some way? The whole endeavour sounded fraught with risk. How awful, to go looking for your father, and find yourself rejected – at Christmas, too.

Phoebe came into the kitchen, frowning. 'God, Olivia's so moody,' she said.

'Darling, she's had an awfully difficult time,' said Emma, tipping purple peelings into the compost. 'And now this poor friend of hers is in hospital – we must be sympathetic.'

'I am sympathetic. But does she have to be such a downer?'

'Come on, Phoebs, that's not quite fair. She just needs a nice cosy week, after everything.'

'She did choose to go there,' said Phoebe.

Emma couldn't think what to answer. The trouble was it had been so long since Olivia had been back for any length of time that Phoebe – who still lived at home – had come to assume undivided attention. She'd essentially been an only child for a decade. Emma looked at her, fiddling with the sapphire on her left hand. It looked frightfully expensive. If George had asked Andrew first, she had rather wanted to offer Great Granny's ring, which was beautiful. But it probably wouldn't have been George's taste. She got the feeling he thought antiques were rather awful and crusty.

'Any more wedding thoughts?' she asked.

'Not really. I'm Skyping George in a bit.'

'I had such a nice chat with a young man at the airport yesterday,' said Emma, hoping to distract her daughter before the mood put down roots. Phoebe had inherited Andrew's formidable capacity for sulking. 'We were both waiting. He was from Los Angeles. Terribly handsome.'

Phoebe looked up. 'Cougar,' she said.

'I'm pretty sure he was gay, darling.'

Emma thought of the man's searching brown eyes. He must have been in his thirties, but his boyishness had made her feel positively maternal. Maybe it was her latent yearning for a son. Big lanky arms to hug her from above. Madness. She'd had the change years ago.

Phoebe

. . .

Phoebe had arranged to Skype George at four. She still hadn't told him, officially, that she wanted the wedding at Weyfield. She balanced her laptop on a pile of books, so that the camera wouldn't give her a double chin, and mussed up her hair.

'Hey Titch,' said George, appearing on screen. Why, she wondered, when she was so used to him, did she sometimes feel like they were meeting for the first time? Maybe it was the weirdness of speaking on camera. He was wearing an ironic Christmas jumper and hugging Boris, the Marsham-Smiths' new Labrador. With his skiing tan and Fox's Glacier Mint eyes, he reminded her of 'Mr December' in her old tween calendars.

'You look pretty,' he said. 'That colour suits you.'

'It's yours,' she said faux-coquettishly, shrugging slightly so that the sweater she was wearing slipped down over one shoulder.

'What?' he leaned closer to the screen. It wasn't a great angle for his nostrils. 'Hey that's my Lyle & Scott! I've been looking for that. Don't go giving it booby dents, will you?'

'I wish.' She also wished he wouldn't say 'booby', but didn't say so.

'Small but perfectly formed. Like the rest of you.' He grinned.

'I'll take that. OK – wedmin,' she said. 'My dad's going to try and get us Sexy Fish for engagement drinks, but we should probably send the save-the-date soon so people can start booking accommodation.'

'Sure.'

'So, also, I was thinking . . . How would you feel about having the wedding here?'

'What, in Norfolk? I thought we agreed that?'

'No I mean here, at Weyfield.'

'At yours? But if we're thinking December we'd have to be inside?'

'Yeah. The drawing room's massive, if you open the double doors to the dining room. We had my eighteenth here, and Mummy's fiftieth. And my parents got married here, obviously. Plus people can stay.'

'How many was that?' Even on screen she could see panic in his eyes.

'Easily a hundred and fifty.'

'Sitting down? What about dancing?'

'We had a dance floor for my eighteenth. And Mummy had a sit-down dinner. You just have to move the piano and all the stuff out.'

'OK.' He screwed up his face. 'Just . . . I was thinking Gunston Hall. The food's meant to be awesome. Or Mum suggested Delling Abbey. Will and Poppy got married there.'

'Delling? But that's just like here, except, you know, we've got no connection to it. It's like, generic.' Will and Poppy were a pair of deeply basic friends of George – if it was possible to be rah and basic.

'That's a bit harsh.'

'I don't want to have a wedding someone else could have,' she said. 'I've always imagined I'd get married here. Ever since I was little.' She hadn't expected George to have plans of his own. He'd always seemed quite taken with Weyfield. Usually he was the one joking about her 'country pile'.

'Wouldn't it be a massive ball ache for your parents?'

'No way. They'd love it. Especially Mummy. She's expecting it to be here.'

'Is she? But we hadn't, like, talked about it.'

'I know, but it's a given. Birch weddings are always here. I mean, Hartley. Can't believe you're being funny about it.' She knew she sounded like a sulky child.

'I'm not, Titch. It's stunning, you know, the outside. I'm just not sure it's kind of wedding-like inside. It's more of a home, you know?'

'But that's why I want it. It would be personal. And once you had all the flowers and stuff it would look wedding-y. Anyway, I don't want my – our wedding to look like "a wedding". Or be in some hotel where another couple is getting married the next Saturday.' She stopped, realising she was on the point of insulting George's world.

'I thought you liked hotels?'

'I do, but this is different. It's our wedding.'

'Why is that any different? Plus, just in terms of logistics. The bar, and loos, and stuff. How would it work?'

'Logistics? It's not a work conference. Anyway, we could sort all that out.' She knew this wasn't the real problem. He thought the inside of the house was weird. It was true, the decor needed updating, but in photos that passed for shabby chic. At least it had character – unlike his barn conversion.

He rubbed both hands over his face, up into his hair.

'Will you look at Gunston and Delling, before you write them off?' he said.

'I haven't written them off. Anyway, what did you get Tom and Matt?' she said as a kind of peace offering. She knew she'd get her way in the end. Arguing wouldn't help her cause. George was soon recounting a recent pub quiz victory with his brothers, 'Team Marsham-S', and she felt the tension had been put aside.

'Anyway Titch, look, I should go,' he said when he'd finished his story. 'We're heading to The Woolmaker's.' George's Christmas Eve drinks with his siblings was sacred. Phoebe usually went too, and half of her resented Olivia for making it impossible. The other half was relieved to miss an evening with his sister Mouse, and Tom's wife Camilla. Something about the girls' uniform of rugby shirts and pearl earrings made her feel simultaneously superior and out of place.

After the call, she went downstairs to moan to her mother. Emma was in the kitchen, listening to *The Archers*, in a fug of boiling beetroot. Every Christmas Eve she made the same meal, a thick fuchsia borscht, marbled with sour cream and studded with porcini. Phoebe always felt it was unpleasantly close to baby food. She slumped on one of the benches, her head on the table. Her mother looked over. 'Daddy's set me up on you-player!' she said brightly, pointing to her iPad. 'So clever.'

'It's *i*-Player,' said Phoebe. 'George doesn't want the wedding here.'

'What?' said Emma, turning. 'But wouldn't it work wonderfully, with the Marsham-Smythes so nearby?'

'Smiths. Not Smythes,' she said, for the millionth time. Why, after six years, couldn't her mother get her head round George's surname not being as posh as her own? 'I don't know, he just didn't seem into the whole idea.'

'Where does he want it?'

'Gunston Hall. Because of the food. Or Delling. That's what Linda wants.'

'But . . . this is your home.'

'Ish. But he, his family don't really get that. They're different.'

Her mother looked down at the Aga. Phoebe could see she was battling Granny's voice, saying something about the Marsham-Smiths' new money. She knew Mummy prided herself on not being as snobbish as Granny, but it still came out. Especially when she was annoyed. Phoebe suddenly felt strangely defensive of George.

'What if we had it here, but got Gunston to do the catering?' said Emma.

'It's not only the food. It's just, the Marsham-Smiths do things in a more, kind of, traditional way.'

'Traditional? Isn't it more traditional to have a lovely wedding at home than in some hideously expensive venue?'

How could she begin to explain? Her mother had no idea that weddings had become an industry, that most people got married in a venue now.

Andrew walked in. 'I think what Phoebe is trying to say,' he said, 'is that the Marsham-Smiths prefer to throw money at a problem.'

'Hey! They're not like that,' said Phoebe, thinking of George's mother and her Mulberry handbags, and knowing he was right. He was always right.

Andrew took a Satsuma without saying anything, and strode out again.

'It just seems rather a pity. We've got all this space. Why would we spend God knows how much when we have somewhere with such sentimental value?' said Emma. She waved a spatula around to make the point.

'Let's just look at Delling', said Phoebe. Why was she now on George's side, she wondered, when she'd come down for support and got it?

They sat down together with Emma's iPad. Looking at stuff online with her mother was always exasperating. Emma typed any Google search in full, usually making several typos, and then wondered why it didn't work. Delling Abbey's website appeared, and they clicked *Get Married At Delling*. There was a picture of a woman wearing beauty-pageant make-up with her hair in crispy tendrils and a man in shiny morning dress. They were grimacing and ducking in a blizzard of confetti. The idea that she and George might become that couple was surreal. A banner ad on the side steered them to another site called Wedding Bee. Here, all the brides said how intent they were on making the wedding unique, but all had a photo booth and moustaches on sticks. Her mother kept hooting with laughter. Phoebe felt her blood pressure rise, even though she agreed with Emma that the weddings looked terrible. She wanted to say: 'If you'd just spend some money on this place, instead of leaving everything to rot, then George wouldn't be freaking out.' But she knew this wouldn't go down well. She would have to convince her mother to re-do the dining room and drawing room at least. Her father would understand.

She left the iPad to Emma and returned to the mood board she had begun that morning. She was using the back of Olivia's homecoming banner, the green fitting her Christmas theme neatly. The table was soon covered in tusk-shaped fragments of *Brides* magazine, as she snipped round photos of winter flower arrangements, white fur capes and the occasional, non-disgusting dress. 'Ooh, this is a jolly idea,' said her mother, 'a cupcake tower – a sort of pile of fairy cakes. I suppose traditional wedding cake can be rather stodgy, can't it?'

'Yummy!' said Phoebe. Her mother wasn't to know that the world had reached peak cupcake years ago. She needed to be extra sweet, if her campaign to get Weyfield redecorated was to work out.

Olivia came in, looking tired. 'Can we move this thing? There's nowhere to sit,' she said, gesturing at the mood board. Phoebe took the board and leant it against the window. She'd moved on to a wedding playlist now anyway. She was thinking either 'Baby It's Cold Outside' or 'Let it Snow' for the first dance, and her all-time favourite 'Please Come Home for Christmas' for the last dance. Or even Mariah. George wouldn't object; he had typical public-school cheesy taste in music. Olivia sat, pushing a mince pie into her mouth as if in a trance, and pulled a property supplement towards her – the way she used to hide behind the Shreddies at breakfast.

'How's your poor friend?' said Emma.

'No news,' said Olivia, barely looking up. 'Though the press have gone to town on him. Including Andrew's colleagues.'

He's our *dad*, thought Phoebe. Why d'you have to call him 'Andrew'? After a moment of nobody saying anything, she gathered her lists and went upstairs. She knew it must have been stressful in Africa. But everything was so much easier, and nicer, when Olivia wasn't around.

Jesse

. . .

It was Dana who told Jesse that staying in wasn't an option on Christmas Eve. He had called in a nostalgic mood, seeking sympathy, after catching *It's A Wonderful Life* on TV. They used to watch it together, eating Mom's spiced shortbread, he'd reminded Dana. But she hadn't indulged him. 'Jesse, you made this decision – you need to own it. Go make some new memories,' had been her exact words. So he had showered, cologned and stepped into the cold, to see how the locals celebrated.

Now, sipping a self-conscious pint, he couldn't tell if The Woolmaker's Arms, Blakenham, was playing tricks on him. It seemed to be pure Ye Olde England – close and carpeted, with tiny, diamond-paned windows and such a low beamed ceiling that he had to stoop. The seats were dark as church pews, and the beers had crazy names like 'Woodfordes' and 'Bullards'. Back home this would have been a replica – like the dude ranch in Montana where he'd stayed with his ex, Cameron. He didn't want to be the gullible tourist, taken in by a sham, but something about the The Woolmaker's suggested it was the real deal. He semi-regretted not bringing his camera, but he felt conspicuous enough as it was.

The bar was packed. Christmas Eve was clearly a big party night in Blakenham. Jesse wondered if this was the kind of topsy-turvy evening when lords and peasants mingled, like in *Titanic*. A group of three young guys with 'posh' accents dominated the room. With them were two blonde girls, giggling uncontrollably. They were all sitting by the fire, braying with laughter at an anecdote Jesse couldn't catch. The men reminded him of frat boys at college, but their bodies were different – with bigger necks and barrelled thighs. Two wore striped shirts, sleeves rolled up to show meaty forearms, the other had on a V-neck that just stretched over his broad chest. Their table was covered with empty glasses. The one with his back to Jesse stood and turned, and Jesse saw it was the guy who had jogged past him that morning. Their eyes met, fleetingly. Jesse watched him walk to the bathroom, and resisted the impulse to follow, to see if he would acknowledge him were it just the two of them under strip lighting.

Moments later he reappeared right beside Jesse at the bar, looking straight ahead. He had a preppy little snub nose, and a fine, almost feminine jawline – at odds with his athlete's beat-up ears. His hair-line was wet – he must have smoothed it back in the bathroom. Jesse looked at his wrist, the blond hairs against his tan, muscles twitching as he fiddled with two notes. A gold ring shone on his pinkie, and beside his Hublot watch was a string of pale green prayer beads. Funny to see that the LA influence even made it here. "Nother three Woodfordes and two G&Ts please, mate,' he said to the barman. He had a deep, garbled voice that reminded Jesse of Prince Harry – top of the 'celebrities I am allowed to sleep with' list he'd had with Cameron. The guy turned to Jesse and raised his eyebrows.

'You were out running this morning, right?' said Jesse, before he could stop himself.

'Ha, yeah. Unsuccessfully,' he said.

'How come?'

The guy seemed confused. His cheeks coloured slightly.

'Oh, uh, y'know. "Suboptimal terrain",' he said, and Jesse could hear the air quotes in his voice, but wasn't sure what he was alluding to. This must be the famous British sense of irony.

'Sure,' said Jesse.

'You on holiday? Sorry – "vay-cation",' said the guy, in a twangy New York accent.

'Kind of. I'm also working.'

He could feel his adoption story about to spill out again, like in the airport, and stopped himself.

'Doing what?'

'Research,' he said. 'I'm making a short film.'

'Cool,' said the guy.

Jesse waited for him to ask what it was about, or to question why he was working over Christmas, but he said nothing.

'Are you from around here?' said Jesse, fearing the conversation might end.

'We have a house here.'

'Cool. Must be a nice place to relax.'

'Yah. So beautiful. I love it here, the sea, the air. Awesome.'

'It's beautiful, right?'

The barman set down the drinks. 'And a pint for this fine gentle-man,' said the guy, gesturing to Jesse.

'Hey, cheers – I appreciate it,' said Jesse. His 'cheers' still sounded off.

The guy mock bowed, but said nothing as he put the two notes on the bar and tried to pick up all the drinks at once.

'Let me help you,' said Jesse, taking the gin and tonics.

'Thanks – George, by the way,' said the guy.

'Jesse.'

'Jesse. Good to meet you, mate.'

He followed George through the crowd, feeling the fizz of being invited to the popular table in high school.

Putting down the gin and tonics, he was unsure if he was expected to join the group or go back to the bar. They all seemed too drunk to notice either way. One of the men, who appeared to be the alpha male, was mid-story.

'And then,' he gasped, voice shrill with supressed mirth, 'Chingers sits up and promptly says: "Mmmm Toby, why are your testes in my mouth?"' As if taking a cue, the table erupted with laughter.

'Guys, this is Jesse,' said George.

'Jessie? I'm sorry, your name's *Jessica*?' said Alpha Male, dissolving into more guffaws.

'Stop it,' hissed the girl beside him, slapping him on the arm. 'Sorry about this one – can't take him anywhere,' she said, putting a hand over the man's mouth. 'Hel-lo,' she added, looking at Jesse properly. 'And where are you from?'

'Los Angeles.' Jesse had learned long ago that this got a better response than 'Iowa'.

'So what in God's name possessed you to spend Christmas in Blakenham?' said Alpha Male. He talked like a fifty-year-old man, though he looked around thirty-five.

'He's in film,' said George. So he had taken in what Jesse said after all.

'Christ,' said Alpha Male. 'What are they filming here – period drama?'

'Uh, it's more documentary.'

The girls were looking at him eagerly. They probably thought he was an actor. Women often did.

'Where's the rest of your crew?' said the other, younger-looking girl. She had the same profile as the three men, and he guessed she was their sister.

'I came early. Wanted to get a feel for the place.'

'So you're on your own at Christmas?' said the first girl.

'It's all good – we just celebrated Thanksgiving back home. Plus it seemed like a nice opportunity to travel.'

'You can't be on your own at Christmas! We'll look after you,' said the girl he presumed was a sister, shifting up the bench to make room for Jesse.

She began introducing the table. Her name was Mouse, inexplicably, and the three men were her older brothers, as he'd guessed. Alpha Male, real name Tom or 'Tommo', was the oldest. George was the youngest, and the middle brother was named Matt. The girl beside Alpha Male was Camilla, Tom's wife. By the way Mouse was tossing her hair, he guessed she didn't have a refined gay-dar. But people didn't always realise Jesse was gay, straight off. The looks Matt was shooting him suggested he thought Jesse was sharking on his little sister. Just as well Matt didn't realise Jesse had a crush on his brother. A couple of times he sensed George looking at him on the edge of his vision, but whenever he checked George either wasn't or had just looked away. He was by far the cutest of the three brothers. He was the only one with the cool, swimming-pool eyes. He wondered if George had guessed he was gay.

'Drinking game!' bellowed Alpha Male. 'I Have Never. The Christmas round.'

Everything they said about Brits drinking was true. Shots were summoned from the bar and they played a few rounds of 'I Have Never', where it transpired that Matt had thrown up on his boss's back at an office party, and Alpha Male had taken a dump in someone's shoe at boarding school. Jesse wasn't sure what the point was, since they clearly all knew each other's secrets.

'OK, my turn,' said Camilla. 'I have never given my ski instructor a blow job,' she crowed, looking at Mouse.

On impulse, Jesse knocked back one of the honey-coloured shots on the table. His throat burned.

He blinked to find the whole group staring at him, stunned. His eyes met George's, just for a second.

'What?' he said to them all. 'Don't tell me you had me down as straight?'

Alpha Male began chuckling and beating the table with his hand, his laughter rising to a crescendo. 'So it's *that* kind of film,' he spluttered. 'Well, fuck me. Christmas drinks in The Woolmaker's descends into gay porno. Fuck me.'

Jesse tried correcting them but it was no use fighting the current – they wanted him to be a porn star, and so he was, even though he had no answer to Tom and Matt's increasingly explicit questions.

The game moved on to everyone's porno name, but the mood had shifted. Mouse's hair tossing stopped. Matt was obviously repulsed by Jesse's revelation, several times describing something as 'gay' and then pointedly apologising. Alpha Male was so drunk he looked like he wouldn't care if Jesse had stated a sexual preference for chipmunks. The girls, he guessed, were keen to appear liberal. He could already see them telling the story in years to come: 'Remember when we got talking to that gay porn star in the pub?'

It was bullshit, of course. He'd barely been skiing. But he needed to know if what he sensed about George was real, or if his brain was addled by alcohol and too much alone time. Straight-seeming jock types had always been his weakness.

George was drinking hard. It looked like he was on a mission. Jesse had seen him finish two pints, a glass of mulled wine and a bunch of shots, and now he was back from the bar with more beers – one for him, one for Jesse. Everybody else had refused his offer of a final drink. Camilla returned from the bathroom. 'Guys, I'm shattered. Home,' she said firmly, looking at her husband.

'Me too,' said Mouse. Alpha Male and Matt both stood, unsteadily.

George stayed sitting down. 'I'm gonna finish this one. I'll catch you up,' he said to them, slurring slightly.

'Suit yourself,' said Alpha Male.

'Make sure he gets home safe,' Camilla said to Jesse. She seemed to be Mother Hen already.

'No sexy time,' added Alpha Male, and George gave him the finger. Matt looked appalled.

Now it was just the two of them. George was sitting back in his seat, eyelids drooping.

'Last orders!' shouted the barman.

'They're closing already?' said Jesse.

'This is Norfolk, mate. You're not in Manhattan now.'

'LA. I'm west coast.'

'Same difference.'

Was he just being a dick, or was it a clumsy attempt at flirting? A ringtone broke the moment, and George reached into his pocket. He looked at the cell phone for a second, switched it to silent, and let it sit, buzzing, on the table.

'Go ahead,' said Jesse, sipping the cool foam from his fresh pint. He'd nursed the first one for hours, and it had grown warm and stale.

'Nah, I'm leaving it.'

'Your girlfriend?' said Jesse. He'd spent enough time with straight men to read the signs.

'Fiancé.'

'Woah. Serious.'

'I know. Not entirely sure how it happened, if I'm honest.'

'I'm guessing you put a ring on it?'

George grunted. He was staring at the phone, looking spaced out.

'How long have you guys been together?' said Jesse.

'Six years. Don't get me wrong, she's an awesome girl. Hundred per cent. But it's a massive commitment, y'know? There's still a lot I want to do before I settle down, do the whole two-point-four kids thing. Guess you wouldn't know.'

'Drink up boys, we're closin',' said a hefty, middle-aged barmaid.

'Where are you staying?' asked George, abruptly.

'The Harbour Hotel.'

'Would the bar be open?'

'Maybe.'

'Quick one there, for the road?'

'Won't your family wonder where you went?'

'They know I can take care of myself.'

'OK. Sure.'

They walked out into the night.

· 4 ·

Christmas Day 2016

Quarantine: Day 3

Olivia

. . .

Haag Blog 10:
What Happens In PPE Stays In PPE

So here I am, back on British soil, after three months in Liberia. For the rest of the world it's Christmas Day, but for me and my colleagues this is another twenty-four hours of quarantine. Twice daily, we must report our temperature to Public Health England. We have been supplied with 'emergency Haag response' kits, packed with bleach, rubber gloves and a mysterious little orange trowel, presumably for some kind of emergency burial . . . With these tangible links to Haag, it's not easy to switch off and feel festive.

Because it turns out that coming home can be lonely. Friends and family either don't want to hear about the things you've seen, or they don't ask, for fear of upsetting you. 'How was it?' they say. 'You know, um, eye opening,' you reply, groping for some palatable truth. 'Of course. Must have been awful,' they say, looking uncomfortable, and some-how, at that point, the conversation always moves on. They mean well. But in trying to spare you, and themselves, they unwittingly make it worse. With no outlet, memories fester like untreated wounds.

There's another shock in homecoming: the flashback. My colleague, who had more practical experience in treating epidemics than me, used to say, 'What happens in PPE stays in PPE,' and I now understand what he meant. Let me explain. The Red Zone, the ward where Haag-positive patients were treated, could only be entered in full PPE. For the uninitiated that's Personal Protective Equipment: a hazmat suit, goggles, wellies, heavy-duty apron, double rubber gloves. Anything that went into the Red Zone had to be bleached, or incinerated, on exit. We dressed with a buddy, to check – and triple check – each other's kit. It took at least twenty minutes. The deeper you both got into your PPE the harder it became to communicate, until you were two shapeless monsters performing a strange dance of exaggerated thumbs-up gestures. If you've ever been scuba diving, you'll have some idea of the process. And, just like going underwater, PPE muffles the senses. Within minutes your goggles are steamed up, you can't smell anything but yourself – your own sweat, your own breath. Your hearing is foggy. Touch is blunted. It once took me five minutes to ascertain whether a woman was dead. Out of PPE, it would have taken me five seconds.

Then you enter the Red Zone, and do what you have to do. From inside your bubble you see terrible things. Children, screaming and screaming for their mothers – who are crying because they can't touch their child. People begging you not to let them die, when all you can offer is a few words of badly accented Kreyol. Patients haemorrhaging so fast that within minutes of changing their sheets their beds are drenched with blood. Corpses lying unmoved for hours because there isn't time to prioritise the dead over the living.

By the time your shift finishes, you are emotionally spent. You and your buddy leave the Red Zone and are immediately sprayed with chlorine solution, before painstakingly doffing your PPE. A chlorine shower follows. Next, you must wash your hands three times, wash the tap you used, change into clean, bleach-mottled scrubs and dry wellies. But during this time, something happens. The hour of ritual undressing, washing and redressing acts as a buffer between the Red Zone and reality. And the strange thing was, the memories did stay in that underwater PPE world, just as my colleague promised.

Except now, safely home and with time on my hands, the worst things I saw keep resurfacing. They haunt my dreams, and ambush me over family lunches. In Liberia, I slept soundly, lulled by the hum of a generator and the racket of Monrovian streets: shouting, dogs barking, cockerels crowing. But here, in the quiet of the English countryside, peace is evasive. When I shut my eyes, all I hear is children crying.

I will never forget a man who had recovered from Haag, only to lose his three-year-old son Abu to the virus soon after. I had become too attached to Abu myself – it was impossible not to. Right up until the day when he was fighting for his life, he would grin and offer his little starfish hand for a high five when I did my rounds. I remember, when Abu died, his dad just sat, weeping and rocking, saying that it should have been him, that he didn't want to live any more, that he would drive himself off a cliff. I covered Abu's tiny body in a white cloth and said a prayer while I held his father's hand. The prayer was for the man's benefit. It would be difficult to believe in any God that afternoon.

But it is desperate memories like these that make me determined to return to Liberia. Every day that I am doing nothing in England, I am conscious of people dying, whose deaths I could have prevented. At the very least, I might have made their final hours more comfortable. As British aid workers, we are only allowed to treat Haag for twelve weeks. Since most of us volunteers arrived in October, we leave the treatment centre dangerously short staffed. What happens in PPE may stay in PPE – at least at first – but our work is by no means finished.

Olivia posted the blog and flopped back on her pillow. It had been cathartic to write, but she longed to credit Sean – to say it was he who coined the PPE catchphrase, and he who had been her Red Zone buddy. She remembered how the donning and doffing was laced with sexual tension, weeks before anything had happened between them. But she couldn't risk naming Sean online, now that he was a news story. Their secret crawled under her skin like goose bumps. Since his diagnosis, checking her temperature had taken on a sharp, adrenaline-spiked significance. Even the normal reading, which she'd taken at 5 a.m., had been small relief – she'd seen plenty of patients develop Haag symptoms without a fever. Now, it was only 6.30 a.m. She had never felt less Christmassy.

Andrew

. . .

Andrew had woken just before five – as so often these days. He wanted to blame the birds, but it was silent outside, and no light penetrated the pond-green drapes around the bed. He had never liked the four-poster they slept in at Weyfield – previously Emma's parents' – just as he didn't like Weyfield's cavernous master bedroom. He had a fear that one day he would be taken ill, and a doctor would arrive and see the eccentric bed and write him off as a kind of squalid, senile lord. It had taken years of complaining about his back just for Emma to replace the horsehair mattress – so soft one longed for a snorkel. There was no way she would ditch the bed itself.

Beside him, Emma snored. Years ago, he used to find the sound rather touching. As a young man, he'd felt honoured to hear the inner workings of Emma Hartley, who looked like a china doll but snored like a drunk. Now, it was just a cruel reminder that he couldn't sleep himself. Of course Emma could sleep. Her conscience was as virginal as the day they'd met. Emma never lied, never concealed anything. Perhaps this was why they'd grown apart. He lay looking up at the canopy over the bed, the ebb and flow of Emma's breath raking at his ears. He tried to picture her snores as three-dimensional objects, thinking it might make a writing exercise. They had jaunty peaks – like meringues, or dog turds. Occasionally, a snore rose to a curly flourish, as if someone were piping it out of an icing bag. He flopped onto his side, his back to her, and savoured the cool patch of pillow. The bed was oppressively stuffy. Perhaps she was having a hot flush, for old times' sake, he thought, as the snores reached an abrupt hiatus. Then they began again, louder than ever.

But it wasn't the dawn, or the bed, or Emma's snoring that had woken him. Deleting Jesse's emails hadn't felt as final as Andrew had hoped. It didn't change the fact that the man was here, less than a mile away. And Jesse's voice, calling from Andrew's past, had unlocked a Pandora's box in his mind – memories of Beirut he had long buried. Ever since Jesse's second email, his dreams had echoed with the jabber of gunfire and the crooning call to prayer. He saw things he hadn't seen for years – smoke mushrooming from rubble, apartment blocks ripped to cross section, people running from flames, blood-stained pavements. He found himself startled by the rifle-click of Weyfield's front-door latch and sitting with his back to the wall – as if a sniper might be lurking in the larder. Madness. But he could no more help it than expect anyone to understand. He kept seeing the broken body of the child he'd watched flung into the air by an explosion. It was probably for the best that Jesse hadn't grown up in Lebanon. At least he could destroy Leila's letter soon. As predicted, Emma had requested a bonfire after a 'Boxing Day Sort Out'. He'd feel better once it was out of the house.

A ringing blasted the darkness, and he jumped. Beside him, he felt Emma fumbling for her alarm clock and getting out of bed. What on earth was she doing? Then he remembered – stockings. Even now, she and Phoebe remained oddly attached to this childhood ritual.

'D'you mind if I put the light on?' she said, blinding him with her bedside lamp before he could answer.

He watched her crouching over two crammed woollen socks,

wearing one of the tent-like nightdresses she now slept in. It was a pity, because she had kept her in-and-out figure, unlike so many of his friends' wives. But what did it really matter, since he only saw her undressed by accident, and they hadn't had sex for months. He remembered past Christmases when they had managed a hurried morning encounter while the girls were busy with their stockings. But at some point, years ago now, he had become aware they were having sex *because* it was an occasion, as if she felt obliged to tick it off the list along with making a perfect Christmas dinner and festooning the house with bits of twig.

It was around the same time Emma had had the menopause, and they had taken to sleeping under different-tog duvets. It was a small shift, but it felt symbolic, cocooning them in their discrete shells. He thought back to last Christmas morning, lying in bed, ruefully aware that Phoebe wouldn't surface for hours and that he and Emma could have had a leisurely shag – if she'd wanted. But Emma had been downstairs, stuffing a whole turkey, just for three.

Emma

. . .

Emma had always enjoyed doing her daughters' stockings. When the girls had been little (well, until they'd been teenagers), she used to creep into the room they shared wearing a special red dressing gown. Laying their stockings at their feet, bending to look at their sleeping faces, she remembered feeling overwhelmed with tenderness. Now that they were grown up they all opened their stockings together, over breakfast. For years, Phoebe had sweetly made stockings for Andrew and Emma too, so that everybody had one. Emma had gone to extra effort with Olivia's this year. She had put in several tubes of swanky hand cream, a Georgette Heyer that she thought would make cosy reading, and some leather gloves she grabbed in a kind of daze in John Lewis, after meeting Nicola.

When she looked at Olivia's raw, red hands, she felt that same tenderness flood her – except she knew it wasn't welcome now. All she could do was try to spoil her and will her to open up. She hoped Phoebe wouldn't mind that Olivia's stocking was bigger than hers. Phoebe could be silly in that way. With luck she would appreciate that Olivia had missed out for the past few years.

Emma yawned. It had taken her an age to fall asleep, talking her-self down from a ledge of anxiety at 2 a.m. During the day she could banish thoughts of the lump quite successfully, but they lay in wait – pouncing in the horizontal quiet of the night. She'd only been asleep for a couple of hours when her alarm went off. Andrew had already been awake. He slept so badly these days – perhaps it was all the rich food he had to eat. There was a time when she'd have felt duty bound to make love on Christmas morning, but not now. For the past eighteen months Andrew seemed to have stopped even trying. She didn't particularly mind; in fact it was rather a relief not to be pestered. But it wasn't like him. Funny how the more you went without sex the less you missed it. She held the rustling, multi-jointed stockings in her arms like babies, to stop them stretching all over the place. The stairs by the kitchen smelt of last night's borscht. She opened the door, and let out a little yelp of surprise. Phoebe was sitting at the table looking at Emma's iPad, crying. Emma's first thought was that she'd argued with George. 'Phoebs! What's wrong?'

'You have cancer!' Phoebe was sobbing extravagantly now, her lips turned down like a sad clown's face.

Emma sat sideways on the bench to hug her, and for a while they rocked together, Phoebe weeping into Emma's neck. She smelt of sleep and shampoo. Emma's side was killing her, but Phoebe was clinging to her neck like a toddler.

'I'm OK, darling, I'm OK,' Emma kept saying, until Phoebe emerged.

'I'm sorry, I know I shouldn't have read your emails but I was putting out your stocking, and I wanted to check something on that Delling link, so I went to your history and then I saw all the searches. All the Hodgkin Lymph stuff. So I looked at your emails and I saw one from Nicola. Why didn't you say, Mummy? Why didn't you tell us?'

Bother, thought Emma. If only she hadn't left her iPad lying around.

'I was going to. I was. I was just waiting until this quarantine is over. I wanted us all to have a nice Christmas. No point ruining Christmas!' she said.

'You wouldn't be ruining it. You can't keep something like that secret.'

'But I feel fine, sweetheart. This is Olivia's week.'

Phoebe hiccupped. 'Still! What are you going to do?'

'Well, I'm ... I'm with a very good doctor, angel, the best doctor for these things. I will probably have to have chemotherapy, but he says I should make a full recovery. It's not a very bad cancer.' She knew this wasn't quite what Mr Singer had said, but protecting Phoebe was a reflex. She was still so vulnerable, so young, compared to Olivia.

'Will your hair fall out?'

'It may do. But that's a small price to pay.' She forced her face into a bright grin. 'I'll save a fortune on haircuts.'

Phoebe gave a valiant smile. 'Will it have grown back for the wedding?'

She hadn't thought of this. What an image – mother of the bride, bald as a vulture. That is, if she was here at all.

'Hopefully. Just as well one wears a hat!' she said. 'Now come on, stop this, I'm going to be absolutely fine. I need to be – you're getting married!'

This didn't seem to fortify Phoebe as she'd hoped. Her daughter sat staring at a poinsettia on the windowsill, sniffing.

'Daddy knows, right?' she asked.

'Not yet,' said Emma, trying to keep her tone light.

'What? But shouldn't he ... shouldn't you two—'

'I'm going to tell Daddy and Olivia when the quarantine is over,' Emma said, before her daughter could offer any marital advice. 'I want Christmas to be happy. It'll only upset them. All of us sitting here fretting, cooped up with nowhere to go. I'll get the next test results in a few days – that'll be the time to discuss it.'

'But—'

'Please don't say anything, will you, Phoebs? Can we keep this just between us, for now?'

Making Phoebe feel special had always been the way to win her over, even when she was very small. Her forehead softened.

'OK. But do you promise to tell Daddy, straight away, afterwards? And Olivia? She's the doctor, for God's sake. She'll probably piss off to Africa otherwise.'

'Phoebe. That's not nice. Yes, I promise. Now you go back to bed. I need to do some last bits and bobs down here.'

'Shouldn't you go back to bed, too?'

'I'm not an invalid.'

'Can I help you? Lay the table or whatever?'

'No, no. Just being you cheers me up.'

Emma sat for a while after Phoebe had gone upstairs. The effort of sounding upbeat had left her drained. She made a cup of Earl Grey, and looked out of the window at the croquet lawn. She thought of her own parents and her childhood Christmases here. All at once she wanted, more than anything, to talk to Mama. It was funny how, even once you had children, you never stopped needing your mother. If anything, they made you need her more.

Phoebe

THE GREEN BATHROOM, 7.30 A.M.

. . .

Phoebe knew she wouldn't be able to get back to sleep. She ran a rose-fragranced bath and lay looking out of the window at a square of white sky. The words she had seen on her mother's iPad made her feel squeamish: tumour, growth, biopsy, CAT scan. They were words that belonged in other people's lives. She realised that a tiny, awful part of her resented Christmas being ruined. And next year. It was meant to be her year, the run up to the wedding, and instead everything would be clouded. She could hardly ask her mother to redecorate Weyfield now. She knew this was not a generous way to think.

She considered calling George, but he would still be asleep. She pushed down the voice that piped up: 'You should be able to call your future husband at any time, especially with something like this.' Instead, she went outside for a jog – turning up a gym playlist full volume. Miley Cyrus sounded tinnily out of place on the croquet lawn. As she ran laps, she found herself obsessing about whether George had got her the Dinny Hall hoops – the last thing she should be thinking about. But the thought that he might get her present wrong, like he'd got the ring a bit wrong (OK, a lot wrong), made the crying lump rise up in her throat again.

Worst of all, she hated herself for still being such a brat. Would she ever grow up and be like Olivia, and stop caring about *stuff*?

Olivia really annoyed her at breakfast. Even while they were doing stockings, she kept sneaking looks at her iPad under the table. Phoebe wanted to shake her and say: 'This could be Mummy's last Christmas! At least look at her, instead of the news, for five minutes.' She didn't say anything, though, even when Emma had to ask Olivia three times if she wanted panettone.

Afterwards, she went upstairs to call George. His phone rang to voicemail, as it had done twice last night. She would have to call the Marsham-Smiths, which meant talking to George's mother.

'Hello, Dalgrave Barn?' trilled Linda.

'Hi Linda, it's Phoebe. Happy Christmas.'

'Phoebe! The bride to be! Merry Christmas! How *are* you?'

It was odd how her voice was different to George's watertight drawl. Linda always sounded too loud and too posh, bar the occasional clanging vowel.

'Fine! Quarantined, haha, but fine.'

'Of course you are. How's your sister? Must have been pretty primitive over there? Do they have running water, toilets?'

'She's fine. She just has to take her temperature the whole time.'

'Does she? That's good. Did she know the Irish boy?'

'Sorry?'

'You know. The one who got it.'

'Oh right, er yes, a bit, I think.' Why did Linda always have to ask a billion questions?

'He really should've been more careful, shouldn't he? It's just irresponsible, putting us all at risk like that. Now let me see if George is up yet. They all had *rather* a late night.'

'Ah,' Phoebe tried to sound knowing. She heard Linda shouting for George.

His 'Hey, Titch' when he answered was hoarse.

'Hey. Happy Christmas.'

'Oh yeah. Happy Christmas, babe.'

'Your mum said it was a big one last night.'

'Did she? Not specially, just The Woolmaker's.'

'Oh. Anyway, George, can you go somewhere on your own?'

'I am.'

'OK, I have bad news. I just found out –' she paused, to make sure he registered the crisis in her voice, 'that Mummy has cancer.'

'What? Your mum? Shit.' He sounded distracted.

'Yes. Hodgkin Lymphoma. No, wait, Non-Hodgkin Lymphoma.'

'What, she does or she doesn't?'

'It's *called* "non", that's like the name of the cancer.' She found tears rising again and exaggerated her sobs slightly to make sure George didn't think she'd just gone silent. She didn't often cry in front of him, considering how easily she wept with her family.

'Don't cry. She'll be OK,' he said, stiffly.

'What if she's not? This is like my nightmare! She can't, she can't not be OK.'

'Don't think like that.'

'I just found out by mistake. I was looking at her iPad and I saw all her searches, and then this email from Nicola.'

'Nicola?'

'She's her best friend. You've met her. Blonde, shouty?'

'Oh right, her. Look Titch, I'm really sorry, I have to go. We're doing champagne breakfast. I'm sure she'll be OK. Talk later.'

And he hung up.

Jesse

. . .

Jesse woke up fully clothed on top of the bedspread. His head was throbbing. He was craving a cold-pressed juice, but the only remotely cleansing thing in the minibar was a camomile teabag. He stood, sipping its thin, floral brew, looking out at the marshes. It was hard to believe it was Christmas Day. The room smelt of George's cologne, woody and young – perhaps Chanel Egoiste or Boss. He lay down and stared at a yellowish stain on the ceiling, replaying last night in his head.

They had left the bar. He remembered George pulling on a beanie, but having no coat, and how his athlete's shoulders looked strong and powerful in the cold. The moon was so full it cast shadows. A pheasant shot out of the undergrowth with a frenzy of squawking and flapping, and their arms bumped as they both instinctively ducked. The rest of the time, the only sound was their footsteps on the frosted road.

'You close with your brothers?' said Jesse, for want of something to say.

'Sure. They're, like, my boys. My buddies. We were shipped off to boarding school when we were seven, so we kind of clubbed together.'

'Seven years old?'

'Mmm-hmm.'

'Jeez. I'm sorry.'

'Don't be. It's all good.'

They walked on in silence, turning onto a lane so overhung with branches that it was more tunnel than path. George had been the one to suggest they keep drinking, but he didn't seem to want to talk. Jesse couldn't work him out. He was straight – publicly – but sometimes the straightest-seeming guys were the ones who wanted to experiment. Why else would he have suggested they go back to Jesse's hotel? Unless he was just drunk. His profile was expressionless. Jesse tried a different tack.

'Do you think that's why you proposed to your girlfriend? Looking for security? Righting the wrongs of your childhood. All that shit.' For a moment, as George's head whipped round, he wondered if he'd overstepped the mark. But George just looked bemused.

'What wrongs?'

'Your parents sending you away. Abandoning you. Maybe you wanted to, I don't know, fix it with your own happy ending.'

'Ha. Happy ending.' He sniggered, like Jesse had said something dirty. 'Do there have to be reasons for everything?'

'Everything happens for a reason.'

'Right ... so you're like a Scientologist?'

'Nope. But I'm a film maker, and we get pretty deep. Human condition and all that.'

'I thought you were in porn?'

'Hell no! That was your brother, jumping to conclusions. I did some acting when I started out, but I prefer being behind the camera. Besides, I'm too tall to be an actor.'

'So what've you been in? Anything I'd know?' The question came with a slight sneer, as if to undercut any inferred interest – either in Jesse's acting or superior height.

'Mostly US shows. *Spring Break*? *Willow Drive*? I had a walk on in *Curb Your Enthusiasm*.'

'Woah! Did you meet Larry David?' His excitement made him sound younger.

'Sure. I mean, we didn't talk a whole lot but we met.'

They reached the hotel. The security light revealed a deserted lobby, and a metal screen over the bar. Jesse sensed the mood evaporating, and George having second thoughts. 'I have booze in my room,' he said, on impulse. He must have been drunker than he realised. Or perhaps he just needed company. It was days since he'd had a real conversation.

George followed him up the stairs. He was suddenly very aware of the other man's body, the corridor so narrow that they switched to single file. Up in his room, they both sat side by side on the edge of the maroon bed. Jesse emptied two Jack Daniels miniatures into tumblers.

'Chin chin!' said George.

'Merry Christmas,' replied Jesse.

'So, what, you're spending Christmas *here*?' asked George, leaning back on his elbows and surveying the room.

'Looks that way,' said Jesse, switching on MTV but turning the sound way down.

'How come?'

'I didn't plan on ... I mean, it wasn't supposed to turn out this way,' he said.

George looked confused.

'OK, here's the deal. I'm adopted, right?' said Jesse. 'And I'm looking for my birth father. He lives around here. The whole idea was that I was going to spend Christmas there, at his home, but it turned out I'm not welcome.' He knew he was oversharing again, but he was too drunk to care. He could hear his therapist's monotone asking:

'Do you think you "blurt", Jesse, because you want to free yourself of something?' Shut up, Calgary, he thought.

'Wait – what? So you're looking for your real, as in, biological father and he told you to piss off?' George seemed more animated than he had been all evening.

'Not straight out. But I sent him a bunch of emails, and he didn't reply.'

'Nothing?'

'Just, I don't know, silence. I told him I was working in Norfolk, that we could meet somewhere neutral. It's cool. I had to be here for work anyway. I knew I was taking a chance.'

'Dude, that's really poor form. Have the decency to reply, for fuck's sake.'

'He might not have gotten the email.'

George didn't look convinced. 'D'you know where he lives?' he asked.

'Uh, yeah. It's not far. Do you think I should, like, go to his house?'

'You have his actual address? Then sure, why not? Look – either he got the email and he's ignoring you, in which case he's a douche and you should call him on it. Or he never got it, and you're losing out on the chance to meet your father.'

'I guess. I'm not sure it's so simple.'

'Mate, what have you got to lose? I always say this, you regret the things you didn't do, not the things you did do.'

'Right – you're the first person *ever* to say that.' Jesse grinned to show he was joking. The conversation had gotten too intense. George smiled back. His lips were stained with mulled wine. Jesse wanted to taste them. He sat up and pulled his sweater over his head, careful to make it look casual. As he emerged, he saw George checking his abs where his T-shirt had ridden up, as he'd known he would. He leant back on his elbows, too, so that they were both staring straight ahead at Beyonce gyrating on TV. George collapsed down on the quilt beside him. Their legs were still over the edge of the bed, feet on the floor.

'I am properly wasted,' said George, into space.

Jesse looked across and down at him. 'Room spins?' he said.

'Room fucking teacup ride, mate.'

'You can crash here, if you want.' Jesse lay back, flat out, like George. Their heads were inches apart on the bed.

'Might have to.'

George shut his eyes, so Jesse did, too. He was almost nervous to breathe. Was it his imagination, or was that George's arm, shifting closer to his, so that he could just feel its hairs mingle with his own, and George's knuckles, brushing his hand? He pushed back, just enough, with his own hand. They lay like that for what seemed ages. Jesse stretched to switch out the lamp, so that the room was lit only by the flashing TV screen. He could smell the whiskey on George's breath. He modified his own breathing to sound like he was falling asleep. And then he felt George turn, and his lips against his neck, in the dimness.

They must have slept, because he was woken by the click of the door handle. The clock by the bed said 05:08. George was by the door, with his back to Jesse. He was moving with a kind of hunched stealth that told Jesse he didn't want to be seen. Jesse shut his eyes again and heard the door creak open, then softly close. George's steps retreated down the corridor outside. Jesse lay still, wondering if he had imagined everything that had happened in the watery dawn light, until his bladder overcame his need to stay horizontal.

Olivia

. . .

Olivia had only checked the news an hour ago, but already her fingers were itching for her iPad, as if it was a link to Sean. There were no updates on his condition today, and the headlines were dominated by forecasts of 'the soggiest ever Christmas'.

'No news is good news, surely?' her mother had said, as they opened stockings over breakfast.

'It just means he hasn't deteriorated, or improved. And he was critical yesterday, so that's not great.'

'I hope you might still manage to enjoy Christmas?'

Olivia made herself smile and pretended to be interested in the Fortnums marmalade, and credit-card Swiss army knife emerging from the red sock in her hands.

Now the four of them were in the drawing room, her father pumping at the hearth with a pair of wheezy bellows. He stopped to tell a story about lighting a fire in the desert with a magnifying glass, during the Soviet–Afghan war. Olivia knew he was going to tell it even before he sat back on his heels to say, 'Y'know, this reminds me of . . . ' He never talked about the Afghan people, or the politics at the time – just his own boy-scout memories. But that was the way it was at home, everyone sticking to a script, wheeling out the same, exhausted anecdotes. *Carols From King's* was playing again, 'Silent Night' bleating from the speakers. The air was dense with woodsmoke and a sickly mix of orange peel and furniture polish. It seemed indecent to be sitting here with the radiators on full as well as the fire. The only thing that helped to take her mind off Sean was planning a return visit to Liberia next year. She felt slightly crazed with the need to do something.

Phoebe dived towards the tree, pulling out shiny parcels and distributing them, until everyone had a little mound of presents at their feet. Olivia slid her iPad out from under the sofa and swiped the screen, refreshing her search for Sean Coughlan. Nothing new.

'OK, this is for you from Mummy,' Phoebe said to Andrew, choosing a present for him to unwrap. 'And this is for you from me,' she said to Emma. She eyed Olivia's pile. Unlike when they were children, it was noticeably larger than Phoebe's, though Olivia would gladly have given Phoebe the lot. 'That's just from Irina,' said Phoebe, pointing at a gaudy gold parcel.

'Who's Irina?'

'Irina The Cleaner,' chorused Emma and Phoebe, and burst out laughing. Olivia wasn't sure why this was funny. It kind of appalled her that they had a cleaner when her mother didn't work. And that the poor woman was spending her wages on gifts. Irina (she now dimly remembered a Romanian woman scurrying around Gloucester Terrace) had given Olivia a box of Lindt chocolates and a glittering card wishing her safe return from Africa. Her mother had probably been talking about it non-stop. At least she no longer wrote her round robin, which always began 'Olivia has reached new academic heights'.

Olivia offered everyone the chocolates, though only her mother took one. She reached again for her iPad, hiding it behind the cushion on her lap, and pretended to watch the others open their presents. Her mother met each one with a noisy show of delight or hilarity. Andrew kept pulling the same nonplussed face he always made on receiving gifts, until he came to Phoebe's, and looked genuinely thrilled with a wine aerator.

Phoebe was holding a small, professionally wrapped present. 'OK, now George's,' she said. She uncovered a tiny turquoise box. Her lips puckered, like when she was about to cry as a child.

'Ooh, Tiffany! More sparkles!' said Emma.

Phoebe opened it and sighed. 'I knew he wouldn't get them,' she said.

'What's wrong, angel?' said Emma. 'Let's see.'

Phoebe held up a pair of pearl studs.

'Oh sweet! Very nice, very classic. You'll have those for ever.'

'I never wear pearls.'

'Perhaps George would like you to,' said her father. 'Nice pashmina and pearls, sounds right up his street.'

Emma shot him a look.

'It's just I asked him specifically for these Dinny Hall hoops. I sent Mouse the link and everything. I knew she'd be useless.'

'Oh well, these are lovely too. Let's see them on! Perhaps the hoops can wait?' said Emma.

Phoebe sat back on the sofa, biting her bottom lip. 'Can you put that away?' she suddenly snapped at Olivia. 'It's Christmas!'

'OK, calm down. There.' Olivia made a show of turning her iPad screen face down and covering it with a blanket.

'You never get it, do you?' said Phoebe.

'*I* don't? I'm not the one crying because I got some ridiculously expensive earrings, when millions of children are malnourished.'

'Oh my god – do you always have to bring it back to Africa?'

'It's not just in Africa. Although, since you mention it, hundreds of people have died of Haag this month.'

'Girls, come on, please,' said Emma. 'Now, here's one for Daddy.' She handed a floral package to Andrew, and he gave her a clumsy pat on the arm as she leaned down to plant a loud kiss on his cheek.

He took ages to open it, using his penknife as if they were on a survival course. Finally, he eased a book out of the William Morris paper, held it at arm's length and announced: '*Where Chefs Eat: A Guide To Chefs' Favourite Restaurants*. Marvellous, I shall enjoy that. Thank you, my sweet,' he said, scanning the blurb.

Olivia wondered why her mother had bought him a book on the one subject he knew inside out. But it wasn't really about that, she knew. It was about going through the motions of giving each other more and more stuff, every year. Her mother had given her about twenty tubes of hand cream – all of them overpoweringly perfumed. Phoebe had bought her a jumper that looked like something she'd wear herself, and was probably made in a sweatshop in Bangladesh. And her father had given her a pointless photo album – no doubt chosen by Emma. He'd written in the gift tag: *Olivia, Haagy Christmas, A.* What was wrong with him? Did journalists find it that hard to resist a pun? She looked at the floor, scattered with newness and wrapping paper and ribbon, and realised it was actually making her feel sick. She mumbled an excuse, and went upstairs to check the news in peace.

Andrew

. . .

It was nearly dusk outside but they were still finishing lunch, wearing paper crowns from their crackers. Andrew had protested that it made them look as if they were in an old people's home. But Emma and Phoebe had insisted, and Olivia had just looked pained – no change there. Was there anything, thought Andrew, more dismal than a family of adults wearing paper hats? He felt uncomfortably full. The turkey carcass sat on the side, the tar-like pudding still on the table. They'd followed it with some unnecessary Stilton, and Emma was now passing round Charbonnel et Walker truffles. Writing about food, eating out all the time, Andrew had come to feel that less was more. In his foreign-correspondent days, they'd often made do – cheerfully – with Ryvita and boiled water.

Emma put a fuzzy recording of 'White Christmas' on the old LP player in the corner. He remembered dancing to it with her soon after they had met, and knowing he would marry her. Now it just sounded schmaltzy.

Phoebe was clamouring for charades, when the doorbell rang with the long pressure of a stranger. Nobody ever used the bell. A heavy knock followed.

All four of them looked at each other.

'Who's that?' said Phoebe.

'Didn't they see the sign at the gate?' said Emma.

Andrew stood up quickly. He knew he should have replied to Jesse's last email, should have fended him off. 'I'll go,' he said. But already there came the sound of someone grappling with the front door.

'Keep them outside,' said Olivia, sharply.

'I will,' he called back, guts contracting as he rushed through the kitchen, the quickest route to the hall. He jumped as the latch clicked – louder than ever, it seemed.

But before he reached the hall, a voice called out 'Meeeeerry Christmas one and all!' and he found George, pulling off his gilet.

'Mr B!' he said, with a slightly crazed grin. 'Couldn't stay away!'

Andrew wondered if the boy was drunk. He seemed to be slurring, but perhaps that was just his obnoxious accent.

'George . . .' He couldn't think what to say, but luckily Phoebe appeared.

'Tiiiiitch!' he said.

'Bae! What are you doing here? You're not allowed!' She was tipsy, too. She rushed up to him, and he lifted her off the ground. 'Thank you for my earrings,' she said. 'Love them.' He kissed her, full on the lips, as if he was eating her.

Andrew coughed. 'Charming though this display of festive affection is, children, we Birches are in quarantine. George, should you be here?'

George looked at him. He had Phoebe's lipstick all over his mouth, but he wore it like victory. Emma and Olivia walked in.

'What the—? He shouldn't be here,' said Olivia.

'Lovely to see you too, Liv.'

'We can't see anyone till the thirtieth. Didn't you explain?' Olivia said to Phoebe. She sounded unusually flustered.

'Of course I did! He knows. But he can stay till then, right?'

'I'm family! Nearly,' said George, his joker smile widening.

'Well he has to,' said Olivia. 'They've just exchanged God knows how much bacteria.'

'He *has* to stay?' said Phoebe, hopefully.

'Yes! It's a public health risk if he leaves now,' said Olivia. 'And you won't be able to go anywhere till Friday, you know that, right? Even leave the grounds. We all have to stay here.'

Emma seemed to rediscover her default hostess. 'Of course you must stay, George – not that there's any real risk. How lovely. Will you have some coffee? Take it you've had lunch?'

They walked back to the dining room, Phoebe and George whispering behind Andrew.

'I can't believe you came! You're literally insane,' she said, in the same little-girl voice she used to ask Andrew for money.

'I missed you, Titch,' said George. 'And I was worried about you. You OK now?'

'Mmm. Thanks for coming.'

Andrew briefly wondered what George was talking about, but knowing Phoebe it was probably nothing more than a broken nail. She was always having a melodrama about one thing or another. Still, he was surprised George had risked Haag for one of her crises. Andrew didn't have him down as the type. Maybe he knew he was in the doghouse about the earrings. Perhaps he was just deeply stupid. Anyway, he supposed he had to get used to having George around.

Emma

. . .

Emma stood by the sink, hand washing the special plates. Everything had gone to plan, but the timings of Christmas lunch had left her exhausted. Even for four, it felt like a military operation. She was always afraid the turkey would be undercooked or that she'd end up 'nuking it', in Andrew's words. Still, Ottolenghi's sprouts were a success, and the pudding lit up with blue flames like a witch's spell and, best of all, nobody had argued. Emma had feared the girls would bicker after their quarrel by the tree. She saw both their points and felt stretched between them. Phoebe could be a bit spoilt, but Olivia didn't know her sister was fragile because of what she'd seen earlier. And Olivia's way of looking at her iPad, when they were meant to be having family time, was rather rude. On the other hand, she might have some kind of post-traumatic stress disorder, like a soldier. Emma knew, from Andrew's war correspondence, that she could never understand what Olivia had seen. Still, she wished she didn't have the feeling that Olivia looked down on their Christmas fun as slightly grotesque. She began squirting Dettol over the worktop and had a sudden urge to clean the toaster tray. She wasn't like this usually, she thought, giving the fridge handle a furtive wipe. She did hope she wasn't getting that syndrome Phoebe talked about – OCDC, was it? Or was that a band?

The phone rang – it was Nicola.

'Emma, darling, Happy Christmas. How *are* you?' she said, in her new bedside manner.

'Terrific! We've had such a jolly day. Gorgeous weather here, too. And tell me about you, how are all your boys?'

But Nicola would not be drawn on her life. She kept bringing the conversation back to Emma and Weyfield.

'Have you told them? The girls and Andrew?' she said, in a stage whisper.

'Well, not yet – remember I didn't want to put a dampener on Christmas? But Phoebe found out, unfortunately. This morning. She saw our emails from yesterday.'

'Oh poor thing. Was she terribly upset?' Nicola sounded as if she rather hoped she had been.

'She was, I'm afraid. But George turned up to surprise her after lunch, and that seems to have helped. I think she must have told him. I did ask her not to. But discretion was never Phoebe's forte.'

'George? What about the quarantine?'

'Well, he has to stay here now, with us.'

'Oh. Young love! Rather sweet, risking his life.'

'Well, yes, I suppose. Not that there's a great risk. He must have realised she was low. I was a bit surprised, I must say. You know how I've never thought he was all that . . .'

'Sensitive?'

'Mmm. I thought he was a bit more,' she lowered her voice, 'stiff upper lip, army type.'

'I thought he was in finance?'

'Well, the father's military, or was, before he made his millions. And his brother's in the marines. Anyway, just from what Phoebe's said, I get the feeling the whole family don't really "do" feelings. Though I suppose Andrew and Olivia aren't huge emoters. Phoebe and I make up for them with our waterworks.'

'And how *is* Olivia?' Nicola was back to her bedside voice. 'I saw her new blog today. One doesn't think about the difficulty of coming home, does one?'

'Her blog? I thought she'd finished it?'

'It was about being back in England.'

'Oh golly, I should have read it. What did it . . . did she say it was awful to be home and we didn't understand her?'

'No! Of course not. She just – you know, it's a huge adjustment, I suppose. You mustn't catastrophise, Em. It's not good for you.'

Emma had the feeling Nicola was backtracking. She knew she needed to look the blog up, now. She made an excuse about clearing away lunch, and then wished she hadn't, because Nicola reminded her to 'take it easy' and 'be kind to herself', which was rather irritating. Waiting for the blog to load, she thought of what Nicola had said about young love and how dismayed Olivia had looked at George's arrival. She wondered if she minded not having a White Knight of her own. She did hope Olivia would meet someone and have babies soon. Wasn't that what life was all about? But Olivia always seemed so self-contained that Emma rather doubted she felt the same.

The internet connecter – or whatever it was called – seemed to have gone on strike. She would read Olivia's blog later, she promised herself.

Phoebe

· · ·

Phoebe felt sluggish with daytime drinking and more food than she usually allowed herself. She and George were in the bungalow, which backed onto the drive. Her mother always talked about doing it up as a guesthouse, but never had done. Phoebe rarely came here any more. It belonged to a different, teenage time, serving first for sleepovers with her best friends Saskia and Lara, and later for spliffs and snogging. There were still relics of that era – Paris Hilton's face on old magazines, a ping-pong table and a lingering stench of tobacco and Febreze. Olivia hadn't been part of the bungalow back then, although Phoebe remembered her attempting a party here with her lame medic friends. Trust her to do stuff a decade late. She hadn't even got a boyfriend until Cambridge, while Phoebe's love life had started at a respectable fourteen.

It was much warmer in the bungalow than the arctic main house, once you had both heaters on. Phoebe curled up beside George on the sofa, where, years ago, she had lost her virginity to Seb, a boy from the year above at Westminster. She reached for a chocolate and tried to think of something to tell George or ask him.

'Stop me eating!' she said, after a while. 'Seriously, I'm going to be obese by the wedding at this rate.' She wasn't really worried – keeping herself under eight stone was second nature. But she kept finding her eyes drawn to Olivia's model-skinny legs. Her sister was as thin as she had been at school, when Phoebe lived in constant fear of Olivia being scouted (luckily she wasn't pretty enough).

George moved the chocolates and took one of the pearl studs between his finger and thumb. 'They're beautiful. Like you,' he said, wiggling her earlobe. He was being mushier than usual. Now that he was here she'd got over the Dinny Hall hoops. The worst thing was that she knew Olivia was right; it was bad as an adult to care so much about getting the right present, or that George had written 'lots of love' not 'all my love' in the gift tag. But she couldn't help it. So, on top of disappointment, she had to feel ashamed of herself, too – like a sandwich of rank feelings.

'I can't believe you came,' she said again, resting her head on his shoulder. She'd thought he'd barely registered the news about her mother. But perhaps that was just George – he was all about actions, not words. Put that way, it sounded kind of manly and hot. George didn't answer. He was fiddling with an old lighter from Phoebe's gap year in Paris. 'You sure your parents aren't freaking out that you're here?' she said.

'They're chill. If we get Haag, we're getting it together,' he said, pulling her closer.

'Your mum sounded pretty anxious when I spoke to her this morning.'

'Did she? She shouldn't read the *Mail*. I'll call them again in a bit.'

'You knew you'd have to stay, right?'

'Course! That's why I came. I wanted to be held captive with you.' He kissed the top of her head.

Phoebe nestled into him. This wasn't like George. Apart from holidays, she wasn't sure they'd ever spent more than two consecutive nights together. He always needed to get to work, or the gym, or some sporting fixture. But she liked it. Besides, they'd have to get used to living together when they were married. It was still an unreal thought.

'I'm feeling better, by the way.'

'Sorry?'

'About Mummy.'

'Oh, right. Yeah, that's shit.'

'D'you ever worry about your parents, like, getting ill?'

They didn't often have conversations like this, and she wanted to keep it going.

'Not really. Bit morbid.'

'I guess. Just, I don't know what I'd do, if . . . If . . .' Just thinking about saying the words 'if Mummy died' she felt tears jam her throat, like someone was digging in it with a spoon.

'Hey, stop it. It's all going to be OK. We're getting married, remember?'

She sniffed everything back. 'Maybe you'll come round to having the wedding here, after being quarantined?'

'Like Stockholm syndrome?'

'What's that?' She knew what it was, but playing dumb was second nature with George. It seemed to make him happy.

'Don't worry.' He kissed her, a slow, determined kiss on the lips. He was stubbly, and as she pulled away she noticed mauve shadows under his eyes.

'I love you, Phoebe Birch.'

'I love you too,' she said. She wanted to jump up and do a victory lap round the bungalow. He had said it. He had finally said the words.

Jesse

. . .

After a damp walk and a slimy 'Vegetarian Roast' in the Harbour Hotel's dining room, Jesse spent the afternoon on his bed. He'd watched the Queen's speech and three episodes of an impenetrable comedy called *Only Fools and Horses*. This wasn't how Christmas was meant to be. He was supposed to be at Weyfield Hall with his new family – although the whole idea now seemed stupidly naive. Calling home, lying to his parents that he was having fun and hearing everyone laughing in the background, had only made it worse. Especially the sad note in his dad's voice, as he said: 'Well, take care, son. Don't do anything I wouldn't.'

There was still no reply from Andrew. The Glenmorangie Jesse had bought in the airport, knowing it was Andrew's favourite, sat on top of the closet. Every time Jesse saw it, he felt small. If he wasn't so hungover, he'd have opened it himself. He still hadn't filmed anything. The idea of returning home with reams of footage of Norfolk, and none of his birth father, was too depressing.

He thought about George saying: 'What have you got to lose?' It had sounded trite, but maybe the guy had a point. Perhaps, aside from a brief physical thrill, the universe had sent George to Jesse for that exact reason – to prompt him to go see Andrew Birch. He looked up at his dumb Duty Free gift and felt a new defiance stirring inside him. Perhaps he was still drunk. Whatever, why not just go to Weyfield? If not to knock on the door, at least to see the place, maybe get some fresh inspiration for his film. Besides, he needed to know the house was real, that this whole thing wasn't in his head.

Finding Weyfield Hall was not as straightforward as he'd assumed. Since he had no cell signal, he was forced to use the tiny, photocopied map in his room information pack. The sidewalk seemed to fizzle out as he left Blakenham, and there were no signs anywhere. He asked the two couples he passed for directions. The first were French and couldn't help. The second kept saying 'just bear left and head for the sea,' which was hardly more use. It was dark, and a few lone flakes of snow bobbed in front of him. His feet were rigid. Too bad he hadn't inherited the British imperviousness to cold. Just as he was about to give up, half-relieved, he saw four chimney stacks sticking out of a cluster of trees, across the field by the road. That had to be the house. By the map, it looked like it was in the right spot. His pulse began to pick up. Fuck the roads. He ducked under the barbed-wire fence and strode straight across the frosted stubble.

Beyond the field he found the entrance to a gravel drive. The gates looked like they were always open, one hanging off its hinges and overgrown with ivy. There was a note tucked into the gatepost, which read: *Please leave all deliveries here, as we are unable to sign. Thank you.* Bizarre. Maybe they weren't here after all. The whole place was more run down than he had expected. It was actually kind of ghostly in the twilight, skeletal trees like black lace against the sky. Or was that just his nerves? Before he could chicken out, he began walking briskly up the drive, past some outbuildings, reminding himself he could always turn and run if he saw anyone. He rounded a corner, and there, twenty yards away, was the house.

For a moment, he just stood looking up at the huge rectangular facade, several windows glowing with life. His heart was pumping like he'd done an hour in the gym. It was definitely Weyfield; he recognised it from the *Country Living* shoot. It reminded him of the doll house Dana had as a kid, like you could just swing the whole front wall open. He walked closer, slowing down, trying to stop his feet crunching too loud in the silence. The house came into focus – red brick, with long stately windows and a shallow stone porch, coated with lichen. He stood by the front door a while, holding his breath, straining to hear sounds from indoors over his pulse. But all he could hear was the wind in the bare trees, and the whoosh of distant cars.

'My father is in this building,' he said, in his head. 'My father is on the other side of this door.' He decided against the mossy doorbell and lifted his hand to touch the knocker instead, just to feel it, not sure if he had the balls to knock. It was shaped like a lion, a sprig of mistletoe clamped between its bared teeth. A light snapped on in the window directly above the door, followed by the sound of steps inside. He froze. They were the urgent steps of someone hurrying, right up to the door, as if they knew he was outside. Who was coming? What the fuck should he say? He was on set with no script – totally unrehearsed and unready.

He jumped back, as the letterbox spat out a piece of paper, and caught a glimpse of fingernails as it clicked shut. The note by his feet was scrawled in gold pen: 'Hi. We can't answer the door. Call landline.' Jesse suddenly felt utterly freaked out. What had he been thinking, coming here, unprepared? What was this place, where people wrote in liquid gold and refused to answer the door or accept the mail? He turned and hurried down the drive, certain he was being watched. When he came to the field he broke into a run across the open ground. He found the spot where he'd ducked the wire fence before, and this time vaulted over it, accidentally grabbing a barb and swearing out loud – with frustration as much as pain.

Already he was cursing himself for being such a pussy, for not shouting out to the person on the other side of the door. But what else could he have done? It was a relief to see headlights swinging down the coast road, and the cottages near his hotel, windows flashing with Christmas TV. It was even good to be back in his crappy little room, he thought, rinsing the graze on his palm under the weak tap. The British were seriously eccentric. At least he'd have a story for Dana.

· 5 ·

Boxing Day 2016

Quarantine: Day 4

Olivia

. . .

Now that there were no more presents to wrap, the Porch Room could become Olivia's sanctuary. She used to read here as a child, to escape the glacial swims and long boat trips demanded by a gung-ho little Phoebe. Boats always made Olivia throw up – painfully conscious that she was the gross one, spoiling everyone's fun. Now she folded herself into the deep window seat and pulled the curtains shut, just as she had when she was nine. It wasn't comfortable – she could feel every knobble in her spine against the panelling – but it was private.

She looked out at the bare garden, so different from Liberia's tropical foliage. In just three months she'd grown used to its wild, accelerated fertility. She remembered how tendrils crept into the treatment centre within days of being hacked back, how insects seethed over carrion. At the time, it seemed disturbing. Now, Norfolk's slow safeness, its brittle twigs and absence of predators, felt as unnatural as Mars. She wished she could talk to Sean about it. She'd written him another email yesterday, trying to sound positive, determined to write daily, even though he wouldn't read her missives until he was out of isolation. But one-way correspondence was hard. She would email later, she decided, when she had more to say. She tried to read an e-book, but her fingers kept Googling his name. A critical stance towards him was growing in the press. One columnist had accused him of 'a treacherous disregard for Great Britain'. Every newspaper seemed to have run an opinion piece, questioning why Sean and other Irish aid workers were permitted to wait at Heathrow when their follow-on was delayed – as if this was Sean's fault. Her Christmas blog was meant to be her last, but now she found herself logging back in.

Haag Blog 11:
Why Does Our Press Delight In Taking Others Down?

I wasn't planning to blog again, but I'm angry. Christmas jingles on (and on), but my colleague Sean Coughlan's positive test has destroyed all hope of celebration. What angers me, though, is the British media's response to his diagnosis. Our focus should be on Sean's courage and recovery. Instead, many reports have chosen to cast blame – speculating that Sean must be at fault. The cruelty of Haag is that it is transmitted by compassion. Mothers catch it, because they can't bear to leave a vomiting child alone. Nurses are infected by patients they have tended too well. Nobody knows how Sean contracted Haag. But I can assure you we were all subject to the strictest protocol. None of us, including Sean, would knowingly have put ourselves at risk. Bottom line: we were trying to contain a deadly virus with basic resources.

Unlike those commentators who have seen fit to question Sean's professionalism, I worked alongside him. He was one of two paediatricians at the treatment centre and a favourite among staff and patients. It wasn't just his expertise that inspired us. It was his humanity. I saw him sit with grieving mothers long after his shift had finished. I saw him make sick children laugh as he inserted their cannulas, all while dressed in monstrous PPE, and persuade bewildered toddlers to drink their rehydration salts (no mean feat, as any parent will tell you). And I saw how he returned to our furnace-like conditions day after day with a smile, when others were at breaking point. So I would challenge those journalists who accuse him, on no evidence, of 'selfishness', to do the harrowing, hot, messy job Sean did.

Jane Falcon, a columnist for *The World* magazine, describes us aid workers as: 'naive idealists, risking British health to indulge their own post-colonial rescue fantasy'. She goes on to advise that we 'let Africa sort out its own political cesspits, breaking the cycle of hand-outs'. Both of these clichés have become convenient excuses for the West to sit on its hands. Yes, any aid sent to Liberia will always be complicated by a colonial hangover and, more importantly, a deeply corrupt status quo. But is this reason to turn a blind eye? And why does our press delight in taking down a hero? Is it so hard to believe that some people are motivated by a genuine desire to do good? Perhaps Falcon and her ilk cannot comprehend altruism, because they themselves are driven by nothing more than the screech of their own voices.

The world's indifference towards Africa has long frustrated me. This time, though, the crisis is becoming harder and harder to ignore. I hope that, if any good can come out of this cruel disease, it might be that the West will wake up to fellow suffering. Or, at least, that journalists might think before they shout.

She pressed post. She knew she should leave it for an hour, check it over later, but fury made her impatient. Just sending out a small seed of truth into the scaremongering felt better. She hoped her father would read it. He was complicit, she felt, by dint of working for *The World* – even if he'd chosen to wield his journalistic power by ruining restaurants. But what did it matter, since he never would read it, and if he did would most likely respond with some argument for free speech.

Just another three days, she told Cocoa, who was lying on her lap. His drowsy eyes looked like he understood. And now George was here. Olivia had never liked George. She sensed the feeling was mutual. It was baffling what Phoebe saw in him, besides their history. He was loaded, and attractive if you liked that public schoolboy look (depressingly, her sister obviously did). But that was hardly enough in a life partner. He reminded her of the rugby players at Cambridge – only stupider. What was he doing turning up, like quarantine was a silly, optional formality? It riled her that Emma had ushered him in, too.

That was why, when she'd seen a stranger approach the house last night, from her vantage point above the porch, she'd shoved a note through the letterbox warning them away. It could have been anyone (although who knocked on doors on Christmas Day?), but she feared the man was one of George's relations, out searching for him. The last thing they needed was a George clone in the house for the next three days.

He and her sister had been unbearable last night. Phoebe had made everyone watch *Best Ever Christmas No.1s*, which George kept saying was 'banter', instead of the *Lord of the Rings*, which Olivia loved. Later they'd gone off to the bungalow, like teenagers. But then, she'd never understood Phoebe's choices. How her younger sister could be fulfilled working in TV, or fashion, or whatever it was she did now, confounded her. It wasn't like Phoebe was driven by money: she earned so little she still lived at home – though she seemed in no hurry to leave. Olivia had fled Gloucester Terrace on finishing Cambridge. She'd chosen an elective out of wi-fi contact in rural Uganda, then lived in halls at UCL, to her mother's dismay. Phoebe couldn't even drive. Judging by the awful 'mood board' in the kitchen, her only goal was marriage. Work was something to fill the days until then. Olivia watched the rain slanting down outside. It was strange how such a big house could be so claustrophobic.

'Wiv, are you coming?' shouted her mother from the corridor. Emma had declared today an 'attic clear-out'. Olivia felt drained at the prospect. The attics gave her the creeps. It was Phoebe who used to love playing up there, trying on talc-scented dresses, sometimes emerging in full period dress when their parents had guests, so that everyone could coo and get the camera out.

'In a sec!' she shouted back. She had ignored her mother's summons twice now. She would have to haul herself up there soon.

The attics at Weyfield spanned the whole top floor, but the rooms were dingy and low ceilinged – at the eaves even Phoebe had to bend double. There was one main room, three other rooms, and various cell-like bedrooms, which her mother said had belonged to teenage maids. It made Olivia feel grubby, as if she was implicated in a caste system against her will. She found Emma and Phoebe in the main room, cross-legged on the splintery floor, beside a box of yellow papers.

'Liv! It's our reports,' said Phoebe. 'This is me in year seven, chemistry, Dr Spiro. "Phoebe is a dithtraction to otherth,"' she read out, with a pompous lisp. '"Unlike her thithter, she lackth focuth. Phoebe would do well to remember that thcool is not a thocial occathion, but an opportunity to learn."' She had Dr Spiro's voice spot on. She'd always been a good mimic.

Her mother was wiping away tears of laughter as she read out, 'Autumn term, 1991: "Olivia's performance as a turnip, in the lower school's production of *Harvest Hooray*, was outstanding."'

'Oh my god, that play! I was a fairy!' shrieked Phoebe.

Olivia vaguely remembered it too, but not in the razor-sharp focus that Phoebe seemed to have recorded every moment of childhood.

'Now, there's a huge pile of your things over in that corner, Wiv,' said her mother. 'What do you want to do with the compact discs? And your A-levels, do you still need all that?'

Olivia began looking through the boxes. Here were her lower-sixth biology notes and first CDs – Blur, Coldplay and The Verve. She recalled a bitter row with Phoebe in the back of the car, about the musical merits of David Bowie against Britney Spears, when they must have been about fifteen and twelve. That had been the start of realising that Phoebe was fundamentally misguided.

She could hear her sister now, talking about whether she should get married here or in Gunston Hall, and how here was more 'her', but maybe Gunston would better achieve the 'Winter Wonderland' theme she wanted. Her sense of entitlement was mind boggling. Not just Phoebe's – this entire country's. Olivia shunted the box she had emptied to one side, and there, beneath it, was a loose floorboard she recognised. She and Phoebe used to hide things in the space beneath it, when they still played together. Prising it up, she uncovered a nest of Kinder Egg wrappers and a Start Rite shoebox. It was labelled, in Olivia's own childish script, *TIME CAPSULE 1992 DO NOT OPEN UNTIL 2092*. Without thinking, she shouted, 'Phoebe, I've found our time capsule!'

Her sister darted over, shrieking, 'No way, I remember that so well! Open it!'

Olivia peeled back the Sellotape, gooey with age, and took off the lid. Inside the box was a Sylvanian rabbit, a tube of rock-hard Opal Fruits, a photo of their first cat, a smelly eraser, a bath pearl, a Save the Rainforests pamphlet, a blank cassette and Olivia's treasured Filofax. In the middle was a jam jar, with an inch of grey water at the bottom.

'How old were we, eight and five?' said Phoebe.

'Guess so, if it's ninety-two.'

'You got the idea off Blue Peter. I thought it was so cool.'

'What is *that*?' said Olivia, reaching for the jar.

'Our perfume, remember? Rose of the Valley.'

Olivia saw the tiny label reading *Rose Of The Vally*, in her best italics. They looked at each other, and Olivia saw Phoebe as her little disciple again, following her everywhere.

'Wow, that must smell rank,' she said.

'It was pretty foul at the time, wasn't it? Dare me to?' said Phoebe, thrusting the open jar under Olivia's nose before she could answer. Her half-laugh, half-shriek, as she batted Phoebe away, made their mother look up in surprise.

'Hey, here's the letter,' said Phoebe, unfolding a piece of Disney notepaper. '"To the person that opens this time capsule,"' she began reading. '"Our names are Olivia and Phoebe Birch, we are eight and five. We go to St Edward's School. When I grow up I'm going to be a doctor, and Phoebe wants to be a pop star. We like playing Operation, Fimo, Sylvanians and Pass The Pigs. Our Mummy and Daddy are called Emma and Andrew, and we have a ginger cat called Freckles. The tape is a tape of our songs, from our band Sugar 'n' Spice."'

'Sugar 'n' Spice!' they shouted in unison, both reaching for the tape. 'Mummy, we've found the tape from when we had our girlband,' said Phoebe. 'Where's that Walkman?'

But now that Olivia had started giggling, she couldn't stop. She wanted to say, 'Do you remember "Rainbow of Love"?' but she couldn't speak. Her cheeks were hurting, and tears were starting to squeeze out of her eyes at the memory of the two of them putting the camera on timer and trying to pose sexily.

'You're crying!' said Phoebe, dissolving into giggles herself, and then warbling: 'Raaaainbow of Lo-ve, you're red like a ruby,' before standing up to do the dance routine. She put the tape in a dusty Sony Walkman and, miraculously, it began to whir. A sound like a cat came screeching out – Olivia, aged eight, warbling: 'Laaaand Ahoooooy! Laaand ahooooy.'

'It's the boat song!' said Phoebe, but Olivia was shaking with silent laughter. At last she composed herself and lay on the floor, gasping. She felt lighter, like when she was holding Sean's hand.

Andrew

THE SMOKING ROOM, WEYFIELD HALL, 10 A.M.

. . .

Andrew sat in the smoking room with a bowl of porridge, feeling banished. He had been eating in the kitchen until George came in and helped himself fulsomely to breakfast – even frying eggs. The boy had then sat down with a stack of toast (Andrew had resisted a comment about quarantine rations), and begun munching through it without speaking. Andrew had never known anyone to eat toast so loudly. It sounded like fireworks going off. When the noise became intolerable, he had claimed a work call and taken his porridge to the smoking room. Scraping the last mouthful, he did what he always did when he was frustrated – emailed his editor about the subs.

SUBJECT: Re: Dec 27th copy
FROM: Andrew Birch <andrew.birch@the-worldmag.co.uk>
TO: Gibbs, Sarah <sarah.gibbs@the-worldmag.co.uk>
DATE: 26/12/2016 10:05

Sarah,
I've just seen my proof for the 27th – too late, I might add, to have any input. May I ask why subs (I'm presuming it was Ian Croft) saw fit to remove the word 'briny' from the

phrase 'flap of briny irrelevance'? I need hardly spell out that, without the adjective, the entire sentence falls flat. It pains me to have to explain that I paired 'briny' and 'flap' precisely because, as a couple, they convey a certain double entendre (pertaining to the female genitalia). 'A flap of irrelevance' is meaningless – and, as such, entirely unfunny.

I work extremely hard to write prose that people will want to read, and then reread, and I don't appreciate it being mucked about with. If you absolutely need to cut words, as a fit issue, then please email me and I will gladly oblige. What maddens me, Sarah, is having my words butchered by illiterate subs. No doubt, in this instance, someone decreed that only the sea, or contact-lens solution, may be accurately described as briny. Which is why their powers should be limited to hyphenation.

I know you will think me precious. But what you all seem to forget is that it is MY byline on the page. The buck stops with me, as dear old Barak might have said.

Happy Christmas,

Andrew

PS. Not wild about the schmaltzy standfirst, either. What about the quarantine angle?

He pressed send and waited to feel better. He'd been on edge all morning, after a clammy dream about Jesse Robinson shinning down the chimney, dressed as a sniper Santa Claus, and shooting Phoebe. Preposterous, but the fear it had triggered had been all too real. Looking at his desktop calendar, he remembered that today was Jesse's birth date, according to Leila Deeba's letter. The letter – the attic! They were all up there, rifling through everything. Bugger.

Andrew shot up the stairs. He needed to get to the briefcase before Emma or his daughters. Bounding up the final narrow flight he heard everyone in the biggest room, and burst in to find his daughters convulsed with laughter. It was so unlike them that he was momentarily distracted. And then he saw Emma, holding his briefcase and adeptly flicking the locks.

Emma

. . .

Emma relished Boxing Day. The build up to Christmas was such fun, of course, but it was always a relief to collapse in an armchair on the 26th. This was the day when everyone could potter about, read their books and help themselves to leftovers. It saddened her that Andrew never seemed to embrace it, as she did. The year Phoebe was born he'd gone haring off to Beirut on the 26th. They'd had a vicious row as he left for the airport, and she had placated Olivia with Frosties so that she could scream into a cushion unseen. She remembered ranting to Nicola about how everything fell to her, and how Andrew had taken no interest in Olivia's presents, and Nicola saying that perhaps she felt 'abandoned' (this was when Nicola had begun couples therapy).

Looking back, Emma saw it had just been his incurable restlessness – and his discomfort at Weyfield. They didn't fight like that any more. At some point she had accepted she couldn't win, and so the shouting had stopped, along with the kissing and making up, and the holding hands, and the talking in bed. They still had a few shared jokes, always instigated by Andrew, usually at someone's expense. But when she'd mentioned this to Nicola, hoping for approval, Nicola had said that humour was a defence mechanism – a way of keeping emotion at arm's length. She was right, Emma feared. Andrew's irreverence only seemed to highlight the gulf between them. Even her book club knew more about her daily concerns than her husband did.

She had woken feeling more than usually tired. She prayed it had nothing to do with the lump, knowing it almost certainly did. Mr Singer had classed her 'asymptomatic', and she clung to this like a buoy in choppy water. She might have cancer, but she didn't *feel* like she had cancer. She didn't even *look* cancerous. Although what one thought of as 'looking cancerous' came later, she supposed, with chemotherapy. She had lain in bed for ages, fighting the fatigue that seemed to have settled behind her knees and shoulder blades, before wrenching herself up. If she collapsed in an armchair she might stay there indefinitely, so she had rallied the girls to tackle the attic. She had been longing to have a session up there for ages, since both girls seemed to use Weyfield as an unofficial storage hangar. She was so glad she had – even though they kept getting sidetracked. Phoebe and Olivia were truly laughing together. She realised she hadn't seen them like that for years. She watched them doubled up with giggles over some box of treasures and found her eyes blurring. When she died, and left them to fend for themselves, she needed them to be each other's family. She hoped they realised that. What if she had just had her last Christmas?

Her thoughts were interrupted by footsteps on the stairs, and Andrew charging in. 'Emma!' he barked.

'What? What's happened?'

'Nothing, just, I just – would you like coffee? I was about to make some,' he said, sounding short of breath. 'Isn't that mine?' he added, looking at his old briefcase in her hands.

'Yes, you don't still need it, do you?'

'Well – I can't chuck it! It's practically an artefact now. A museum piece. Christ, to think we all carried these!' he said, grabbing it off her. 'And now it's just god-awful iPads.' He stood, clutching it to his chest.

'I was just about to see if there was anything in it,' said Emma.

'There's nothing. I remember emptying it when you first stowed it up here. It was a seminal moment. This case came everywhere with me.'

So he still hadn't forgiven her, thought Emma, as Andrew skulked off to one of the side bedrooms with his precious case. She crouched over a box of old kitchen gadgets, but she couldn't concentrate.

When Andrew quit his Beirut post in 1987 and became so chippy with her, she had blamed motherhood. He minded her shift in priority, she'd told herself. But she could see, now, that his real gripe had been her insistence he come home. It was galling to think he hadn't accepted it, after all these years. She resented being cast as the party pooper – particularly since she'd sacrificed her own career when Olivia was born. She could have made quite a success of catering. She'd had dreams of launching her own company, Emma's Eats, or just Emma's. The fact that Andrew had never become a household name as a columnist wasn't her fault.

Andrew

. . .

Hugging the briefcase, Andrew sat on Emma's school trunk in the garret where he had hidden on Friday. His fingers shook, as he unlocked the catches and tucked Leila's letter in his breast pocket – vowing to burn it on tomorrow's bonfire. Thank God he'd got up here just in time.

Waiting for his pulse to slow, he saw a stack of old copies of *The Times* in a box by his feet. The top one had his byline on the front page – a 1985 report on Hezbollah and the hostage crisis following Alec Collett's abduction. He read it hungrily, and the others beneath. This was the stuff he should have kept writing, not drivel about tasting menus. He had known so much at that time, had been so intent on getting the truth published, read, understood. The idealism of youth, he supposed. He finished the last cutting and delved deeper. At the bottom of the box was a bundle of old-fashioned blue airmail letters. Some were in his own handwriting, the others in Emma's. He unfolded one of his:

4th April 1981

Brown Eyed Girl,
    I'm writing this from the camp, where we've been holed up for forty-eight hours. Our usual crummy hotel would be unimaginable

luxury by comparison. We've been on rations for two days, nothing but crackers and boiled water and dehydrated astronaut food. I ought to be filing a piece on the Mujahideen, but all I can think about is you. It's hopeless — even when the editor chases my copy, I just think how much I need to hold you again, to kiss your elegant neck, to feel you beside me. I want to be touching you, always. I miss you so much, Emma. And I want to show you off. I wish I'd never broken the Bunty story, that we'd never got into this secret mess. You were right, we should have told your parents at the start. Now I've made everything more complicated. What do you think about the Royal Wedding idea? We could start over, they needn't ever know about last year. You will wait for me, won't you? I have nightmares that you're going to go off with some chinless baronet your parents would approve of. You won't, will you?

Oceans of kisses,

Ax

PS. Your Royal English Rosiness would need a lot of sun cream here. It's just as well you're safe at home in darkest Battersea. I'm not going to give up on moving you north of the river, by the way. One day, you'll see the light.

He remembered writing it at the camp where he'd briefly been stationed during the Soviet–Afghan war, instead of his usual post in Beirut. He opened up the next one, from Emma.

10th April 1981

Dearest Andrew,

I adore posting letters to you, it feels so romantic and old fashioned. And I love getting your spidery handwriting back — I

*think your ts and ks look like you, all tall and skinny. I should
be quick because I have to get to the kitchens in a second
(Arabella and I are doing a swanky kiddy party tomorrow and
they've requested Mr Men chicken kievs), but I had to answer
your poor letter – is it swelteringly hot? Are you really living
on Ryvita and Cup-A-Soup? I can't bear it! Shall I send you
something nice to eat? What shall I send? I can't wait for you to
come home. I miss you so much, too. I wish you were kissing me
RIGHT NOW. I can't concentrate at work because of it, either.
I nearly made meringues with salt yesterday, and it would have
been <u>all your fault</u>.*

Please be careful, won't you.

All my love X

*PS. Let me think about the wedding idea. Wouldn't it be better
just to tell the truth? Maybe Mama and Papa won't mind about
Bunty?*

*PPS. I won't go off with a baronet. I hate baronets, chinless or
otherwise.*

PPS. I'll never be persuaded up to Camden.

There were several boxes of them, dating from 1980 to 1984, when
Olivia had been born and the letters had been replaced with sporadic,
distracted phone calls. By the time he'd read the whole lot, his neck
was stiff and his foot was fizzing with pins and needles. He felt as
if he was surfacing after hours underwater. Emma must have kept
the letters – he hadn't seen them since they were written, though he
vividly recalled their composition in the shimmering heat, and the
thrill of ripping open a blue envelope from Emma. So why did he
feel as if he'd been reading about a pair of strangers?

Phoebe

. . .

It had been nice to laugh with Olivia for once. Phoebe remembered giggling with her sister when they were children. But their private jokes had stopped around the time Olivia got tall and lank looking. Phoebe wasn't sure how exactly, though she remembered her sister getting more earnest with every birthday. Even at fourteen she had been permanently outraged about climate change, until her laugh had come to sound like a rusty, rarely used machine – surprising everyone, including Olivia. Phoebe's own memory of her teens was one long paroxysm of stifled hysterics – mostly in the back row of lessons, lolling against Saskia and Lara. She didn't laugh so much now, she realised. But perhaps that was just being a grown up.

They'd carried on sorting after lunch, not talking but occasionally showing the other something funny that set them off again. It had taken her mind off Non-Hodgkin Lymphoma too, which was a relief. George was right – there was no point in worrying when there was nothing she could do. He had come up to the attic at midday and stood in the doorway looking blank, until Phoebe reassured him that he wasn't needed. She wasn't sure she wanted him to hear the Sugar 'n' Spice tape, or see her frizzy-haired school photos. They didn't quite reflect the image she'd painted of her teens, as a wild day-school girl (still, incomprehensibly, an exotic concept to George). When the sky outside the dormer window turned yellow, she and Olivia had gone downstairs, leaving a satisfying mound of stuff on the floor for the bonfire.

Phoebe hoped Olivia would come and sit with her in the kitchen, but when they got to the top of the back stairs Olivia said she had to check her temperature first. Phoebe made a pot of jasmine tea, and took three sticky Medjool dates from the box on the side. She added a vintage tiara to the mood board. It would have been easier to do it on Pinterest, but seeing all her collages and drawings up in the attic had reminded her how much she used to love crafty stuff. Art was the only subject she was good at – or better at than Olivia, anyway.

Olivia came in, her brow furrowed. She stood over the table, flicking impatiently through the *FT Magazine*. The mood from the attic seemed to have evaporated. 'Why do they get this?' she said, looking up at Phoebe. 'It's obscene.'

'Daddy needs it for work. I should read it too; I'm meant to read all the papers. But my brain can't handle financial stuff. I only just found out the FTSE 100 isn't spelt like playing footsie.' This line always made her father and George chuckle, but it didn't mollify Olivia – even though she openly despised bankers.

'What's the *FT* got to do with reality television?'

She sensed Olivia wanted a fight, and more annoying, she could feel herself rising to it.

'It's not reality, it's *dramality*. We don't just rig up CCTV, some creative thought does go into it.'

Olivia didn't seem to have heard. She was looking at the mood board. 'I thought you weren't getting married till next Christmas?'

'Yeah. But that's quick. Loads of people take eighteen months or longer.'

'Why?'

'Cos, there's like a million things to sort out.' Surely Olivia knew this stuff. She had friends, she went to weddings, didn't she? Or did she? Phoebe didn't know much about her life beyond her work.

'For a party?' Olivia said 'party' as if it disgusted her.

'Yeah. Venues get booked up way in advance.'

'I thought you wanted it here?'

'I do, but – look, it's just normal for a wedding to take a year to plan. You don't have to make me feel like I'm doing something terrible!' The last word came out with a babyish tremor. Tears, when she was angry, had always been her Achilles heel.

'Normal? You think *this* is normal?'

'Yes! If you were more normal you'd get that.'

'I'm so sorry I'm not "normal" enough for you, Phoebe,' said Olivia. She cut a ragged hunk of panettone and walked out, muttering, 'For the record, this house is *not* normal.'

'I didn't mean this *house*,' shouted Phoebe. 'I meant WEDDING PLANNING.' It sounded so silly out loud that she was glad Olivia didn't answer.

'Woah! All clear?' said George, emerging from the larder with a plate of Stilton and Bath Oliver biscuits. Phoebe started, she hadn't known he was in there.

'Sorry about that,' she said, propping her chin on the table and looking up at him. 'She can be so weird.'

He sat opposite her. With his elbows out he seemed to fill half the table. 'Sounded pretty savage,' he said, through a mouthful.

'We were actually having fun just now, in the attic. You're so lucky you're close with Matt and Tommo. Me and Liv are too different. It's like our childhood is all we have in common.'

'Cabin fever. You've been stuck here too long,' he said, reaching for her hand and kissing it, leaving a tiny crumb of Stilton on her knuckle. Ever since he'd shown up yesterday he'd been unusually affectionate. They'd had sex this morning as well as last night, which was unheard of. George didn't want sex as much as her exes. But, as she'd told Saskia, the one time she'd discussed it, wasn't sex about quality, not quantity?'

Saskia had enquired after the quality. Phoebe had said she 'didn't have any complaints'. Which wasn't exactly a lie, but made it sound better than it was.

'You need to get out, Titch. Charlie Ingram's having a party tonight,' said George. 'He's only in Glandford. We could walk.'

'Bae! We're in quarantine.'

'Come on. Really? You said before this whole thing is OTT.'

'I know. But we can't just leave. Olivia would go psycho.'

'Why can't we? Seriously, I don't get how it works,' said George. 'She walked through a massive airport and then drove all the way here, right?'

'Yeah, but that was unavoidable. She had to get home somehow.'

'But if it was genuinely a public health risk, surely they'd quarantine her in Liberia?' George leaned forward, looking at her intently and playing with her left hand. His signet ring gleamed on his little finger. His dad had got them made ten years ago.

'I guess. But—'

'But what? Clearly, your sister doesn't have Haag. So what's the problem? Why put yourselves through quarantine when no one's ill?'

'Isn't there, like, the incubation thingy?'

'Fuck that. I need to get out of here. Your family's intense.'

'You go, then.' How come he was allowed to comment on her family, when she never criticised the Marsham-Smiths? Not to his face, anyway.

'I can't go without you! I want everyone to see my stunning bride. Pleeease.' He opened his pale eyes wide, so that he looked like a photo in negative.

'Maybe,' she said, but already she could feel herself giving in. She felt like flirting and getting drunk, forgetting about cancer. Andrew always said parties were her oxygen.

'Go on ... Escape with me?' he said.

'Guess if I said we were sleeping in the bungalow they wouldn't find out,' she said.

'Genius! I'll tell Chingers,' said George, standing up.

She let him. The thought of flouting Olivia's inflicted rules was too tempting. Served her right for being such a bitch.

Phoebe peered into the mirror in the dank bungalow bathroom. She'd left a note on the kitchen table: *George and I are eating dinner in the bungey. Will stay there tonight, got bedding etc. P xxxx*

She was 99 per cent sure this would put anyone off coming to bother them, with its suggestion of 'Date Night'. She'd blow-dried her hair (it was a useless Weyfield hair dryer but better than nothing), and in her dress felt like she was emerging from a loungewear chrysalis. She'd only met George's friend Charlie Ingram, aka Chingers, a few times and had always found him a bit awful, but he'd been very drunk. All the other girls there would be like Camilla and Mouse – blonde, boarding school, blah blah. She'd probably have met them before, and forgotten.

She walked out of the bathroom to find George smoking a joint. He looked her up and down approvingly.

'Where d'you get that?' she said. She hadn't seen him smoke since his insomniac phase, years ago.

'Present from Matt,' he squeaked, holding down a drag. He held it out for her.

She didn't want it – weed always sent her to sleep. But to refuse would deflate the conspiratorial mood of the evening. She sat beside him, breathing in his 'going out smell' of Chanel Egoiste and chewing gum. Her three pecky tokes went straight to her head. By the time they crept through a gap in the hedge onto the road (safer than walking down the drive) they were sniggering like teenagers. Bent double in the darkness George nearly tripped over, setting them both off even more. Straightening up on the road, he shouted, 'Liberaaaaaation! Yes!'

'You've only been here twenty-four hours, you dick!'

'Longest twenty-four hours of my life,' he said, bolting away from her singing George Michael's 'Freedom'.

'Hey waaaaait! I'm in heels!' She tottered after him, enjoying the night air on her face, and the rush of taking a risk. But as she neared George, she felt a bicycle whizz up behind them and screech to a stop. Olivia got off the bike. She looked so angry that Phoebe burst out laughing again. 'You followed us! Ha, I can't believe you literally followed us.'

'Phoebe! What are you doing?'

'Oops . . .' said Phoebe, trying to stop smirking.

'Oh, it's funny, is it?' said Olivia.

'Hey, chill,' said George. 'We were just going for a walk. We weren't going to infect anyone with your deadly lurgy.'

'Right. In high heels,' said Olivia, looking at Phoebe's feet.

'We got dressed for din—' Phoebe started, but began giggling again at the idea of eating dinner in the bungalow in black tie. The laughter began to take over her body, aching in her chest and ribs and face, until she couldn't remember why she was laughing any more and was just trying not to pee.

'You're drunk,' said Olivia, sounding disgusted.

'I'm not. I'm not. I'm . . . we,' began Phoebe, but thought better of telling Olivia what they'd been smoking. She'd managed to stop now, but her legs were still weak.

Olivia looked furious. 'Fucking hell, Phoebe. When are you going to wake up to yourself? You don't just go skipping out of quarantine cos you feel like it. It's only a week, for God's sake! Can't you put someone else first, just for a week?'

'Put who first?'

'Everyone! Everyone other than you, and your boyfriend,' she said, looking at George for the first time. 'This is a public health issue. We shouldn't even be out here. You definitely shouldn't be going wherever you're going.'

'How come I saw your dad out on Christmas Eve?' said George.

'What?' said Phoebe and Olivia together.

'Andrew. He was walking to the beach, day before yesterday. We spoke.'

'Daddy! He kept that quiet,' said Phoebe.

'Oh my god,' said Olivia, clasping her forehead dramatically. 'This whole family is so . . . so fucking self-absorbed. What's wrong with you all?'

'We're the self-absorbed ones?' Now that the hilarity had faded, Phoebe felt quite clear headed – and angry. Who was Olivia to come and play chaperone?

'Yes! The fact that you can't even see it says it all. Utterly, utterly self-absorbed, self-obsessed bunch of egotists.'

'Us? Just because you're always doing your missionary work, doesn't mean you're Mother Teresa. You're so busy freaking out about the third world you don't even notice what's going on with your own family.'

'What do you mean, what's going on?'

'Mummy has cancer! And if you were a good doctor, you'd have noticed.'

She knew she had gone too far. But shocking Olivia into silence had been irresistible.

'What? What kind of cancer? How long?'

'Ladies, I'm gonna leave you to it,' said George, turning and walking down the road.

'Wait! Where are you going?' said Phoebe.

'Yours. Weyfield. Can't be "risking public health",' he shouted without looking back.

Olivia glared after him. 'Mum has cancer?' she asked again.

'Yes. Non-Hodgkin Lymphno … lympho …' she couldn't remember how to say it.

'Lymphoma?' said Olivia.

'Yes. She found out just before Christmas. She has to have chemo in the new year.'

'Shit. What stage is she?'

'What? I don't know, she didn't say anything about that. She just said she's having more tests.'

'Why didn't she tell us?'

'She didn't want to ruin Christmas. For us all to be worrying. She said it's treatable.' Her voice had gone shaky. 'She has a really good private doctor.'

'It's OK,' said Olivia, putting an arm round her, and trying to support her bike at the same time. It felt unnatural, her head level with Olivia's neck. 'NHLs have a good recovery rate. Which consultant is she with?'

'I don't know, I didn't ask.' She hoped Olivia wasn't going to go off on one about the evils of private healthcare.

'But didn't this consultant advise her not to … I mean, it's a risk, for her, being around me this week.' Olivia looked scared. Phoebe realised that she hadn't heard her sound uncertain about anything for years.

'Is it?' said Phoebe. 'She didn't say that. I bet she didn't tell him. She was so excited about you being home, all of us being together. You never come home for Christmas.'

Olivia said nothing. Phoebe hoped she'd made her feel guilty. She should feel guilty. Everyone came home for Christmas. That was just what you did.

They started walking home in silence. Olivia kept her bike torch on. Its beam, spotlighting the road ahead, made the woods either side seem even thicker and darker.

'Liv?'

'Yeah?'

'Don't tell Mummy I told you, will you? She didn't want me to say. She hasn't told Daddy.'

'Really? How come she told you?'

'She just needed a shoulder to cry on, I guess. She's only told me and Nicola.'

'Nicola?'

'Your godmother.'

'Oh, right. That Nicola.'

'Which other Nicola would it be?' She felt the anger bubble rise up again. 'How can you just *not know* who your godmother is? Who Mummy's friends are? It's like you're proud of being crap. It's rude.'

'Phoebs, can you give me a break? It's not OK to just pick and choose when you do quarantine, but I'm not having a go at you, am I?'

'You are! That's exactly what you're doing. You followed us here! Because you don't have anything better to do than spy on me and George.' Phoebe remembered the party. She didn't feel like it now anyway. Her shoes were already killing her. But still.

'Believe me, I have better things to do than chase after you and your boyfriend.'

'Fiancé.'

'Christ. Sorry – how could I forget that you're getting married?'

'Just because you don't care about that stuff doesn't mean I can't.

Most girls, people, want to get married, you know? It's not like, a *weird* thing.'

'Right. God forbid I suggest you're weird.'

Phoebe couldn't think of a comeback, so she said nothing. This used to be how childhood arguments always ended, Olivia taking the last word, while Phoebe stood opening and shutting her mouth like a furious fish, before shouting, 'I hate you!'

They walked on for a while, saying nothing.

'Do you know when Mum *is* planning to talk about it?' said Olivia.

'Once your quarantine's over.'

'It's not just my quarantine.'

Phoebe was about to disagree, when her heel skidded sharply on the icy ground. She grabbed at Olivia's sleeve to stop herself falling, but her ankle went over sideways under her. She felt something crunch inside.

'Ow ow ow. Shit. Ow,' she said, clinging to Olivia's arm, and holding her foot up limply. It was throbbing, the pain spreading over her ankle like heat. She felt slightly dizzy, with pain or the effects of the weed, or both, she couldn't tell.

'Here, hold this,' said Olivia, turning her bike handlebars towards Phoebe and crouching to look at her foot with the torch. 'Can you put any weight on it?'

Phoebe touched the road with her toe and winced as pain shot up her calf.

'Agh, no! It's broken! I've broken it!'

'It's probably just a sprain. They can be very sore. Take your shoes off,' said Olivia, putting her arm round her back to support her.

'I can't. I can't walk. It hurts too much.' She reached down to touch the top of her foot, the flesh already puffy and tender.

'OK, we'll both go on the bike – you sit in front.'

They began riding slowly back to the house, Phoebe's knees folded away from the wheels, and Olivia behind her, peddling.

By the time they'd got into the bungalow and located some ice cubes in the prehistoric freezer, it felt wrong to carry on the argument.

'Sorry about before,' Phoebe said.

'It's fine,' said Olivia, briskly. 'You'll sleep here, then? Might be better, with no stairs.'

'True. Did Mummy and Daddy know you went after us?'

'I didn't tell them you'd left, no. They weren't around.'

'Cool. If you see them now, just say you've been hanging out with me and George.'

Olivia looked unimpressed, but agreed.

'And tomorrow, we'll just say I slipped in the garden, OK?'

'Fine. Keep it elevated.'

Typical Olivia not to say sorry back, thought Phoebe. So much for their sisterly bonding in the attic. She limped into the bedroom. George was already face down in the bed, snoring.

Jesse

· · ·

It had been a bad birthday. Worse, even, than Christmas Day. Jesse had gone for a bleak run in the morning, half-hoping to encounter George. In the afternoon he'd taken a cab to a celebrated town named Cromer, and wandered for an hour checking his email every time he got a signal. Still nothing from Andrew. He'd gone to an empty cafe on the pier and ordered a mug of black tea (what was with the milky tea here?) and a rigid scone, too hungry to forgo refined carbs. Afterwards, he'd stood for ages on a shingle beach, watching gulls dive-bomb the charcoal sea. Then he'd sat through a terrible Christmas blockbuster, where he and a shady-looking man in a parka had been the only people in the movie theatre. When he'd first arrived in Norfolk, the Regal Cinema would have tickled him, with its tiny screens and commercials for local fish and chip shops. But now, the way everything looked about thirty years old was depressing. He hadn't taken his camera out of its bag. There didn't seem to be any point.

Back in the Harbour Hotel, he began to pack. His train didn't leave until mid-morning tomorrow, but he needed to do something practical. All day he'd toyed with going back to Weyfield. But what would he say if they deigned to open the door? 'Oh hi! I'm your uncouth American bastard, showing up uninvited!' Except . . . if he didn't go, what then? Was he really going to quit, fly home, and pretend like the whole trip never happened? Chalk it up to experience: 'The Lousiest Vacation Of My Life'? And to think he'd pictured himself making a breakout documentary about his journey. He'd barely filmed anything the entire time he'd been here, just a couple of shots of the beach. His camera had been a dead weight, following him around while exactly nothing happened. Nothing except George. And that made him feel kind of gross, looking back. The guy was engaged – the whole thing was sordid, not Jesse's style. At least it hadn't gone further than kissing.

He emailed Dana: 'No cell signal, Skype me asap.' That should appeal to her sense of drama. It was just midnight, meaning Andrew's weekly restaurant review would be online. Jesse slumped on the bed, unsure if he even wanted to read it, and clicked on *The World*'s website. The headline for Andrew's new column was up on its homepage.

The Most Wonderful Time of the Year (ho ho)

Chefs, you can stuff your alternative turkey. Kinfolk come first at Christmas, says Andrew Birch, ahead of his week en famille in Norfolk.

Just as he was about to click Read More, Dana's number and profile picture flashed up in the corner of the screen. He answered and talked through his dilemma again.

'So now I have no clue what to do,' he finished. 'I don't want to just leave, without trying once more, after everything. But when I went to the house yesterday . . . I don't know, I just can't go through with it again. Not after no reply. I need some, like, certainty. I need to draw a line under this whole thing.'

'Sure. I get that,' said Dana. He was grateful that she didn't say 'I told you so,' even though he knew she was thinking it.

'I can't send *another* email. And I can't find the number for the house anywhere.'

'How 'bout a letter? You could deliver it by hand tomorrow. You know somebody's home. So you mark it "Private" and "Please forward to Andrew Birch" or whatever. And that way you can be sure he'll get it, plus—'

The screen darkened, and her speech blurred. 'Dana, you're breaking up,' he said, but Dana's face was replaced with an error message. The wi-fi was down. Again. Fuck this place, he thought. Why did nothing work in Norfolk?

Maybe Dana's suggestion wasn't so bad. A letter had a certain gravitas. He could deliver it tomorrow morning, before catching the train. Besides, the headline to Andrew's latest column felt like a sign. He could still see it on *The World*'s homepage, though the text was now maddeningly out of reach, as the little wi-fi fan refused to fill up. He read the headline again. It sounded like Andrew was definitely here in Norfolk. And it didn't sound like his usual cutting tone. 'Kinfolk come first at Christmas.' That had to be a message from Fate, right? He took a sheet of the Harbour Hotel's notepaper and began to write.

· 6 ·

27 December

Quarantine: Day 5

Olivia

. . .

Olivia lay in the dark, knees drawn up to her chest. She'd barely slept. The row last night shuttled round her head like a trapped wasp. Usually arguing with Phoebe left Olivia feeling vindicated, but yesterday had caught her off guard. She kept hearing her sister say: 'If you were a good doctor, you'd have noticed.' Emma seemed no different to usual, though. Frenetic, but that was her default setting. Still, Olivia felt shaken. Her mother was never ill.

On top of everything else, her latest blog about Sean had garnered a stream of spiteful comments. Olivia had first seen them when she'd taken her temperature yesterday, on her way down from the attics. She felt bad now for taking her anger out on Phoebe's bridal collage. Her sister was obviously just looking for distraction, unable to deal with anything more than a tiara dilemma. Which made it even stranger that Emma had confided in Phoebe – the last person Olivia would want in a crisis. She knew why Emma hadn't told her, though. Phoebe was right, Emma was afraid it would put Olivia off doing her quarantine at Weyfield. That she'd skip another Christmas. It wasn't a comfortable thought.

Hunger growled inside her. Or was it a hungover, sick feeling? Her stomach, which had definitely shrunk in Liberia, must be thrown by the onslaught of rich food and daytime drinking. It was probably stress, too. Stress always went to her stomach, Olivia reminded herself, recalling how she used to throw up, without fail, before exams. She took her temperature just to be safe, despite the normal reading an hour earlier. The thermometer seemed to take for ever. She realised she was holding her breath. Eventually, it flashed a cheerful 37°C. See? she told herself. You're fine. Feeling a bit off post-Christmas is hardly remarkable. Don't be paranoid. You need to stay rational, for Sean.

The pips on the radio signalled the news, and Olivia groped to turn it up. She had taken to keeping the World Service on all night, so that when nightmares jerked her awake she met the soothing burble of the shipping forecast. The newsreader's voice shifted gear, indicating a positive story.

'Sean Coughlan, the Irish doctor diagnosed with Haag, is said to be improving. Doctors say he is in a stable condition, sitting up, eating, and able to read.' Olivia yanked her iPad off its charger. All the headlines said the same: Sean was stable – still Haag-positive, but likely to make a full recovery. She caught sight of herself in the mirror, lit by the white glow of the screen, beaming madly.

SUBJECT: READ THIS FIRST! Not previous emails!
FROM: Olivia Birch <olivia.birch1984@gmail.com>
DATE: 27/12/2016 07:05
TO: Sean Coughlan, <SeanKCoughlan@gmail.com>

Hi Pekin,
You're OK! So so happy to hear the news this morning (you're a hot topic, by the way). I know you won't see this today, as you'll still be in isolation with only *Heat* magazine and other combustible reading matter. But I'm writing

anyway, so you get this as soon as you're out. I want to be your first message. I've been so worried about you, baby. This will probably come out wrong, but you testing positive made me realise how much I care about you. I mean, not that I didn't realise! Agh I told you it would come out wrong – I'm rubbish at this stuff. I just can't believe that four months ago I didn't even know you existed, and now I'm never not thinking about you.

Sorry in advance for my hysterical email on Christmas Eve (which if you've followed instructions in this subject line you won't have seen yet. On second thoughts, maybe ignore it altogether.)

How are you feeling? Rough, I expect. Like I said I've been going quietly mad here, wishing I could do something, or just be with you. But besides that I'm fine, don't panic. Fingers crossed I'd know by now if anything was wrong. It's been so strange reading about you and hearing your name but not being able to speak to you, or even tell anyone about us. Hoping you haven't said anything either? There didn't seem to be any point freaking my parents out, potentially getting us in shit etc. But it's been pretty hard to act normal – or as normal as anyone could be expected to act, post Red Zone. Not that my dear family seem to get that. Thanks for ruining the nation's Christmas, by the way. Joking.

So just as you get better, I've had bad news. It turns out my mother was diagnosed with an NHL last week. I had no idea – my sister sprang it on me last night. Basically her boyfriend George gatecrashed our quarantine on Christmas Day, so he's now staying here with us (not sure if the whole thing was planned, wouldn't put it past them). Anyway, last night the two of them got pissed and decided to go out ... I know ... I saw them leave and followed them on my bike, and Phoebe and I ended up having a massive row, and she dropped this bombshell in the middle of it.

Apparently my mum didn't tell me because she didn't want to 'ruin Christmas', which is typically mad of her. But, obviously it's not ideal that she's in the house with me, with her immunity, when I'm high risk. I don't want to scare everyone by mentioning you and me, though, when there are only two days to go. Phoebe said my mum's waiting for test results, so will probably start treatment asap. Hard to know whether to say anything, because she wants it kept secret and I feel like I should respect that. But since I only got my sister's garbled version I have no idea what stage she is, how fast it's moving etc. Often feels like I'm the last to know anything about my own family. As in, the fact that I have a life and don't live at home with arrested development like Phoebe, means they don't need to tell me stuff. OK rant over. Sorry to dump all this on you when you're probably still drugged up. It's just a relief to put it all down in words. Your parents must have been so worried. Are they in London, at least? I promise I'll come and see you as soon as you're out of your isolation tunnel, and I'm free from this madhouse. Can't wait.

Get lots of rest. I love you.

Olivia XXXX

PS. Not quite sure how I'm going to break the news to my parents – remember Sean Coughlan off the news? We hooked up in Liberia. And I'm crazy about him. Hohoho.

She pressed send and turned the iPad over – the screen was burning her eyes.

'Wiv,' her mother called from downstairs. 'Are you up? We need to do the bonfire before it rains! Come down! I've done scrambled eggs.' Olivia's stomach turned slightly at the thought of warm, lumpy egg. She couldn't refuse Emma's giant breakfasts now, though. Feeding the troops was probably all that was keeping her mother sane.

The bonfire was a Weyfield Christmas ritual. Olivia remembered hopping around it as a child with Phoebe, both in manic Rumpelstiltskin mode, but as a teenager she'd pleaded revision to avoid the whole thing. She was surprised the others were persisting with it now. Still, it was good to be outside in the fresh air. She felt fine now that she was up, so it must have been low blood sugar earlier. Her father had built the fire in the usual spot at the bottom of the orchard. He was walking down the grassy slope from the house, now, carrying a stack of boxes. Her mother was standing beside the heap of branches, looking through old magazines and schoolwork from the attic. Surprisingly little had been deemed disposable in the end.

'Fabulous,' said Emma. 'This is going to be really cathartic. Now, haven't you got any Haagy gubbins you want to burn, sweetie?' Clearly her mother hadn't quite grasped the concept of contamination. But she must have a lot on her mind, Olivia reminded herself.

'Everything got burned or bleached while we were out there,' she said.

'Of course, of course. Silly me. Perhaps I should go and get Phoebs,' said Emma, half to herself. Olivia tried to observe her professionally. She didn't appear to have the visible fatigue that typically affected cancer patients – or any discernible weight loss.

Andrew staggered towards them, almost dropping his load. 'Golly, you've done well!' said Emma. 'I had no idea you had so much down here.'

'I was ruthless. It's mostly work bumpf. And one appalling attempt at a novel. A thriller, I'm afraid. Christ knows why. Did I tell you at the time? Can't remember now. Anyway, the less said about my foray into fiction the better. Right then, pyrotechnics!' he said, beginning to arrange the branches into a wigwam shape.

Olivia thought of him sneaking out for a walk on Christmas Eve. Sometimes she felt like she had no respect for her father. He was as bad as Phoebe – both worshipping the frivolous, making careers out of it, pleasing themselves above all else. The fact that he was apparently oblivious to his wife's cancer only confirmed his grotesque ego. A small, bobble-hatted figure came limping over from the bungalow.

'George's still in bed,' said Phoebe, when she got near enough to be heard.

'Good-oh,' said her mother, running over to take her arm. 'Nobody need feel they have to do anything. We're very relaxed. How's your poor foot?'

So Phoebe had filled everyone in on her injury, thought Olivia. Just as well, since she hadn't wanted to lie for her. Phoebe kept making agonised grimaces as she clung to Emma, and then moved onto Andrew. She was wearing sparkly mittens and avoiding Olivia's eye. She probably hadn't forgiven her for last night. Typically child-ish. Especially after Olivia had got her home, sorted out her foot and agreed not to tell anyone.

Andrew threw a match into the pile of dry wood and paper, and the fire launched with a greedy crackle. 'Seems extraordinary that we had to make do with a magnifying glass, in that camp,' he said. Her mother began tipping boxes onto the flames, with little whoops. Phoebe seemed to forget her foot in the thrill of igniting Tricolore textbooks, too. Olivia stood back, breathing through her mouth to avoid the acrid smell. It reminded her of the mass cremations the Liberian government had ordered in November. Was the whisper of nausea back? Don't think about cremations, she ordered herself. Sean's getting better, and you're fine. Stop being silly.

Jesse

. . .

Weyfield Hall was different in daylight. Jesse stood at the turning in the drive looking up at it. The air felt swollen with impending rain, and pale light slanted through low, grey clouds. Against it, the house looked spectacular. Even the weeds on the drive struck him as romantic. He took the letter from its unsealed envelope for a final read.

December 27, 2016

Dear Andrew,

I am writing this letter because I believe you are my birth father. My late birth mother was a Lebanese woman named Leila Deeba, who I think you met as a reporter in Beirut, 1980. My mother had me adopted soon after giving birth, and I was raised by my adoptive parents in Iowa.

I sent you two emails reaching out before Christmas, as I have been working in Norfolk over the holiday season. I was hoping you might be curious to meet, but since I didn't hear from you, I can't be sure if you didn't receive my emails, or if you would prefer not to make contact. I hope it is the former, but I understand if you don't feel comfortable meeting me. I have no idea if you even knew my birth mother had gotten pregnant, so I appreciate that this letter may come as something of a shock. However, since I am in Norfolk, and I can't be certain my emails made it, I am taking the liberty of delivering this letter by hand. I hope you will forgive my forwardness.

Some background on me: I now live in Los Angeles, where I produce documentaries, primarily on health and wellbeing. I am gay and currently single. Like you, I enjoy great food and travel (I never miss your column!). My email address is jesse.iskandar. robinson@gmail.com, should you wish to make contact.

With best regards,

Jesse

It would have to do. He'd gotten so late, writing and rewriting it this morning, that he'd wound up stopping at Weyfield on his way to catch the train. He still wasn't sure of the final paragraph, which read like a dating profile, but he needed Andrew to know something about him, in case this was the end. A speck of rain blotted the paper, and he stuffed it into the envelope as the drops quickened. He walked up the drive, feeling naked. There was only one light on, but the same cars were parked in the drive as on Christmas Day. Perhaps they were sleeping in.

Out of nowhere sheet lightning lit up the house, followed by a shudder of thunder. Jesse was used to storms in Iowa, but the torrent that fell next took him by surprise. He dashed the last twenty yards to Weyfield's front door, pulling his coat over his head, and pushed the envelope through the letterbox, eye to eye with the lion knocker. It was done. Gone. He turned to shelter under the shallow porch for a moment. The pediment barely covered him – rain was blowing sideways, soaking his hair and clothes. He pressed his back harder against the door and, as he did so, felt it shift under his weight, so that he half-fell into the house. Grabbing for the door frame to steady himself, he straightened up. He knew he ought to walk back out into the rain, pulling the door to, as it had been left. His letter lay on the mat. He had done what he came here to do. But something made him pick the envelope up, instead, and look round into the shadows of the hall.

Olivia

. . .

The four of them hurried up the garden towards the house, Olivia in the lead. The rain was different to the fat, warm drops in Liberia, lashing down in icy rods. The front door was open, as usual, and she rushed straight through into the hall. Her scream of surprise at the tall man standing inside sounded uncharacteristically girlish.

'Sorry! I'm sorry – I startled you,' he said in an American accent. He was holding an envelope and looked about her age. As her eyes adjusted to the light, she saw his face properly. There was something disconcertingly even about it, so that he didn't look quite real. He had large, dark eyes, like a manga cartoon.

'Hey,' he said. 'Is this – are you Olivia?'

'Yes. Who are you?'

'Uh, is Andrew home? I was hoping to speak with him.'

'Look, you shouldn't be here. How did you get in?'

'I, the door was, like, open.'

She was about to answer when her father appeared. The colour left his face. He and the man stood staring at each other, as if they were alone. Andrew opened his mouth, but just made a kind of croaking 'ah' noise, as Emma walked in.

'Golly, I'm drenched!' she said, shaking out her sleeves, and then saw the man.

'Hull-o!' she said, sounding shocked but delighted, as if they'd met before. 'How did you—?'

'Oh, shi-it,' he said, dark eyebrows shooting up his forehead, and his eyes bulging like headlamps. 'Oh my god, this is crazy. This is insane. I didn't realise, I mean, I had literally no idea—'

'What's going on?' said Olivia. 'We're in quarantine, we can't—'

'Shh,' said her father. 'This is . . .' he hesitated. 'This is . . .'

'Jesse,' said the man.

'I know,' said Andrew.

'Oh – wait – oh my god,' said Emma, her face falling. 'Oh Christ, *Andrew*!' She looked at Andrew beseechingly.

'What's happening?' said Phoebe, from the doorway. 'Hi,' she said, seeing the man and switching on her strangers smile. She pulled off her hat, reaching up to smooth her hair.

'Girls, go upstairs please,' said Emma.

'Why? What's going on?' said Phoebe.

'Nothing,' said Emma. 'Just, could you go upstairs, darling?'

The man was looking even more uneasy, his doe eyes flitting around the four of them.

'He shouldn't be in the house—' Olivia tried again. Why did none of her family grasp what quarantine meant?

'Olivia, please. Just go upstairs. We'll sort all that out,' said Emma.

Her mother's face told her she had no choice.

'Come on,' Olivia said to Phoebe.

She put an arm out for her sister as they climbed the stairs. Nobody in the hall said anything. When she and Phoebe reached the first landing, they heard their father say, 'Have you two . . . have you *already met*?'

'Wait – shh,' said Phoebe, stopping. She leant over the banister to listen, so that Olivia had to stop too.

'At Heathrow, when I was fetching Olivia,' said Emma, shrilly. 'We spoke! Now, do come on through, Jesse. Tea, tea, tea.'

'What? Who *is* he?' whispered Phoebe. Her little hand was vicelike on Olivia's arm.

'What's she doing, just inviting him in?' said Olivia.

'Miserable weather!' they heard Emma say, as their parents walked into the kitchen with the man. The door closed and the voices faded. Phoebe sat down on the top step. 'Who is he?' she said again.

Andrew

.   .   .

Sitting by the fire, Andrew kept scanning Jesse's face for the girl he remembered, dimly, from Beirut. He couldn't really see her, though, and he certainly couldn't see himself – besides the man's height. He could just see a startlingly handsome, young American, separate from them both. Jesse was sitting on the sofa, Andrew on the armchair. On the table between them were two mugs of very sweet tea, which Emma had made as if they were in *EastEnders*. He could hear her now, clattering around in the kitchen where they'd left her.

The absurdity of Jesse meeting his wife at Heathrow hit Andrew afresh. Never mind *EastEnders* – this was pure telenovella. Emma bustled in and out again, with hushed apologies for interrupting and two wodges of Christmas cake. Her offerings sat untouched beside the envelope, which Jesse explained he had been planning to leave for Andrew. His letter said more or less the same as his emails, but struck a defeated note. It read more like a goodbye than a greeting, with its sad little summary of hobbies, marital status and sexual preference. Andrew tried to put this last fact aside to deal with later. Not that it had to be 'dealt with'. Andrew had lots of gay friends, and not just through work. He was an open-minded metropolitan, a writer – oh shut up Birch, he told himself. Just shut up.

Jesse leant forward and took a polite sip of tea.

'Sorry about that,' said Andrew, gesturing at his mug. 'It's a British response to shock – dreadful tea. Brandy might be more to the point.'

Jesse laughed. He was wonderful looking, Andrew kept thinking, rather stunned that he could have produced such a perfect specimen. The picture he'd found online hadn't done his son justice. Even his eyebrows were extraordinary – as if someone had stencilled them on to his face. And he had those very white American teeth like piano keys. Jesse's adoptive parents must have seen to that.

'I'm a shock?' he said.

'Well. It's not every day a long-lost son comes out of the wood-work, so to speak.'

Why was he taking up this odd, jovial tone? Andrew wondered.

'So you didn't get my emails last week?' Jesse asked, after a second, looking at the letter.

'Ah, I did, I did, I'm sorry. I should have replied sooner. I was going to. I had every intention of doing so. But we're in rather an, um, unusual situation here. Did you read my column this morning?' He was gabbling. He tried to breathe from the diaphragm.

'Your column?' Jesse looked confused. 'Uh, I tried to, but I couldn't get online since last night. Did you write about my emails?'

'Your emails? God, no. No, my column was about us Birches being in what's called "voluntary quarantine". My daughter Olivia has been working in Liberia, you see, treating Haag victims, and we're supposed to avoid contact with anyone for a week – or the next three days, now.'

'Oh shi— shoot, I totally forgot,' said Jesse.

Andrew was thrown. 'Forgot?'

'Emma told me when we met at the airport. Is it, like, OK that I'm here?' said Jesse, glancing at the door.

'Oh yes. Absolutely. It's really a formality. The NGOs are just being doubly careful. No need to panic.' Now that Jesse was here, he could hardly send the boy back out into the rain. And he wanted him to stay, he realised. Still, what a mess. And quite a shock to find he'd fathered someone who inserted 'like' between every word.

'So you didn't reply because you didn't want to infect me with Haag?' said Jesse.

'That, and also . . . Well – it's complicated.' Andrew stopped. He'd prefer not to go into sordid details, but the quarantine excuse sounded flimsy, face to face. 'The night I—' he stopped again. How did one explain to someone that they were the product of a meaningless fuck, and that their father was a cheating bastard? 'That night your birth mother and I, er, met, Emma and I were already an item. A couple, as it were. So . . . Not my finest hour.'

'But, wait, I thought you and Emma met the summer of eighty-one? I found this whole article about it. You were reporting on the Royal Wedding, and she was a guest, right?'

'That was what we told people, at the time. But we had in fact been "courting", so to speak, in secret. For well over a year. I'd broken a scandal about Emma's uncle – in the press, I mean – and I knew her family would recognise my byline and disapprove of me. So we kept schtum to begin with, and then, when that became unsustainable, I was introduced on the pretext that we'd just met at the Royal Wedding. Idiotic, in retrospect. I doubt they bought it for a moment. We were young, in our defence. And we were both at the wedding – that was true.'

Stop gibbering, he instructed his brain. He was making himself sound worse and worse. All Jesse needed to know was that Andrew had been unfaithful to Emma, with Leila. Which was bad enough. What a start.

'Jeez, I'm sorry. If I'd known I would never have just shown up. Does Emma know?'

'Ah, no. No she doesn't.'

Jesse pushed his hair back, and Andrew saw himself in the gesture – and his own, square hairline. Proof at last that he had contributed to this Adonis.

'I see why you came. I'm sorry you didn't hear from me sooner,' he said. 'I had every intention of writing to you.' Out loud, it sounded hopelessly gauche.

'That's OK. I get it,' said Jesse. For a moment, Andrew thought he might rise for a manly, back-slapping embrace. But he just took another sip of tea.

'So where *did* you and Emma meet?' said Jesse.

'Me and Emma?' The question threw him. What did it matter to Jesse? 'She was catering a media bash I had to go to. She dabbled in the canapé business back then. Eyes meeting over a tray of vol-au-vents, sort of thing.'

'Awesome!' said Jesse, as if it was a huge relief to respond positively again.

Andrew fought the impulse to point out that vol-au-vents hardly inspired awe, in the true sense of the word.

'How is Emma, by the way?' asked Jesse, after a moment.

'Sorry?'

'I mean, how's she doing? Did she decide about treatment?'

'Treatment?'

'Chemo. For, like, the cancer. She told me when we met.' His face took on the appalled look it had in the hall. 'Oh, wait, shit. You don't know?'

Phoebe

. . .

It felt like they'd been sitting on the top step for ages. Phoebe's buttocks were numb, and she needed to pee. She wasn't sure what they were waiting for, and she suspected Olivia wasn't either. But there seemed to be a tacit agreement to stay together.

'Oh my god, Mummy *told* me about him,' Phoebe had said once their parents and the man were in the kitchen. 'This random she started chatting to in the airport. She said he was gay. D'you think he's like, Daddy's *boyfriend*?' She shuddered, thinking of the day Andrew had taken ages to get the Christmas tree. Perhaps he'd been calling his toyboy. She'd known something was up.

'Phoebs! There's probably a totally reasonable explanation.'

'But why was Mummy being so weird? Should we go and see if she's OK?'

'No! Leave her.'

Phoebe feared Olivia was about to quiz her about Emma's diagnosis again. She wished she hadn't told her sister last night. The more people that knew, the more real it felt. But instead Olivia said, 'They will understand that he can't leave the house now, whoever he is. Won't they?'

Phoebe realised how rarely her sister asked her opinion on anything.

'Guess so,' she said. 'They let George stay after he'd been here about five seconds.'

'True.'

'Why are you so stressed about the rules? I thought it was just, like, a precaution to be safe. That's what you said, before you went.'

'I'm not stressed. It's just, with Sean and everything.'

Phoebe looked at her sister's profile. Her jaw was clenched.

'Sean?'

'Sean Coughlan,' said Olivia slowly, looking round at Phoebe as if she was stupid. 'My colleague with Haag. Don't you ever read the news?'

'Oh right. Him. Sorry, I just, I think of the news and real life as, separate, I guess.'

'Exactly. Not your problem.'

'That's not fair. It's cos, when I read about it it's so sad, and there's nothing I can do, so . . . ' she knew Olivia would think this was feeble. 'I just don't work in news, so I'm not thinking about it all the time.' She could feel the fight from last night resurfacing. She didn't want to argue. Whatever was going on downstairs, she felt instinctively that they needed to stick together.

'It's not whether you "work in news" or not, it's . . . Sorry, I'm just—' Olivia took a deep, huffy breath, like she couldn't get enough air in. 'It's like this constant, relentless anxiety,' she said. She was still staring straight ahead, not looking at Phoebe.

'But wasn't Sean Coughlan going into schools, and that's why he caught it? Plus Mummy said this morning he was getting better,' said Phoebe.

'Yes. He was. And he is. But, still.'

She stopped, as if her own voice was choking her, and at once Phoebe realised.

'You didn't hook up with him, did you?' she asked. She'd seen the doctor in the papers and he was pretty hot. By her sister's standards.

Olivia said nothing, but pursed her lips as a single tear leaked over her cheekbone. So that was why she'd been such a bitch all week.

Phoebe shuffled up to hug her, and they sat in a stiff side-on embrace for a moment. It occurred to her that Olivia was a massive hypocrite. She'd been preaching about Phoebe skipping quarantine – when she'd been busy shagging a Haag-infected colleague. It was nice to have the moral high ground, for once.

'I'm sure you'll be totally fine,' she said, trying to sound confident.

'It's not only me. I'm worried about Mum, now. Just in case,' said Olivia.

'Mummy's OK. She's tough. Anyway, you're not going to get Haag!' Phoebe knew her certainty didn't ring true. 'So was it serious with Sean? Can I see pictures?'

Olivia nodded, wiping her nose on her sleeve. 'I've got loads on my iPad. Show you later.' It crossed Phoebe's mind that the smear could be contaminated with Haag, and she moved minutely. Sometimes she even shocked herself with how nastily her mind worked. Olivia was right – she was selfish.

'When did you get together?' she said.

'Just five weeks ago. But it feels like we've known each other way longer.'

Phoebe thought how often she felt like she was meeting George for the first time. She'd always told herself it was romantic.

'He's a really, really amazing person,' said Olivia, looking round. 'He was in charge of paediatrics. What he did with the ward – it was incredible. He got all the paperwork reorganised, all the protocol. He saved so many children's lives.' Her voice went thin again.

'Oh Wiv. He sounds amazing. I'm sure he'll be OK.' She'd never seen her sister like this. Whenever she talked about her ex – Dull

Ben, as Phoebe and Andrew privately called him – she sounded like she was talking about a dry relation.

'Yeah. I know,' said Olivia. 'He'll want to go back out there, even after this. That's the kind of person he is.' A wood pigeon outside cooed its folorn chorus.

'Don't tell Mum or Andrew, or George, will you?' added Olivia. 'Or anyone? I could get in serious trouble. There was a No-Touch rule out there.'

'Course not,' said Phoebe. In the past, any glimpse into Olivia's personal life had been relayed to Emma immediately. Her mother was usually pathetically grateful. This time, though, Phoebe decided to honour Olivia's secret.

'What about you? Excited about getting married?' said Olivia. She always did this – changed the subject when she'd been talking about herself. It had put Phoebe off asking her stuff years ago.

'Of course,' said Phoebe.

'Are you going to move out of Gloucester Terrace before?'

'Maybe. It's quite convenient being at home, with all the wedmin. Since Mummy and Daddy are paying.'

'Wedmin?'

'Wedding admin.'

'Ha. Oh right.' Phoebe knew what she was thinking: how can you marry someone you've never lived with?

'Anyway,' said Phoebe, 'I think it's kind of nice, to move in together *after* you're married. It's more special, like the olden days.'

'What, like dying in childbirth and getting an allowance from your husband?'

'Exactly! I'd love an allowance. No more shitty TV work.'

'D'you get on with his family?' said Olivia. It had taken her six years to ask this, Phoebe thought.

'Yeah. They're OK. They're quite—' she stopped. She knew Olivia wouldn't get the shorthands she used with friends. 'They're just quite different to us, I suppose.'

'In a good way?'

'Not good or bad. Just different.'

'But he's British, your age, university educated, they have a second home in Norfolk and he grew up in London. So not massively different?'

'South London.'

Olivia laughed. 'You're ridiculous,' she said, but for once it sounded affectionate.

'It *is* different,' said Phoebe. 'It's a huge difference.'

'Where is he anyway?'

'Still asleep. He never gets up before eleven.'

She prayed the man downstairs wasn't her father's gay lover. She needed to know what was going on, so she could spin an acceptable story for George – or at least something funny. Why did her family have to be so weird?

Emma

. . .

Emma leant her forehead on the worktop. Her mind felt like the old cake mixer beside her, churning and churning, until her thoughts spun together in a gooey clump. Andrew and Jesse had been in the smoking room for over an hour. Emma had been hovering in the kitchen, unable to sit still. She had no idea where Olivia and Phoebe were. She hoped they'd stay away until she'd had a chance to speak to Andrew.

Thinking of her daughters, she reminded herself that she was the parent. She'd had a shock, but she mustn't be hysterical. She pressed her cheek to the cool marble and tried to get a grip on the facts. Andrew had another child – a son who looked much the same age as Olivia. What if he'd known about this other baby, this other firstborn, all along? Her throat tightened, as she remembered how he hadn't seemed to share her elation at Olivia's birth. Perhaps this – at last – was the reason. He had already fathered another child, and he knew it. Then again, she thought, jerking up, Jesse might be younger than Olivia. Which would be worse still, in a sense. Had Jesse's mother been a one-off or a long-running affair? Had there been a string of other women while Emma was stuck at home with two small children? This was why she despised secrets. When they emerged, as they always did, they opened up a whole labyrinth of other unknowns. She gave a little sob of fury. How had everything spun upside down in the space of an hour? Her fingers slipped into her shirt and under her arm, fondling the bump under the skin like a worry bead.

She still couldn't believe that she'd met Jesse at Heathrow and had that long chat. It would be funny, if it weren't such a lurid mess. Seeing his luggage by the table, Emma had a thought – his passport would reveal his birth date. It was wrong, but excusable, to rummage. Unzipping the smaller bag, she found the passport in a pocket, with a bill from the Harbour Hotel. The identity page read *Jesse Iskandar Robinson, DOB 26 Dec 1980*. He was older than Olivia. But if Jesse was born in December 1980, he must have been conceived during that year. She and Andrew had first kissed on the 4th January 1980 – the date etched in her memory. Which meant he'd either met this woman soon after Emma or had been involved with her already, while telling Emma he was unattached. Bastard. *Bastard*. She studied the passport photo again. Jesse looked like a film star. His mother must have been a knockout. So, on top of everything else, Andrew had gone and fathered a child more beautiful than either of their daughters, without her. Stop it, Emma! she scolded herself. Don't you even entertain that thought.

She replaced the passport, palms sweating, and registered that it had been Jesse's birthday yesterday. Poor thing. What a wretched day he must have had, alone in the Harbour Hotel. She thought back to what he'd told her at Heathrow. Hadn't he said he wasn't sure if his birth father knew he had a son? She definitely remembered him saying that his father hadn't replied to his emails. Why on earth hadn't Andrew replied? And why hadn't he shown Emma these emails? They were married – she had a right to know. No wonder he'd seemed so distracted and taken no interest in Olivia's homecoming.

She heard the smoking-room door open and stepped away from Jesse's bags, marshalling her face into a smile. None of this is Jesse's fault, she said to herself again. He deserves to know his father – every child deserves a father. Andrew, of all people, should appreciate that. Besides, hadn't she been worrying about Jesse all this time? It was hardly fair to shun the boy now, just because his birth father happened to be her husband. The least they could do was give him a proper Weyfield welcome.

Andrew

· · ·

Emma was still in the kitchen when Andrew came to find her. He'd left Jesse gazing round the smoking room. The news of Emma's diagnosis, the fact that she'd kept it from him, had been like a punch in the face. How many shocks could a man take in a morning? he wondered, thinking it would make a neat first line to something. Emma was leaning against the Aga, with a brittle smile.

'I've looked at his passport,' she said. 'In case you were going to try and cover that up, too.'

'Emma,' he said, without much idea what he'd say next.

'Who was she?'

Close up, he saw that her eyes were glassy. He realised he hadn't seen her cry for ages, not since her cousin's funeral, last year. The cousin had died of cancer. Why hadn't she told him she was ill?

'Emma, listen,' he said, again.

'Actually, you can explain yourself later,' she said. 'Where is he, anyway? Where did you leave him?'

'In my study.'

'The smoking room?'

'Yes.'

'And now what? Did you tell him that he'll have to stay, now he's here?'

'Well, we touched on it, but we had other—'

'Andrew! You need to explain properly. I'll go.'

Back in the smoking room, Jesse was standing up, looking at a hunting print.

'You have a beautiful home,' he said to Emma, as they walked in.

'Thank you, Jesse,' she said, smiling warmly. The way she could switch her anger off, for good manners, was formidable. It was a product of her breeding. 'Now, this boring quarantine business,' she began.

'I remember!' said Jesse, 'The banner you made for Olivia – we talked about it.'

'You're too sweet,' she said. 'That's it, you see – now you're in the house, you really shouldn't leave until we're all clear. It's just until the thirtieth. So you're stuck with us, I'm afraid.' She laughed, a little wildly. 'We've been calling it Haag Arrest!'

'But, uh, my flight leaves this afternoon.'

'You'll have to book another one,' said Emma. 'We'll pay, of course. It's the least we can do. You don't have anything pressing to get home for, do you?'

'I guess not,' said Jesse. 'But are you guys sure? I don't want to impose. I feel bad . . . you probably need some space . . .' he tailed off.

'Not at all! It's our pleasure,' said Emma. 'I'd been wondering how you were getting on. What an absolutely *incredible* coincidence. We'd have insisted you stay anyway; you're family.'

She was taking the Pollyanna act a bit far now, thought Andrew.

'It's very low risk,' she carried on. 'But we just need to be doubly cautious, because one of Olivia's poor colleagues went down with it on Christmas Eve. He's on the mend, but he's not out of the woods.'

'Sean Coughlan?' said Jesse, his eyes widening.

'That's right, the Irish boy. But he was going into schools and taking all sorts of risks, whereas Olivia's been terribly careful. Anyhow, I think the Rose Room is ready. Why don't we go up and you can unpack?'

It wasn't the time to correct Emma's theories on Sean Coughlan. As far as Andrew could make out the man had been unlucky, not reckless, but presumably Emma felt safer thinking this way.

They followed her up the back stairs, Andrew carrying the luggage, Jesse caressing the banister as if it were solid gold. He probably thought he'd landed in a stately home, thought Andrew, rather than a draughty, slightly decrepit manor house.

Up in the Rose Room, Jesse turned, beaming. 'This is so nice! Thank you,' he said. The Rose Room was Andrew's least favourite in the house. It was too chintzy, and dominated by a mahogany wardrobe the Hartleys called Monster. Opposite the bed was a portrait of Granny Gwendoline, who used to glare at Andrew over torturous afternoon teas.

'You're welcome,' said Emma, with a faint American nasality. It always happened when she spoke to foreigners. It was her empathy, her selflessness, he thought, with a rush of admiration. Emma was a trooper.

'You're in the Green Bathroom with Phoebe – it's on the left, just down the passage. I'll put clean towels in there. Is there anything else you need?'

'I'm good for now. Thank you so much, Emma, I appreciate it. I'll rebook my ticket, give you guys some time. You'll need to talk to Olivia and Phoebe, right?'

'We shall,' said Emma. 'But do make yourself at home. Lunch at one-ish.'

Outside, Andrew followed her mutely to their bedroom. She shut the door and sat on the chaise longue. He stayed standing, arms crossed, shifting from foot to foot.

'So. When were you planning to tell me?' she said. 'Or did you think, if you ignored him, he'd go away?'

'Emma. Honestly, I had no idea about any of this. He emailed me out of the blue, before Christmas, and that was the first I'd heard of him – ever.'

'Honestly? You'd never heard of him?'

'Honestly. You saw the dates. When it – uh – happened, you and I had only just met. And I can't tell you how insignificant it was. A drunken, one-night, utterly meaningless mistake. I was in Lebanon, missing you. I mean, we were so young. And it just sort of happened, I don't know why. I'd never met her before, never saw her again. No wonder she never told me.'

'She wasn't a . . . you didn't *pay* for her, did you?'

'Christ, no! Emma! What d'you think I am? Look, I know I should have said something at the time. I wanted to. But I'd only taken you out a few times. I didn't know how to tell you. I was afraid I'd lose you. It wasn't worth that. I'd only have been telling you to assuage my conscience. It would have been selfish, in fact.'

'But Andrew! It's not so much that it happened; it's that you didn't tell me. It makes me wonder what else you haven't told me.'

He wanted to bring up her unmentioned cancer, but perhaps it wasn't the moment. 'There's never been anything else, or anyone else, I swear to you, Emma. On Phoebe's life. I loathed myself afterwards. Truly. I've never forgiven myself.' He knelt down to be level with her, and his kneecaps screamed in protest. She said nothing, but as he looked straight into her large, light brown eyes, he felt that she believed him. There was relief in coming clean, after so many years. Almost clean. Clean enough.

'Well, it's all so long ago, I suppose,' she said, eventually, picking at a thread on the chaise longue. 'But what about poor Jesse's emails? You should have told me the minute you heard from him. I'm your wife, Andrew. We're meant to share everything! And you should have replied to him. Whatever else, I didn't think you were a coward, or that you'd—'

'Now hang on,' he interrupted. 'That's not quite fair. I'm not the only one with secrets. Jesse told me about your diagnosis. For God's sake, Emma! If we're meant to share everything, I'd say that was pretty important.'

He saw the shock flash behind her eyes – it was rather satisfying. She opened and shut her mouth like a goldfish. Phoebe did the same, when you caught her out on a fib. Funny how genetics worked.

'That's entirely different,' said Emma.

'How?'

'I *was* going to tell you. I just didn't want to ruin Christmas.'

'Emma – I'm not a child! If I'd found a, something, or been diagnosed with anything, you'd be the first to know.' I'd need you to know, he thought. I'd need your help. Why didn't she need him?

'Well, you know now. I start treatment in the new year. Right, I should speak to the girls,' she said flatly, standing up.

He didn't feel they'd resolved anything. But if she was prepared to explain everything to Phoebe and Olivia, he wasn't going to stop her. He wouldn't have known where to begin.

'Shall I come with you?' he asked, knowing she'd say no.

'Rather you didn't,' she said. She left, and he stayed kneeling on the rug. She was right. He was a coward.

Phoebe

. . .

'Gosh, I just can't get over all this,' said Emma, folding napkins with a slightly panicky precision. Phoebe felt like she was stuck in a messed-up dream. She wished her mother hadn't laid the table in the dining room. It always made meals weirdly formal – as if lunch with Jesse wasn't going to be awkward enough. Her father appeared to be hiding. The thought of him shagging some random woman made Phoebe feel like throwing up. Even worse, her first thought on seeing her half-brother was that he was hot.

'Isn't it extraordinary that I met Jesse?' said Emma, brightly. 'D'you know, I'd been thinking about him, and hoping he was all right, ever since. I do wonder if perhaps I *knew*, on some level.'

'Are you all right, though, Mum?' said Olivia. She was using her doctor voice, as if to ascertain whether Emma was having a nervous breakdown. Their mother did seem freakishly upbeat. She'd explained everything earlier, sitting between Phoebe and Olivia on the stairs. But before they'd had time to absorb it, she'd corralled them down to the kitchen, to make 'a lovely lunch for everyone'.

'D'you know, I'm just fine,' said Emma, stopping and straightening up, as if to reflect on how she felt. 'People do silly things, when they're young. Daddy should have told me. But the point is, none of this is *Jesse's* fault.' She'd made the exact same little speech, ten minutes ago, in the kitchen. Sometimes it was like she had amnesia. 'I felt quite strongly, when I met Jesse at Heathrow, that he deserved to know his father – and his new family. So, what sort of person would I be if I forgot all that? Just because Daddy made a silly mistake? It was decades ago!'

'You'd be normal,' said Phoebe.

'Phoebs, don't be difficult.'

'You do get how genuinely devastating this is?'

'I know it's a shock, angel, but we're all grown ups,' said Emma, briskly. 'Now, will George be joining us?'

'No. He's still not up,' said Phoebe. She had called the bungalow while her mother was laying the table, primed to tell George about Jesse. But George had announced that he was too knackered for lunch, so she'd decided to explain everything later. She still wasn't sure how.

'Good-oh. You all right, Wiv? You look rather washed out,' said Emma.

Her sister did look a bit rough. Maybe she was in shock, though Olivia always seemed to take everything in her stride. Before she could answer, Andrew and Jesse walked in. The only giveaway that they were father and son was their identical height. Side by side, they looked like chopsticks.

'Now everyone must just help themselves – we're very relaxed here,' said Emma, retossing the salad and adjusting the angle of a baguette. Phoebe caught Olivia's eye.

'This looks incredible,' said Jesse, sitting down. 'Thank you.'

She'd only seen him in his coat before. He was wearing skinny jeans, a cashmere cardigan and a lame little scarf. He looked like a Uniqlo model. No way was she going to welcome him. If possible, she wouldn't even speak to him.

'Did you try arnica?' he said, looking at her foot. 'Your mom told me about your fall.'

She looked at her father. They had an in-joke about the pointlessness of arnica. But he was studiously carving wafers of ham.

'Now, Jesse, you must try this gammon. It's from our local farm,' said Andrew. How could he be acting like Jesse was a normal guest?

'I'm actually vegan,' said Jesse, apologetically. 'Well, that's my goal. But anything vegetarian is fine, I'm easy.'

'Vegan? *How* interesting,' said her mother, as they all sat down. 'Vegan food has become quite fashionable now, hasn't it? And remind me, you aren't allowed to wear leather, are you? Is that tricky with shoes?'

'Well, I don't take it to that level. It's more the nutritional aspect for me.'

'So this endeavour is for health reasons, rather than animal sentimentality?' said Andrew.

'Both, I guess. My sister and I, my adopted sister, we were raised around animals. Plus there are so many vegan places in LA now. It's practically the norm there.'

Nobody spoke for a moment. Everything about his ready smile and slick answers grated. He could at least have the decency to feel uncomfortable, thought Phoebe, barging into their house without knocking.

She glanced at Olivia, wanting to exchange another look, but her sister was just gazing at her plate, not eating.

'Don't vegans get rather low on iron? Or is it calcium?' asked her mother.

He looked as if he might launch into a spiel on nutrients, but the door opened and George walked in. Bollocks. He was meant to be in the bungalow.

'Oh! Wow – hey!' said Jesse, looking up at George.

George looked shocked, too. Phoebe wished she'd warned him now.

'I mean, like, hey, I'm Jesse!' he added, giving a little wave. Americans were so fake. Greeting strangers like friends.

'Hi,' said George, stiffly.

She needed to take charge before either of her parents said anything.

'Jesse, George is my fiancé. George, this is Jesse – our half-brother.' Put like that, it sounded convincingly normal. Perhaps George would just think she'd told him about a half-brother and he'd forgotten.

For a moment, George looked stunned – understandably. Then he seemed to recover himself. 'Good to meet you, mate,' he said.

'Likewise,' said Jesse.

'All alright, George?' said her mother. 'Phoebs said you weren't feeling a hundred per cent?'

'Yah, no, better thanks. Hair of the dog!' he said, reaching across Phoebe for the wine. 'Top up?' he asked Andrew, who was the only one drinking.

'Why not?' said her father.

She noticed George staring at Jesse twice. But there were no questions about where the surprise sibling fitted in, and no quizzical looks thrown her way. Sometimes Phoebe felt like she barely knew him.

Olivia

. . .

'There you are,' said Emma. 'I thought we might all have tea. What are you doing?'

'Getting kindling,' said Olivia. 'The log basket was empty.'

'Oh. OK. Thanks, sweetheart.' Her mother looked surprised, as if it was out of character for Olivia to be helpful.

They stood just inside the woodshed, a former privy with a large hole in the roof. Behind them sat a stately Victorian lavatory, cobwebs tightroping from cistern to curved wooden seat.

'Gosh, that must have been nippy!' said her mother, staring at it.

Olivia was about to answer: 'The entire developing world still has outdoor loos,' but stopped herself, seeing how tired Emma looked.

'Anyway, Wiv, I wanted to tell you something. I know you've already had a shock today. A real shock. But, well I should have told *you* first, really – I mean – you're a doctor!' she said, with an odd soprano laugh.

Olivia prepared to look surprised.

'I've, um, well a couple of weeks ago I found a lump, you see, just here,' Emma went on, fingers leaping to her armpit. 'And it's, it's cancer I'm afraid.' She stopped with a little gasped breath. 'Non-Hodgkin Lymphoma. Anyhow, I'm only telling you this because—' she stopped again. 'I mean, I was going to wait to tell everyone after quarantine but Phoebe found out the other day, and now—'

'Found out?'

'Yes, by accident. And also, it sounds barmy I know, but when I met Jesse at Heathrow I told him all about it. And he presumed Andrew knew, so the cancer's out of the bag!' She laughed the tinkly laugh again. 'I'm sorry, I know I should have told you all immediately. I didn't want to cast a shadow over Christmas. I couldn't bear to think about it myself, to be quite honest.'

Olivia knew this was her cue to say something reassuring. It wasn't fair to press her mother on how Phoebe had 'found out'. Or to scare her, by pointing out the risk of being quarantined together. It was too late now anyway.

'That must be frightening for you, Mum,' she said carefully. 'I'm glad you told me. But this type of cancer is very treatable, you know. There's every chance of making a full recovery.'

'Yes, he said. My consultant.'

'What stage is it?'

'Just early, hopefully. But I'm waiting for more results.'

'Which ones? Did you have a CT scan?'

'Yes CT, MRI, lots of blood and things. But I won't find out until the new year.'

'And has he talked you through the treatment options?'

'He touched on them, yes. But not to worry. We'll cross that bridge when we come to it,' she said, picking up the log basket as if the conversation was at an end. 'We've got enough on our plates, what with Daddy and Jesse.'

They walked back across the sodden lawn, side by side, her mother chattering about how Andrew and his son had doppelganger ears, and had Olivia noticed that they both had the same way of pushing back their hair, and wasn't it uncanny that they were both interested in food. The sun was sending fat fingers of grey light down to the horizon. Olivia remembered her mother saying – after Granny died – that they were slides from Heaven. What if she hadn't caught the cancer early?

'Well, if you're unsure of anything I'm happy to advise,' said Olivia as they reached the porch. Why did she sound like she was speaking to a patient, not her mum? She thought how different Phoebe and Emma sounded when they talked. Though it was interesting that her mother hadn't confided in Phoebe after all. Typically sly of her sister to make out she was the chosen one.

'Mmm,' said Emma. 'Thanks, lambkin. Must get some WD40 on this bloody door.'

Jesse

. . .

Jesse lay on his bed, looking round the Rose Room. The bedside lamps cast an amber glow, like an old sepia photograph. With the antique closet and ancestral portraits, he felt like he'd stepped back in time – although when he'd tried to film the room, it looked strangely sinister, and his own voiceover sounded ludicrous. Perhaps daylight would be a better time to get footage. He'd planned to shoot the house during the afternoon, but it had seemed kind of rude so soon after arriving. Tomorrow, maybe. He needed to pee again – Andrew kept refilling his glass at dinner – but the cistern was so loud he decided to wait. In his room he felt safe, like it was his little haven. The fact that he was here, at Weyfield, was enough to process – never mind the coincidences the cosmos had thrown his way. He'd nearly choked when George had walked in at lunch.

He switched off the hilariously old-school heater Emma had brought up, anxious that he'd get 'chilly'. The room was roasting. He tried to crack open a window, but the ivy growing up the wall outside had pinned it shut, so he stripped to his briefs instead. He took out his iPad – Dana had replied to the short email he'd sent before lunch, and would be waiting for a response. In his alien surroundings, it was a relief to have a link to home. He read her email again.

Subject: Re: Big news
From: Dana Robinson <danar_1985@hotmail.com>
Date: 27/12/2016 17:03
To: Jesse Robinson <jesse.iskandar.robinson@gmail.com>

Jesse!!! I'm freaking out, please promise me you won't go
getting Haag! Are you sure the risk is minimal? Didn't some
Irish doctor just get it already? Mom would have a fit if she
knew where you are. Also, that is INSANE that you already
met Andrew's wife in the airport!!!!!! It's like God wanted
it to all work out. Although I hope it's not too intense that
you have to stay? Do you feel like your birth sisters are cool
with it? What are they like? Tell me everything.

Happy for you,

D XOXO

Subject: Re: Big news
From: Jesse Robinson <jesse.iskandar.robinson@gmail.
com>
Date: 27/12/2016 23:05
To: Dana Robinson <danar_1985@hotmail.com>

Don't freak out!! I promise you I won't get Háag. They
told me the quarantine is just a formality, it's pretty hard
to infect somebody with it. You have to literally exchange
bodily fluids. Plus the house is huge (the dining room is
the size of your apartment), so it's not too intense. I now
fly home Jan 1st – can you make some excuse to Mom and
Dad? I owe you!

It's just bizarre how I was all set to leave today, without

even hearing from Andrew, and now I'm a house guest . . . Emma has been super welcoming, which makes sense because she was the same at the airport. I still can't believe I didn't realise who she was, but we didn't swap names and we barely talked about her family. Plus she looks nothing like that photo online. I guess I was picturing 'The Honourable Emma Hartley' to be more aloof and aristocratic or something.

I get the feeling the others need longer to warm up. Olivia doesn't say a whole lot, but she's clearly very smart. She's tall and skinny, like Andrew (and me!), and basically exactly like her dad. Phoebe is adorable – she looks like her picture and seems like fun. Her fiancé is here, too. Andrew is sort of terribly British and stiff upper lip, like I expected, although he opened up a little when he showed me 'the grounds'. He's pretty different from Dad – so far the only similarity I see is the universal male fascination with fire building. But I think they could get along, if they were to meet someday.

One thing that's not so great – turns out Andrew was already with Emma when I was conceived. They were having some kind of clandestine relationship way back before the Royal Wedding. I don't fully get it. I think Andrew was afraid Emma's parents would disapprove of him. But essentially he cheated on Emma with my birth mother, and Emma had no idea until today. She's acting like she's cool with it, but obviously it makes me feel very uncomfortable. Plus I messed up by asking Andrew about something she told me in the airport – that she has just been diagnosed with cancer. I assumed he knew, but it turned out he had no idea (?!). It's very weird, and I

know it's not my fault, but now I feel like I've come in and
caused problems.

Jesse stopped. He wanted to be honest, but he was making Andrew
and his family sound bad. Dana's judgements were swift and lasting.
If he confessed to feeling as out of place as excited at Weyfield, she
would never warm to the Birches. Especially if he told Dana that his
birth sister appeared to hate him. Phoebe had barely looked at him
during lunch, and he hadn't seen her or George all afternoon. At
'supper', the two of them had eaten separately in the summer house
they called the bungalow. It made Jesse feel pretty shitty. He had
eaten with the other three in the big, cosy kitchen – Andrew quiz-
zing him about Trump, as if to avoid discussing anything personal.
Olivia didn't say much, even when Jesse tried to engage with her,
although he got the feeling that was normal. It was kind of strange
in a doctor, though. Weren't they meant to be able to communicate?
Even stranger was the way nobody mentioned Emma's cancer. His
own family would be the opposite. When his mom had a minor
operation last year everyone had pulled together, fussing over her,
restocking the refrigerator, doing extra chores so she could rest up.
But perhaps silence was the British coping mechanism.

On top of everything, there was the George situation. Jesse still
hadn't told Dana what had happened on Christmas Eve, just that
he'd befriended some British guys. He felt even scuzzier about it now.
He definitely wasn't about to start explaining all that shit today. All
Dana needed to know was 'so far, so good'.

The door opened and Jesse jumped, pulling the blankets over his
crotch. It was George. He came in, turned the rusty key in the lock,
and stood with his back against the door.

'Hey,' began Jesse. 'About before . . .'

'Listen, mate,' said George. His eyes looked a little crazy. Jesse wondered if he was drunk again. 'The other night, it didn't happen, OK?' he said, lowering his voice. 'I was shitfaced. I don't know what I was – that wasn't *me*, OK?'

'Sure, sure. I get it. I was your experiment.'

'You weren't anything! Nothing happened, mate. I never met you.'

'Fine. So I've never seen you in my life.'

'Right.'

'OK. Wait, how come you were out? I thought the quarantine started on the twenty-third?'

'I wasn't here then. I came over on Christmas Day to surprise Phoebs.'

Guilty conscience, thought Jesse. 'And you're sure you want to go through with this?' he said.

'Through with what?' said George.

Jesus, the guy was obtuse. 'With getting married.'

'What the fuck? Of course I do! Like I said, that wasn't me that night. Haven't you ever done anything stupid when you were pissed?'

Pissed meant drunk here, Jesse reminded himself.

'Sure, but I never stopped being gay.'

George took a deep, angry breath through his nose, his little nostrils quivering. Jesse wondered how he had thought he was cute. He looked like a flushed, balding pug.

'If you say anything about *any* of this,' said George, tendons flexing in his outsize neck, 'I will personally fucking kill you. OK?'

'Dude, calm down. I'm not about to say anything. That's your call. I just think you have some pretty deep thinking to do. You're getting married—' Down the passage, a door closed. He lowered his voice. 'You're marrying Phoebe and that is a huge commitment. You don't want to be having doubts as she walks down the aisle. That's all I'm saying.'

'I don't have doubts! Listen, I don't know what you're playing at just rocking up here, but Phoebs is devastated.'

'Hey, you *told* me to come here, remember?'

'I'm sorry? Why the fuck would I do that?'

'Forget it. What do you mean, Phoebe's devastated?'

'What d'you think? You've destroyed her entire image of her daddy. She worships the ground he walks on, and now you show him up as the prick he really is. She just told me the whole story.'

'Hey, that's my father you're talking about.'

George made a snorting noise. 'Ha! Your father for all of five minutes. Why couldn't you have written to him first, like a normal adopted person, and met in private, for fuck's sake?'

Somewhere, a flush set off a symphony of gurgling pipes.

'Anyway,' said George, in a tight whisper. 'Just don't say anything, OK?'

'Believe me, I won't.'

'Good.'

He left, and Jesse lay looking at the scalloped valance. He felt bad for Phoebe, marrying such a dick. He wondered if the other Birches liked George. The things he'd said about Phoebe made Jesse feel terrible. He hadn't planned any of this – the front door had opened, literally, and somehow it had all just happened. Besides, if Andrew had replied to his emails, he would have met up with him in private.

An alert flashed up on his iPad – Jesse still hadn't read Andrew's latest column. The review was of a pub called The Perch, but mostly it was about being in quarantine. The 'family first' headline was a red herring. If anything, Andrew sounded kind of scathing about families. It was interesting to read his birth father's writing again, having finally met the man. He had the same arch tone in person, but Jesse felt there was something warmer underneath. It was just buried.

Andrew

· · ·

Walking out of the Green Bathroom, Andrew was surprised to find George in the passage. He'd been under the impression that the lovebirds had defected from the main house altogether. George was kicking a spider by the skirting board, but looked up and said, 'Just getting Phoebs an extra blanket, bungalow's bit cold,' before marching into the Grey Room. Andrew wondered what George, with his painfully conventional worldview, must make of Jesse's arrival. He hoped Phoebe wasn't too mortified, but he feared she would be. For all her bravado, his younger daughter could be rather conservative – hence her choice of husband.

Andrew walked down to the smoking room. His next column wasn't due for days, but he'd told Emma he had an early deadline to avoid coming to bed. The thought of lying beside her, neither of them speaking, was grim. Easier to go up once she was snoring. Or perhaps he'd just camp in the smoking room. He knew he'd never sleep anyway.

Andrew poured himself a large glass of port, aware that he'd already drunk more than enough, and sat at the desk in near-darkness. He took a long, sickly swig, as he tried to recall a meal at a new Middle Eastern place in St John's Wood. He remembered Phoebe turning heads in a short dress, and how proud he'd felt of her, and the owner making her baulk by assuming she was his trophy wife. He remembered talking to her about how the media wasn't what it once was, and that she'd do well to extricate herself. And he remembered her saying that she just wanted to do something *fun* and funny for work, like Andrew did, and that life was too short to do a serious job. But he couldn't remember a single thing about the food. Had it been small plates (Phoebe's favourite), or Emma's beloved sharing platters? Or his personal bugbear, 'street food'. His meal blanks struck more and more often, these days. He began to write anyway – he could ask Phoebe what they'd eaten tomorrow. If she'd answer him.

Hourani & Co, Welbeck Street
Food ??
Atmosphere ??

Beirut: 1980. The sun bathes the carcass of a primary school in silvery dawn light. The droning adhan, blasted through loudspeakers, heralds a new day. A man balances a beaten copper tray of cakes on his head, cubes of filo and pistachio drenched in perfumed honey, as he picks his way through the rubble

Andrew deleted the lot. He wasn't in lyrical mode. He began again, this time typing:

Readers of this column will know me as a food critic – the main occupational hazard of my job being heartburn. But between 1977 and 1987, I worked in Beirut as a war correspondent. For all its tortured history, Lebanon remains one of the most

He deleted that too. He was too drunk to write anything factual. He tried another tack:

You say Taboul-eh, I say Taboul-ah,

He preferred this, except he couldn't think where to take it from there. There weren't really two distinct pronunciations of tabouleh, anyway. Andrew had always been scornful of writer's block – if one was a writer, one wrote. But now he was at a loss. Many columnists he knew would use Jesse's arrival as copy. It would certainly make a neat preamble to a Middle Eastern restaurant. But something was stopping him. The idea that he was the man's father still made no sense. He hadn't expected to feel so detached, as unlike Jesse, as he did. The boy seemed so cheerful, so grateful, brimming with 'positive energy' – so unlike Andrew. He was a vegan, for Christ's sake. He was the kind of person that Andrew and Phoebe sniggered at, who probably practised mindfulness. It couldn't just be his American upbringing. They were made of entirely different stuff. If anything, Jesse was more like Emma.

Andrew had tried to expand on this observation to Emma earlier, up in their bedroom, but it had sounded pompous. Emma had said sharply: 'Andrew, I don't quite understand. He's a sweet young man with good manners. I'd have thought you'd be relieved?' When Andrew had protested that he had nothing against Jesse, he just couldn't believe that the man was his flesh and blood, she had gone back to crisis management, repeating that they *owed* it to Jesse to welcome him, adding: 'It's the least you can do after all this time. You're his father.'

It was like being punished with politeness. She probably thought Andrew minded Jesse being gay – which, of course, he didn't. Or if it did make him feel just slightly off-kilter, it was only because it wedged another difference between them. What did trouble Andrew was Phoebe's response to Jesse – saying nothing at lunch and then hiding in the bungalow. But when he'd broached this with Emma, she'd got into bed and said: 'Andrew, you know Phoebe. She's had a fright. It's up to you to lead by example. You're the adult. Right, I must get some sleep.' He'd taken this as his cue to leave.

He drained the last of the port – it tasted of tomorrow's headache. How had they reached a point where his wife could be diagnosed with cancer and not tell him?

· 7 ·

28 December 2016

Quarantine: Day 6

Olivia

. . .

Subject: PHEW!!
From: Olivia Birch <olivia.birch1984@gmail.com>
Date: 28/12/2016 09:18
To: Sean Coughlan <SeanKCoughlan@gmail.com>

Just heard the news – you're officially Haag-negative!
Jubulani!! How are you feeling? Hope they get you out of
isolation asap so you can read my email ramblings, and
write back. Missing you so much. I miss your voice. I miss
you saying everything's 'grand', even when it's about as
un-grand as humanly possible. I'm still fine, by the way,
don't worry.

   More drama here in sleepy Norfolk: this American dude
came to the house out of nowhere yesterday, claiming
to be my dad's son … As in, I have a half-brother I never
knew about … In fact, nobody knew about, not even my
dad until recently. Basically, he got some woman pregnant
when he was working in the Middle East in the eighties
and she had the baby adopted, without telling my dad
anything. Probably for the best, since my parents had

just got together at the time (don't judge). Anyway the child – now adult male called Jesse – traced my father and emailed him but got no reply (typical of my dad). He probably hoped if he did nothing this illegitimate son would disappear. But instead Jesse finds our address and just walks in ... Which sounds a bit psycho on paper, but I get it. He'd come all the way here from California, so he must have been desperate. Anyway, once he was in the house the only option was to finish the quarantine with us.

Even more improbable, my mother somehow met Jesse and spoke to him at Heathrow on the 23rd – seriously, what are the chances? He landed in London the same day we did, and they were both waiting in Arrivals (having said that, she talks to practically everyone). She's being pretty tolerant of my father's 'indiscretion' (her words). I feel bad for her though, as she must be a nervous wreck as it is. She told me about her diagnosis yesterday, at least. But since she's carrying on being the perfect hostess it's hard to know how to help. I'd like to be some support, but I find myself defaulting to work mode, like she's a patient, and I don't think she wants that.

The weird thing with Jesse is knowing he's my brother, that we share all this DNA, but seeing a complete stranger. I can't even view him like a distant cousin – it's like there's no connection at all. He seems perfectly nice, though. He asked me some proper questions about Liberia, unlike everyone else here. He must be mid-thirties, and all I know otherwise is that he's gay, brought up in the Midwest, but now works in LA – in film or TV or something. My sister has really taken against him – partly because she's fundamentally irrational, but also because she's such a Daddy's girl and now she has to accept that our father's not this demi-god ... Think it's easier for me because I've never hero-worshipped him like she does. Until now I'd sort of forgotten that he used to work in a war zone. Not that I can talk. What we did was pretty silly ... I'll never regret it though.

Anyway, hope all this adds some interest to your convalescence. Probably seems like nothing to you, with your tribe of fifty-seven siblings (all of them 100 per cent legitimate, of course). Next instalment coming soon.

Love you and miss you too much,

O x

Olivia pressed send. Writing her one-way emails to Sean came naturally now, but the thought that she might get something back this time was making her smile inanely, alone in bed. She nearly added a PS explaining that Phoebe had guessed their secret, but decided against it. Sean could be indiscreet – if he knew she'd told her sister, he might start telling people before it was safe. The news had taken her mind off the sick feeling she'd woken up with again. It wasn't like she was actually about to vomit or anything. It was more like a clawing inside, as if her stomach was slowly turning inside out. She pushed away the thought that nausea was the major first Haag symptom. Besides, she'd felt fine yesterday, once she'd had breakfast. Most likely it was just another hangover – her father had been topping everyone up compulsively last night.

There was a knock on her door. It was her sister. She never usually came into Olivia's room.

'Hey. What'cha doing?' said Phoebe.

'Writing an email.'

'To Sean?'

'Yes. Nosy.'

'Is he OK?'

'Yeah, he tested negative – it's all over the news!' Olivia was too relieved to berate her for knowing nothing. Or to grill her on how she'd 'found out' about Emma's diagnosis.

'Oh! Cool! So he's better?'

'Not *better* better. But he's not high risk any more. They'll be able to move him out of isolation.'

'Amazing. Yay,' said Phoebe, wanly. She sat on the edge of the bed, and sighed.

'What?'

'I don't know. I just, I don't like him. Jesse.'

'You don't like *him*, or you don't like the fact that he exists? What Andrew did?'

'Him, everything about him! And that. Both, I guess. It's scary to have everything you believed in just, shattered.' She flopped on her back, her hands behind her head, at Olivia's feet. 'To find out we were all living a lie.'

'We weren't "living a lie". There were just things we didn't know. That's how it is in families.'

'Is it? Anyway, whatever, Daddy isn't who we thought he was. Can't believe he would *do* that to Mummy.'

'He made a mistake when he was young. I know it's hard to think of him like that. But nobody's perfect.'

'I'd never do that. I wouldn't *marry* someone and not tell them I'd cheated.'

'But he probably knew it would only upset her. If something meant nothing, why make someone miserable by bringing it up years later? It's not like he knew the woman got pregnant. And it sounds like he and Mum had only just met.'

'Doesn't it make you wonder what else he's done?'

'Not specially. He's worked from home since you were born. When would he have had these torrid affairs?'

Phoebe examined a split end, not looking at her.

'Anyway, you can't expect to understand other people's relationships,' Olivia added. That was the thing with Phoebe. She thought she had a right to know everything about everyone.

'Liv! They're not "other people" – they're our parents!'

'Still. Everyone's entitled to privacy. Just like Mum didn't want to talk about her diagnosis until she was ready. She told me yesterday, by the way.'

She looked straight at Phoebe, wondering if she'd admit to lying about the way she'd found out. But Phoebe was on a roll.

'That's different,' she said indignantly. 'It's got nothing to do with it. Anyway, she was always *going* to say, just not before she had to. She didn't want to upset everyone before Christmas.'

'Isn't that exactly what Andrew did? Why would he mention it until he had to, if it would only upset everyone?'

'So we could have all been prepared! I just think Mummy's right, Daddy should have replied to Jesse's emails. Then it wouldn't have been such a shock. For us.'

'I get it. He didn't want to rock the boat. Not until we were done with quarantine.'

She got out of bed, and as she did so felt another lurch of queasiness. Her stomach plummeted, as saliva pooled in her mouth. She'd confront Phoebe about her lie later.

'Are you OK?' said Phoebe, nervously.

'Fine. Just – it's weird, I feel really hungover. I didn't know I'd even drunk that much.'

Forming words felt like an enormous effort. She tamped down the nausea rising in her throat.

'Oh my god, I know what you mean. I'm such a lightweight. I can have literally one glass and feel like shit the next day. It's probably cos you're so skinny now.'

'Yeah. Maybe,' said Olivia, pulling on her dressing gown. Her hands felt clammy as she tried to knot it.

'Porridge always sorts me out,' said Phoebe, following her out of the room. It reminded Olivia of how she used to tag along everywhere when they were little.

As they walked downstairs, the smell of bacon drifted up from the kitchen, and Olivia knew, abruptly, that she had no choice but to be sick. She mumbled something to Phoebe about getting her iPad and sprinted to the bathroom. Three foul heaves hijacked her body. She knelt by the loo, trying to slow her ragged breathing, eyes clamped shut so she wouldn't have to see the contents of her stomach in the bowl. After a moment she stood up and looked in the mirror, gripping the sink to stop her arms from shaking. Her face was a greenish yellow, and her eyes were shot with blood from choking up her empty insides. Fuck, fuck, fuck, she thought.

Emma

. . .

Cooking, and Jenni Murray's voice on the radio, felt like anchors to normality. Emma had made one pan of mushrooms and tomatoes for Jesse, and another of bacon and eggs for everyone else. With breakfast sizzling, she started to prepare lunch, a vegan curry she'd found on Google. Andrew had slept in the smoking room last night. Emma had found him already up and dressed with Jesse when she'd come down earlier. The two of them had gone to look at the gun room, at Andrew's suggestion, so Emma had begun to cook for everyone on her own. At least Andrew was making an effort, after whinging last night – idiotically – that he and Jesse had nothing in common. She realised that a small, rather mean, part of her wanted it to be hard work for Andrew. He never did anything he didn't want to.

Phoebe appeared, enveloped in one of George's jumpers. Emma hadn't seen her since lunch yesterday. She hoped she'd come round to Jesse soon. It was embarrassing, her daughter sulking like a teenager.

'What's that?' said Phoebe, inspecting the casserole on the Aga.

'Aubergine curry. Not a speck of meat.'

Phoebe rolled her eyes.

'I thought you were rather keen on vegan food?'

'Me? No. Although "hashtagcleaneating" *is* a handy cover for anorexia,' said Phoebe, in the faux chirpy voice that made Andrew laugh. She had a lot on her plate, Emma reminded herself.

George came in, wearing a little woolly hat. He kept it on, even though the kitchen was steamy. She suspected it must be to hide his receding hairline, poor thing. How awful to lose one's hair, she thought, and then remembered her looming chemotherapy.

'Morning Mrs B. Yo Titch,' said George. 'Thought I smelt bacon.' Emma still hoped he might change his mind about having the wedding at Weyfield. Perhaps she could play the cancer card. Linda Marsham-Smith wouldn't have much answer to that.

'Where's Daddy?' Phoebe asked Emma.

'In the gun room. Showing Jesse Papa's shooting things.'

'Guns? Guess he is American,' she said, as if it was an embarrassing medical condition. George straddled the bench by the table, and Phoebe sat on one of his thighs. Cocoa, who was lying by George's foot, stood up and stalked off.

'Thought he'd be too gay for firearms,' said George.

Phoebe tittered. It wasn't like her – she had several sweet gay friends she referred to as her 'walkers'. George took a banana from the fruit bowl and shoved most of it into his mouth in a single bite. Even though they were adults, Emma had to stop herself saying: 'I'm just cooking a lovely breakfast and you're going to spoil your appetite.'

Instead, she said, 'Anything wrong with being homosexual?' She kept her tone light, but realised she was holding a wooden spoon rather threateningly.

'Hey there,' said Jesse, coming in. His grin suggested he hadn't overheard – thank goodness. But George looked unusually alarmed, like a trapped animal.

There was a strained pause, until Phoebe squawked: 'Hey, is that the last banana? It is, you knob! I always have one with my porridge – you know that.'

'Sorr-eee,' said George, batting his eyelids and offering her the bit in his hand.

'Waitrose doesn't deliver again till tonight,' she said.

'Oopsies.'

Phoebe said nothing, but managed to execute a hobbled flounce out of the room. George gave his hat a nervous tug, as Phoebe shouted back, 'I'm going to have a shower. In the bungalow. Stairs hurt too much.'

Emma wondered if she ought to go after Phoebe, encourage her to eat breakfast, but decided against it. Yesterday, seeing how Phoebe had taken Jesse's arrival, she'd realised she babied her youngest. Perhaps it was because Olivia had always refused to be molly-coddled. And the result was that Phoebe threw a wobbly over a banana. Still, it wasn't terribly chivalrous of George.

'Aren't you going to check that she's OK?' said Jesse. He was fabulously direct, thought Emma.

'Phoebs? She's fine. Just needs to chill – read a bridal magazine or something.'

Emma looked at George, engrossed in the jigsaw she had started down one end of the table. He had the kind of face that wouldn't age well, she feared. She remembered how the snub nose and fine jaw had looked boyish when he and Phoebe had met, but a heaviness was settling around the features, now. His eyes were still very pretty, though she'd always found their wolfish pallor rather disconcerting.

'Can I help, Emma?' asked Jesse, but she batted his offer away. 'So, uh, how did you guys meet?' said Jesse to George, sitting on the bench, his back against the table. His legs trailed over the floor and he crossed one over the other, just like Andrew did, as if to tidy them away.

'I'm sorry?' said George, looking up as if he'd been alone.

'You and Phoebe.'

'At uni, in Edinburgh,' said George. 'Car-lege, to you,' he added in a strange American accent that sounded more West Country.

'Did you know she was The One, straight off?'

'*She* did,' said George.

'They were peas in a pod from the word go,' said Emma, feeling this was the right thing to say, with George being so terse. In fact, the start of the relationship had been fraught with uncertainty. Emma remembered thinking it wouldn't last. But, somehow, she'd been proved wrong, and George had become a permanent fixture. She'd never fully discussed it with Andrew. The times she'd tried, he'd always said any disapproval would make Phoebe keener. She suspected that this was a veiled dig at her own parents, and had taken the hint.

'Where did you take her for your first date?' said Jesse.

'What is this, twenty questions?' said George. 'There was no "date". We hooked up at a dive called The Mock Turtle. Gangstas and Hoes night,' he smirked. Emma couldn't think what Gangstas and Hoes might involve. Was it some kind of hoedown, like reeling? Jesse seemed to know, so it must be American.

George stood up, tossed the banana skin into the waste-paper basket and pulled down his hat. Emma made a mental note to move the peel to the compost, later. 'I'll go and get Phoebs,' he said.

Neither Emma nor Jesse said anything, as his loafers slapped down the hall.

'Are you happy she's marrying him?' said Jesse, when the sound stopped.

Maybe Jesse was a bit too direct, thought Emma.

'Well, it's not up to us. And he's a good influence on her. He doesn't put up with any of Phoebe's nonsense.' This had long been her line on George. It was true, in a sense.

'Who doesn't?' said Andrew, coming in.

'George. Isn't that right?'

'One way of putting it,' said Andrew. He put an arm around her waist and sniffed the pan she was stirring. She froze slightly, in his grasp.

'And that,' he said, 'smells absolutely delicious. D'you realise, Jesse, in all the years I've been reviewing Michelin-starred chefs, Emma's food is still the best I know?'

'I don't doubt it,' said Jesse.

'Considering what a meanie you are about most places, I'm not sure I take that entirely as a compliment,' said Emma. Andrew's body against hers felt at once alien and familiar. What were they doing, carrying on as if everything was hunky dory?

'Now that's hardly fair,' said Andrew. 'If a dreadful place opens, the public deserves to be warned. There are few greater let downs than a bad dinner out.'

'You don't hold back, that's for sure,' said Jesse. 'I was kind of intimidated to meet you, after reading your columns.'

'I do hope I didn't disappoint?' said Andrew.

'You're different, in person,' said Jesse, after a pause. 'You seem, I don't know, pretty frustrated, in your reviews.' The way he stressed the first syllable, 'frus', made the word sound more exasperated. It was odd to see a stranger get to the point so easily.

'Journalism is a frustrating business,' said Andrew, releasing Emma. 'Everyone tinkering with your words. D'you know, in my last column they took the word "briny" out of my phrase "flap of briny irrelevance"?' He looked at them both, eyes wide with disbelief. Then he added, not sounding at all like himself, 'You're right, though. It's not worth fussing over. We have more important things to worry about. Speaking of which, how are we on the coffee front?'

He took the spoon from Emma and pulled the bench out for her, before silencing them with blasts from the coffee grinder. She sat, pretending to read India Knight's column. So this was how they were going to ride this storm. Least said, soonest mended.

Olivia

. . .

Olivia shifted on the little stool she and Phoebe used to stand on to brush their teeth. She was pretty sure that she wasn't going to be sick again. Slowly, she raised her head from between her knees and breathed. The bathroom smelled of Pears soap and the mouldy patch on the wall. After a moment she felt steady enough to stand up. She found an old mercury thermometer in the cabinet over the sink, and checked her temperature. It was normal. Should she say something anyway? No. No point. It would only panic everyone – especially her mother, which was the last thing Emma needed on top of Jesse's arrival. They'd demand she get checked out, and she'd have to tell them about her and Sean, and before she knew it an air ambulance would be landing on the croquet lawn, costing the NHS thousands, and she and Sean would be crucified by the press – and most likely it would all be for nothing. After all, she didn't have any other symptoms (tiredness didn't count – of course she was tired).

It had to be the wine last night. Besides, being sick wasn't even unusual for her. In any other circumstances she'd put it down to stress. The acid taste in her mouth took her back to being little, her mother stroking her back when she was ill. She remembered a miserable night when she had eaten a bad mussel, and they had sat in this bathroom together until dawn. She could hear her mother downstairs now, trilling above everyone else. She'd have to go and join them at some point, she thought, leaning her forehead on the window and trying to rally herself. Tears threatened, as she yearned for Sean's chest and orang-utan arms wrapped tight around her. Surely home shouldn't feel so lonely?

By the time she made it downstairs only Emma and Jesse were in the kitchen, loading the dishwasher. She paused in the doorway for a second, as she realised what they were talking about.

'They've *proven* that cancer cells feed on sugar,' said Jesse. 'They did this study where they had one group of cancer patients eat their regular diet and another group go sugar free, and their tumours practically vanished.'

'Golly,' said Emma. 'Oh dear. Me and my sweet tooth.'

'Hey – no – don't blame yourself. Sugar is disguised. It's everywhere – ketchup, bagels, even fruit. People assume fat is the bad guy, but it's sugar we need to cut back.'

'Well I don't eat a vast amount of ketchup, at least!' said Emma, with a forced laugh.

'You should look up this TED Talk. I'll email you the link,' said Jesse.

'Oh yes, fab!' said Emma. Olivia could bet she had no idea what TED was.

'There are actually a ton of natural remedies for cancer, but nobody knows about them because it's not in the pharmaceutical companies' interests. There's like a whole underground movement for fighting cancer without chemo.'

'Really? Is that wise?' said Emma.

'It's extreme, sure. But it has to be up to the individual. Nobody should feel obligated to accept an aggressive treatment – right?'

'I suppose so.'

'Even just alkalising your diet a little can be helpful.'

Olivia backed out of the kitchen before they'd seen her. She stood by the door, wondering what to do as they prattled on and on about juice fasts and superfoods – Emma cooing as they Googled 'eat to beat cancer'. Usually, Olivia would have walked in and confronted Jesse – asked him to back up his vacuous theories with proof, shown him some WHO survival rates. But he was her dad's son, her new brother; it would be massively awkward. And right now, she felt too drained for an argument. Still, maybe Phoebe had a point about him after all.

Phoebe

. . .

One more day of this hell, thought Phoebe, lying on the sofa. One more day, then she and George could flee to London. She'd skipped breakfast to make a point, and was hungry now, but she could hear her mother and Jesse still in the kitchen. It wasn't fair that she was forced into hiding in her own house. At least she'd lose weight, avoiding so many meals. She leant forward to prod her puffy foot, half enjoying the pain that roared back, and peeled away her sock to examine the bruise. The skin was a storm of green and lilac, slightly pearlescent, like cheap eyeshadow. She lay back, letting Cocoa lounge on top of her, and stared at the Christmas tree.

Everything seemed so different, so grown up. She'd given George the backstory to Jesse last night, and it hadn't gone well. She knew he was judging. When she tried to explain why Jesse riled her, George just said she couldn't deal with a gay brother. That wasn't the problem – Jesse was. His happy clappy Californian-ness was the problem. The Eager Vegan, she thought, knowing this would make her father laugh, in different circumstances. Even Jesse's J-Crew catalogue face was annoying. Olivia didn't under-stand stuff like that, but at least she was prepared to talk about him – unlike George. Come to think of it, her sister still hadn't made it downstairs. Phoebe considered going to check if she was OK. But her foot hurt too much. Olivia was probably reading the news somewhere.

She watched a couple of YouTube first dances to take her mind off everything. The couples were all cheesily American, like Jesse. Then she leafed through the copy of *Brides*. It always fell open at the same page, headed 'How To Make Your Wedding More *YOU*'. She'd decided on her Winter Wonderland theme, but she couldn't seem to get beyond that. Whenever she pictured the wedding, she always imagined walking up the aisle with Andrew, or everyone crowding round her – alone – at the reception. George never figured in her mental images. She'd thought being quarantined together would be a chance to brainstorm ideas. But every time she mentioned the wedding he said, 'Bit early, isn't it?' He'd been tetchy since yesterday, after being so soppy at Christmas.

She wondered idly if Olivia and Sean would get married, remembering how smitten Olivia had sounded yesterday. She'd never seen her sister like that. She wasn't sure she'd ever been like that herself, about George. Reaching for her laptop, she Googled 'Shaun Cofflan' before she could dwell on this thought. It replied reproachfully: 'Did you mean Sean Coughlan?' There was a picture of Sean, surrounded by laughing black children, wearing Saintly-Person-In-Hot-Country clothes: combat shorts and Velcro sandals. He had a big nose, but nice eyes and a good body.

Olivia came in, and Phoebe minimised the search. Her sister looked tense, even for her. 'Can we go somewhere private?' she said. 'Attic? I need to see a different four walls.'

'Sure. If you help me with the stairs.'

Phoebe was surprised that Olivia was coming to talk to her, for once. And pleased, she realised, as they climbed the final flight arm in arm.

They went into the room where they'd found the time capsule and sat on some lumpy eiderdowns – the ones that would cost £50 each in Portobello.

'I'm worried Jesse's giving Mum quack advice,' said Olivia. She was panting more than Phoebe. All those evening runs with George must have paid off.

'Quack?'

'Misinformed.'

'About what?'

'Her diagnosis!'

'Oh,' said Phoebe. The last thing she wanted to discuss now was cancer. George hadn't mentioned it, and mostly she managed to push any tumour thoughts down, like a horrible jack-in-the-box. She wished she'd never told Olivia. She kept thinking of how Nicola's emails had referred to a 'growth'. Just the word made her feel sick.

'I mean, I overheard him in the kitchen saying she could "beat" cancer with superfoods. Even talking about refusing chemo. And he has no medical training. It makes me so angry.'

'What? She'd never refuse chemotherapy, would she?'

Olivia flopped back against the eiderdowns. 'You never know. We see it all the time, patients self-diagnosing, believing any old rubbish online. It drives us insane.'

'Wait – how come Jesse knows, anyway?'

'She told him when they met at the airport. Because she's mad like that. And Jesse told Andrew, so everyone knows now.'

'Oh. I thought she didn't want to talk about it yet.'

'She didn't really tell me anything. She was just like: "I'm still waiting for results, so we'll cross that bridge . . . " It's not unusual, in cancer patients. They all have different ways of coping.'

'But she'll talk about it to Jesse?'

'Sometimes patients find it easier to talk to strangers. Frustratingly, since I am actually a doctor. I acted surprised, by the way. Didn't say you'd told me.'

'Oh. Thanks.' She felt a bit mean for letting Olivia feel like the last to know. She traced the swirls on the eiderdown.

'At least it's out in the open now,' said Olivia. 'I'd like to be some use. Stop her listening to Jesse.'

'Ugh, he's such a dick. Why is Mummy being all nice to him? If I was her I'd tell him to piss off.'

'I don't know. I thought he was OK at first. But now I'm wondering. It's dangerous, the stuff he's telling her.'

'But – won't she listen to you, if you tell her it's dangerous? It's your job.'

'Not necessarily. She was lapping it up, Googling faddy diets. Plus she can't see me that way. Like, an authority on anything. We're just "the children" to her.'

'Can't you talk to Daddy about it, ask him to speak to her? She'd listen to him.'

'Um. Not sure that would work.' Phoebe looked round at her. Olivia was staring ahead, the bulb above casting shadows under her cheekbones. She was now 'worryingly thin', thought Phoebe, enviously.

'Why not?' she said.

'Just. Me and Andrew, you know, it's not like you and him,' said Olivia. 'We don't talk much.'

'Maybe you should. He hates alternative medicine. He's obsessed with this book called *Bad Science*.'

'Is he? I love that book!' said Olivia, turning. She looked pleased, as if she had no idea she and Andrew had anything in common.

'You two are too alike, that's the problem,' said Phoebe.

'How d'you mean?'

'Stubborn. Obsessed with the news and the third world. Don't talk about feelings.'

'Hey, I told you about me and Sean.'

'Only when I asked you straight out. Do you miss him?'

'Just wish I could talk to him. Hearing his name everywhere, like he's just this phenomenon, it's so weird.'

'D'you think you'll get married?'

'What? I don't know. Why does everything have to be about getting married?' Phoebe could see she was trying not to smile.

'You do! You're going to marry him!'

Olivia was grinning now. Phoebe took the chance.

'Liv, I'm sorry, but I only found out about Mummy being ill by accident. I saw this email on her iPad about it and asked her. I should've said. It wasn't cool.'

Olivia said nothing. Phoebe didn't chance looking at her.

'I didn't mean to make you feel bad, I was just really pissed off you'd followed me and George,' she added, the words rushing. 'But I get it, we shouldn't have left the house. It was his idea, by the way.'

'S'all right. She told me you found out by mistake. But thanks.'

'Oh. OK then.' Phoebe's cheeks burned. Why did she still get herself in these situations at twenty-nine years old? She felt better for apologising, though. Her phone pinged, and she grabbed for it.

'No way! I had no idea I got signal up here!' she said, her voice coming out squawked. It was a text from George. All it said was *Sorry*. She tapped back *You can make it up to me. But don't go pinching my banana again x* and told Olivia she was going to find him, relieved to escape the awkwardness of confession.

Since Jesse's arrival, the bungalow had become their refuge. It was fun, playing house down there with George, even though he was so anal about mess. He was always huffing about her leaving clothes on the chair. His army dad had made him weirdly OCD. One day, she fantasised that they'd live in one of the big white houses on Primrose Hill, and she'd have a dressing room. But when she got down to the bungalow, hopping on her good foot, it was dark. She opened the door and switched on the lights. It looked different, and she realised that all George's stuff, even his bag, had disappeared. There was a piece of folded paper on the ping-pong table. Something about it chilled her. She opened it and read, in his cramped schoolboy handwriting:

Ph, *Titch, I'm sorry but I don't think I can do this any more. I need some space to think, on my own. I guess this won't come as a shock to you, but it's all moving too fast for me. I hope you understand. Please don't contact me, I need time to work stuff out.*

G

ps. Don't worry about the ring.

She looked around, to see if George would jump out of a cupboard shouting 'Fooled you!' but the silence in the room was too real. She felt like she'd been winded. What did he mean, it wouldn't come as a shock? She picked up the bungalow's phone and called the main house. Emma answered, and her voice unlocked Phoebe's sobs.

'Darling? What's wrong? What's happened?'

'Come here,' she croaked.

A minute later she heard boots and voices outside the door. She'd thought her mother would come alone, but everyone, even Jesse, was there. They all looked very concerned. Through her tears she found this mildly gratifying.

'Look,' she said, thrusting the note at them. She threw herself face down on the sofa to carry on crying. She didn't even care that Jesse could see.

A hand began rubbing her back, and she saw through the chink between her face and the cushion that it was Olivia. The others were standing around the ping-pong table, reading the note.

'What a . . . pig,' said her mother. 'What on earth does he mean, "moving too fast"? He just asked you to marry him!'

'What about quarantine? He shouldn't be—' began Olivia.

'Do his parents know about this?' interrupted her father.

'Just found it,' said Phoebe, into the cushion. It still smelt of George – of his scalp and his neck, and she began crying so hard she felt like she was choking. I want to choke, she thought. That would serve him right, if I choked to death, crying because of what he's done. Her thoughts seemed to be on fast-forward, each fresh humiliation crowding out the one before. The plans for engagement drinks. The save-the-date email she'd sent a hundred people. The dreadful, shaming sympathy. Single. Back at square one. She started to cry again with new, hysterical force.

'Phoebe – breathe,' Olivia was saying. 'Where could he have gone? Can you think? We ought to get him back – he can't just *go*.'

'I'm half-inclined to call up his odious parents and tell them what a little—' Andrew paused. 'What a little twerp their son is. A note! And a badly written one at that!'

'Maybe I put too much pressure on him,' said Phoebe. She had no idea where he might have gone – home probably. That was the least of her problems. She'd quite like the whole Marsham-Smith family to get Haag. She still had her eyes shut, so that she could just feel the damp cotton against her face, and smell George and hear her family.

'Hey, this isn't your fault!' said an American voice. Jesse. She peered round. 'I mean, you shouldn't blame yourself. This is about George,' he said.

'What?' It was the first time she'd spoken to him directly, beyond 'hello'.

'I mean, this is his action – he needs to own this.'

'I'm sorry?' said Phoebe, looking up properly. She knew she was being rude, and she knew she looked rough – and she didn't care. On second thoughts, it really pissed her off that Jesse had come down.

'I just meant, this is a hundred per cent his issue.'

'What issue?'

'Well, seems like he has some work to do on himself.'

They were all staring at Jesse now. He looked uncomfortable at being the centre of attention. So he should.

'Work? Is this some LA therapy bullshit? You only met him yesterday!' It was satisfying to snap at someone.

'Phoebe . . . ' said her mother.

'I'm sorry, I just meant—' began Jesse.

'Now, I think perhaps it's best if Phoebe and I have a chat on our own,' interrupted Emma. 'We'll be up later. You three can sort your own lunch out, can't you? There's plenty of ham and cheese in the larder. Jesse, you could reheat some of the risotto we had last night.'

Her mother only told people to feed themselves if there was a crisis. She registered that Emma had been specially cooking the aubergine thing, and that she was abandoning it to stay here. As the others left, and she sat sobbing into Emma's shoulder, she realised that it wasn't just George she was crying for. It was the thought of coping with stuff like this, with everything grown up, without her mother.

Jesse

. . .

Andrew and Olivia were sitting on one side of the table, and Jesse on the other, like they were interviewing him. The aborted vegan curry sat on the worktop. Andrew was picking at a single slice of ham, with a blob of gold-leaf mustard that looked like paint. Olivia was eating more white toast with her gross-smelling Marmite – same as she had yesterday. Didn't British doctors know about processed food? Jesse chewed through a mound of claggy risotto, as instructed. He had no clue how to reheat it in the range they called the Aga, and nobody offered to show him. It didn't matter – the moment in the bungalow had blunted his appetite anyway. Why couldn't he keep his mouth shut? Nobody had mentioned the way Phoebe had spoken to him just now. Perhaps that was how they dealt with shit here.

It was dim with rain outside, and Andrew leant forward to light the angel chimes on the table, saying: 'Mustn't let standards slip.' He held up the match to watch the flame dwindle, and said, 'D'you know, Jesse, when I was reporting from Afghanistan, I learnt to start fires with a magnifying glass.' He'd said the same last night – Jesse guessed it was one of his refrains. His own dad, Mitch, did the same. He was about to ask Andrew to elaborate, but seeing Olivia's glare guessed that she had probably heard the story ten thousand times already.

'George shouldn't just be out there at large,' she said, out of nowhere. She was wearing glasses, but the shadows under her eyes were unmistakable. Her time in Liberia must have been pretty harrowing, even though she never said so. Clearly, it was all about Phoebe in this house.

Andrew poured himself a second glass of red, and another for Jesse. Olivia refused, and Jesse wished he felt able to, too, especially after the biting G&Ts Andrew had mixed at noon. His head was already fluffy, but he didn't want to be rude. He felt bad enough for eating differently. Then again, it was kind of liberating how his birth father drank at any hour of the day. And he could use a drink right now.

'Sorry about all that, Jesse,' said Andrew, ignoring Olivia's comment. 'It's not usually quite so dramatic around here. Phoebe wouldn't have meant anything by it.'

'Hey, it's all good. She's in shock.'

'What a cretin,' said Andrew. 'Slinking off like that. And that appalling note. Despicable. People that can't write, shouldn't,' he added, as if George's prose style had offended him more than the content.

'Did you realise there were problems?' said Jesse. He guessed Phoebe had no clue that George was bi, or gay – but perhaps her family had suspected something.

'I never thought he'd do this,' said Andrew. 'Perhaps I was naive.'

'Did you like him?' said Jesse to Olivia. She stopped chewing, as if startled that he was asking her opinion.

'I thought he made Phoebe happy,' she said. 'Except when he bought her the wrong earrings.'

'Earrings?'

'She asked him for these particular earrings for Christmas, and he got the wrong ones. She threw a tantrum about it,' said Olivia wearily.

'That's what I meant,' said Jesse. It seemed safest to build on what she'd said. 'I know I only just met him, but I got the feeling they hadn't fully connected. It felt kind of forced. Like they were playing at being a normal couple.'

The second he'd said 'normal', he wished he could swallow it back, but Emma's entrance distracted Andrew and Olivia.

'Poor Phoebs,' she said, sitting on a corner of a bench, beside Andrew. Jesse was now faced with three of them across the table. 'She's beside herself.' She shot up again, as if she shouldn't have sat down at all. 'Now, I was just going to make her a sandwich. She might want it later.'

'Emma, won't you sit down for a moment?' said Andrew.

'Yeah, I'll take her something, Mum,' said Olivia.

Emma looked doubtful, but sat down again.

'What did you mean, "normal couple"?' she said, looking at Jesse. Shit. He'd just promised himself he wouldn't get involved.

'Nothing – I mean, I had no idea he was planning to bail on Phoebe,' he said. 'I just sensed that maybe he wasn't totally ... certain.'

Olivia looked up, her face sceptical.

'I have, kind of, a radar for this stuff,' he added. Why did he make things worse every time he tried to explain himself?

'What stuff?' said Olivia.

'For when guys are, like, confused.' The second he said 'guys', rather than people, he realised there was no going back. 'I mean, people,' he added.

'Are you implying he's *gay*?' said Olivia. Her eyes, flinty now, looked just like Andrew's.

'No! Yeah, no, I mean, maybe. Or bi. Nobody's one hundred per cent.' Fuck wine. He wasn't used to drinking all day. It was making him say things he wouldn't ordinarily.

'Based on what, precisely?' she asked.

'Nothing explicit,' said Jesse. 'It's just, like, an energy I got from him. Right off the bat.'

Andrew took a sip of wine and said nothing.

'It's a pretty big accusation to come out with, based on "an energy".'

'I know it sounds that way. But intuition can be very powerful.'

'So it's a hunch? No actual evidence?'

'Like I said, you get a feeling for these things.' He resented Olivia interrogating him. He could hardly say: 'I was making out with him in my bed three nights ago.'

'What the hell? George isn't *gay*!' came a voice from the doorway. It was Phoebe, bedraggled and puce faced.

'Hey – I wasn't accusing him of anything. I just said it was a possibility. A lot of straight guys are confused. It's not uncommon.'

'Please! This is actually fucking disrespectful. This is my fiancé you're talking about. What – did you fancy him yourself?'

'Jesse – I'm not sure this is helpful,' said Emma quickly. 'George and Phoebe have been together for years. He proposed to her. It's fairly obvious he's not gay, or he—'

'You did, didn't you? This is your little "public schoolboy" fantasy!' Phoebe interrupted.

He could feel all their eyes on him, trapping him in a mess he had created. An old, familiar indignation came broiling up – the hot temper he tried to purge, for years.

'Don't shoot the messenger!' he said, way louder than he meant to. 'It's not *my* fantasies you need to worry about. It's your fiancé's!' He knew he'd passed the point of no return. They were all staring at him.

'Don't shout at me!' Phoebe screeched back. 'You have no idea what you're talking about! Why don't you piss off back to Minnesota?'

The angel chimes dinged in the shocked pause.

'What is he even *doing* here?' she said, turning to Andrew. Jesse felt like they were acting a scene.

'Phoebe, calm down,' said Emma. 'Jesse, perhaps we might have a minute?'

He stood up, legs weak as a string puppet. 'Sure,' he said, taking his still-full plate to the sink and trying to walk normally. He felt them all watching his back, waiting for him to go.

For a moment, he stopped in the dark passage behind the kitchen wondering if anyone would say something about him. But there was just the sound of Phoebe bursting into noisy tears again. His skin pricked with mortified sweat. He took the oak staircase three steps at a time – as if this might help him escape the house and everyone in it. The long corridor upstairs felt oppressive, and his room horribly foreign. He lay on his side in bed. He had destroyed everything. He had only himself to blame. It was like the oversharing – he'd always struggled to contain his thoughts, his emotions. He'd trained himself to act so grounded the whole time, but then his feelings came spewing up, like a geyser – regardless of where he was or who he was talking to. They would all hate him now, even Andrew. His birth father was bound to be on Phoebe's side. This wasn't how it was meant to be.

Emma

. . .

'Let me do the dishwasher, sweetie,' said Emma to Olivia. Her daughter was putting everything away in the wrong place – no doubt a misplaced effort to make Emma relax.

'It's fine, Mum. Why don't you sit down, or go and check on Phoebe, or something?'

'Seriously, Wiv, it's no trouble. I like to know where all my bits and pieces are. *You* go and sit down.' The last thing Emma wanted was to cede control of the house now that her diagnosis was out. Sometimes it felt like the kitchen, her realm, was all she still had to herself. At least Andrew had slunk off after the unpleasantness at lunch.

Olivia put a spatula into the pot of wooden spoons by the Aga. Emma moved it to the drawer where she kept spatulas.

Olivia sighed, as if Emma was a contrary child. 'OK,' she said. 'Shout if you need any help.'

'I'm fine, Wiv,' said Emma. People never understood how domesticity could be soothing. She couldn't have abided her grandmother's Weyfield with servants doing everything for her.

She carried on clearing up, mulling over George's horrid note, and the quarrel, just now, with Jesse. Poor Phoebe had been inconsolable afterwards. Emma had seen a new side to Andrew's handsome son – at best idiotically insensitive, at worst, a stirrer. She'd always had reservations about George, but he'd never struck her as in the closet. What Emma couldn't get over was how the note had come with no warning. Just this morning George had seemed his usual (admittedly slightly obnoxious) self. She thought of the squabble over the banana. It was rather frightening that someone could carry on as normal, cool as a cucumber, when they were planning such a thing. Sociopathic, almost. Surely that was the problem, not his being gay.

With the dishwasher purring, Emma went upstairs to call Nicola. She'd had a long chat with her only last night about Jesse's arrival, swearing her to secrecy for the time being. Nicola's view on Jesse (typically) had been that Emma must 'talk her emotions through' with Andrew. All very well in theory, but easy as talking to a donkey in practice. Nicola had also kept asking if Andrew had been 'behaving at all unusually', as if Emma should have seen all this coming. Rather tiresome, but then Nicola was tiresome – in the sweetest possible way. It was only because she cared. Emma dialled her number, barely waiting for Nicola's too-loud 'Hullo?'

'Nic, it's Emma. The wedding's off. George has left Phoebe.'

'What? He's left? No! Oh poor little Phoebs! What happened? It never stops at Weyfield, does it?'

Emma explained about the note, and the cross words at lunch.

'Well, George might be gay, I suppose,' said Nicola. 'And Jesse might be more able to pick up on it than Phoebe – or you lot.'

'D'you think? He's not the least bit camp. Though gays can be very macho too, can't they?'

'Isn't he rather homophobic?' said Nicola. 'There might well be an element of denial.'

'But why would he propose, if he wasn't sure?'

'Well, presumably he doesn't *want* to be gay – if he is. That's the problem. Otherwise he wouldn't have spent all this time with Phoebe.

Do you know if their sex life was fulfilling? Did Phoebe ever talk about it?'

'No!' This line of questioning was annoying Emma. Why did she always call Nicola for sympathy, only to come away feeling cross?

Andrew walked in and she used him as an excuse to hang up. He was holding a cup of tea and mince pie – for her, she guessed, since he never ate between meals. He was still grovelling, then.

'Where's Phoebe?' she asked, as he set the cup down on the dressing table. She fought her mother's voice, telling him it would make a ring on the wood. He'd never understood about good furniture.

'Earl Grey, Madam?' he said.

'Thank you. Where's Phoebe? Is she all right?'

'She's on the sofa looking sorry for herself, eating Nutella out of the jar.'

'OK. That's good. She's eating.'

'Now you must stop worrying about Phoebe and look after yourself,' said Andrew.

'And where's Jesse?' she asked, ignoring him. How could she not worry about Phoebe? 'You didn't leave the two of them together, did you?'

'No sign of Jesse. Keeping a safe distance, I'd have thought,' said Andrew.

'I'm sorry Andrew, but I just can't believe he would suggest such a thing – to Phoebe's face. George isn't gay!'

'It was unfortunate she overheard, I know. You look very regal, sitting there,' he said.

'Unfortunate? It couldn't have been worse. She's distraught, thanks to him.'

'Now hang on – it's George who's to blame here, not Jesse. Phoebe was hysterical long before he said anything. Anyway, isn't this whole business a good thing, ultimately?'

'Good?'

'Come on, Emma. Neither of us was wild about George. We only tolerated him because if we'd said anything it'd just have made Phoebe keener.'

'Well. I know he was a little bit . . . ' she paused, not sure how to say what she meant without sounding snobbish. It was too soon to be having this conversation, anyway. George had barely left. They might well get back together.

'A little bit of a cunt?' said Andrew.

'Andrew! You know I hate that word. And no, that's not what I meant. What I meant was, I sometimes worried that he didn't listen to Phoebe,' she said. She didn't add, 'and his parents were a bit Brexit,' but she wanted to.

'Same difference. Jesse said they struck him as not having quite gelled, as if they were "playing" at being a couple. I thought that was rather incisive.'

'Oh,' she said, not wanting to agree, although he was right – Jesse was spot on. Andrew rarely praised anyone else's opinion on anything.

'They did seem a little mismatched, sometimes,' she conceded.

'Emma, they aren't, weren't, remotely suited. He's a rugby-playing Hooray Henry. That's not Phoebe, cheering on the sidelines with the other little wives. Far better that they get this over with now, than go through a miserable divorce in five years' time.'

'Well. But still, this gay business. That's just absurd. And so insensitive!'

Andrew scratched his nose vigorously. 'Didn't you even wonder if Jesse's right?' he said, turning to face her. 'Speaking of rugger buggers?'

'No! Of course he isn't. We'd know if he was gay. Why would he be with Phoebe?'

'You're forgetting what kind of people the Marsham-Smiths are.

This isn't Primrose Hill. Or Los Angeles, for that matter. His parents would be furious.'

'But he's nearly thirty! Surely he can be gay if he wants. Honestly! They've got all those other sons.'

'Apparently it's rather common for third sons to be homosexual. No other way to distinguish themselves.'

She decided not to dignify this fatuous theory with a response. It was all a bit near the knuckle, anyway. She suspected Andrew was rather shocked that his own son was gay, despite himself.

'Jesse and I were talking about it earlier,' Andrew continued. 'He had a dreadful time, coming out as a teenager in the Midwest. Must have taken great courage.'

Emma clenched her toes. Don't say anything, she ordered herself. But it was hard to hear Andrew quoting Jesse when he struggled to mention Olivia. Besides, where had this enthusiasm for his new child sprung from? Yesterday she'd been pushing Andrew to give Jesse a warm welcome.

'Well I'm sorry about that, and I know he's your son, but once this quarantine is over I think it's best he leaves,' she said. 'Phoebe needs some breathing space – we all do.'

She stood up, taking the cup with her, to show the conversation was over. Andrew might be carrying on as if everything was normal between them, but she needed more time.

Olivia

. . .

The queasy feeling had faded to a background hum, as if Olivia had just stepped off a boat. Anxiety – that's all it was. She had nearly emailed Sean after being sick, but it would only freak him out. It hadn't happened since. And she still had no fever. She'd been tempted to email him after lunch, too. She knew Sean would get why she was so annoyed by Jesse's ridiculous theories. But she should probably try to play it a bit cool – at least wait for Sean to reply once before writing again. She had no idea if he'd even received her messages, though he ought to have his phone now he was out of isolation. Her whole body felt edgy with missing him.

Phoebe was still hiding, and dinner with Jesse and her parents had been strained. At least Jesse had had the grace to keep quiet. His comments on George, based on no evidence, still infuriated her. It reminded her of his anti-chemo advice, and how Phoebe had asked her to speak to Andrew about it earlier. She felt bad for her. Phoebe had looked terrified when Jesse had implied George was gay. Olivia wanted to get back at him. How dare he kick her little sister when she was down?

'Yes?' said Andrew, when Olivia knocked on the smoking-room door, and then: 'Olivia! To what do I owe this pleasure?' She wished he didn't always speak to her in that fake, formal way. He didn't do it with Phoebe. A pillow and blanket were pushed to one end of the sofa. He must have slept down here last night. Perhaps things between her parents weren't as amicable as they appeared.

'Um, I wanted to talk to you about Jesse. About some ideas he has.' Why did she sound so timid? She needed to be the grown up she was at work, to imagine her father was a colleague.

'Ah. His gay-dar, you mean?'

She was still hovering by the door, while he craned round from the desk.

'Not that. Though perhaps it's part of the same thing.'

'Come in then, child.'

She sat on the old linen sofa, avoiding the grey head-shaped patch on the back. Its springs gave under her weight, folding her knees up to her chin. The room, with its teak panelling and heavy rugs, still smelt of cigars and chestnuts – so that even the air felt dark brown.

'He was spouting all this pseudo-science at Mum this morning – about her diagnosis.'

'Was he?'

'Total rubbish, about how you don't need chemo. That you can "beat" cancer with an "alkalising diet", whatever that means. All this alternative holistic stuff.'

'But Emma doesn't buy into that, surely?' he said.

'She seemed to be. They were Googling juice fasts, and every-thing.'

'I expect she was just humouring him, being her usual charming self. And a few kale smoothies can't do any harm, can they?'

'If they stop her accepting chemo they can. Cancer patients can be very suggestible. They're desperate.'

Andrew said nothing, but walked over to the sofa. A cloud of dust motes mushroomed up as he sat down.

'I'm sure he means well, you know,' he said. 'He'll only be trying to help.' Close up, he looked drawn and unshaven. He'd dropped the formal tone now.

'Maybe, but it doesn't stop it being irresponsible. He doesn't have a clue about medicine. The stuff he's advising, the World Health Organisation has officially discredited it. There are no significant studies on alternative cancer treatments, it's just a load of charlatan nutritionists with no idea what they're talking about.' She stopped – it wouldn't help to rant.

'Olivia, you don't need to convince me. I'm a rationalist, too. We journos like facts, proof – just like you scientists.'

'But Mum doesn't think like that. If it's in a magazine, it's true.' She realised too late that she had just undermined his line on journalism. 'Will you talk to her about it?' she added. 'She'll listen to you.'

'I can try – but, your mother and I . . . ' he hesitated and seemed to change tack. 'I mean, after all that business with Phoebe earlier, she's very down on Jesse. I don't think you need worry about her hanging on his every word.'

'Oh. OK, that's good, I suppose.'

'Well. Perhaps, in this instance. But it's a pity things appear to have turned sour so quickly.' He said this to the fireplace, instead of her.

'It was always going to be complicated,' she said tentatively. Her father looked very tired. She felt a bit sorry for him.

'You're a mistress of understatement,' he said, using the artificial voice again, but looking up at her and smiling. His face bore shadows of Jesse's, when he smiled. She caught a glimpse of him as the young man he must have been in Lebanon. 'I hope this quarantine hasn't been too arduous for you,' he said after a moment. 'I know you're not a fan of the Weyfield Christmas. I used to feel the same. Usually engineered to be working by the twenty-seventh. Something else we journalists and medics have in common – always on call.'

'Well, it's definitely been eventful. And now Phoebe and George. He really shouldn't just be out there when I'm not clear yet.'

'Don't fret about that. I'm sure it'll be fine. As far as I'm concerned he can give his dreadful family Haag.'

She found herself smiling, despite herself. His certainty was comforting.

'And you?' he said, looking straight at her. 'Not easy coming home, is it?'

'Did you, did you used to find it hard, too?' she asked.

'Of course. Made all the harder by the fact that it ought to be a relief, to have running water, safe roads, decent food, all the rest of it. But it isn't, necessarily. One gets used to the simple life, I found. And your mother, fussing over me, with the best will in the world. I see how she does that to you now.'

'Mmm. It's mostly Sean. Coughlan, I mean,' she said, although he'd perfectly summed up the strange discomfort of Western luxury.

'Of course. It must be difficult, hearing his name on the news. I hope you don't mind me drawing comparisons, but my cameraman was shot in Beirut, and seeing his name everywhere was – well, it twisted the knife.'

'Was he OK?'

'No. No, he died. I was with him at the time.'

'That's awful.'

'It wasn't much fun.'

'Was that why you stopped?'

'Partly. It was more that your mother demanded it, when Phoebe was born. You didn't use to recognise me when I came home, and she minded that.'

'Really? Sorry. I never knew that.'

'Don't be – you were tiny. Why should you when I was always buggering off?'

'Still. Was it hard to stop?'

'Well. It's not easy to give up something you feel strongly about. If the press hadn't been in Lebanon, lots of people would have ignored the whole conflict. Emma didn't really want to know the details. She was just terrified I'd be kidnapped, become the next Terry Waite.'

'Has Jesse made you remember things?'

'In a sense. Not that I'd ever forgotten. I was in and out of Beirut for ten years. But memory is very odd, or mine is anyway. You block out the worst moments, for the most part – sometimes almost as they happen, just to get through it. And then you think of them out of the blue, years later.'

They looked at each other for a moment. It was like he'd read her mind, or her PPE blog. He reached out and patted her hand, awkwardly. She remembered how small her palm used to feel in his when they crossed the road, after Phoebe was born and he came home.

Emma

. . .

Emma walked back from the bungalow, a torch lighting her through the mulchy orchard. Phoebe had refused to sleep in the main house. Emma knew it was because Jesse was there, though Phoebe hadn't said so. Why else would she want to sleep alone in the poky bungalow? As it was, Jesse had hidden in the Rose Room all afternoon, only joining them for supper, when he'd barely eaten. He'd apologised for speaking out of turn – and Emma didn't doubt he was sorry. But still. Her spring of forgiveness was starting to run dry. It was agonising to see her youngest so miserable. She wished Phoebe could still be comforted with hot chocolate and Harry Potter.

Passing the remains of the bonfire, something made Emma pause. She remembered what a jolly time they'd had there yesterday. That had been the last time they'd stood together as a family of four – the last time they ever would, in a sense. Just us, she thought. Blissfully ignorant. Or, rather, she and the girls had been blissfully ignorant. Who knew what Andrew had been thinking, with Jesse's emails on his conscience?

Nicola's question from the other day came floating back. 'Had Andrew been behaving unusually?' Because now Emma thought about it, standing in this spot again, she *had* noticed Andrew seeming not quite himself by the bonfire. All that stuff about writing a book – a novel she couldn't remember him ever mentioning before. And he'd kept patting his pockets, the way he did when he was looking for something, so that she'd almost asked him what he'd lost. But she'd been distracted by Phoebe limping up with her sore foot, and then by the fun of the fire, and then it had begun to rain and then – well, then Jesse had appeared and she'd forgotten everything else. Thinking back, though, Andrew had seemed nervy yesterday. It reminded her of the way he'd come rushing into the attic on Boxing Day, and grabbed his briefcase from her. She hadn't thought anything of it at the time. She'd had no reason to, then. But he'd looked rattled, which wasn't like him. And what had he been doing in the garret afterwards? He'd stayed in there for ages. She stood staring at the heap of ash and charred wood, mulling it over. And after a while, the urge to go and look in the briefcase – right now – became impossible to ignore.

The attics were as cold as the garden. In the near-darkness, she almost tripped over the zig-zag of boxes still on the floor of the main room. Andrew had taken the briefcase into the right-hand garret, hadn't he? She walked into the tiny tent-shaped room, shutting the door behind her, and switched on the top light – its shade flecked with dead moths. Scanning the floor, she saw the briefcase immediately. It was under the bed, just in view between her old school trunk and some gummed-up tins of Farrow & Ball. She swallowed, throat dry. What was it doing down there? Why try to shove it out of sight? She'd known she was right. Feminine intuition. For all they might have drifted, she could still tell when Andrew was hiding something. The thought gave her a kind of grim satisfaction.

She took the briefcase from the floor and sat on the bare mattress, the case on her lap. The feel of its smooth sides and sharp corners took her back to another era – when she seemed to be permanently standing in the hall in a dressing gown, handing Andrew his work things and restraining an infant Olivia. Was that when things had started to go wrong? Something like sadness heaved inside her. She realised she was still rather tipsy from all the wine at dinner. Her fingers fiddled with the brass catches, as she pondered what she might find inside. Adoption papers for scores of other bastard children? Fistfuls of photographs of Jesse's beautiful, exotic mother? Or perhaps something more prosaically sordid – a spare mobile phone, the better to lead a double life.

She bent closer, to see the little combination locks. One Nine Five Zero – even her soupy brain knew it would be his birth date. The catches clunked open. She parted the case, breath suspended. And then – nothing. It was empty. She picked it up by one handle so that it flopped fully open, then took both handles and turned it upside down with a shake. Then she laid it flat out on the bed and rummaged through every pocket. Still nothing. All she found was a crumpled receipt from Boots, Gatwick, dated 1987.

She sat back on the bed, feeling a total fool. It was like that scene in Northanger Abbey, she thought, when Catherine Morland opens an old, gothic chest and finds nothing but bed linen. Who had she become, first checking Jesse's passport, now snooping through her husband's briefcase? She didn't want to be this woman. Damn Andrew. This was what his hiding Jesse's emails had turned her into – a jealous wife. She felt almost tearful as she relocked the case, and put it back exactly where she'd found it. Walking through the main attic, she stopped to ram all the boxes on the floor against the wall, out of the way. Why didn't the girls ever tidy up after themselves? It was only when she was halfway down the back stairs, that she remembered the briefcase had a secret pocket in the lining.

Andrew

· · ·

Andrew stayed sitting on the sofa, thinking. His oldest daughter, who usually shunned him with evasive eyes and brief answers, had opened up. They had had something amounting to a real conversation. Then he remembered why – she'd come to complain about Jesse's misplaced advice. In twenty-four hours, Jesse had managed to alienate Andrew's entire family – first Phoebe, then Emma and now Olivia. Yesterday, Andrew had naively assumed that Jesse was doing rather well. Emma had warmed to him, Olivia appeared to accept him – and no doubt he would have charmed Phoebe in time. If anything, Andrew was the one struggling to make sense of this sunny stranger.

But today, Jesse had messed it all up with his well-meant opinions and advice. It made Andrew feel unexpectedly defensive, as if he'd known his son for much longer. Besides, he was convinced Jesse was right about George. He thought of the boy's vile, openly expressed homophobia – not to mention his obscene Lycra. Phoebe had really had a lucky escape. But when Andrew had put all this to Emma for a second time, before dinner, she'd shut him down. 'It's very normal that you're making sense of your own son being gay, but that's nothing to do with George,' she'd said. Bloody condescending. When he'd protested, she'd changed gear and said that Andrew was obviously 'infatuated with Jesse'. She never stuck to a linear argument. And he wasn't infatuated with Jesse. In fact, Andrew decided, he'd show her that right now, by telling Emma about his talk with Olivia. He didn't really expect Emma to take Jesse's dubious medical advice seriously. But this was the first thing Olivia had asked of Andrew since she was a child. He wanted to keep his word.

Emma

. . .

Emma almost smacked into Andrew in her hurry to the smoking room, just as he was walking out of it. He put a hand on her elbow to steady her. She recoiled, and barked, 'Come to the cellar!'

'What?'

'The cellar.' He looked baffled, and she didn't care. It was a Hartley tradition to have tricky conversations in the cellar – it guaranteed privacy in a house full of servants. Not that she and Andrew needed to consider such things. She switched on her torch as she opened the cellar door and began to descend the stone steps, their edges rounded by her forebears. There was something comforting about the cellar, the buried depths of the house. She breathed the distinctive, musty smell, like a church, looking round the bell-shaped space at the bottom of the stairs. A wine rack to her right still held the last of their wedding claret, which Andrew was saving for God knows what.

'This,' she said, handing him the handwritten letter she'd found in the briefcase lining. He seemed to recognise it at once.

'How did you ... oh, Christ,' he said, sitting on the bottom step and rubbing his forehead.

'Well?' she said, looking at the sheet in his hand.

'Emma, I'm, I'm a fool. I'm so stupid, I—'

'A *fool*? Incompetent, certainly. I presume you never intended to tell me? You thought that would be an end to it?'

'It just, it seemed better that way. I thought it would cause you needless pain. I was planning to burn it, if you must know. But then—'

'Better to *burn* it? To lie, to cover your tracks like a snake in the night?' she knew she was muddling her metaphors, and she didn't care.

'Emma – if you'll let me finish – I was planning to burn it, but then Jesse arrived and I thought, well, I thought he deserved to see it, one day. It's all he'll have of his mother.'

'Oh right. How noble of you. So you think you deserve a medal, do you?'

'Emma – please don't be sarcastic. You have to understand, I didn't even believe that letter when I got it. I thought it was a hoax, or that the woman was delirious. It wasn't until Jesse emailed me that I realised it was genuine, and that—'

'But you'd still kept it all that time?' she interrupted. 'Hidden away, for over a year. Just in case?'

'Mmm.'

Neither of them spoke.

'I never replied to her,' said Andrew eventually. 'We never had any correspondence.'

'Andrew! You still don't understand, do you? I wouldn't have given a flying fig if you'd replied to that poor woman – in fact that would have been the right thing to do, for fuck's sake!' It was exhilarating to swear. Her heart was pummelling her rib cage. 'It's your lying that's the problem. Hiding things, burning things! What sort of man does that? How can I trust anything you say any more? Anything you've *ever* said?'

'Emma—'

'Don't! I don't want to hear your feeble excuses! I thought you were a decent man, despite everything.'

'I'm sorry? Despite everything?'

She realised she was in too deep to go back.

'Yes. How you've treated me, all of us.'

'How I've *treated* you? How have I ever been anything but the supportive husband?' He stood up, looming over her. His face was indignant, now. She was glad. She wanted a fight, a real fight. She needed him to be angry, not contrite.

'Ha! Supportive?' she said. 'Do you have any concept of the sacrifices I've made for you? D'you know what it's like to give up everything you've worked for, to look after small children, so that *you* could do what you wanted? And you repay me by, by—' she didn't want to lose momentum. If she gave him a way in, he'd remind her that she'd stopped working by choice. 'You repay me by sulking, snapping, moaning – forcing us all to walk on eggshells every time the subs remove a word from one of your snarky columns.'

'So that's what you think of my work?' he said quietly. His eyes were slits. 'You think this is what I wanted? To be reviewing restaurants, when I could be reporting on the real world? You're not the only one who gave something up, y'know, Emma!'

'Christ, you still haven't got over it, have you? I'm sorry I dragged you back from a *war zone*, when you had two daughters! I'm so sorry I spoiled your fun, because I wanted them to grow up with a father, not a hostage, or a . . . a headstone.'

'Civil war isn't fun, Emma. It is important, though.'

'More important than your own daughters?'

He said nothing.

'Some father you've been, anyway,' she added. She wasn't ready to stop yet.

'What?'

'Surely you're not oblivious to *that*, too?'

'To what?'

'You and Olivia! You barely speak to her! You never even try to, not properly. It's always been you and Phoebe. How do you think Olivia feels? Why d'you think she's never here?' She wondered if she'd gone too far.

'I'm sorry you feel that way, Emma,' he said tightly. 'For what it's worth, Olivia and I had a very enlightening conversation earlier. I was just coming to find you to tell you about it.'

Emma hesitated. She wanted to know what they'd talked about, but didn't want to ask.

'She hasn't had an easy time of it, being back,' he went on. 'No doubt you're congratulating yourself on making a fuss of her. But you don't know the first thing about what she's going through – what she's been through.'

'Oh, and you do?'

'I have more idea than you.'

'I'm sorry, Andrew – but what does that have to do with you keeping something like this,' she snatched the letter from him, 'secret from me?'

'You brought it up, Emma! And for the record, I'm not the only one in this marriage with secrets. God knows when you were planning to tell me you had cancer. If Jesse hadn't said—'

'Jesse? Jesse! What about the rest of us? What about me?' She felt her grip on her temper loosening, years of composing herself unlocked. She yanked the neck of a bottle from the wine rack on the wall and held it up above her head, feeling like she was watching someone else – someone unhinged. Everything slowed down as she let go, and it met the stone floor with a crash. Andrew flinched at the explosion of crimson and broken glass, the wine splashing onto his socks and the bottom of his trousers.

'What the hell has got into you?' he shouted, backing up the steps.

Emma looked at the mess and burst into wild tears and giggles, all at once. A tiny voice in her head wondered if the flagstones would stain, and whether she should fetch the salt.

Olivia

. . .

Olivia drew the curtains, stopping for a moment to look out the window. She could just see the puddles on the marshes, gleaming like black glass. Cocoa slalomed through her legs and she gathered him up, leaning her cheek on his silky, prism head. She used to hug him this way as a teenager – whispering grievances in his folded ear, taking his purr as sympathy. It was around that time she'd stopped calling Andrew 'Daddy', part of her hoping he'd object. But only Emma had seemed to mind. It had been strange to hear him talking as if they were allies, just now. For as long as Olivia could remember he and Phoebe had had their private thing. And Olivia had got used to that. Phoebe was the enchanting one. But perhaps her sister was right – perhaps Olivia and her dad were more alike than she knew. She'd long assumed that Andrew had quit war correspondence by choice, not Emma's coercion. It was like looking at a room she'd always seen from one side, from the opposite wall. Phoebe and Andrew had all their media in-jokes, but his early work in war zones was a lot more like Olivia's. And it had seemed, just now, as if he'd wanted her to see that. She felt warmer at the thought. Warmer, and disconcertingly weepy for her teenage self. The too-big fourteen-year-old who used to sit hugging the cat, listening to Andrew and Phoebe leave for yet another restaurant.

Her iPad chimed, and she released Cocoa to refresh her email. Everything inside her jolted at the name in bold, at the top of her inbox: Seán Coughlan. She opened the message and began to read.

SUBJECT: Re: PHEW!!
FROM: Sean Coughlan <SeanKCoughlan@gmail.com>
DATE: 28/12/2016 23:00
TO: Olivia Birch <olivia.birch1984@gmail.com>

Olivia Birch! So I'm back in the land of the living … With an iPad and everything … I won't lie, it's not been the merriest of Christmases. Mostly because I was so worried about you. Are you sure you're OK? Promise you'd tell me if anything is wrong. I felt awful that I had no way to contact you, or even check if you were all right.

It was so good to read your blogs (thanks for sticking up for me!) and get your emails. So it sounds like it's been an eventful quarantine … How are the Birch family dealing with your man Jesse showing up? So sorry to hear about your mother, that has to be hard. Guess you just have to keep trying to talk to her.

I've not told my family about us either, but I might have to. They'll realise by this stupid grin I can't keep off my face. Counting the hours till your quarantine is up, and I can see you again.

I have to go, my nurse is hovering – we've to do a lumbar puncture. I think she has a crush on me, as a minor celebrity. FYI she's at least sixty.

Missing you, Stóirín. Happy Days Haag-negative kisses.
XXXXXXX

Olivia kept reading and rereading. She wished she could bottle this feeling – a delicious Venn of joy and relief. Coming after the chat with Andrew, it was like the day had turned around. She would email Sean first thing tomorrow, she decided, curling up under the heavy blankets. A barn owl screeched outside. For now, she wanted to savour not waiting for a response.

· 8 ·

29 December 2016

Quarantine: Day 7

Andrew

. . .

Andrew couldn't get comfortable. The sofa appeared to have potholes. He ripped off his airline eye mask, pressing his face into an itchy embroidered cushion instead. The fight still seemed utterly implausible. It was so unlike Emma – the accusations, the histrionics, the bottle smashing. It had been a 1980 Margaux, too. And all because of his sheer idiocy, in assuming he could keep Leila's letter from her. What had he been thinking?

Mentally, he retraced his steps. The morning of the bonfire he had buried the letter in a box of newspapers, ready to throw on the flames. But he had sensed Olivia watching him and stalled – the box still at his feet. And then Jesse had arrived. And with every passing hour, Leila's words had needled more fiercely. '*If, some day, he contacts you, please tell him that not a day passed when I didn't think of him. My dying wish is that he has been happy.*' How could he burn those words – the only words Jesse might ever have from his mother? It felt too final. And so he'd retrieved the letter from its newsprint coffin and hidden it in his briefcase again, last night. He still couldn't think how Emma had found it. He'd gone to the absurd lengths of flushing a lavatory on his way down from the attic to excuse his creeping around. As far as he knew, he'd only encountered George torturing a spider. Not that it really mattered. She knew now.

A stab of remorse, as he relived the row in the cellar, bled into dozens of tributaries. The way he'd taken Emma for granted, exploiting her good nature and capacity to keep cogs turning. The way he'd allowed their love to drift from the besotted notes in the attic to their rubbing along today – shrouded in forced jollity. He thought of what Emma had said about how he never talked to Olivia, knowing it was true. What stopped him from telling his daughter that her work was remarkable? He'd had the chance earlier. Dawn leaked through the curtains, and he flopped onto his back to start dissecting his own life. Why had he given up on any drive to do good when he'd resigned from *The Times*? What had happened to his ambition, his grit? He thought of all the poor restaurant owners whose businesses he'd wrecked for a snigger in his column. That snide voice wasn't really him. Or at least, it hadn't been. It was a pose he'd learned to put on for the job, just as he used to pull on his flak jacket and go in search of the truth. Each regret seemed to summon another, as if he'd turned over a log in his mind and revealed a writhing mass of woodlice.

Except, hadn't there been something strangely invigorating about the clash with Emma? It was years since they'd voiced raw feelings, uncensored. Even their exchange by the chaise longue, after Jesse's arrival, had been restrained – as if they'd both looked over a cliff and decided to teeter on the edge. There was relief in seeing Emma lose it just now, dropping the head-prefect act. She used to get angry, sometimes, when they were young. He'd found it sort of sexy at the time. But when Olivia arrived, she took to damming any conflict with a hissed: 'Not in front of the *baby*.' And then, at some point, they'd given up on fighting along with everything else. Part of him longed to crawl into bed beside Emma now, as if her body might soothe his fevered thoughts. It used to, years ago, when he was woken by dreams of bombs and bullets and bodies in dusty roads. But he knew she wouldn't want that.

Phoebe

. . .

Phoebe stood on one leg in the drive, hoping to catch some signal. The cold wormed into her ears and stiffened her fingers. Still, it was better than being indoors. She couldn't face her family, or – worse – Jesse, and she couldn't bear the bungalow, where George's aftershave haunted every breath. She thought she could actually feel a pain in her heart, like a shard of glass, somewhere behind her left breast. She'd lain in bed for hours this morning, trying to absorb what had happened, raking over the past weeks. What had made George change his mind? She'd tried so hard to be the perfect girlfriend. Her bikini line had remained pristine for months, while she waited for him to propose. All that smarting agony, and this was what she got in return.

She kicked out at some dry leaves in rage, forgetting too late not to swing her sore foot, and yelping with pain. Was it all the drama this week at Weyfield that had freaked him out? She shut down the voice that told her George should be able to deal with illness, secrets, arguments. Approaching the road, she caught a bar of signal. She stared at it, willing it to grow, to bring a message from him. But when a lone text came it was Lara, asking *What are you and G doing for New Years?* and Phoebe realised, with a bump, that she was no longer part of 'you and G'. She was just Phoebe, with nothing to show for herself but an embarrassing job. 'You and George' had been part of who she was for so long now. Being half of a couple was the only thing that made her a grown up.

A grey Audi, like his, swept past and she contemplated another bout of sobs. She was already sick of crying, of the puffy feeling in her face, the stinging eyes, the aching throat – and it had only been a day. She still hadn't contacted him, on her mother's advice. She didn't know what she'd say anyway. It was hard to disentangle her pride from her heart, to know which had taken the more crushing blow. She felt sick when she thought of trying to tell everyone that the wedding was off. But the same voice at the back of her mind kept asking: 'Are you surprised, really?' She thought of the way she'd struggled to picture their wedding, their children, George as an old man. Perhaps she'd never truly believed it was going to happen. And then she thought of the thing Jesse had said, which she knew, deep down, made too much sense not to be true. The way George was so disgusted by gay men, but always pointed them out in public. Calling everything gay all the time. How he'd never been that fussed about sex. The hot humiliation of it crawled over her skin. She would ask him outright. She might not be able to see his face, but she'd be able to tell by his voice. She deserved to know. He owed her that much.

Jesse

. . .

Jesse had never felt so homesick. Or so hungry. He'd barely eaten since breakfast yesterday. And he'd been awake nearly all night, replaying everything in his head. Whichever way he turned, the multiple sheets and blankets tangled round his shins, like a net. Didn't the British have quilts? Now, staring out at the grey morning, he yearned to press rewind. He didn't belong here, and he was dumb to think he could slot in. The whole idea of his 'adoption story' documentary seemed laughable.

He knew he had to leave the Rose Room. But the thought of encountering any of the Birches flooded him with fresh shame. Dinner, last night, had been quietly excruciating. He contemplated fleeing, like George, but if he left now he would effectively end any relationship with Andrew – period. Besides, it would infuriate Olivia, who was so big on finishing quarantine. He had to stay and salvage things, today. That was what his mom and dad, back home, would tell him to do. He would apologise to Phoebe, and again to Emma. And he would try to redeem himself in Olivia's eyes by asking again about Liberia, the way none of the others seemed to. That was the plan.

Now was a good time to grab something to eat, because he'd seen Phoebe limp down the drive five minutes ago. He felt so bad for her. He remembered how he'd felt when Cameron had left him. He'd stayed in bed for two days – Phoebe was doing well to get up at all. Knowing he was the likely catalyst for George's decision made him feel even shittier. But the whole relationship was doomed, he reminded himself, engagement ring or not. If it hadn't been Jesse it would have been someone else.

He checked his reflection in the fussy gilt mirror before leaving the room. His skin looked like oatmeal. He needed to get back to the sun. He took a long centring breath, and opened the door.

Olivia

· · ·

The email came from Dennis White, Olivia's supervisor at HELP who had co-ordinated the volunteer programme in Liberia. Seeing the subject 'Sean Coughlan', she assumed it was a group email to all the volunteers on their final day of quarantine. She would open it in a second, she thought, shutting her eyes against the screen. The hum of nausea was back, more insistent now. Was that saliva pooling in her mouth? She curled up on her side on the rug to ease the fatigue in her legs and forced back the thought that sickness, drooling and exhaustion were textbook early Haag symptoms. If she had caught it from Sean she would know by now. In just a few hours quarantine would officially be over. She opened Dennis's email to distract herself. It was addressed to her alone.

SUBJECT: Sean Coughlan
FROM: Dennis White <dennis.white@HELP.org>
DATE: 29/12/2016 09:15
TO: Olivia Birch <olivia.birch1984@gmail.com>

Olivia,
I have been trying to call, but your mobile appears to
be switched off. I have reason to believe that you and

Sean may have been physically involved in Monrovia.
Not wishing to approach Sean in his current state, I'm
approaching you in the first instance.

I need hardly explain what a serious breach of protocol
this constitutes. Please could you call me, as a matter of
urgency, to confirm whether or not you and Sean were
in a relationship, and, if you were, how strictly you have
observed quarantine over the past week. Once I hear from
you, I will be obliged to discuss what action to take.

Dennis

Olivia sat straight up, her heart hammering. How could Dennis
know? She thought of Sean's offhand comment about his nurse's
crush on him. Could this nurse have snooped through his emails?
Sean had always been less careful than Olivia. She remembered
the time she'd WhatsApped him a photo of herself in a bikini, and
he'd left it out in full view of their colleagues. She scrolled back
through all their messages, wondering if she could claim they had
become close, but hadn't had any physical contact. It was obvious
they were a couple. She pressed the heels of her hands into her
eyes, willing the world to disappear, to leave her alone with nobody
except Sean.

The door opened and Jesse came in, holding a mug. The last
thing she felt like was small talk. She stood up, and as she did so a
warm, churning nausea flushed through her again, from her scalp
down to her knees. Stars danced at the edge of her vision, and as
she reached out for the sofa the whole room blurred. She heard
the blood swoosh in her ears, and Jesse's voice, sounding a long,
long way away, as if he were calling down a tunnel, saying, 'Olivia?
Olivia, are you OK?'

Andrew

. . .

When Andrew heard the thud he assumed a Hartley portrait had taken a kamikaze leap off a wall. He hurried down the passage to the drawing room, where he thought the sound had come from. From upstairs, Emma shouted, 'What was that?' At least, then, it hadn't been his wife hurling an oil painting in a fit of pique. He had a gruesome vision of Cocoa flattened by a Victorian bureau. But when he got to the drawing room, the cat was cowering outside. Then he heard Jesse saying, 'Hey, hey, can you hear me?' and saw Olivia lying face down on the floor by the Christmas tree. His mind grappled to catch up with the scene his eyes were relaying. Had she tripped over, been knocked out? Young women didn't have strokes or heart attacks, did they?

'Call 911!' Jesse barked at him. 'Now!'

'What, what happened?'

'She passed out, she's unconscious. Just call 911. We need help.'

Andrew couldn't seem to move. He stood, staring at Olivia's upturned back. Her top had fallen forward, so that a strip of creamy skin showed above her pyjama bottoms, and her limbs were splayed out like a discarded rag doll. How had the drawing room become an episode of *Casualty*?

He heard Emma's sharp breath behind him.

'Emma, call an ambulance now,' said Jesse, looking past Andrew. 'Tell them she passed out, breathing, weak pulse.' He was moving Olivia into the recovery position with professional efficiency. Andrew just stood watching as Emma yanked the phone towards her and said: 'Ambulance, please ... Weyfield Hall, NR25 7FB. My daughter's fainted, I mean she's unconscious ... yes, she's breathing. And she has a pulse but it's – it's weak.' Her voice constricted. 'No, but she's been in Liberia treating Haag ... she's been back seven days – today's the last day of her quarantine ... No, no other symptoms, I think ... OK. Please hurry.'

'It's coming,' she said, as she knelt near Olivia. 'What happened?'

'I came in and she just literally passed out right in front of me,' said Jesse. 'I don't know if she was, like, sick or what. I walked in, she collapsed.'

Phoebe came in next and screamed, as Olivia began coughing and spluttering on the floor. 'Oh shit, she's throwing up,' said Jesse, levering Olivia up into a sitting position. It was horrible to watch. Her head lolled to one side, as clear fluid gushed down her chin and over Jesse's hands, which were clasped round her waist. He didn't move.

'Hey, Olivia, you're OK, you're all right,' he kept saying. Her head tipped back against his chest, and there was a gargling noise as she seemed to vomit again and began gagging and choking. Jesse laid her down on her side, swiping round the inside of her mouth with his finger and repositioning her head. Her eyes batted open briefly, rolling back in their sockets so that only the whites showed.

Andrew felt dizzy. Emergencies were always false alarms, weren't they? Surely, surely he was not to be the father who outlived their child? He watched Jesse continue to help Olivia, moving her hair out of her face and saying over and over again: 'You're gonna be just fine. The ambulance is on its way. You're gonna be OK now,' as he held her hand, while Phoebe stood over them, whimpering. 'Andrew, go flag them down,' said Jesse, and Andrew jogged down the drive, grateful to be given a task. He was useless, he thought, looking left and right even though the ambulance could only come from the left. Manifestly useless. What would they have done without Jesse – helping Olivia without a thought for the deadly virus she appeared to have?

Emma

. . .

Emma hadn't seen inside an ambulance since Olivia's birth. Her labour had started a week early, while Andrew had been on an assignment in Israel that she'd begged him to refuse. Now, thirty-two years on, she watched as her daughter was swallowed into another ambulance – its neon sides too garish against Weyfield's muted palette. It seemed impossible that Olivia was lying on a stretcher with an oxygen mask over her face. Emma had spoken to her on the stairs, just an hour ago. Please let it not be Haag, please, she begged silently. She was too terrified to attempt her usual expect-the-worst bargain with Fate. Why, oh why, had this had to happen here, when in Camden they were so near the Royal Free – the country's designated Haag hospital?

'Y'all right?' said one of the sweet paramedics. She nodded at him, dazed. She was still in her dressing gown and a pair of too-large wellies. She must look completely bonkers.

Olivia had come round just as Andrew had gone outside, but appeared confused, fainting again when Jesse tried to get her to sit up. Moments later, the ambulance crew had entered the drawing room in ominous white suits and heavy-duty gloves. 'Just a precaution,' one of them said, seeing Phoebe's face. 'Case we got any nicks or grazes on our hands.' That was when Emma had first seen Jesse look nervous, gently lowering Olivia's hand to the floor. He'd been heroic, explaining everything to the paramedics, while Andrew stood back and Phoebe and Emma clung to each other. Then had come a second shock, when Phoebe said: 'She was seeing Sean Coughlan, the Irish doctor. I mean, they were in a relationship – she might have caught it from him.'

Emma couldn't believe she hadn't guessed. It was obvious, looking back. She was also rather stunned that Phoebe knew – she thought her daughters didn't talk that way. What on earth had Olivia been thinking? It wasn't like her to be so reckless. Or was it?

Emma had told the ambulance men that Olivia had shown no symptoms until today, prompting Phoebe to say that Olivia had been feeling sick for days. Now, watching the paramedics flit round her daughter, Emma thought how often Olivia had refused food and stayed up in her room. Had these been signs that she was sickening – signs Emma had missed? She had been concentrating on Phoebe as usual. Poor Olivia hadn't wanted to worry them. The thought made Emma ache with guilt. She stared at her daughter's chalky face, and tried to get a grip.

'She'll be fine, Emma,' said Jesse. 'They'll get her into ER. Everything will be OK.'

'Gosh, Jesse,' she said. 'Thank goodness you're here. What would we have done?'

'Just did what anyone would have.'

'Well, none of us did! Where did you learn all that?'

'Waiting tables. First aid is mandatory. I never had to use it, though,' he said, smiling.

She looked at his hands and saw they were shaking. She could see the tiny cut on his palm now – the one he'd shown the paramedics, anxious that it might pose a risk of infection. He said he'd done it on a barbed-wire fence nearby, out in the dark on Christmas Day. She felt horribly responsible. What would Jesse's American mother think? He'd come to Norfolk, cut his poor hand, and might now catch Haag – all because he was the only one with enough sense to help Olivia.

Nearby, she heard the senior paramedic calling 'the Red Phone' at Norwich Hospital for advice, and rattling off cold medical terms: 'Vomit following faint, BP one forty ninety, appears hypoglycemic, high risk Haag-positive.' He walked further down the drive, almost out of earshot, but she caught the words 'body fluids', 'isolation', 'open wound', and 'medevac' and her heart started thrumming even faster. She wondered how Olivia numbed herself to this stuff every day at work.

'Right,' said the paramedic, striding over. 'We haven't the facilities to test conclusively for Haag at Norwich, so we're going to stabilise her there, then get straight to London. They're preparing two RAF planes at Lakenheath,' he said, looking unduly excited. Norwich hospital obviously hadn't expected to put its Haag drill into practice.

'Two planes?' said Emma, feeling faint herself. 'Why two? One for the rest of us?'

'No, you won't be able to accompany her, I'm afraid.'

'What? But I'm her mother! I can't stay here if she's going to London!'

'Just until she's had the all-clear. We'd ask you to stay in the house, but not to enter the room where she had the vomit. Presume she had her own bathroom?' he said, glancing up at Weyfield's huge facade.

Emma agreed, though she had no intention of hanging around at Weyfield. They would drive straight back to Gloucester Terrace the minute the ambulance had gone.

The paramedic turned to Jesse. 'You're higher risk, because of the contact with body fluids. Her vomit, I mean, with that cut on your hand. You need to come with us now. The second plane is for you.'

Phoebe

· · ·

Phoebe and Andrew managed to lock up Weyfield and bundle themselves into Andrew's car in a record forty minutes, remembering Cocoa just in time. Emma had already hurtled on ahead in her Golf. She had decided that the three of them should stay at Gloucester Terrace until Olivia had tested for Haag.

'Shouldn't we do as the paramedics said?' Andrew had asked. But Emma had overruled him, and he'd let her. It wasn't like him not to put up a token fight.

'But what if she's positive? Won't we be in trouble for leaving?' Phoebe had asked. It was the first time she'd registered that they might all be in danger. She felt sick already.

'Cross that bridge when we come to it,' her mother had said, slamming her car door and reversing down the drive. She sounded firm, but Phoebe could see she was freaking out.

'So, Phoebles, now I know you don't *need* a whole day to pack, can we make this a precedent?' said Andrew, as he revved round a corner. He always made jokes when bad things happened. It was his way of coping, and for now it suited Phoebe. She'd prefer to be here with her father, making bad jokes, than her mother, panicking.

Or – worse – in the back of the ambulance with Olivia and Jesse. She felt bad for Jesse, though. She had to admit, he'd been amazing. The paramedic said his first aid had prevented Olivia choking on her vomit. She hoped Olivia would forgive her for telling them about Sean.

Andrew switched on the radio. 'Baby It's Cold Outside' was playing – one of the songs from her first-dance shortlist. She realised that she hadn't thought of George since Olivia's collapse. The raw crisis of the morning seemed to have blasted everything else sideways. And actually, she was glad George hadn't been around. She'd never seen him in an emergency, apart from the time his friend had staggered off the rugby pitch with a gory nose, and George had gone white and done nothing. If he couldn't deal with that, she doubted he'd have been much use earlier.

Andrew began humming along to the male parts in the song. 'Curious lyrics, aren't they?' he said.

'I'd been thinking of it as our first dance,' said Phoebe.

'First dance?'

'At the wedding. Me and George. The wedding that's not happening.'

'Oh! Right, right. Well, I'm not sure about that. Isn't it a sort of rapist ditty?'

She laughed.

'Rather camp, too, I'd have thought,' he said, and then hurriedly added, 'I mean, not that George was camp – is camp.'

'It's OK, Daddy. It's not important now,' she said.

Andrew just nodded slightly, as they whipped round the roads to London.

Jesse

. . .

Ordinarily, Jesse would have been psyched to see inside a military plane. But this, he thought as they took off, was a long way from *Top Gun*. It was eerie to be the only passenger. If he'd known he'd wind up here, in a medevac bubble, he wondered if he'd have emailed Andrew at all.

You still would have, he thought. You'd still have wanted to know him – to know them. He stared out the window at the British countryside below. The quilt of little green rectangles, stitched with hedges, looked so tame. He wished he could stay suspended up here forever, never to face everything on the ground. He willed Olivia to be OK. The last time he'd seen her, before she was wheeled into her plane, she'd been wrapped in a silver blanket, her face a dead greyish colour. A doctor had been trying to give her a glucose drink. He was dressed in a full hazmat suit, like everyone they'd encountered since leaving the ambulance. It was like they'd been thrown into a CSI episode – he and Olivia the victims. His ring finger found the cut on his palm. How could something so tiny, so insignificant, be so huge? Would everything be different if he hadn't grabbed the fence at that exact place? The possibility that he really might have contracted Haag fluttered inside him.

You had to do what you did, he told himself. You had no choice. You can handle this. Besides, if you've caught it, you won't even know yet so there's no point worrying. He tried to practise his relaxation techniques, consciously softening his forehead, unclenching his jaw and hands. But a cold, creeping fear was fast replacing the adrenaline from before. He wanted to wash his hands – to bleach his hands. He realised his nail was in danger of gouging the cut deeper, making things even worse. Was the nausea welling up inside him nerves, or the start of something?

Andrew

. . .

It had been impossible to talk to Emma when they'd got back to
Gloucester Terrace. Phoebe had sat with them in the kitchen for
ages, as if she was afraid to be alone, periodically announcing how
worried she was. Eventually she'd gone up to her room, leaving
Andrew and Emma alone. Last night felt like a dream. He knew he
ought to acknowledge the things that she'd said – or at least grovel
for hiding the letter. But the image of Olivia being wheeled out of
Weyfield on a stretcher, and Emma's face as she watched, was all his
mind could contain.

'I'm sorry about before. What I said yesterday,' said Emma, as if
she was thinking the same.

Her hair still looked slept on, and she reached up to pat it with one
hand. It was a gesture she'd always had, inherited by Phoebe. They
both looked straight ahead, through the window to the modest paved
garden – so unlike Weyfield's sprawling lawns.

He offered her his whisky – she took a sip and handed it back.
Something in the gesture felt more intimate than they had been in
years.

'You had every right to be angry,' he said. 'I wish I'd just shown you that bloody letter when it arrived. Or told you about that night, what happened, at the time. If I'd known then how much trouble it would have saved . . . but I just, I didn't want to ruin—'

'Don't,' she said. 'It doesn't matter any more. It was all so long ago.'

'But you do believe me that it was a one-off, don't you? That there was never anyone, anything like that afterwards? It was just a freak, a stupid, stupid mistake.'

'I believe you. I know you, Andrew. Besides, if Jesse hadn't been there today, I don't know what . . . I can't imagine . . . ' He put an arm around her shoulders and she let him pull her closer. 'The thing is, I realised that I've kept secrets from you myself,' she said. 'And once we got like that, it felt easier to carry on that way. But I shouldn't have.'

He wanted to ask if she'd really meant what she'd said about how he treated Olivia, but he was afraid of digging up the fight again.

'I should have been more open with you about still wanting to work, after the girls were born,' she carried on. 'I know you haven't been happy at *The World* for years. And I should have said something, because you just soldier on, and it's no good. For any of us.'

'It's not your job to tell me. And besides, those aren't secrets. That's hindsight.'

'Maybe. But I definitely should have told you when I found the lump. It was weeks ago. It was just easier not to, to spare everyone, until I had to. It would've made it real, when I could barely think about it myself. But it's still no excuse. And it's not so different from the things you kept from me. It's all talking, or not talking. "Communication."' She over-enunciated the word, to acknowledge that it was the kind of therapy-speak he loathed. How well she knew him.

'I thought about what you said, about Olivia,' he said. 'It's not that I . . . favoured Phoebe.' He dropped his voice. 'At least, I hope not. It was a difficult time for me, when Olivia was born, reconciling myself to responsibilities here – knowing I ought to leave Lebanon, but not wanting to stop. I was wrong to keep that from you, too.'

'I still knew.'

'I know. I know you did. It's just that, when I came home, I already seemed to have missed the boat with Olivia. And then it was so easy with Phoebe. We always laughed at the same things. But Wiv never seemed to need me – even to . . . to like me all that much.' His voice shrank at the thought of Olivia in hospital, and the possibility that he might never be able to make it right.

'Andrew, don't!' said Emma. She reached up, her arms circling his neck, and kissed him on the lips, as she hadn't for years. He pulled her against him. The reality of her diagnosis, of her death, reared up in his mind with a terrifying force. 'I'm sorry,' she said into his neck. 'I should never have said those things about you and Olivia. I was just angry. They aren't even true. It's different with every child, every parent.'

He composed himself just in time to hear Phoebe coming downstairs. 'Have you heard anything?' she yelled.

Her sing-song brought Andrew back to normality. 'Nothing yet,' he shouted back, relieved to hear his voice back on a baritone keel.

'We'll call you the second we do, angel,' added Emma. They were still wrapped in each other's arms, the phone balanced on the windowsill beside them.

Jesse

· · ·

Jesse caught a second of an old *brring brrring* ringtone before Emma's breathless, 'Hello?'

'Emma, it's me, Jesse. It's OK,' he said.

'Oh thank God. So it's not Haag?' He could feel her relief down the line.

'Nope. She doesn't have Haag. So I'm all good, too. It's over one week since she left Liberia, so there's zero risk now. We were put in isolation separately, so I had, like, hours alone where I heard literally nothing. And then this nurse comes in and tells me Olivia just tested negative. Man, I was so happy! I was seriously beginning to freak out in this little tent—'

'So is she all right?' Emma interrupted. 'What was it? Just a nasty tummy bug?'

'Not exactly. Why don't you speak to her – she's right here. I'm going to put you on loudspeaker. She has an IV in her hand.'

He put the phone on the bedside table near Olivia's face. Her skin was still waxy, but she was smiling.

'Mum?' she said.

'Wivvy! Darling!' came Emma's voice, muffled. 'How are you? What *was* it?'

'Well actually I'm, um, I'm pregnant, Mum,' said Olivia. She looked at Jesse, her smile getting wider.

'Pregnant?'

'Yup. Seven weeks. But I honestly had no idea. I'd been feeling sick, but I thought ... I mean I didn't even think of that. I thought I hadn't got my period because I'd lost weight. It's happened like that before, and it always comes back when I put the weight back—'

'And it's ... it's Sean's, presumably?' Emma butted in.

'Of course!' Olivia said, almost laughing. 'I'm not that stupid! Jesse said you knew about us. Me and Sean. I know it was a bit—'

'Oh sweetheart. Yes we did know, we did. But all's well that ends well. What happy news.'

She was being very cool about it, thought Jesse, considering all they really knew of Sean was that he'd gotten Haag. But Olivia had told him a bunch of stuff about Sean that afternoon, and he sounded incredible.

'And the baby, will it be OK after this morning?' said Emma.

'Yeah, they did an ultrasound in Antenatal, and it all looks fine. But it's still early.' Olivia stopped for a second and then said, 'They found a heartbeat,' and her face crumpled into a half-laughing, half-crying grimace as she tried to say, 'Sorry, I think it's the hormones.'

So that's what she looks like when she feels something, thought Jesse.

Phoebe

· · ·

Olivia was passed around them all. Her mother kept saying, 'Oh Wiv!' before passing the phone to her father, who just said, 'Congratulations, old girl,' in his funny, stiff way, and then turned round, away from Phoebe and Emma, to face the window. Phoebe spoke to Olivia last, taking the phone out of the kitchen so their parents couldn't hear.

'Thanks for stealing my jilted-at-the-altar thunder,' she said, knowing her sister wouldn't be into squeals.

'Yeah, sorry about that,' said Olivia. 'Fainting seemed to be the only option, with all your drama.' She sounded different – her voice was weak, but it had a new brightness.

'God, Liv, it was so stressful! How do you work in a hospital every day? You were like the one person who'd know what to do, and you were lying there being no bloody use!'

'Well, Jesse was there. Seems like he handled it pretty well.'

'True, take bac—' she said, before remembering she was on speaker and chirping: 'Shout out to Jesse!' instead. Cringe. 'So anyway, you're PREGNANT!' she ploughed on.

'Yup. I'm that idiot you read about that has no idea.'

'And you're a *doctor*! Did you genuinely not realise? Just cos you're such a skinny bitch?'

'I'm always irregular. And we used protection – obviously. If you must know.'

'Nothing's a hundred per cent! Didn't you read *Sugar and Bliss*? To be sussed is a must but sex is, um . . . ' She couldn't remember the rest.

'No! I had better things to do. Anyway, it's still early days. I'm just "a little bit pregnant", for now – OK?'

'Sure. Am I allowed to be "a little bit excited" then?'

'OK.'

Olivia was to stay in overnight for observation, but Emma insisted Jesse stay at Gloucester Terrace until his flight on New Year's Day. Yesterday Phoebe would have been furious, but now it seemed natural – like it would be wrong for him to go anywhere else. Walking back from the corner shop where she'd been sent for milk and eggs, she broke into a lollopy skip on her good foot. She bounced down the pavements, joyously hard underfoot after Weyfield's muddy paths, buoyed at the sight of so many lighted windows, so many parked cars, so many people packed into one space. The wreath she'd hung on their door in early December had withered, and she yanked it off. Inside, she breathed the smell of the house, always more noticeable after a week away. It was like number thirty-four's own essence, its paint or its radiators or something, with a hint of Emma's Chanel and Cocoa's litter tray.

I'm going to be an aunt, she thought, hanging her coat on the Eames hooks. She could already see herself as Glamorous Auntie Phoebe, a kind of gift-strewing fairy godmother. She'd always assumed she'd be the first to have babies, while Olivia travelled the world. But this way round felt right, after all.

The doorbell rang right behind her – it was a rumpled-looking Jesse.

'The hero of the hour!' said Andrew.

'Where's the taxi? Did you have enough cash?' said Emma.

'I took the Tube,' he said, pronouncing it 'toob'. 'I wanted to see the real London. And I got dinner. I figured you'd be craving Japanese after Norfolk. Don't worry, it's not all vegan,' he said, holding up an Itsu bag, as if he'd read Phoebe's mind. She hadn't really felt like the omelette her mother had suggested.

'Well, this calls for champagne,' said Andrew, once they were all down in the kitchen. He opened the empty fridge, where a bottle of Veuve Cliquot lay on its side.

'To Olivia's happy news,' he said, filling four flutes, 'and to you, Jesse!' They all raised their glasses, and Jesse moved forward to clink, and Emma looked rather startled and then clinked so enthusiastically she spilt her champagne.

The four of them had a little celebratory picnic, sitting on stools around the island, using the disposable chopsticks and plastic spoons in the bags. There was silent, contented munching and slurping for a while.

'Mmm, this is yummy. Thanks Jesse,' said Phoebe. She wanted to offer some kind of olive branch, but the thought of mentioning the argument yesterday felt too weird. He looked up at her, noodles trailing out of his mouth, which he swiftly sucked in, splattering soy sauce on his white T-shirt. She preferred the soy sauce-splattering Jesse to Uniqlo-campaign Jesse, she thought.

'That's OK. Just wanted to give your mom a break,' he said.

It took a second to see what he meant. Perhaps she'd been a bit too efficient at blocking out cancer thoughts. Or perhaps she'd just been lazy, letting her mum do everything out of habit.

'Yeah, I'll clear this up, Mummy,' she said. 'You should relax.'

'Thanks, sweetie pie,' said her mother. 'That would be great. Then I can drive a kit bag straight down to Olivia. It's all packed.' Phoebe met Andrew's eyes. Clearly, Emma wasn't going to be a natural at chilling out.

After dinner, Phoebe and Jesse were left alone in the kitchen. 'That was exactly what I felt like,' she said, shoving cartons into the bin.

He looked over at her from the sink, where he was dabbing at his T-shirt. 'I needed it too. Not that Emma isn't an awesome cook.'

'Sorry about yesterday, by the way,' she said, straightening a tea towel so she could turn away from him.

'Hey, I should be the one apologising. I should never have stuck my nose in. I was most likely wrong anyway.'

'Don't worry. Doesn't matter,' she said truthfully. It was strange how George was already beginning to feel like a part of her past. Maybe the loss was yet to hit her, but somehow she didn't think so. She looked down at her finger, freed from its ugly ring, and thought of the bill for the Proposal Package. She'd be able to laugh about that one day, she knew. For now, it made her want to tense every muscle in her body.

'Did you hear from him yet?' asked Jesse.

'No. I wouldn't have expected to.'

'He has to contact you at some point, though, right?' said Jesse. 'Don't you have a ton of each other's stuff?'

'Not really. He was always funny about me leaving things at his. And he didn't even keep a toothbrush here. He had to bring it every time he stayed, in this wash bag with his school name tag inside.'

'Seriously? Jesus.'

'I know. He would have had no idea what to do this morning. Which seems like a pretty big sign he wasn't marriage material.'

'For sure. Sickness and health and whatnot.'

'For better, for worse . . . How about you, are you seeing anyone?' she asked.

'Not right now. I broke up with someone last year, when I found out my birth mom had passed away. It was kind of similar to what you're saying. I felt like he couldn't handle emotional shit. Like I was always emoting for the two of us. And that won't work, long term.'

'Mmm.' She knew now was her chance and mumbled: 'What made you think George was gay, by the way?'

'Nothing specific. I just wondered. But like I said, I was probably wrong.'

'You might not be. I probably just got so angry because I'd some-times wondered myself. It would explain some stuff.'

'I had the feeling he wasn't big on communication, right?'

'S'pose so. He was more the strong silent type. Actually just silent. Weak and silent.'

'And you're not like that. So if he was gay, straight, whatever, you need someone who can talk. Next year's going to be tough, right? You're going to have to be there for your mom. You need someone who gets that.'

'True.' She hadn't thought of this either, she realised, with a jolt of shame. Until yesterday, 'next year' in her head had been all about the wedding.

'Anyway, look at you. You're so beautiful! You could do so much better.'

'Aaaahh. Thanks, Jesse! You're so American!' She wasn't sure if it was the champagne, but she reached up and gave him a hug.

'And you're so bloody British!' he said, in Dick Van Dyke cockney.

Once Emma was back, the four of them slumped in front of an old *Downton* Christmas special. 'I thought I'd just escaped *Upstairs Downstairs*,' groaned Andrew, but Phoebe noticed how he put his arm around her mother, and kept topping up her mint tea and cracking walnuts for her. It was nice to be back, squashed up on the sofa in the TV room. Watching Maggie Smith glare at a butler, she realised that Weyfield might have the roaring fires and four posters, but only Emma was truly at ease there. Gloucester Terrace wasn't special like the Norfolk house, but it was home.

Jesse

. . .

Jesse looked around the rooftop room where he'd be sleeping. It had been Olivia's bedroom, and though her stuff had gone, vestiges of a younger Olivia remained – a lava lamp, some terrible clogs, and a graduation photo of endearingly dorkish friends. Now that he had seen the Birches' tall, narrow London house, with its Danish chairs and Andrew's political cartoons, he realised that Weyfield wasn't really them. The place was all Emma, her childhood in aspic. And it was only now, seeing the Birches in their home, eating takeout and watching TV, that he'd started to feel like they were in some way family – not his foreign-exchange hosts. Or maybe it was everything that had gone down today that had broken the barriers.

It was nearly midnight, but his mind was still whirring. He lay on the single bed, looking at the starless skylight, thinking about the chat with Phoebe in the kitchen. It had reminded him of talking to Dana, though Phoebe was sharper. Of course she was – she was Andrew's daughter. He would call Dana tomorrow, he decided, and tell his mom and dad the entire thing once he was back home. The quarantine stuff might take some justifying, but they'd get it. He realised he was excited to meet Sean, Haag survivor and another foreigner in the Birch clan. Potentially his brother-in-law. He wondered if Sean and Olivia would get married before the baby was born, if there would be a family wedding after all. Too bad he never got started on his adoption film; Olivia and Sean's first dance could have been a neat closing scene. Outside, Jesse could hear traffic, sirens, drunken shouting. Even the subway journey from the hospital had been a relief after Norfolk. It felt like coming up for air, or cracking a window in a stuffy car. Maybe he and Phoebe could go shopping in the West End, he thought happily, as he stretched under the atlas-print bedding, and turned out the light.

· 9 ·

30 December 2016

Olivia

. . .

Olivia leaned against the hard hospital bed, bags at her feet, impatient to be discharged. The thought that Sean was in the building, just floors away, had been dancing inside her all night. She'd felt such a fool in front of the doctors yesterday when her urine came back teeming with progesterone. Until now, she'd barely considered when she wanted children. It had always been 'one day, not yet'. A family would tie her to London, stop her working abroad. Settling down was for Phoebe.

But now that it was happening with Sean, she felt different. Nervous, but ready – as if they'd been together for ages. She remembered him saying, offhand, that he wanted lots of kids, and how she'd teased him about being broody. Secretly, though, she'd hoped he'd been testing the water, gauging how serious they were.

She had sent a text earlier, promising to visit, but hadn't said she was here in the Royal Free. It would be cruel to announce she was in hospital without explaining, and she wanted to tell him she was pregnant face to face. Dennis White had written again this morning, demanding she contact him, but conceding that there was no longer a risk, now her quarantine was over. She hadn't been able to face replying. She would have to kowtow, she knew. It could wait. She rechecked her cautious strokes of mascara (Phoebe had sent a make-up bag with Emma last night), and willed the nurses to come and set her free.

An hour later she was on Sean's high-observation ward, visitor's pass in hand. She breathed the safe NHS scent – bleach and mopped floors, and the ghost of school dinners. Being in a hospital as a patient was disconcerting, like going from actor to audience. Two young doctors passed and she wanted to explain that she was one of them, usually in scrubs, too. Rounding a corner, she saw a barrel-shaped, middle-aged woman with spiky hair and gold earrings, by a vending machine. 'O-livia?' she said, in a deep Irish accent.

'Yes?' said Olivia tentatively. 'Are you ... with Sean?' It hadn't occurred to her that his family might be here. She felt about ten years old.

'I'm his Mammy! Kathy. He's told us all about you. I recognised you from The Facebook. Come here, love!'

Olivia allowed herself to be embraced, and then held at arm's length as Kathy beamed at her. She could see Sean now in his mother's grey-green eyes. It crossed her mind that this woman was her baby's grandmother. Potentially her mother-in-law – part of a whole new family, a new life. How could that night on Cape Beach have led them here so soon?

'Not your average Meet The Parents, eh?' said Kathy. 'But it's great to meet you, Olivia. You're as lovely as Sean said. Now you've to see y'man inside!'

'How's he feeling?' said Olivia, as they set off down a long corridor, shoes squeaking, Olivia holding doors open.

'He's grand. He's a fighter, our Seany. But he's awfully thin, you should know. He's been so worried about you.'

'Yeah. It was a risk, us . . .' she tailed off, not sure how to put it, but Kathy laughed.

'Ah, young love! He's a naughty boy,' she said, fondly.

'This is him,' said Kathy, stopping at a door, and sanitising her hands up to her forearms before knocking. There was no reply, and she opened the door just enough to see in.

'Ah, he's asleep,' she said, sounding like a new mother admiring her baby.

'That's OK. I'd like to see him anyway,' she said.

'Y'grand, you take your time, love. He might wake up when he hears your voice,' she said, eyes creasing like Sean's.

Olivia walked into the sterile room. There he was, propped against pale green sheets, deep in a jungle of drips and wires and monitors. Still Sean, but different. She couldn't believe how much weight he'd lost. Even after Kathy's warning, and seeing so many Haag patients, it caught her off guard. His face was hollow, and his arms, flopping out of the hospital gown, had shrunk so that his elbows looked too big. Bluish dots peppered his throat – the remnants of the Haag rash. Their size confirmed that he had been Haag-negative for over twenty-four hours. She studied the ICU screen beside him, relieved to see respiratory rate, pulse, oxygen and temperature were all in the normal parameters. A clipboard at the end of the bed recorded his meals, sleep, urine. She considered summoning a nurse and asking to see his bloods before he woke up, and told herself to let go. She needed to stop – to be here as his girlfriend, not his doctor.

Clearly, not everyone shared the media's negative view of Sean. Get Well cards crowded the bedside cupboard, and the floor was heaped with presents. She put her gifts from the hospital shop on top of the pile, and then took them back again. She wanted to give them to him properly. She'd chosen a new Robert Harris, and a big box of

Maltesers – which he'd craved in Liberia. She realised it was the first time she'd enjoyed picking a present for somebody.

Flat, regular beeps from the monitor punctuated the steady rasp of his breathing. She sat on the visitor's chair, wondering if she should wake him up to make the most of her time here. Now she was with him, at last, it felt cruel to have to leave again. She said 'Sean' a couple of times, but he didn't stir. He'd always been an enviably heavy sleeper. She had imagined, stupidly, that she'd hug him on sight, but he looked too prone – too battered. Instead, she took his fingers in hers, careful not to dislodge the cannula by the knuckles. His hand was cold, and she remembered how much she'd wanted to touch it that first night at the beach bar. She was about to nudge his shoulder, to wake him, but stopped. She wanted to just look at him for a while longer. Your baby's father, she thought, trying to absorb what it meant. The two of them, combined in a whole new person.

'Sean,' she said again, louder. He still didn't stir. She felt unexpectedly shy. What if she'd got everything all wrong, what if he was horrified at the news? What if he said it was all too soon? He wouldn't, would he? She'd just tell him now, she decided. At least this way she could try the words, out loud, before he woke up.

'Sean, I've got news,' she said. She paused, though he was still asleep. 'I'm pregnant. We're having a baby.'

His eyelids flickered. She carried on.

'I've been feeling sick, but I never thought – we were always so careful. I've already had a scan, because—'

His eyes half opened and closed. She held her breath.

'Anyway, it's so different when it's you, not a patient. It was just this little lozenge, this tiny heartbeat flashing.' She remembered the throb of new life with a thrill, the pulse sound they'd picked up, like a bird's beating wings.

'O-livia,' he said, and his thumb stroked her hand.

'Sean!' She squeezed his hand back, and leant forward so that she could rest her cheek against his gaunt face.

'We're having a baby. Fantastic,' he whispered, and grinned, with his eyes still shut.

Andrew

. . .

SUBJECT: copy 10th Jan
FROM: Andrew Birch <andrew.birch@the-worldmag.co.uk>
DATE: 30/12/2016 16:09
TO: Gibbs, Sarah <sarah.gibbs@the-worldmag.co.uk>;
Croft, Ian <ian.croft@the-worldmag.co.uk>

Hi both,
Copy below – decided on a Japanese place I visited
before Christmas, over Hourani & Co, which was dreary.

I'll let this one speak for itself, but suffice it to say I think
the time is right. Despite my occasional tantrums, some of
which I blush to recall, it has been a pleasure to work with
you both. Sarah, I owe you a good lunch. The Ivy?

Andrew

PS. Ian, would you humour me by leaving the deliberately
split infinitive 'having boldly fallen' in situ? It's a *Star Trek*
reference – this being a tale of 'The Next Generation'
(ho ho). Which, it so happens, was my daughter Olivia's
favourite childhood TV programme.

Thanks.

Yukiko's Table, Belgravia
Food 5/5
Atmosphere 4/5

And how was your Christmas, New Year, all the rest of it? Unremarkable as ever, passing in a fog of bad TV, superfluous Stilton and unwanted presents? Readers, I can only tell you that mine was life changing. You may remember that Chez Birch was a no-go zone over the festive season. My heroic daughter Olivia spent the run up to Christmas treating Haag in Liberia, obliging us to spend a week in quarantine in North Norfolk. Quite a shock for the modern family, as you can imagine. Not least because a son I fathered as a young man (and to whose existence I was hitherto oblivious) turned up on our doorstep. Or, to be precise, in our hall, having boldly fallen through the front door – plunging himself into our quarantine.

If this sounds like an abysmal modern play, it gets better. On the final day of quarantine my older daughter fainted, and might have choked on her own vomit in the manner of Jimi Hendrix, had not said long-lost son tended to her. While the rest of us flapped like the proverbial decapitated poultry, he risked contracting Haag without hesitation. Don't worry, the happy ending's coming. Olivia tested negative for Haag, transpiring, in fact, to be suffering from morning sickness and thus redeeming herself, in spirit, from junkie legend to the Duchess of Cambridge. In a nutshell, I have not only gained a son, but am shortly to gain a grandchild.

I know, now, that life is too short to sweat the small stuff. Because to sweat the small stuff, day in, day out, is the great quotidian tragedy of our cosseted Western world. When I was a young man, I wrote about the big stuff. Wars, famine, human suffering. I thought a freshly slaughtered Masai goat the height of culinary elan. At Olivia's age, I too would have been in Liberia, reporting on the crisis my daughter has been working so bravely to contain. But for nearly thirty years, I have written about . . . new restaurants. New restaurants are not the big stuff. They are the ultimate small stuff. If this Christmas showed me anything, it is that my heart is no longer in this column. I would like to apologise to every chef whose efforts I may have lampooned for good copy. I would not like to apologise to the Michelin-starred hellhole that turned me away for wearing jeans.

Yukiko's Table is a fitting end to this column, being staffed by one family. I went the week before our quarantine, conscious that sushi would be in short supply in our Norfolk plague house. I was seated at a low table, in a room just a shade too bright, while a charming waitress hurried to bring me a cup of bracing, blood-temperature sake. Prawn tempura, light as mermaid's farts

Andrew stopped, and deleted 'mermaid's farts'. It was time to stop aping other critics' puerile humour, and just write. Then he went back and changed the too-wordy bit about headless chickens, before pressing on.

Prawn tempura followed – plump, and fresh as rain in batter jackets, with a pool of silken tamari. Then came yamucha: sensitively cooked, steaming pillows of umami. I could have happily eaten two baskets more, but left space for the teriyaki salmon – which had none of the 'catfood in treacle' quality of its poor imitations. I finished with a boule of Jasmine green tea ice-cream, a little ho-hum, but really, who goes to a Japanese restaurant for the puddings? Readers, run and eat at Yukiko's Table, and tell them a friend recommended you. Farewell, and bonne degustation.

Andrew read the column back. Was it too corny? No. He had shied away from corniness for too long. And it gave him enormous satisfaction to erase George from this parting family portrait. Should the little shit ever read the review (doubtful, but still), Andrew hoped George would be piqued at his own absence. As a bonus, he had written it in one sitting. Usually his column was a laborious routine of drafting, scrapping, rewriting, tweeting and coffee making. This one had written itself – a sign, he felt, that his decision to leave *The World* was right. He would call Sarah in the new year. For now, this was his notice. He wasn't sure what he would do instead. A new freelance gig was bound to turn up. He'd always rather fancied travel writing – assuming Emma was up to it. Or why not aim higher, have a go at writing his memoir? Imagining life without the fortnightly tug of his column was a revelation. Besides, many of his friends were already retired.

It was a relief to be back at his Ercol desk, out of the smoking room with its glinting decanters and miasma of Hartley Male. From his compact, bay-windowed study, its walls a minty green chosen by Phoebe, he could see Primrose Hill. He decided to walk there later, before it got dark. Perhaps he would start to do so daily, he thought, adding this to a general intention to do better, be better. He wasn't about to start writing New Year's resolutions. But he had some plans. He wanted to take Olivia and Sean to Lemonia on Regents Park Road for lunch, and to visit Jesse in Los Angeles, and to be Emma's rock through whatever ghastly treatment she might need.

He thought of Phoebe's paean to his heroic 'restaurent' reviews. It had been too easy, for too long, to let Phoebe cast him as a hero. Olivia's serious stare, her laudable ideals, had made him feel more Judas-like every year. That was why he didn't ask about her work. It wasn't that he didn't care. It was just painful to remember his younger, intrepid self, his dreams of making a difference. He'd been jealous too, he could admit now. Jealous of her freedom – the way she used her freedom. He pressed send on his final column and sat back. His stock of pithiness had run out.

Andrew had volunteered to go and collect Olivia from the Royal Free. In the hall he met Phoebe, coming up from the basement. She sat on the top step, watching him put on his coat.

'Daddy,' she said. 'Look at this message – what d'you think it means? He's one of the presenters at work. No idea how he knows I'm single,' she said, sounding gratified that he did. She showed Andrew a text that read: *Hi Phoebe, I heard you're newly single. Before you get snapped up, I'd like to take you out for dinner. How are you fixed for tomorrow night – pre parties? Caspar x*

'Sounds promising,' said Andrew.

'He's really nice. But I'd never thought of him in that way, because of George.' Andrew doubted this, by the moony way she was looking at the message. 'He's super talented, though.'

'Well, there you go. See what happens,' said Andrew. He didn't want to get drawn into one of Phoebe's long dissections of her life and be late to the hospital. 'I'm just about to pick up Olivia,' he said. 'You coming?'

'No thanks. Hospitals give me the creeps,' she said, wedging her small body against the banister and stretching her legs so that they took up the whole step.

'Right. Well, we'll be back for lunch.'

''Kay,' she said, gazing at her phone as if it held all the secrets in the world.

Driving downhill from the Royal Free to Camden, Olivia in the passenger seat, Andrew automatically reached for Radio Four, and then stopped himself. They had just had a very interesting talk about corruption in Liberia, the nightmare of a system rigged by bribes. He had managed to ask lots of questions (the trick was to imagine he was interviewing her to avoid butting in), and learned things he hadn't from the news. She returned his questions with a couple about the Middle East, which he felt he answered well, considering how long ago it was. He was just trying to think of another enquiry about her future plans – interested, but not invasive, when Olivia said: 'I saw Sean this morning.'

'Marvellous!' Andrew felt as if he'd been thrown a lifeline. 'I imagine he looked rather different from when you last saw him?'

'Mmm. He's lost weight. And he still has the Haag rash, so he looks pretty rough. But he's just weak really. Once he was awake he was totally lucid. Talking, eating, everything.'

'And you told him the happy news?'

'Yup. I woke him up with it.'

'Did you? Terrific. He sounds like a very decent chap. Perhaps I could do, I don't know, some sort of interview with him for *The World* – once he's fully recovered. Set the record straight, sort of thing. Such a lot of rubbish was written. Just a thought, anyway. Your call.'

'Maybe,' she said. He couldn't tell if she liked the idea or not. After a moment he added, 'I'm sure he'll be an excellent father. Better than me.'

He glanced at her, but she was staring at the windscreen. He'd always thought she had the misfortune to look like him and not

Emma, but she had Emma's nose, he realised – straight, guileless. It was Phoebe who'd inherited his beak, albeit in miniature.

'You're not that bad!' she said, looking round as if he'd been joking.

'I could have been better. Almost missed Jesse altogether.'

'There's plenty of time. You've only just met.'

'There is, there is,' he said. 'With you all,' he added, in a half-mumble.

They sat at a red light.

'And where does Sean live when he isn't in Liberia?' said Andrew.

'Dublin. But we talked about that. He's going to move here in the spring, ready for the baby. There's room in my flat for now.'

'Good for him,' said Andrew. But he was thinking, she's staying put. She's not trying to escape any more.

· 1 0 ·

New Year's Eve 2016

Emma

. . .

It was early afternoon before Emma got round to the snowdrift of post by the front door. On top of the late Christmas cards and Oxfam flyers about Haag was a white, bill-shaped envelope, addressed to her. She knew it was her test results, before she had seen the 'Private & Confidential' stamp or Mr Singer's address on the back. She stood looking at it for ages, not wanting to know what it held. She would open it alone, she decided, in the loo on the landing. She was still holding it when Olivia came down the stairs.

'Is that your results?' she asked, as if she was psychic. Or perhaps she'd just seen enough patients in Emma's position to know the signs. She was wearing the jumper Phoebe had given her, not her usual hoody.

'Mmm,' said Emma. 'Yikes!' It was meant to sound cheery but it came out strangled.

'Why don't we open it together, in the kitchen?' asked Olivia. 'Then we can look at your options.' She sounded different from usual, sort of professionally positive. It was rather nice. Like a doctor, thought Emma, before remembering that her daughter was a doctor.

'Um. Yes,' she said. 'Yes, OK then.'

*

'Happy Noo Years!' boomed Jesse, coming into the TV room holding brown paper grocery bags, like the male lead in a rom com.

Somehow, it was already teatime. Emma and Olivia had slouched on the sofa for hours, while the others flitted in and out, offering cups of tea.

'Hey, guys, I found my favourite tofu balls!' said Jesse. Phoebe had sent him to Whole Foods on Parkway, for a vegan alternative to the chicken Andrew was preparing. He looked disproportionately thrilled by this outing. 'Man, London is so beautiful! I just walked to the top of Primrose Hill. Seriously, it reminds me of that movie *101 Dalmatians*. I love this time of year! It's, like, a chance to start fresh.'

He was right. Emma felt galvanised. A new baby was something to live for. She looked at Olivia, her face the most relaxed Emma had seen it in ages, despite the daunting chat they'd had earlier over her results. Still, the plan Olivia had drawn up for her chemo, down to designated drivers for Emma's appointments, was better than the limbo of the past days. Better, too, than Jesse's well-meant, but rather cranky-sounding theories. All Nicola's fighting talk around cancer seemed appropriate, after all. *I may lose my eyelashes*, she thought, *but it's a small price for knowing my grandchild.*

'The hill's so pretty at sunset, isn't it?' said Emma.

'Incredible!' said Jesse. 'How're you feeling, Olivia?'

'Better, thanks,' she said. 'Though I have new sympathy for pregnant women.'

'Right! So, Andrew and I are waiting on you ladies tonight. You two need to rest up. No helping, Emma. We'll take care of everything.'

He left. Olivia and Emma looked at each other, and for once she felt like they were sharing a joke.

They carried on watching *Poirot* in easy silence, until Phoebe appeared in the doorway, wearing a kimono. Her hair was wrapped in a towel turban, eyes pulled into slants like a bad facelift. She managed to make even this look rather chic.

'Mummy, really sorry, but I don't think I can stay for dinner now. Party starts earlier than I thought, so ... Plus I'm getting ready at Lara's.'

'Oh, Phoebs! That's a bit rotten. The boys are doing everything specially. D'you have to get there right at the start?'

'No, but I'm meeting this guy first. He wanted to take me for dinner, but that seemed a bit intense, so we're going for a drink and then on to this party. Anyway, I haven't been out for a week. Literally. Or a date, for six years.'

'Caspar?' said Olivia.

'Mmm-hmm,' said Phoebe, not looking at all like a girl who'd just been chucked.

Emma was rather amazed that she seemed to be moving on so quickly. It was a good sign, of course, but she couldn't help feeling deflated. She knew Andrew wanted supper to be a special family meal, to mark everything that had happened in quarantine. Olivia kept her eyes trained on the TV.

'Well, do let Daddy know,' said Emma weakly. 'I'm sure he'd like to open some bubbles before you leave.' Andrew could probably persuade Phoebe to stay for supper, she thought. Besides, she ought to line her stomach.

'OK. But it'll have to be soon,' said Phoebe, turning to leave.

'All right, lamb,' said Emma, trying not to sound disappointed.

Jesse

. . .

Andrew was already in the kitchen when Jesse came in with the groceries. He marked a page in a yellowing paperback and smiled. Lately, just since yesterday, Jesse had come to see his own face more in Andrew's. Emma had said the same.

'D'you know Claudia Roden?' said Andrew, holding up the book.

'Is she, like, a British chef?'

'British Egyptian. She really brought Middle Eastern food here, in the eighties. There's a wonderful chicken recipe in this book that Emma and I used to do. And here's the pilaf I thought we might have with it,' he said, showing Jesse a page headed *Saffron Rice with Raisins and Almonds*. 'That falls within your remit, doesn't it?'

'Sure,' said Jesse, scanning the recipe. He had gotten used to the way Andrew talked. He made a mental note to tell Dana that he actually spoke a lot like he wrote, that the prose wasn't fake, though he was less catty in person. More real, once you knew him.

'Excellent. I thought we should do something from that part of the world, for your final evening,' said Andrew. It was the third time he'd said so since breakfast. Tonight must be a big deal for him.

Jesse made a start on his contribution, sweet potato brownies, while Andrew chopped herbs and weighed out spices, putting everything in tiny bowls as if they were on a cookery programme. He was whistling 'Driving Home For Christmas', with nerves or contentment, or both, Jesse couldn't be sure.

'I read your article about your mom,' said Jesse, between pulses of the Magimix. 'She sounds awesome.'

'Did you? She was, she was. In the true sense of the word,' said Andrew. 'I'm sorry you didn't get to meet her. She was very fond of Olivia and Phoebe. Olivia, in particular. They were rather alike, in fact. Fiercely self-reliant.'

'Right. That figures.'

'She had to be both parents to me, in a sense. I never really knew my father,' said Andrew. 'But I knew *of* him. I imagine being adopted, that must be – ah – complicated in a different way. Just, not to know.'

'I guess. My parents – my adoptive parents – were always very open, but there was literally nothing they could tell me about you. Until I looked up your name you were just, like, a void.'

Andrew's mouth twitched as if he was about to say something quippy, but then didn't.

'I was planning to make a film about it,' Jesse continued. 'I was hoping to shoot some more at Weyfield. But I kind of got sidetracked.'

'Events intruded, rather, last week.'

'For sure!'

'Well, if you do make it, I hope you'll consider a cameo from Camden. Over Skype or something. We're very glad you came,' he said, looking intently at the digital scales.

Jesse took this as his chance.

'So what was she like, Leila? My birth mom?'

Andrew's neck reddened as he looked up, and for a moment Jesse wondered if he'd crossed a boundary. But his face relaxed as he said:

'Well. Terrific looking, I recall. Good move on your part, taking after her. And bright, going places. But I can't tell you a great deal beyond that, I'm afraid,' he said, looking sheepish. 'We didn't, um, talk an awful lot.'

Jesse laughed. 'I get it. Where did you meet, if you don't mind me asking?'

'My hotel bar. Sounds dreadful, put like that. But a war zone, human crisis, it heightens everything. Makes one behave out of character. Take risks, I suppose. Look at Olivia and Sean.'

'Right. Carpe Diem.'

'Quite. I didn't make a habit of, er, picking up women in bars, by the way,' he said, looking uncharacteristically earnest. Jesse guessed this was his way of saying he'd been faithful to Emma throughout their marriage. 'But look what it brought us!' said Andrew, reverting to his usual wry tone and holding up his mug to Jesse.

'Hey, you were a young guy.' It was funny how he felt like he could talk to Andrew as another adult, but Andrew clearly couldn't quite do the same. Jesse knew he would never see him as his father, the way he saw his dad Mitch, but that was OK. Healthier, probably. 'She was a news anchor, right?' said Jesse.

'Yes, at the time. She became quite a senior producer at Al Jazeera, I believe. But you probably know more than me. You Googled her, I imagine?'

'I did, but there wasn't a whole lot.' He was surprised Andrew had kept tabs on Leila Deeba.

'There's something I've been meaning to show you, actually,' said Andrew, turning a pan down to a simmer. 'Now's as good a time as any. Come up,' he said, and Jesse followed him to the first floor.

*

He hadn't seen Andrew's study yet. It was nothing like the dark, cluttered smoking room. A bay window overlooked Primrose Hill, and two walls were lined floor to ceiling with books, even over the door. The only furniture was a spartan desk and ergonomic chair. The whole effect reminded him of somewhere, he thought, before realising it was his own apartment. Dana and his folks had always teased him about being the neat freak in a sloppy family.

Andrew opened his desk drawer and unfolded a sheet of cream paper. 'I should have shown you this when you first arrived,' he said. 'But, well, it was complicated because I stupidly hadn't mentioned it to Emma. She knows now, though. Have a look. You should keep it. It's for you, really, I think.'

Jesse took the sheet of paper and saw it was a handwritten letter. He looked at the signature – it was from her. His birth mother.

Dear Andrew,

It has been many years, but I hope you remember meeting me, Leila Deeba, in Beirut. I am writing to tell you that, after we met, I discovered I was pregnant with your baby. He was born 26 December 1980. I chose to have him adopted, as I felt unable to raise a child alone. I would like to sincerely apologise for not having informed you. I was young and afraid, and my career, at that time, was my obsession. Beirut was a dangerous place for a child. I thought it would be easier for you if you didn't know.

But I am writing to you now, Andrew, because I am sick. I have a terminal disease. I have accepted that I will probably die without meeting my son. For many years I hoped he would try to find me, but he has not. I never had any other children.

If, some day, he contacts you, please tell him that not a day passed when I didn't think of him. My dying wish is that he has been happy. Please believe this letter, for his sake. You will know him if you see him. He was beautiful. I named him Iskandar.

> *Yours,*
> *Leila*

I wish you well, and I hope that life has been good to you.

He heard each line over and over in his head. He had always assumed the orphanage staff had called him Iskandar – 'defender of the people' – but it had been her all along. *Not a day passed when I didn't think of him.* He leaned against the desk, forgetting Andrew and everything in the room. The dull, empty sadness he'd felt on hearing she was dead was back. But this time there was something else, too. She had named him. She had hoped for him. She had never forgotten him. And it felt like a circle completing – a circle that had been a C-shape, for as long as Jesse could remember.

Andrew looked away, straightening the post on the windowsill.

'Wow,' said Jesse, when he trusted his voice.

Andrew put a clumsy hand on his shoulder. 'Lucky, I'd been planning to—' he said, and then seemed to change tack. 'Drink?'

Phoebe

· · ·

Phoebe paused by the kitchen door. She'd felt bad, seeing her mother look crestfallen earlier. Especially after the big chat they'd all had about her treatment. The outlook was good, apparently, but Emma would need chemotherapy. Phoebe had made it her resolution to stock the freezer with Marine Ices sorbet – which Olivia said was all chemo patients could stomach – and to be a grown up, and not freak at Emma's hair blocking the plughole.

But still, she didn't have to cancel Caspar, did she? Nobody knew, but the two of them had had a long-running game of eye contact across the office. She wondered how he'd got her number, liking the idea of him searching it out. He'd left a voicemail earlier, confirming their date, and she'd found herself listening to it over and over. If she cancelled their drink, or changed the plan to meeting at the party, it would send the wrong message. Surely Andrew would be fine with her skipping dinner. Then again, after that cheesy column he might try to guilt-trip her into staying. Everyone else had cheered when he'd announced he was quitting *The World*. Phoebe had been secretly sad – she loved their one-on-one meals in restaurants she couldn't afford. Even the bad ones were fun, forming jokes for years afterwards. She'd hugged him and said it was the right decision, because her mother and sister were saying so. But it stung that she hadn't got a mention in his parting column, when everyone else had. She was the daughter who'd always been there – if you were getting all #familyfirst about it. Olivia had only come home because she had nowhere else to sit out her quarantine.

She opened the kitchen door. Jesse and her father were surrounded by ingredients, both wearing aprons that barely reached their thighs. Andrew was refilling two glasses of whisky and ice cubes. The smell reminded her of the Southern Comfort George drank at Edinburgh. He called it So-Co, she remembered, cringing. The urge to confront him about Jesse's theory had already faded. He'd never admit it, even if it was true.

Andrew raised his glass as she came in.

'Daddy,' she said, 'Dilemma – it's not a big deal for me to miss dinner tonight, right?'

'What?' he said jovially.

'It's OK if I'm out tonight, isn't it?'

'Of course – so long as you're here for the fatted calf. Cornfed chicken, rather.'

'The thing is, I'm meant to be getting ready at Lara's to catch up on everything, and then I'm meeting Caspar for a drink at nine, so . . .'

'I don't quite follow,' said Andrew. The new, alien smile dropped a fraction.

'I'm just going to take a shower. You're good to do the zucchini, right, Andrew?' said Jesse, moving past them discreetly.

'Quite right,' said her father, sounding distracted.

Phoebe thanked Jesse silently – she needed Andrew alone if she was to get her way. She perched on a stool at the island, waggling geranium toenails.

'I mean, I can't stay for supper. I don't have time,' she said, beginning to feel frustrated. 'It won't work. I can't change the plan with Caspar this late. Sorry, Dada. I assumed we wouldn't bother doing a big thing for New Year.'

'It's not quite a normal New Year. I'm sure Caspar will understand, in the circumstances.'

'But I was really looking forward to it. Why is tonight a major thing? We've all been in each other's pockets all week.'

'I thought you said you had a dilemma. You seem to have made your mind up.'

'You don't have to be like that about it,' said Phoebe. 'I'm just trying to get out there again. It's not easy, you know, finding out the last six years of your life was a sham.' The last bit came out as a tremble, and his eyes softened. They always did when she threatened to cry.

'I know you're keen to get out on the razzle again,' he said, taking off his glasses and rubbing his forehead. 'But there's plenty of time. It would be a nice gesture to join us tonight. Jesse and I planned to do a sort of feast, you see. Fatted calf, as I said.'

She said nothing, not wanting to snap, or cry.

'Prodigal son? Scripture lessons? Ring any bells?' he said.

'Yes, I get it. It's Jesse's last night. But it's not like we're never going to see him again. I thought you had the whole plan to visit next year?'

'Not Jesse – Olivia,' said Andrew, looking down at a recipe.

'What? Because of the baby?'

'No, Phoebe. Don't you see? Until now, your sister and I – well, suffice to say, she rarely came home, as you know. Even at Christmas. And when she did, she and I, we didn't, uh, chat very much – to one another, I mean. And this week, we've, er, we've found we have more common ground than we realised. What with working abroad, and, well, yes, our work.' He kept looking at the recipe as he spoke. Sweat glistened on his temple. She knew she should give him a break, but something made her mean instead.

'God, I could have told you that. You're just both too stubborn to realise it.'

'No doubt. You and Emma always see these things. But still, something to celebrate, no?'

The new touchy feely Andrew was making her feel weird. She preferred the old, grumpy one. Only she could make that Andrew laugh.

'I just want to go out and have fun, forget everything. I'm so stressed about Mummy.'

She didn't feel wonderful about playing this card, despite it being true. It seemed to work, though. He took a sip of whisky. 'Fine. Of course,' he said, the new smile returning. 'Well, off you go. I hope this Caspar character knows his luck.'

Emma

. . .

Emma heaved herself up after a whole afternoon surrendered to the sofa. It was a novelty to be banished from the kitchen, and she had to peek. She hoped Andrew wouldn't be attempting anything too ambitious, or messy. But she was met with a surprisingly professional smell of frying garlic, and much clearer surfaces than she managed. Jesse was stirring a pan on the hob, and Andrew was stuffing a chicken.

Elvis came crooning over the radio. 'You were always on my miiiiinnnd!' warbled Andrew, looking up at her. He'd been almost facetiously jolly since giving his notice with that glorious last column. It was as if the unreal scene in the cellar, and their conversation by the window yesterday – even her diagnosis – had all been leading up to this change. Making love that morning, then watching Andrew whistle while he frothed her cappuccino, she'd been transported back to their honeymoon in Puglia. Perhaps Jesse's Californian sunniness had melted Andrew's sharp edges, she thought, watching the two of them harmonise.

'May I have this dance?' said Andrew, striding up to Emma.

'Haven't you just had your hands up a hen's bottom?'

'Nothing wrong with that,' said Andrew, taking her hand, and clasping the small of her back. 'We avoided Haag. Can't let a spot of salmonella stand in the way of romance.'

He began moving her back and forth, and she remembered what a good dancer he'd been when they used to go to Soho jazz clubs, knowing they wouldn't be spotted by anyone Emma knew. It was like dancing with clockwork, after the Bertie Wooster types she usually met. With Andrew, you just let yourself be led. Jesse whooped in a very American way as Andrew dipped her, and said: 'Still got it, Emma!' which was rather sweet.

'Sorry I couldn't persuade Mademoiselle to stay,' said Andrew. 'No stopping her.'

'Tant pis. Not your fault.'

'OK, bye everyone,' said Phoebe, from the doorway. She had her coat on, and was pushing heels into an overstuffed bag of clothes.

'Ought you to wear those, with your foot?' said Emma.

'Mummy! I'm twenty-nine! It's fine. Doesn't hurt any more.'

'Won't you just stay for a glass of champagne?'

'Can't, I'm late,' said Phoebe. 'You have mine. Plus I don't want to get there pissed. I'm a cheap date,' she added to Jesse.

'It's cos you're like a size two,' he said, and Phoebe looked pleased, as if he'd said the right thing in their private script.

'Right, Happy New Year, guys,' said Phoebe, blowing kisses. 'See you tomorrow. I don't intend to get up till midday.'

She looked so excited that Emma tried not to mind as the front door slammed, jolting the William Nicholson prints on the wall.

'Aaaargh gotta love the King,' said Paul O'Grady, as Elvis came to an end. 'Now we're going to the news, before my next guest, dance maestro Bruno Tonioli.'

The news jingle played, and Andrew released her.

She stood washing her hands at the sink, while Andrew went back to the chicken.

'Sean Coughlan, the Irish paediatrician diagnosed with Haag virus, has died in hospital,' read the woman's expressionless voice. Emma froze, her hands under the too-hot water. 'It is thought he developed an infection, following his removal from isolation on Thursday. A full post-mortem will not be carried out until next week. Coughlan was thirty-three and is believed to have contracted Haag after visiting a primary school, as part of a campaign to educate local children about the disease. Although he subsequently tested negative for the virus, which attacks the immune system, he is said to have been very weak. Tributes have been paid by family, friends and colleagues to a courageous young man who will be much missed. This is the first death of a British aid worker following the Haag crisis. His family have appealed for privacy.'

Emma took the stairs two at a time, cursing the house for being so tall. She shouted 'Wiv!' before she was even close, but there was no reply. When she reached the spare room she saw Olivia lying face down on the bed, her shoulders shaking silently. She sat beside her, saying nothing, just stroking her broad back and her mousey-coloured head. It was the only way she used to be able to get Olivia to sleep when she was a baby. She couldn't tell if Olivia even knew she was there.

'I'm so sorry, darling,' said Emma eventually. 'I'm just so sorry.' She knew it sounded hopeless. Olivia didn't reply, or look up. But after a second she shifted minutely closer to Emma's thigh.

Phoebe

. . .

'I'm still in shock that he'd *do* that,' said Lara, topping up Phoebe's Prosecco. 'Just piss off, after he proposed. It's psychopathic.' Phoebe had given Lara a gabbled account of the week in quarantine, while she did her make-up and Lara smoked out the window. Even in Lara's disconcertingly adult flat the evening felt nostalgic – like when they used to sit in Phoebe's bedroom, talking non-stop and perfecting their Amy Winehouse eyeliner. And it had become clear that Lara had never been a fan of George, despite gushing over the ring two weeks ago. Phoebe felt like an idiot for assuming everyone was jealous of her life. Still, perhaps it was better than the pity she'd expected.

'I know,' she said. 'But it's weird, I kind of feel, just, detached already. Maybe it's everything else going on. It's like I don't mind if I never see him again.'

'Really? Don't you need some kind of ending? Or an apology?'

'I know it makes no sense. It's like how you'd feel about someone you'd only been seeing for a while. Not your fiancé.'

'Like you weren't genuinely that close?'

'Guess. I think I was in love with the idea of being his girlfriend to start with. And then I just got used to being a couple. Except we never really went beyond that dating level. Which was fun, in a way. But not actual love.'

'So maybe he did the right thing by ending it,' said Lara.

'Ish. He could have done it a better way.'

'Yeah, but now you can hate him for being a coward. And it's easier to hate someone than miss them.'

'True.' Could she imagine truly missing George anyway? Wasn't it her pride that she'd been crying for, the years wasted on an idiot?

She'd held back from mentioning Jesse's theory. It had become habit, she realised, to censor everything she told her oldest friends about her relationship. The thought made her say it out loud, in a rush, now. She felt her cheeks flare as she did so.

'Shit,' said Lara. She turned away to tap her cigarette on the windowsill. For a moment she just inhaled and exhaled, saying nothing. Then she said, very serious: 'Too bad it didn't give him better taste in jewellery.' And then they were both giggling so hard that Phoebe had to spit Prosecco into her glass, before she did the nose trick.

She never laughed like that with George, she thought, when they'd both recovered and she had to repair the damage to her mascara. Perhaps she'd cared about having a boyfriend, any boyfriend, too much.

Olivia

. . .

Every part of Olivia's body hurt. Pain seemed to be rushing towards her and around her like an incoming tide – up to her neck and over her head, as she tried to gulp in some air. She opened her eyes, but the room strobed in and out and she thought she might be sick again, so she shut them. Now, instead of the red blackness of her own eyelids, she saw Sean's eyes looking back at her. She could see them in pin-sharp focus – the splotch of gold by one pupil, smile lines fanning to his temples, violet crescents stamped by a night shift. Her heart felt like it might implode, as if her body understood what had happened, while her brain refused to follow. She kept reliving the last time she'd seen him, yesterday. She'd been hurrying, because her father was outside in the car, and had left the room with breezy kisses and a promise to celebrate soon. Why hadn't she asked to check his bloods, to see a lumbar puncture? What was she thinking, taking the ICU monitor's word for it that he was fine, when he'd only tested negative three days ago? She opened her eyes to escape Sean's, and lay looking at the spare-room walls without seeing them.

She remembered a perfect night in Liberia. They'd been sitting on the beach at dusk, barbecuing a fish he'd just caught. He'd looked so proud of himself – like a small boy – that she'd teased him until he'd grabbed her in a fireman's lift and run towards the waves threatening to dunk her. She remembered being pleased, despite herself, that he could throw her around like a fledgling. She liked the way he got into the sea, stumbling through the surf till he fell over, then bobbing up with a seal's slick head and lashes like spears. That night was the happiest she'd ever seen him, and not just because of the fish and the beers and the sunset. He'd told her, afterwards, that it was the moment he knew he was in love. And she remembered feeling the same, and that being so at ease with someone was even more exquisite than the rush of a first kiss.

The enormity of having his baby, the baby he would never see, thudded into her yet again. She tried to push it aside – she was only seven weeks. But the fear that Sean's child would tether her to this day, to Haag, forever was deafening. She clamped her eyes shut again, hating herself for even thinking of her future, for considering life after now. She heard his voice in her head, the way he said 'O-livia'. And she found herself wishing she'd told her mother who he was at the airport. And now it was too late.

Andrew

. . .

The raw chicken sat on the side, naked and chilly looking. It had been ready to go in the oven just as the news broke, but would have to be binned now. Olivia had begged to be left alone, but it still felt wrong for them to feast as planned downstairs. Andrew had no appetite anyway. Seeing him look at the bird, Emma seemed to remember to act like herself – or a caricature of herself. She jumped up as if she'd sat on something hot and yelped: 'The chicken! It'll never cook through in time – quick, put it in, Andrew!'

'But we aren't going to do all that now, surely?' he said.

'We still have to eat,' said Emma. Her eyes had the alarmed look they got in airports. 'Especially Wiv, in her condition. She has to keep her strength up. I can take her a tray – or maybe she'll come and sit with us later.'

Andrew doubted that Olivia would welcome Emma's tray of food. Or that she'd come down tonight – or even tomorrow. All the same, his wife's faith in roast chicken was touching.

'But won't she, uh, *mind* us all carrying on as normal?' he said. He knew how quick Olivia was to take umbrage, and wouldn't blame her if she resented them tucking in downstairs. Their new rapport still felt fragile.

'Of course she won't. Rituals are comforting,' said Emma.

'Emma, really, I don't think ...' he tailed off. 'Couldn't we just put it in the fridge, have it another day? I couldn't eat a thing myself.'

'But it's darling Jesse's last night!' she said, turning to give Jesse a clutchy embrace. The brandy must have gone to her head. Still, it was rather a shame to part on such a bleak note.

'Jesse?' said Andrew.

'Guys, please, don't do anything on my account,' said Jesse. 'Although Emma's right, I guess, rituals can be grounding.'

Andrew realised it was up to him to make a decision. It was a novel feeling. 'Right, well, since it's all done we may as well stick it in and have it cold tomorrow,' he said.

'Good-oh,' said Emma, yanking open the oven and nearly dropping the whole chicken in her hurry. She straightened up, looking for the next task. 'Would she like a bath? Jesse, perhaps you could start running it. I'll go and tell her,' she said.

'Wait,' said Andrew quickly. 'Better she's left alone for now, I think. But Jesse, do see if you can track down your younger sister – you've got her mobile, haven't you?'

And as he said so, he realised it was the first time he'd thought of Jesse as a brother to his daughters.

Phoebe

. . .

Caspar walked to the bar and Phoebe leant back in their booth, watching him. He was taller and wirier than George. She liked how his jeans hung. George's jeans used to cling to his rugby-player haunches – gross. Lara had kept saying how fit George was, as if she was looking for anything positive to say about him. And although Phoebe knew it was true she also knew, deep down, that she'd never liked the way George's bulky body felt on top of her – had never felt her inside dip when she looked at him. But the knottiness behind her belly button, right now, wasn't that how you were meant to feel? She'd noticed people recognise Caspar, and it had gone to her head like the Aperol Spritzes.

She checked her phone while she waited – five missed calls. Three were from the Gloucester Terrace landline, one from her father's mobile, and one from a foreign-looking number. She couldn't be bothered to listen to the voicemails. Her mother always waffled for ages, and she wouldn't be able to hear in the bar anyway. It was probably one of her parents' dumb questions about their own house: 'Phoebe, have you seen the Sellotape?' 'Phoebs, did you throw away our mouldy taramasalata?' She sniggered to herself, rearranging her face into an approximation of sober and sultry as Caspar walked back from the bar, and then ruined it by laughing as he put down their drinks.

'What's so funny?' he asked, putting his arm round her shoulders as if it belonged there.

'Nothing, just my family. They're annoyed I didn't stay for dinner.'

'Ah. Is your dad going to hate me for ever?'

They looked at each other for a long, slow-motion second, and then she was tasting his unfamiliar, Aperol-laced mouth, her hands reaching up to the back of his head and neck, and she knew they'd never make it to the party.

Jesse

. . .

New Year's with Emma and Andrew had been a strange, subdued evening. Olivia was upstairs, unable to face food or company, and it didn't feel right to talk about anything else. The three of them kept lapsing into long, sad silences. Jesse had gone up to see her after the news broke, but by the way she remained rigid in his hug, he could tell she wanted to be alone. Nobody had heard from Phoebe, who was still out on her date. It was pretty harsh, thought Jesse, considering Sean's death had been all over social media. He was beginning to understand how his younger sister operated – she was sweet and fun, for sure, but she always came first.

Nobody had eaten much, though Emma kept imploring them to have some chicken, seeming to forget Jesse was vegan. He was hungry now, but feared that eating would look disrespectful. The batch of sweet potato brownies he'd baked earlier was untouched.

'What about the new year quiz?' said Emma. 'I could do with something to take my mind off ... off—' She looked as if she was about to cry again, and Andrew grabbed a copy of *The World* from the side and began frantically flicking through it.

'It's a little tradition of ours, Jesse,' said Emma, composing herself.

'*The World* publishes a huge quiz on everything that's happened over the year. I'm always hopeless, but it's rather fun anyway.'

'Sure,' said Jesse, thinking it sounded like a bizarre idea in the circumstances. 'We do the same at home, Trivial Pursuit at Thanksgiving.' It was like Emma couldn't decide how to cope – she kept alternating between tears and a kind of forced normality. She was probably in shock. At least Andrew seemed to be keeping it together, unlike when Olivia collapsed. Jesse couldn't have dealt with taking the lead again.

'Right. Here we are. Now, Popular Culture. 'Which female artist sang: "He see me do me. Dirt, dirt, dirt, dirt, dirt, dirt,"' read Andrew, counting the 'dirts' on his fingers. 'Come on Jesse, you're the only member of the younger generation here,' he said, peering over his glasses.

'Was it, Princess Gaa Gaa?' said Emma, anxiously.

They carried on half-heartedly, all of them jumping at any distant creak that might indicate Olivia coming downstairs. It was better than sitting in silence, Jesse guessed. He wished he wasn't leaving them like this. He knew he would worry about Olivia and Emma. As he'd said earlier to Dana, it was strange how he felt like he'd known his new family for months, already. Maybe he could persuade the Birches to come visit next Christmas, and meet his family back home. They were better out of Weyfield. The baby would be, what, four months by then? He'd been thinking how much he wanted to be a part of his niece or nephew's life. Not to be the newcomer in their eyes. Plus his mom adored babies. That was why she'd wanted to adopt, he thought, patting Leila's letter in his pocket. Just knowing it was there felt good.

Andrew interrupted his thoughts by asking: 'Jesse, you'll know this: which popular health-food snack was found to contain traces of arsenic in February?'

Phoebe

. . .

'I have to pee,' said Phoebe, as they came up for air. It was like being a teenager, snogging for ages in public. And kissing Caspar was a revelation. She'd always disentangled herself from George's open mouth and darting tongue within minutes, telling herself it was normal for long-term couples not to kiss. She sidled off Caspar's lap and out of their booth, trying not to stumble, knowing he'd be watching her back view weave to the loos. Once inside, she Instagrammed a photo of their cocktails with the caption 'There may be trouble ahead . . .' Hopefully George, and everyone else, would realise she was on a date – since Caspar's hand was in shot. She scrolled idly through her Twitter feed as she sat on the loo. For a second, her brain, fuddled by alcohol and Caspar, couldn't compute the hashtag #SeanCoughlan that kept appearing. 'Really sad to hear about the Irish doctor', 'Such a shame about Sean Coughlan, the world needs more people like him,' she read. Wasn't Sean better now? Then she saw an unmistakable 'RIP Sean Coughlan, such a waste'.

She sat, paralysed, tights round her knees. No wonder her parents had left all those voicemails. She ought to go home, she knew. But the date was going so well. How could she explain to Caspar without ruining everything? Would Olivia even want her around?

She never knew the right thing to say, even to the people she should be closest to. Then again, if she didn't go home she'd be 'Phoebe who's oblivious to the news', like always. Her phone pinged. It was a text from Caspar.

Have you escaped out the window? X

Shit. She had to choose.

Andrew

. . .

Sitting opposite Jesse, Andrew thought how game his son was – joining in with their quiz on such a sombre evening. It still staggered him, how life could switch. Just hours ago he'd been buoyant with relief at handing over Leila's letter, prancing around, foolishly pleased about the talk he'd had with Jesse. Coming after his chat with Olivia in the car, it felt as if he'd mastered a new language. Even the awkwardness over Jesse's eccentric medical ideas had been smoothed, with Emma promising Jesse she'd try 'green juice', alongside the conventional treatment Olivia advised.

Earlier, he had chilled a bottle of 1984 Dom Perignon, planning to toast Olivia's birth at midnight, possibly even to say a few words. That wouldn't happen now, he supposed. Thinking of her upstairs it was impossible to feel celebratory. And where was Phoebe? It was a new sensation to feel angry with his youngest. He was just skipping a question about Haag, when they heard the judder of a taxi outside. A key turned in the front door above them, followed by heels clacking down stairs.

Phoebe tottered in. She looked sensational, as always – if drunk. 'I just heard,' she said, bending to try to undo her shoes, nearly toppling over, and then seeming to give up. 'Where is she?'

'Upstairs,' said Emma.

'What, on her own?'

'That's what she wants, darling. She won't come down, and she doesn't want anyone with her.'

'I'll go,' said Phoebe, without waiting for any of them to stop her.

They heard her clattering upstairs, and Andrew remembered the Skype call in November, when Phoebe and Olivia had had nothing to say to one another. Perhaps every family should be quarantined together, he thought.

Olivia

. . .

Three floors above, Olivia lay looking at the ceiling. From below, she heard someone coming up the stairs. The steps were too light for her parents, or Jesse, but wasn't Phoebe out on her date? Olivia wouldn't have expected her to know about Sean anyway. Or to cut her date short. It wasn't like Phoebe – or the Phoebe she thought she knew.

It was Phoebe, though. She shut the door behind her and kicked off her shoes, moving with an unsteady conviction. She didn't say anything, but lay down beside Olivia, head to toe. They used to lie like that when they were little, in their room in Norfolk, when one of them had a nightmare. Her feet still only reached Olivia's shoulders. And even though Olivia could feel her not knowing what to say, it was sort of comforting.

Finally Phoebe said, 'He's still here, Wiv. Inside you. I mean, your baby is half Sean. So he's still here, and he always will be.' They lay on the bed for a while in silence, sides touching now.

'You go down. I might come in a bit,' said Olivia after a while. It surprised her that she was able to form a sentence.

Phoebe sat up. 'Yes! Please come down, they're doing that stupid quiz,' she said, and then looked panicked that she shouldn't have said something normal, or revealed that their parents weren't weeping. Olivia wanted to tell her it was OK, but she knew that would embarrass Phoebe more. Sometimes, she thought, she understood her sister better than she realised.

She listened to Phoebe padding downstairs and thought about what she had said about Sean. It flipped around her fear that she was never going to move forward – that the baby would moor her in grief for ever. Because Phoebe was right: there was another way of looking at it. Half of Sean was now going to live on in her care. Perhaps that was why this baby was being born. And the thought shifted something, so that the tide of pain ebbed back, just a tiny bit.

Emma

. . .

Across the table from Andrew, Emma couldn't concentrate on anything – especially the quiz she had suggested. She hadn't even been able to eat, which never happened. All she could think of was Olivia. She hoped Phoebe hadn't rushed upstairs and put her foot in it. It was right that Phoebe had come home, but she seemed rather tipsy and might well say the wrong thing. Emma had already begged Olivia to come down twice now to no avail. After everything that had happened over Christmas she'd hoped Olivia would want them in her hour of need – but it seemed not.

Emma still couldn't believe what had happened. It was always that way, when a young person died. Sean looked so strong, so alive, in his photograph. She wished she'd known everything when she'd met him at the airport. She kept imagining what she would have said, and now never would. Not that her regrets mattered. But it was unbearable to see Olivia in such pain.

Andrew was asking yet another question that Emma didn't have the foggiest about, when Phoebe appeared, in stockinged feet. She seemed less giddy as she put the kettle on.

'Think she'll be down in a bit,' she said.

Phoebe

. . .

Phoebe knew that stuffing herself with Jesse's worthy but not unpleasant brownies wasn't really appropriate. Nobody else was eating, but she had to – she was starving after cocktails on an empty stomach. Seeing her parents' ashen faces she was glad she'd come home. She wished she could erase Olivia's pain as easily as Caspar had hers. It had been horrible to see Wiv, who was usually so composed, crying like that. She didn't even seem to realise she was crying, the tears were just pouring like a tap left on. Everything was going to be so different now, with her mother and sister needing to be looked after. She and her dad would have to be the grown ups.

Her phone buzzed. Thinking it might be Caspar she checked it surreptitiously under the table. But it was a text from George: *Happy New Year, Titch. Miss you.*

An in-breath of cacao powder nearly choked her. *Fuck you*, she typed immediately, then stopped and deleted. She didn't feel angry like that – it was all too distant. One day, she knew, she and George would have to meet for a stilted drink on neutral ground. But it wouldn't make any difference – that whole chapter already felt like memory. Just as she was switching her phone to silent, Olivia came in. And without even thinking about it, Phoebe jumped up and hugged her – not one of their stiff, A-shaped hugs, but a real, boob-meshing hug.

Olivia

. . .

Olivia sat back from the table, holding the token inch of champagne Andrew had poured her. Her whole body still hurt, like she'd been smashed into. But Phoebe had been right to urge her to come down. She'd always thought it was better to cry in private, but now she wondered if she was wrong. Seeing how nervous they all looked, she told them to see in the New Year as usual with the bongs on the radio. She wanted some normalness around her – anything to cushion the feeling of freefall.

With a spark and splintering sound, the room went black. The voice on the radio stopped. 'Power cut!' said Phoebe.

Andrew flicked on the torch in his Swiss army knife, opened the fuse box in the corner and fiddled with the switches. Nothing happened. 'Must be the whole street,' he said, looking out of the window. He took matches and candlesticks from the side, lit a candle, and put it in front of Olivia. He held up the match to watch the flame dwindle. 'Still reminds me of Afghanistan,' he said, and then looked at her as if he shouldn't have said anything.

She took a tiny sip of champagne. 'How come? You never tell us the whole story,' she said.

The candle flared, and she saw Emma, Phoebe and Jesse looking at her in surprise, and then at Andrew. And as he began to tell the story, she thought, It's going to be hard. But I won't be alone.

Epilogue

Seamus Andrew Coughlan Birch
b. 17 August 2017, 1.03 a.m.

Acknowledgements

A huge thank you to my agent Olivia Guest at Jonathan Clowes, for encouraging me to write something longer than an article and for believing in this idea. Without you, I would have put fiction off for years. Thank you also to Cara Lee Simpson for being so brilliant during Olivia's leave, and to Ann Clowes for your time, advice and expertise.

Second, thank you to everyone at Little, Brown for making me feel so welcome, above all, Emma Beswetherick. You are the most enthusiastic, astute and understanding editor anyone could ask for – a fairy godmother of editors – and it has been such a pleasure to work together. I'm also enormously indebted to Andy Hine, Kate Hibbert, Helena Doree, Sarah Birdsey and Joe Dowley at Little, Brown Rights for your tireless work: I'm thrilled to be published in so many other countries. Special thank yous, too, to Dominic Wakeford and Ella Bowman, for your advice and excitement about the book, and to Ursula Mackenzie, Charlie King and Tim Whiting.

Third, thank you to everyone at Berkley in New York – I'm delighted to be part of the Penguin US family. A particular thank you to Craig Burke, Jeanne-Marie Hudson, Claire Zion, Jennifer Monroe and most of all my editor Amanda Bergeron. Your positivity, suggestions and eye for rogue British-isms were invaluable.

Next, I must thank my mother Laura, my husband Luke and my dear friend Laura Cox-Watson. I'm so very lucky to have such clever plot consultants and early readers, close by. I also owe a great deal to my parents and parents-in-law for all the hours you looked after Finlay and Max, which allowed me to keep writing up until my due date, and soon afterwards. I'm deeply grateful to you all.

Finally, thank you to my oldest friends Felicity FitzGerald and Charity Garnett, both for sparking this story through your heroic work in Sierra Leone, and for your help with getting it down accurately. Your courage, kindness and knowledge are awe-inspiring.

And another thank you to Luke, for everything.

Seven Days of Us

Reading Guide

Reading Group Questions

★ Is there one character you relate to more than any other in this story? If so, why?

★ How well do you think Francesca Hornak captures the family dynamic of a week in quarantine over the holidays?

★ Do you think it was better/right for Andrew to conceal his one-off infidelity with Jesse's mother? Or should he have spoken up and told Emma at the time?

★ Why did Olivia stay away from her family for so long? Have you ever experienced the feeling of not being able to be yourself with your family?

★ Can you discuss the sibling rivalry between Olivia and Phoebe? Why do you think we, as adults, fall into old roles when home with family? Have you experienced this?

★ What do you think kept Phoebe and George together for six years?

★ Did you empathize with the way each character reacted to Jesse's surprise arrival? Did you empathize with Jesse?

★ Is there a moral lesson that each character takes away with them at the end of the story? If so, what is that lesson?

★ What are the main themes in the story?

★ Do you like the way the story is told from multiple points of view?

★ The end is tinged with tragedy and hope. How did the ending affect you?

★ What do you imagine or hope would happen next for each of the members of the Birch family after the closing pages of the book?

Behind the Book: A Conversation with Francesca Hornak

What inspired you to write *Seven Days of Us?*

In 2015 my oldest friend went to treat Ebola in Sierra Leone, and afterwards, she and her family had to spend December in quarantine. When she told me, I started thinking how a quarantine would intensify the familiar Christmas set-up, and how that pressure cooker could make a good start to a novel.

The Birch family members feel so incredibly real to life in their flaws and virtues. Do you see yourself in any of the Birch family members and were any easiest to write?

I felt for them all in different ways. I'm the youngest in my family and close to my parents, so on paper I suppose I have most in common with Phoebe (though I hope I'm not quite so entitled). But I relate to Emma as a mother and a worrier, and her impulse to uphold family traditions. And Andrew's rage at his words being edited is annoyingly familiar to me, as a journalist. I found earnest Olivia's head hardest to get into, though I think we can all identify with resenting your family at times and wanting to be the adult you are at work, at home.

Are any of the characters based on anyone in your life?

Not consciously! But my older brother is definitely more intrepid than me, so the dynamic between the siblings has some basis in my own experience. And at university in Oxford I met a lot of men like George Marsham-Smith ... I only had myself to blame, as I chose a sporty college thinking there would be less academic work, which wasn't even true.

If you were forced into quarantine with your family, what would you find most challenging? Most rewarding?

We practically were in quarantine last Christmas because I roped my poor family into intensively potty training my son. We barely left my parents' holiday home for a week. I definitely struggled with my parent's insistence on hoarding mouldy condiments (whenever I try to bin mustard with a 2010 date stamp I get accused of being 'the fridge police'), and my family's tendency to launch into in-depth conversations at breakfast. I should be mature enough to find these things endearing but Christmas makes you regress! The most rewarding thing about being at home is always watching my parents and my children together. Seeing your mum and dad as besotted grandparents is very special – it softens everyone and breathes new life into the house.

The Birches have a whole host of traditions – our favourite in the novel was the digging up and replanting of the same tree every year! Does your family have any unusual or even cringe-worthy holiday traditions or stories?

When my brother and I were little we used to get so hyperactive that we were allowed to open one present under the tree on Christmas Eve. It became tradition to deliberately pick a present that was likely to be a bit rubbish, so you got it out the way and weren't disappointed on Christmas Day. We had certain relations who could be relied on to send a terrible gift – some of our top Christmas Eve openings were a 1000-piece jigsaw just of baked beans, a negligee (when I was seven . . .) and a huge empty box.

I wasn't aware of our traditions being cringey until my husband started spending Christmas with us and was shocked that we still all make stockings for each other when my brother and I are well into our thirties. We also persist with real candles on the tree – even though it once caught fire and my grandmother had to throw the whole thing out of the front door.

The uncommunicative Birches are in stark contrast to the novel's sunny Californian, Jesse. What is your take on the cultural differences between the US and the UK – is that intentional?

From the start I felt Andrew's son should be foreign but English speaking, so I chose to have him from the US. It was only when I started to write in Jesse's voice that I realised his Californian positivity and emotional fluency were a good foil to Andrew's cynicism and the Birch family's stiff upper lip. So it wasn't deliberate, but I was probably unconsciously drawn to portraying those cultural differences as I'm a natural sceptic myself (much as I'd love not to be) and I envy the enthusiasm that seems to be more the norm in the States. The British embarrassment threshold can be painfully low! That said, judging by Instagram there's a new generation of Brits who are already more like Jesse than the Birch family.

What do you hope readers take away from *Seven Days of Us*?

That family dynamics aren't set in stone and that it's never too late for relationships to turn around. I loosely based the plot on the parable of The Prodigal Son, as I've always been drawn to the idea of second chances.

Further Reading – on Francesca Hornak's bookshelf

★ A Visit from the Goon Squad, Jennifer Egan

★ The Catcher in the Rye, J. D. Salinger

★ Notes on a Scandal, Zoë Heller

★ Little Fires Everywhere, Celeste Ng

★ Funny Girl, Nick Hornby

★ Lolita, Vladimir Nabokov

★ The Talented Mr. Ripley, Patricia Highsmith

★ The Dinner Party And Other Stories, Joshua Ferris

★ The Reason I Jump, Naoki Higashida, translated by David Mitchell

★ Hangover Square, Patrick Hamilton

★ This Must Be the Place, Maggie O'Farrell